Synchronicity

IN THE STARS
BOOK TWO

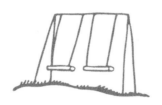

S.L. ASTOR

CW00760002

This is a work of fiction. Names, characters, places, and incidents either are the product of the author's imagination and are used fictitiously. Any resemblance to actual persons, living or dead, events, or locales is entirely coincidental.

Synchronicity Copyright © 2023 by S.L. Astor

All rights reserved. No AI has been used in the creation of any part of this book. No part of this book may be reproduced in any form or by any electronic or mechanical means, including information storage and retrieval systems, without written permission from the author, except for the use of brief quotations in a book review.

For more information, contact: www.authorslastor.com

First edition October 2023

Kindle ASIN: B0CHJC5PRW

Paperback ISBN: 9788989197408

Cover Designer: Murphy Rae www.MurphyRae.com

❀ Created with Vellum

CONTENT WARNING

Please be advised that this is a work of fiction. It contains explicit language and content and explores sensitive subjects surrounding mental health, attempted suicide off-page, neurodiversity, and parental abandonment. It may be triggering for some readers and is intended for audiences 18 years and older.

playlist

You Got It (The Right Stuff)
New Kids on the Block

Kids in Love
Pink (ft. First Aid Kit)

Dandelions
Ruth B.

Back To You
Hannah Mac

Hang You Up
Yellowcard

Drops of Jupiter (Tell Me)
Train

Set The Fire To The Third Bar
Snow Patrol, Martha Wainwright

Take My Name
Parmalee

SNAP
Rosa Linn

See You Later
Jenna Raine

Wish That You Were Here
Florence + The Machine

Two Worlds Apart
Francis Moon

Fall Into Me
Forest Blakk

This Love (TV)
Taylor Swift

Still Falling For You
Ellie Goulding

Outnumbered
Dermot Kennedy

Nights Like This
St. Lundi

How Will I Know
Sam Smith

I Knew This Would Be Love
Imaginary Future

US
James Bay, Alicia Keys

I'll Be Around
Garrett Keto

Safe & Sound
Taylor Swift, Joy Williams, John Paul White

Time After Time
Boyce Avenue

Hold On
Chord Overstreet

Far Away
Nickelback

Girl Harbor
Manchester Orchestra

How Do I Say Goodbye
Dean Lewis

Don't Forget Me
Dermot Kennedy

It's Been Awhile
Staind

The Rose
Bette Midler

After All
Cher, Peter Cetera

I Was Made For Loving You
Tori Kelly, Ed Sheeran

The Bones
Maren Morris, Hozier

Only Time
Enya

Synchronicity I
The Police

To Kim—a guiding light.
Thank you for pointing me true north,
and cheering the whole way.

&

To the caregivers, the caretakers, and the helpers.

&

To the stars in the sky with beautiful minds—
never let the harshness of the world extinguish
your gifts and glow. Keep shining bright.

"Timeless souls need soulmates."
— Amy Harmon

PROLOGUE
SAN FRANCISCO, 2021

The porcelain cup rattled as he placed it on the café table. The memory was old, from a time when the woman sitting across from him wasn't a stranger at all. They had the scars on their hearts to prove it. His eyes had aged, reflecting a hollowness she couldn't recall. She wondered what had put it there—what had become of the boy she once borrowed time with. But some things hadn't changed. The pull between them was the same, strong and magnetic, like a stifled spark that finally caught enough air to go up in flames.

PART I

1991

LOS ANGELES, CALIFORNIA

'I don't believe in magic.'
The young boy said.
The old man smiled.
'You will when you see her.'
— Atticus

1

CHELSEA

*C*helsea Bell knew exactly what to do. By eleven years old, she'd handled her fair share of bloody knees. The first lick always landed the same, sweet and metallic, like Nan's cherry cough drops that came in a tin. She kept a drawer full of them and when Chelsea would visit, Nan made sure to send her home with a red tongue and a five-dollar bill.

What had Mom been thinking? She blew a quick breath over the sting.

"They're the most popular books for your age," she had said in her most melodic pitch. "And the font is just the right size. Your teacher recommended them in preparation for the academic skills camp you'll be attending this summer. It'll be great. A month away from your parents, fresh air. Tutors at your disposal and to be around other kids like you who need . . ." she trailed off, or Chelsea had stopped listening—she wasn't sure.

Chelsea couldn't make sense of what was happening, how they'd gone from happy birthday to a horror show in a matter of seconds. She wanted to beg them to reconsider, but in her house, arguing was useless. All it took was one sharp pin in the balloon—once a decision was made, it was final.

Her mother's voice echoed in her ears. "If you enjoy the stories, it might encourage you to try harder."

That's all Chelsea had ever done. Tried and tried and failed.

She stood up, brushed street dust from the back of her legs, and pressed forward.

Spending the entire summer in a strange place with musty cabins and tutors was punishment enough, but being sent away —hidden like a problem too big for her parents—was too much for her to bear. The truth lodged in her throat, absorbed by every open pore—Chelsea was *different*. She knew it. Her parents knew it. And different wasn't a part of anyone's plan.

Her parents were embarrassed, and a wave of disappointment shuddered through Chelsea's unsteady body.

She didn't remember how it happened, but the room had blurred somewhere between her mom's news and discovering the contents of her present: a plain black helmet and protective pads, and beneath it, a set of books. Each cover image displayed a group of girls, their smiling faces laughing at Chelsea.

That moment, under the watchful gaze of her parents and their "fix it" attitude—an oppressive reality she couldn't accept —was the equivalent of staring into a kaleidoscope of fractured glass. She'd lost complete focus, and the only thing she could do to restore her vision was to escape.

Somehow. Some way.

She grabbed her boring helmet and blades and sailed from the house as fast as she could—speeding across the congested intersection at Sunset Boulevard—not even halfway to the other side when the flashing numbers suddenly appeared. Chelsea pushed past four rows of traffic in both directions, not once looking back.

The bulky knee pads were making it impossible for her to get away as fast as she wanted, so she did something she never did—she ignored the rules. She ripped open the velcro, her thighs and calves on fire, the red hand telling her to stop.

Engines on every side of her roared to life, and a silver Porsche with its top down laid on its horn, jumpstarting Chelsea's heart. Her heel brake caught the lip of the curb, sending her body onto the hard sidewalk, her palms skidding two feet in front of her.

She had some sense to lock her elbows, breaking her fall, motivated by the imagined voice of her mom in her ears. *Not the face.* It would be the end of the world and the obligatory birthday photo if Chelsea came home with more than a pair of skinned knees.

By the time Chelsea made it to the playground, she was ready to burst. She chucked her helmet to the ground, hoping it would split in half, and let out her knotted blond hair. She stared at the deserted blacktop in front of her with every swing up for grabs—the adjacent field lay undisturbed with patches of daisies.

Most kids spent their school breaks at the beach. Not Chelsea. Concrete at her feet, her spring break existed sandwiched between the caramel stucco duplexes of the Los Angeles neighborhood she called home. And now, her summer would be spent trapped in the Santa Monica Mountains with people she didn't know, doing the one thing she hated most.

From infancy, Chelsea's parents had rolled her in bubble wrap, making every decision for her. And not even the poppable kind of packing material that her mom's costume jewelry arrived in. It was boring bubble wrap, just like her helmet and pads and life.

Boring, boring, boring.

Fevered laughter gave way to fresh tears as she remembered the unhelpful, overly eager sales lady pointing out to her mom that the "safety" helmet line would protect three sides of the brain, not two, then promptly asking for her autograph after making the sale.

For Chelsea, there was a true discrepancy between her

mom—the actress—painted in purple and teal eyeshadow, rocking a leather skirt and off-the-shoulder sequined top, and giving her daughter the most basic helmet available, despite knowing which one Chelsea had desperately wanted.

But for Summer Bell, everything came down to safety and education and, Chelsea now realized, keeping up with appearances, too.

It wasn't her fault that she was born to remarkable parents. She couldn't control that fact or rescue the sinking ship in the pit of her stomach.

As she looked at her scuffed up knees, she knew her mom would have something—so many things—to say about the agreement they'd gone over when using rollerblades. But that was a problem for future Chelsea.

She shook free from the impending lecture and her wrist guards, yanking her sweaty feet from the tight casing of the blades. Chelsea chose the swing at the far right, closest to the field. She leaned her body back, pulling on the chains and closing her eyes to the warm sun radiating behind a set of heavy clouds. The mid-afternoon overcast sky tempered the heat hanging off the Santa Ana winds. It had been unusually hot for this time of year.

Chelsea flung her feet forward, tugging hard in an effort to lift higher.

The repetitive back-and-forth motion of her legs expelled in quick bursts. It was like manually pumping air into a tire as fast as possible. As her speed increased, Chelsea's heart once again inflated. She convinced herself that this is what it must feel like to fly.

Moving was the only time the voices quieted down. The faster, the better. And she giggled like someone her age. Like a kid on spring break with their toes in the sand.

Today was still going to be special. She just needed some time alone. She held tight to a huddle of hushed wishes—

eleven to be exact—and planned to set them free. She wanted to see which ones would return to her.

A rush of cool air broke through, tickling Chelsea's lips, peppering her eyelashes and along her arms. Her eyes snapped open to a sheet of rain. Delicious, necessary, soothing rain. Chelsea squealed in delight, halting her swing to catch drops on her tongue.

Rain fell in soft shapes, heavier than a mist but not quite a downpour yet. She followed their path from the sky overhead to the—

Her gaze stopped mid-sweep, body stilled, unable to blink or breathe as warm water melted from her skin, evaporating before hitting the steaming asphalt.

The sight of a boy crystallized before her, a dusting of freckles sprinkled across the bridge of his nose like he'd just got done rolling down a hill and didn't bother washing up.

"Hi there. I'm Seth Hansen," he said.

She caught her puzzled expression in his eyes, barely visible beneath a head of strawberry-blond hair sticking out in every direction from his royal blue hat.

Her hands gripped the chains closer, her chest squeezing into a fist. She didn't know why, but at that precise moment, when he smiled, crooked and soft, she crossed one wish off her list.

2

CHELSEA

"**W**hat are you listening to?" Chelsea's exterior remained calm while her eyes ran laps around this boy, waiting for the rest of the magic trick. What would happen next? A bunny under his ball cap? A severed torso? "How long have you been standing here?"

"I'm sitting." And he was. On the ground, his arms resting over his knees. "What's your name?"

"Oh," she replied, momentarily forgetting herself. "I'm Chelsea."

"Wanna hear, Chelsea?" He popped up and glided over to her, and it took a disorienting minute for Chelsea to realize the rain had stopped and Seth was on rollerblades, too. They were all black like hers, laced up with frayed neon green and yellow thread. His blades had seen some life. Scuff marks scratched the reflective coat beyond its original shine—pieces of warped plastic protruded from the sides. Chelsea dragged her lower lip between her teeth and chewed on her indecision.

Seth settled in the swing next to her, and from this distance, Chelsea confirmed they were definitely freckles and not dirt. And his lashes were thick and his eyes were like honey, the dark kind in the jar that Nan kept away from sunlight and sticky fingers.

He offered Chelsea his headphones, placing them directly between their noses. Curious, she took them from his soil-packed nails into her cautious grasp. When she placed the cushioned speakers over her ears, she remained all eyes on Seth. On his sun-kissed cheeks and wild, yarn-like hair. On his beat-up Los Angeles Dodgers hat.

Seth's head nodded along to the rhythm of the guitar and drums while she listened as a striking male voice poured through the speaker. Chelsea fixated on Seth's mouth as his lips silently followed the lyrics. He had committed them to memory, like she was trying to do now even with the clashing in her ears.

"Is this your band?"

"I wish." His eyes widened. "It's Sting."

When Chelsea's expression remained unchanged, he added, "The Police?" and opened the tape deck, pulling out a cassette.

"Who?" She examined the clear plastic and white letters. There were so many and they appeared out of order. She couldn't read the album title, didn't know the band, and was hesitant to admit it. *Try harder, Chelsea. Sound it out.* Before her frustration could turn into something sour, she returned the tape, wiping her slick palm along her lime green shorts.

"See, here?" He pointed to the cassette again, and Chelsea nodded, mirroring his movement, like she could read exactly what he was talking about—like she was supposed to at her age. "The band broke up, but the lead singer's a legend. My mom's got these cool vinyls and tapes. I listen to them when she's working."

Seth quickly reached over, removing the headphones from her head. He secured them around his neck and latched the walkman onto one of his pockets. "Their music is awesome, isn't it?"

"I kinda hate it." She laughed, mainly from the discomfort of saying what she felt.

Seth's jaw dropped. "What?! Are you kidding?"

Chelsea didn't want to hurt his feelings, but it was exhilarating to be honest. "It's loud—melting my brain loud. Are those drums or garbage can lids they're banging on?"

"It's well before its time. The music breaks all the rules. Give them a second chance. Here," he insisted, popping the tape deck again, handing over the cassette to Chelsea. "Keep it."

"Isn't it your mom's?"

"Music's meant to be shared. Maybe it will grow on you."

She smiled at the tape, accepting the gift—another present she didn't ask for. She seemed to be collecting those today. "Thank you." She tucked the tape into her back pocket.

"Nice wheels and gear," Seth commented, noticing her discarded blades, switching subjects faster than Chelsea could keep up with.

Set back from the street, the playground was as insulated as it got for the city. Suddenly aware of the silence, aside from Seth's rollerblades scraping over asphalt, Chelsea replied, "Thanks. They're new. I got the helmet for my birthday today." She peeked up from the ground to see his reaction.

"No way!" he shouted, both their swings slowing to a stop. "My birthday's this week too. On Saturday."

She drew her head back. "You're making that up."

"Cross my heart." Seth traced an X over the center of his chest. "Can't wait to be eleven."

His mellow laugh had her stomach tying in knots. She blamed it on one too many pancakes that morning.

Not only were their birthdays close, they were also the same age.

"You sure you're about to turn eleven? You don't sound like anyone in my class," Chelsea observed.

"What does an eleven year-old sound like?"

"Not you." She wiggled her toes.

"Well, you don't sound eleven, either." Seth smirked. "What time of day were you born?" he asked, wide-eyed, as if her response came with a prize.

"Who knows that stuff?" She shielded her eyes from the sky. It was bright behind the clouds.

"I was born at five o'clock in the morning. Rise and shine. My mom says I was up before the sun and all of civilization."

"Whatever that means." But Chelsea found the interaction amusing. Seth had a fire in him. And the way his voice emphasized every word he said had Chelsea believing that he meant them, too. "My mom has to drag me out of bed most days. Unless there's pancakes. I'll gladly drag myself for those."

"Syrup or whipped cream?"

"Powdered sugar and a stick of butter." She ran her tongue over her teeth. Her love of butter was tried and true but not something she advertised. She didn't talk to people often—that much was obvious.

The droplets had all disappeared from the pavement now. The air returned to its sticky, heavy heat.

"So, why aren't you at a party or something?" he asked.

"It's just me and my parents. What are you doing for your birthday?"

After a few gentle sways in his swing, Seth said, "I don't know. My dad drives trucks. Mom's a flight attendant. Sometimes, I have to remind them I'm here too. Like I'm an unfinished project they once attempted or something."

Chelsea had the opposite experience. "My parents are glued at the hip and we're together all the time."

"All mine do is fight when they're together." The way his jaw tensed and his smile settled into a straight line made the boy swinging next to her suddenly appear much older. "Ever get the feeling like some people are better off apart? My dad's never here all that much, but when he is, she's gone."

Chelsea had recently heard her parents fight late at night. She listened by her bedroom door to the way her mom's whispers strained and her dad's clipped tone tumbled down the hall. "My parents argue over me sometimes."

Seth didn't jump right in with a response.

"About whether they should have me prepare for my Bat Mitzvah or keep going to Hebrew school. They don't ever ask me what I want. It'd be nice if one of them pretended to be on my side."

His patience was the closest thing Chelsea had to someone listening to her in a while. She shared more than she intended, and faster too. It had all poured out with absolute urgency.

"I'm going to save one of my birthday wishes for you."

"You'd do that for me?"

"Sure." She kept her eyes on Seth, believing it took more than just words to convey the meaning behind them and make them last. "Wanna make daisy chains?"

"Yeah, I do." Seth hopped off the swing with an all-in enthusiasm that motivated Chelsea to do the same. He flipped his hat backward. "You gonna put on your blades?"

"Nope."

"Living on the edge."

As many paces as it took to reach the field, Seth asked Chelsea questions.

"How do you make daisy chains?"

"You'll see. They're kinda like friendship bracelets."

"Well, we should probably pass the friendship test first."

"Test?" Chelsea tripped over her own feet. She was tested at every turn—pop quizzes in the car, over breakfast, and at bedtime. Her mom's favorite saying was, "Practice makes progress. How do you spell *remember, does, because*?"

Seth reached out his hand, but Chelsea recovered her balance. "All right. These are gonna be serious."

No more tests. She couldn't suffer through a single one. "I'm not—" Chelsea's explanation slid down her throat.

Seth blurted out, "Rain or shine?"

Oh. She exhaled. "Um, rain."

He smiled. "Same." Their height was also the same. "Okay, the next one will be tough, and there's only one right answer."

"For some reason, I don't believe you."

"Pizza or burritos?"

"I'm a Californian. Burritos, duh."

"Are you trying to win?"

"Do you want me to lose?"

He bumped into her shoulder, whistling a tune, and kept on with the questions. "Favorite movie?"

"*To Catch A Thief.* My mom loves Grace Kelly and Cary Grant. We always watch old movies and musicals together. You probably don't know it."

Seth turned to face Chelsea. "Are you kidding me? I love classic films. I want to spend this summer watching every movie by the Hitchcock. We should totally have a marathon movie day. There's always some rent three, get a fourth for free deal."

Chelsea giggled. "It's not *the* Hitchcock. Just Hitchcock."

"It will always be the Hitchcock to me." Seth's declaration captured Chelsea. She knew more about Seth now. He didn't accept a thing simply because it was. And Chelsea was curious about that.

"I'd like to . . . you know, watch movies." She accepted his invitation.

They continued toward the field. "What snacks will you bring? Red licorice or Gushers?"

"Grape Gushers."

"Perfect. I'll bring popcorn and Dr. Pepper."

Summer was very particular about who Chelsea played with. She knew some kids in school, but they jumped rope at recess while Chelsea was stuck with extra work in the resource room. And on the weekends, they all had their things—soccer, siblings, family vacations.

No one stayed still anymore anyway. The world rotated around Chelsea at lightning speed. Seth was the first person to slow down and stop in front of her.

"Okay, final question. And this one's the most important. Could ruin everything if you get it wrong."

"It takes a lot of work to be your friend," she teased, not meaning a word of it. She couldn't believe how easy it was to talk to him.

"Only the strong survive." He pumped up his lanky arms like a cartoon character, biceps failing to pop.

"You asking me or not?"

"Right, okay. So Dodgers or Angels?"

"What if I don't like baseball?"

"Not love baseball?" he refuted, licking his chapped lips. "Listen, Chelsea, I think we're gonna be great friends."

"Right here." She led them to the perfect spot. "Let me show you how to pick the best daisies for your daisy chain."

"You mean friendship bracelet?"

She smiled. "Sure. Yes."

The grass was still damp from earlier, and yet there they sat, side by side, with the weight of the world on their shoulders. Two kids about to inexplicably link themselves together.

3

CHELSEA

"There's not much difference between this field of weeds and a baseball field," Seth observed.

Chelsea knew this patch of earth held lots of promise. "Dodgers," she whispered, plucking petals.

"Thank you! I knew it," he sighed, adding, "and you're pretty rad—you know, for a girl." Seth's knee knocked into hers. "Most girls don't like watching classic movies or baseball or blading. Not that I hang with girls other than my mom, and she's a grown-up, so it doesn't really count." Seth was talkative and Chelsea appreciated the distraction.

"What would've happened if I didn't pass?"

"I guess we'll never find out."

She was perfectly happy not knowing because she liked Seth. He was kind and funny and his laugh was a sound she'd like to hear more.

She gathered enough daisies to begin, sacrificing a single flower to wishes. One petal per wish. She dropped her eyelids, about to start, when Seth gasped.

Chelsea's fingers paused from plucking petals. "What?"

"It hurts to watch you do that."

"Do what?" She twirled the wilting daisy between her fingers.

"Ripping the petals off like that. See, look." He stretched out his arm, exposing an eruption of chills over tanned skin and a constellation of freckles.

Chelsea said nothing, swallowing the urge to ask Seth if he thought flowers had feelings like people. If maybe they felt pain like she did, quietly and without protest.

"Here, find the longer stems. Easier to stab." She handed him one from the pile as an example.

"I see."

Chelsea looked over her shoulder and back to Seth. "See what?"

"You."

"Me?"

"Yeah, you. Ripping and stabbing." He laughed, barely taking a breath. "Bet you're trouble."

Chelsea shook her head. "I'm the most—" She stopped herself from saying the first word that came to mind. It started with a "b" and ended in "oring." She rolled her eyes at herself. "My days are pretty uneventful. Anyway, you following along? You can't push too hard or the stem will collapse. Gentle and firm at the same time." She demonstrated with the tip of her chipped hot pink polished nail.

Seth successfully followed suit. "I'm gonna see how long I can make this thing go."

"I once made a chain from my feet to my head. I wanted one as tall as me. But it dried up so quickly. Only lasted a few days."

"My mom always tells me it's best to appreciate whatcha got while you've got it."

Chelsea's cheeks lifted at the idea of being in the present moment. She hadn't been thinking about the summer camp fiasco and chose to keep that thought to herself, too.

Seth leaned in closer to Chelsea. "You get these little lines around your eyes when you smile."

She touched the sides of her face, self-conscious, certain she'd never paid attention to how she looked while smiling. It's not like she sat in front of the mirror all day like someone else she lived with. Okay, that wasn't true. They spent a lot of time together, sitting on the bathroom floor with Summer's eyeshadow palettes scattered around them. But all eyes were on her mom. "Oh, I do?"

"Yes. I like it. That's how you know the smile goes all the way through."

Since Seth arrived—Chelsea had lost count—she found herself smiling again, blades of grass tickling behind her knees. "Do you always come here when your parents fight?"

"I go wherever these bad boys will take me." He slapped the plastic exterior of his blades. "I can't wait to own a motorcycle and get out of here."

"You mean like run away?" Her imagination ran wild.

"If I could, I'd leave today. Wanna come?"

The idea of Chelsea leaving today, out of all days, after everything that happened, equally excited and cautioned her. Could she do it? Grab a bag and go? "What would we do?"

"Anything we want. Think about it—no one telling us where to go or who to be. The sky's the limit, Chelsea. We can be anyone and everything."

Chelsea's fingers trembled as she looped her daisies together, spiraling the strand on the grass while Seth watched her.

She'd never imagined who she could be.

"Wait, you're just gonna leave it here?" Seth asked.

"I guess I'd like to find some way to hold onto it. But it's just gonna die."

"Doesn't mean you let it die alone." He rescued the strand, placing it over his neck. He took Chelsea's hand and wrapped his daisy chain around her wrist—one, two, three times—securing it at the end. "Not bad for my first try."

She nodded, unable to form words. A strange sensation ran the length of her spine. It reminded her of the sugar rush that came after one too many cherry drops.

"So, Chelsea, should we do it? I've got some chore money saved."

"Do what?" she asked, shaking her wrist free from his touch.

"Leave this place."

Chelsea barely knew Seth. She also wasn't sure if he was kidding. She fantasized about doing things on her own but more along the lines of two hours in a dark theater with stale popcorn. "We're eleven. Like, *newly* eleven."

He held the fabric of his white T-shirt at the belly and chuckled.

She wasn't intending to be funny. "Well, you know what I mean. You're almost eleven."

"I know what you meant." Seth sighed. "It'd be cool to have a travel buddy, though. We like the same stuff. We'd never fight over anything."

She didn't think they would, either. Seth seemed to be a pretty happy kid despite his parents' chaos. His heart was unlike hers—hopeful and carefree. And yet they desired the same thing, to escape.

Even if she wanted to leave today, she couldn't begin to know how to do anything that wasn't planned and scheduled and managed for her. Sometimes Chelsea fought the puppet strings, but she always returned to the people pulling them.

"There's a whole world out there," he said, chin tipped to the clouds.

The sky had darkened in a way that told Chelsea more time than planned had passed. She needed to get home soon. She thought hard about what Seth was proposing—she'd do just about anything to avoid that summer camp and the disappointment in her parents' eyes.

After digging her thumb into the dirt, Chelsea's damp palm cooled over the grass. She knew what was behind door number one. Seth was offering door number two. Maybe leaving was not only possible but something necessary, like air or water.

"I gotta get back before my mom sends out a search party."

"Can I walk with you?"

"Um, sure. Let me grab my stuff." Chelsea tried to wiggle back into her knee pads, but it was no use.

"Here, let me hold those for you," Seth offered.

She put on the rest of her gear and blades, saving the helmet for last. "Where's your helmet?"

"I manage. Have you ever thought about blading without the helmet? Get a little wind in your hair."

Sure, like every second.

"Want to try it? Just down the block, then you can put it back on before we cross the street."

She did. It was her birthday. And birthdays were a time to try new things. To be brave.

As Chelsea and Seth turned the corner around the chain-link fence, she ripped off the boring helmet and gave herself something to remember. For Chelsea, blading down the sidewalk was the closest thing to a ticket to anywhere. The heat scraped like nails through her hair, and Seth's cheers and howls echoed beside her.

"Haha, you did it!" Seth boasted. "Way to go."

When they paused at the light, he dipped his fingers under Chelsea's chin, fastening her helmet and securing it tight. He tapped the top of her helmet twice before skating ahead over the bumpy road.

"I live down that way." He pointed as they passed a side street Chelsea had walked by every day going to school.

"Are you starting school when break ends?"

"Yup. It'll be my first time."

"School?"

"We move so much, I learn at home and spend a lot of time in public libraries," he replied with ease.

Had she missed something? His mom worked, his dad worked, and Seth was home alone with his books all this time. The thought shuddered through Chelsea. Somehow, for completely different reasons, they were both trapped in isolation.

Chelsea's cheeks heated with realization. "What will I do about school?"

"My mom says school's an institution, not an education."

She nodded, a nagging pinch in her chest. How far could she get without knowing how to read, anyway? Seth would help. She'd learn in other ways, outside of her cage.

"This is me." She positioned her blade diagonally, slowing as they arrived at Rexford Drive.

"Safe and sound."

"How can I reach you?" she asked.

"I'll give you my number."

"I can memorize it."

"Without writing it down?"

"Try me."

"Okay." He smirked as she repeated the number back to him. "Want to meet me at the playground tomorrow, same time?" He was chewing on his lower lip, his hands buried in his pockets.

The front door swung open to a woman with long blond curls. Her full lips were stained magenta and wrapped around the end of a cigarette. She smelled of floral bouquets and tar. She was beautiful and sophisticated, the kind that dripped of fancy things that most people only see on television. She lit up the porch like it was center stage.

Chelsea never understood how someone like her mom created someone as average as her.

"Chels Bells, I was out of my mind with worry."

Seth leaned into Chelsea. "Chels Bells?"

She ignored him, responding to her mom. "I said I'd be back."

"Hours ago! And hello. I'm Summer." She volleyed her gaze between Chelsea and Seth like chess pieces, impatiently waiting for someone to make the obvious next move.

"You didn't tell me your mom was *that* Summer."

She turned to Seth. "It wasn't a part of the friendship quiz." In truth, she'd been distracted by Seth and daisies and dreaming of the future. And when people found out who her mom was, they treated her differently. It was nice being Chelsea for a minute. "Mom, this is Seth Hansen. He goes to my school. He walked me home."

"Hello, Seth. Thanks for escorting Chels."

"Nice to meet you, Mrs. Bell. My mom loves your musicals."

"Oh, that's so sweet. Thank you, darling, and it's Summer. Call me Summer. Chelsea, what the hell happened to your knees? Where are your knee pads?"

Chelsea went to tell her mom the truth, but Seth stepped forward in his blades, putting himself between Chelsea and Summer.

"It's my fault, Mrs. Bell. I wanted to race and suggested removing the knee pads because they make it hard to go fast. I'm sorry."

Though it was a version of the truth, no one had ever stood up for Chelsea before like this. *Especially not to Summer Bell.* The only person Chelsea had ever seen give Summer a challenge was Nan, and she'd say it's because a mom is always responsible for her kid, no matter their age.

"I don't approve of removing the knee pads, Seth. Chelsea knows the rules. But thank you for getting her home safely."

"Yeah, well, I better be going," Seth replied, facing Chelsea.

"Why don't you come over to dinner sometime soon? We like to get to know Chelsea's friends," Summer insisted.

Seth looked at Chelsea, and Chelsea held her breath. *What friends?*

"Sure, thanks, Mrs.—Summer. That would be great. I'll ask my mom."

Summer smiled, stubbing her cigarette out on the ashtray that lived on top of the window sill. "Come inside now, Chels," she directed, walking into the house.

"Seth," Chelsea whispered, out of earshot of her mom. Her tone was short, laced in shame with how she pathetically stood there and said nothing to defend herself—afraid she'd regret it forever if she didn't take the chance now. She couldn't believe what she was saying or how hot her face felt. "I want to go."

"For real?" he whispered back.

Her throat ran dry at Seth's pleading eyes.

He beamed, locking his gaze on hers. "When?"

"Oh, I don't know." She hadn't gotten that far. "Not today, but before summer for sure."

He smiled. "We can start planning tomorrow."

"Tomorrow," Chelsea confirmed.

"Cool. See ya." Seth pushed off down the block, trailing, "Happy birthday, Chels Bells."

Chelsea stalked around the corner to thank him for what he'd done for her, but Seth was out of sight.

Stretched out on her bedroom floor, Chelsea rolled her ankles in circles, processing the strange afternoon she'd experienced and the exhilaration from their plan—a real adventure, without rules and books and bubble wrap. With care, she unwound the daisy chain from her wrist and put it inside her ballerina music box where she kept the one thing that meant the most to her: a gold chai pendant that Nan passed down to her mom and her mom passed down to Chelsea. A small pearl was pressed into the upper left corner. It was too fragile in Chelsea's mind—such a precious gift—and she was afraid to lose it, so she never wore it. She'd take it out occasionally and return it right away.

Chelsea closed the box and took inventory of her room, of what she'd take and what she'd leave behind.

On her bed, Summer had set out a pink floral dress.

When Chelsea was ready, she put on the dress—wiggling against the scratchy fabric—to face her parents and cake. She avoided eye contact with her mom, convinced Summer would uncover the scandal.

Chelsea's insides had shaken up like a soda bottle. Her disappointment from earlier was replaced with pressurized anticipation. She owed that to Seth—being around him made her worries slip away. She wanted to chase his enthusiasm like she did with butterflies and bubbles, hoping to catch some of his joy.

She closed her eyes as her dad lit the candles and her mom dimmed the lights.

Doubt snuck in, and Chelsea counted the reasons why she couldn't run away with Seth. She'd fail. They'd get lost. Or hurt. Sucking in a deep inhale, Chelsea pushed fear aside and finally set her wishes free.

Summer sliced the cake with precision, even and tidy, not a single smudge of frosting out of place. There it was, directly in front of her, the one and only reason she had to go.

Living in her mom's spotlight and shadow was no life at all.

She was leaving to be as free and as messy as she wanted. She'd be able to eat cake with her hands. She wouldn't be forced inside the resource room or attend school in the summer. She'd be on her own but with Seth, so she wouldn't be alone.

She weighed her options as clearly as she could, not having a crystal ball. Her parents would never forgive her. She knew that. But could she forgive herself?

Chelsea's knees burned beneath her birthday dress, the hem grazing the scrapes. She peeked under the tablecloth at her bony joints. She smiled at the exposed skin, already scabbing over.

Seth kept his word and showed up the next day and every day after that. They made a pact—a pinkie promise—to finish the school year and leave before Chelsea's parents shipped her off to camp. They had plenty of time to prepare.

While they spent the week together, brainstorming ideas, they also played. Chelsea took Seth around the neighborhood to all of her favorite places, pointing out what she'd miss the most. He made her listen to more of his loud music, and she insisted he combine cherry and cola flavors when they stopped for slurpees at the corner 7-Eleven. They traded their best and worst stories, swapped penny candy and poorly executed jokes. They laughed so hard it hurt.

Saturday arrived, and it was Seth's birthday. He had asked Chelsea over for a movie marathon day and ice cream cake. She was shocked Summer was letting her go without having met his parents.

"We trust Seth," Mom stated as she braided her daughter's hair.

"But you don't trust me," Chelsea mumbled under her breath.

She waited nervously for Seth on the stoop, as planned, with a box of grape Gushers and a daisy woven into the tail end of her hair. She hadn't been to his house yet or met his parents.

Seth rolled up to Chelsea's in the same oversized concert T-shirt and basketball shorts he had worn yesterday, stopping at the entryway and leaning against the rough stucco.

Chelsea shot up from the stoop and bladed over to his wiry frame. "Happy Birthday!" Her smile faded as she took in his bloodshot eyes and swollen lids. He'd been crying. "Seth, are you okay?"

His hands landed on Chelsea's arms. "I need to go now."

"Now?" She started to shout but wrangled her words into a low whisper. "Now, now? Why?"

His forehead rested on hers. "I can't take it anymore—their fighting. Today's the worst it's ever been. If I don't leave now, I'm never getting out."

"Where are we gonna go?" Chelsea steadied her shoulders.

"I can't ask you to leave with me like this."

Chelsea's heart thumped so hard, it rattled her ribcage. The base of her neck broke out in a warm sweat. "I want to go. You can't stop me. I'm coming."

"Okay, okay." A slight smile appeared at the corner of his mouth. "Let's head to the bus station and we'll just pick. It's like twenty bucks for a ticket. I have money saved if you don't."

"My nan lives in San Francisco. We could go there."

"Great. Yes. Okay," he rambled, losing his breath. "Listen, I'm going back to grab some clothes and granola bars. Then I'll meet you at our spot in an hour. Can you do that?"

Chelsea squeezed her eyes shut. They hadn't had enough time to iron out a solid plan, but Seth needed her help now. She didn't know how bad it was for him at home, and she didn't want to find out. "Yes, I can do that." There wasn't much for her to take. She had saved some birthday money at the insistence of Nan. It was enough to get out of L.A.

Summer expected Chelsea would spend the day at the

Hansens' after one unnecessarily long conversation with Seth's mom on the phone last night, which quickly went from house rules to gushing about Summer's last performance. By the time the call ended, Summer had autographed a headshot for Chelsea to bring over as a thank-you.

Chelsea knew her mom wouldn't worry if she had no reason to. She'd leave a note on her pillow, telling her parents that she loved them, and by the time they realized Chelsea was gone, they'd be far up the 101. "Please, Seth, be safe," she said, blowing out a shallow exhale.

"I will," he promised, leaning forward, planting a quick kiss on Chelsea's cheek. She wrapped her arms around his chest and gave Seth her strongest hug. The embrace invigorated Chelsea's spirit like hot apple cider.

"I'm so happy we're doing this together," he declared.

"Me too," she agreed, nodding her head.

"One hour, Chels Bells!" Seth took off.

She needed to pack. Timing was everything—and limited. Chelsea raced to get off her blades and back in the house.

"Chelsea, is that you?"

"Yes," she answered, raising her voice over one of Summer's soundtracks playing from the kitchen.

"What are you doing back?"

"Just forgot a sweater in case I get cold."

"Okay, sweetie, good thinking. Have fun. And call if you need anything."

"Bye, Mom," Chelsea replied, pushing past the thickness in her throat. She couldn't be late to meet Seth.

And she wasn't.

Fifteen minutes. That's all the time it took to leave her life behind. It surprised Chelsea how easy it was to disappear when no one was looking.

She arrived at the playground minutes before the hour and opted to wait for Seth at the swings. Her eyes traced over the sun-bleached hopscotch squares in an effort to ignore her watch. She hoped Seth could get his stuff and dodge his parents' verbal bullets.

Chelsea finally looked at the time when she had to pee—two hours had passed. She pulled the daisy from her hair and alternated the phrases—*he loves me, he loves me not*. She couldn't bear to make the full rotation, tossing the flower to the ground. She waited longer, counting the leaves on the trees and the clouds in the sky. She clutched her backpack against her chest, terrified something had happened to her friend.

The chain links shifted, creaking in Chelsea's ears.

Two hours became five.

Her stomach growled. She couldn't bring herself to eat. Instead, her imagination devised worst-case scenarios. Logic trailed behind, demanding that he had simply changed his mind and didn't want to go with her.

The sun was setting when Chelsea wiped her eyes and walked home. She dragged her sore heart and shivering limbs into bed, tearing to shreds the runaway receipt she left on her pillow.

In the morning, Chelsea's hand shook as she unsuccessfully dialed Seth's number.

She tried again and again, each attempt ending in the same piercing tone. *The number you've reached has been disconnected or is temporarily out of service. Try again later.*

PART II

2001

SAN FRANCISCO, CALIFORNIA

"If you have chemistry, you only need one other thing—timing.
But timing's a bitch."
— Robin Scherbatski, How I Met Your Mother

4

CHELSEA

The early bird qualifies for the San Francisco Marathon. The nagging adage pecks at my brain as I smash my protesting palm over the alarm clock and hit snooze for the third time.

Five more minutes, Chels.

But you need to beat yesterday's number.

Fine, I groan at myself, the dedicated part that doesn't like quitters.

Inching my time up every day will get me closer to qualifying. I whimper like I always do when I'm up with the sun, slipping on my running shoes before the procrastinator in me wins out and crawls back into bed.

By mile one, the morning light rolls up skyscrapers, my feet fly over the city sidewalk, and my head's clear.

Even if I hate how it starts, Saturday morning is prime time to run, avoiding the professional lunch rush and stench that swells downtown during the workweek.

Twin Peaks Hill is my usual training route on hill day, but I woke up one snooze too late, and now I need to stay closer to home. It's spring, and a mild winter has made its nod and passed on through, but the first wave of foggy morning air off the Pacific cuts through to the core, and I shiver in a cold sweat.

I started running my freshman year in high school, and six years later, I'm reaching that place where skill and drive mirror some kind of confidence—successfully completing my first half-marathon last summer. I'm on my way to qualifying as a finisher to run the full. I spend as much time as I can running. For me, it's the only time I know which direction I'm going.

My stopwatch reads forty-eight minutes. I fold over into a full-body bend, wrapping my hands around my ankles, satisfied I met my goal for the day. I complete my stretching routine and let myself into the front garden gate of the small apartment/condo I live in with my grandmother.

"Chelsea," Sherryl sings my name from the garden.

"Good morning." I wave on my way inside.

Sherryl and Cher rent the unit above Nan's. They're a part of that fiercely anti-establishment generation that somehow slipped in between the Great Depression and the Baby Boomers and survived. There aren't many who are still alive in San Francisco, but if you're looking for the final whispers of a cultural revolution, this corner of the city is probably a good bet. Every square foot is painted in poetry and vision and guts. A true community that beats to their own rhythm.

"The Sherries," a name they coined themselves, invite me up for dinner at least once a week and dig around my life like their herb garden, turning over the soil for something as interesting as growing up in the sixties. I'd be disappointed if I were them, but they keep inviting me over.

I grab a yogurt from the fridge and warm sliced apples in the toaster oven. While I wait, I draw an X on the wall calendar by the phone, marking my run and adding my time. Today's my day off from the restaurant, and the rest of my to-do list consists of one thing—help Nan at the farmers' market.

The toaster dings as the phone rings. I lift the receiver off the wall and reach over the counter to pull the apples out before they get soggy and I can't eat them.

"Hello?"

"Happy almost birthday, my Chels Bells."

"It's in three days, Mom. Premature much?"

"Well, I'm counting down. Twenty-one is big, and I've been planning," she squeals. "Your father and I are flying in from L.A. on Tuesday. I got us tickets to the Orpheum, then dinner in Chinatown—of course—and Dad wants to stop in Marin while we're there." Her bracelets clatter over the line.

I squeeze the receiver against my shoulder while sprinkling the apples with cinnamon. I shove a scalding bite into my mouth and rest against the counter.

"Okay, well." She keeps on talking while I quietly chew my food, covering the mouthpiece so she can't hear. I wait for her to take a breath or hang up without needing me to reply. At this point, she's carrying on a conversation with herself.

"Chels, we're beyond thrilled. I know we talk on the phone, but birthdays aren't the same without you in the house. I'm gonna get to squeeze my girl in the flesh and take you shopping in Union Square."

"Sounds good. Hey, Mom, I've gotta go meet Nan."

"Yes. Yes. Well, tell her I've made all the arrangements, and she's welcome to join if she wants. And make sure she has some wheatgrass and raw ginger set aside so I can blend my juice. Are you eating enough protein? Should I bring you some homemade nut powder? I've been grinding it myself."

"Hanging up. Love you."

Nut powder has the consistency equivalent of an ashtray. Mom swapped cigarettes for health fads a few years ago. Right now she's into liquifying her meals—last month it was all about kickboxing.

My focus zeroes in on the calendar. I hadn't started counting down. I try not to. I stretch my neck, shaking free from the carousel of apprehension that rolls around this time of year.

She's always made a show about my birthday, never missing an opportunity to throw a Summer-themed production. One year, she even rented a pony—stuck the poor thing in the middle of the street to ensure the neighbors would talk about it over coffee the next day.

In some ways she made my birthday about me, with an annual lemon cake and finding ways to tie in my revolving door of interests to her themes. But it's hard for things not to be about her. I suppose that's expected when your mom had a run in musical theater for two decades, including television and tours.

When I showed little interest in learning in the classroom, she tried to give me access to her world on stage, hoping I might shine like she had.

Maybe it won't be so bad this year. I can legally have a glass of wine now, and I've been working tirelessly to show my parents the progress I've made with training and living on my own. Well, not entirely on my own, but away from everything I've ever known.

"Chelsea, doll—you're here." Nan greets me with a wet kiss. I dab my cheek on my flannel when she looks away. "The jellies need to be made pretty. Will you?"

"Hi, Nan." I drop my messenger bag behind crates of canned jams and twist my quickly rinsed-off hair into a high bun. "Oh, this one's new."

"Boysenberry," she notes, enunciating her Rs. "Not as sweet as the orange or strawberry. Make sure you keep one for yourself." She counts her inventory on the table with a golf pencil and jotting down the total. "And I think it's a keeper, so I'll need you to design a label."

"I can do that."

Brick paths, street lamps, and sweet bay trees surround The Heart of the City Farmers' Market. We typically set up next to the same vendors: Carla's Pastas, who use their family's hundred-year-old recipe to bottle sauces, and Gracie and Yuze Chen, who sell the best homemade hand-pies around, evidenced by the line wrapping around their tent every weekend.

Great neighbors with benefits, we swap goods and help each other out. I try to taste everything when it's offered, partly because I was taught to be gracious and partly to push myself past my comfort level.

When I was a kid, I'd race to the trash, spitting out the contents of my no-thank-you helpings, using the palm of my hand like a wool scouring pad. As a teenager, I'd learned to hold my breath long enough for Mom to turn the corner, and then I'd stash cooked carrots in my napkin.

I pop a piece of grape bubble gum in my mouth and chomp, dissolving the pungent fragrance from childhood.

Fortunately, I've outgrown my aversion to most foods, though Nan says I have a super sense for lots of other things—a nose for the best fruit, an eye for how a table arrangement should look, and the taste for both. She also likes to remind me that I have a twisted sense of humor and that's why she keeps me around. If that's true, I'm pretty sure I learned from the best.

She also keeps me around because I have a decent idea of what people want and can call it from miles away.

Live music kicks on, and vendors have filled their rental spaces with specialty foods, artisan crafts, and farm-grown produce. When ten A.M. hits, two groups of early shoppers stroll through. The first are window shoppers. They come with their coffees and dogs and sometimes step in close but never long enough to incite a hope of a sale. I stay seated for those.

Then there's the skilled shopper, with a planned route of where they're headed. They know exactly what tables to scout before the sun's directly overhead and the paths are too crowded to cut through. They're mostly regulars, so I anticipate what they need by having their orders organized and ready to go. Those I stand for.

Nan insists she makes enough money to come back each week. Once it doesn't sustain itself, she won't do it anymore. I'll believe it when I see it. Cause it's jams, jellies, and honey sticks, and it's Saturday, and we're always here—rain or shine.

I help arrange the table, pushing Nan's bouquets of purple roses to the corners, checking the mason jars to ensure there's enough water, then stage the small jam jars covered in Rainy Days J & J's "Jams and Jellies" stickers. I step in front of the table to inspect. Beneath the merchandise is a gray linen tablecloth with hand-painted white clouds. Beginning left and working their way across the table, jars of fruit and spreads are displayed from red to purple.

I make final tweaks to the roses, taking a long inhale of their candied citrus scent.

"They were cut today," she informs me as I open my eyes.

"I saw a new art exhibit on my way in. There's some photography I want to check out. When the rush settles, I'd like to go, if you don't mind."

"Rainy days." A laid-back voice wraps around me from behind, barreling up my spine. The shock sends me spinning on my heel.

"Hi." My pulse is pounding for no logical reason.

"Hey, there," the guy in front of me replies, his attention darting over my shoulder.

Oh, right. I'm obstructing his view. I step aside and find my way over to the empty chair, bothered that I can't get an immediate read on what he's looking for. The glass clinks as he picks up jars, my line of sight following the fingerprint residue he's leaving behind on every item he touches. *Didn't someone teach him museum rules?* Under my breath, I rattle off Nan's saying —*You breaky, you takey*—thoroughly entertaining myself.

"In the market for something sweet?" Nan projects, her tone nudging me to kindly keep my thoughts locked up or eat the cost of the sale.

"Your business name. It's clever. So, all these ingredients are sourced locally?"

"They are and the very best. She picks them by hand. California's known for its fruit trees," I say with pride.

"Yes, I know," he replies, leaning in.

"Young man, are you sourced locally?" Nan heckles.

"Nan," I bark-whisper, the accusation leaping from my windpipe, landing squeaky and disruptive. I don't know why I care. Nan's just looking for a laugh, and she gets one.

His is deep and carefree, and the reverberation travels from my ears to my toes.

"I go to college on the East Coast. I'm home on break."

"You don't say. My daughter—"

My vision shoots to her again, this time with a raised brow at her feisty attempt to mess with this seemingly nice person.

"I beg your pardon. My granddaughter here—she must be your age."

"Oh, yeah."

I peek at his smirk as I hide my smile.

"Hey," he says, this time noticing me. "Do you have a favorite?" He points to the jams.

My gaze returns to the table. "Grape's my go-to, but we got in boysenberry today. It's hot off Nan's counter. Can't get any better."

"How can I say no to Nan's counter? Do you offer taste tests?"

Nan interjects, "Only to our special local customers home on break."

"Well, then, I'm in luck."

I open one of the boysenberry jars and stick a wooden tester in. He stares at me and says nothing, so I take that as my cue to busy myself with organizing honey sticks.

Out of the corner of my eye, I might catch the way he drops the small amount of jam onto his tongue, and I settle back into the chair, pressing my feet into the ground.

He's methodical in the way he holds the tester up to his nose and sniffs, like he can distinguish the ratio of berries and sugar. I shouldn't be staring.

I'm not one for crushes. I know it's normal to date in your twenties, but I'm not in college and work a lot at the restaurant, so I don't easily meet people my age. I kind of just serve people my age. No one's asking out the girl in the penguin costume rattling off the fresh catch of the day.

I hop off my daydream train when he asks Nan, "Rainy Days —what's it mean?"

"A family secret." Nan winks. "A simple reminder to savor life while you can."

He swallows. "I'm a fan."

I swallow, too. "Of?"

"Rainy days. Savoring." He draws in a breath, "But especially, this jam. I'm experimenting with new recipes, and I think this right here could be the thing that takes it to the next level."

"What kind of—"

"I'll take them all," he states.

"Take. Them. All?" I stumble over my words and shock— dizzy from counting how many Saturdays that will secure Nan.

"Don't have to tell me twice," Nan pipes up. "Got your own bags, honey?"

"Just the one."

"That's okay. They'll keep safe in the crates, anyhow. Chels, will you grab Mr. Locally-Sourced some crates for his purchase?"

I'm smiling as I walk over, hearing a familiar tin can pop open. "Would you like a cherry drop while you wait?" Nan offers.

When I turn around with the crate, this easy-on-the-eyes guy, his face falls like a wrung-out cloud dripping to the ground, and his shoulders drop as his hands slide into his pockets. He blinks, whispering my name as a question. "Chels?"

My giggle is out of place and so are my slippery hands as I load up the jams. "That's me."

He clears his throat. "It can't be."

"What?" The crate slips, and my nose scrunches up in protest. It's a simple task to fill an empty crate, but I still manage to drop a jar onto the ground.

"Chels Bells?" he asks.

Nan's shrug confirms my ears didn't deceive me, and by her blank you-know-as-much-as-I-know stare, it seems between the two of us, we have no clue what's going on.

"I'm sorry. Have we met?" I situate the crate.

"You know my granddaughter?"

His sneakers scrape along the concrete. The shuffling kicks up some dust that's settled, making me sneeze and jogging an image from my mind—*the sound of scraping.*

I watch him pull out his wallet and zip it open. He removes cash, refusing the change.

"Well, ladies, it's been a pleasure. Thank you. For the jam. And the chat."

When I peel my attention from the table, he's all squared shoulders and straight spine, walking away with Nan's entire stock.

"That was one nice, kinda odd boy."

"And all those jams, Nan."

"Guess you can check out the art exhibit sooner than planned," she suggests, locking up her cash box.

"That was strange, right? Knowing my name?" I collect the honey sticks to return to the wagon.

"It sure was. Too bad I couldn't get a good look into those eyes to find some answers. You kids are always covering your bodies with ridiculous oversized slacks and sunglasses and that Dodgers hat. Don't get me started."

"What did you say?" My tongue runs like sandpaper on the roof of my mouth.

"Don't know how anyone can be from this city and call themselves a Dodgers fan."

Rainy days, Dodgers, blades scraping, Chels Bells . . . I leave Nan as she runs down a list of reasons why rooting for a rival team is a disgrace and book it into the swollen crowd—kids riding on shoulders, guitars and drums blaring through speakers, fried dough wafting in the air. I search for a roaming royal blue target, for the boy who disappeared, and all I see are black and orange ball caps and jerseys, yellow and green awnings, rainbow pinwheels, rotating sausage, onions, and peppers . . . everything but Seth Hansen.

5

SETH

"Seth?" Mom calls, her heels tapping on the tile.

I drop my keys on the kitchen island and slide the crate over its slick marble surface. "Hey."

"Oh, I see you're into—" She picks up one of the handheld jars, twisting off the lilac lid to sniff its contents. "That's a lot of PB&Js." She places the jar into its square slot and adjusts the satin handkerchief around her neck.

Every visible square inch of Mom is a pristine canvas—not a single black-coated eyelash out of place.

"There's a sauce recipe I'm working on, and I didn't want to run out." I survey my purchase. Hasty? Sure. "Plus, the sellers were an older lady and her granddaughter." Worth it? No doubt.

"You're a good kid," she reassures herself, patting me on the back.

I noticed her large rolling suitcase by the door when I walked in, nearly tripping over the damn thing. I also noticed an empty fridge when I arrived last night. Can't imagine she's been here for long.

"Sorry I have to get on a flight so soon. You just arrived."

"It's fine, Mom. I'll catch you next month or on one of your layovers in New York."

"You've got the place to yourself. Any plans?"

I eye the dozen jars on the counter.

"Right, well, lock up when you head back to school." Mom slips into a camel trench coat, fluffing her platinum hair out from the collar, double-checking that the sleeves of her navy cashmere sweater cover her wrists. "Enjoy your time home." She proceeds with caution, blowing me a kiss on her way out the door. "Love you."

Today's cyclone from the past has left me grateful for the solitude in the now-empty house my mom owns with her husband. After a string of less-than-desirable living circumstances, she met Ajay mid-air over the Atlantic on her way to London. He's bicoastal, so they swap living abroad and in the States. She's happy, finally, and that means something to me.

Being at school, sometimes our schedules will line up. And sometimes, our relationship's a string of quick phone calls and postcards.

Natural light enters the floor-to-ceiling windows, warming the sterile space—bare walls and monochromatic furniture.

Ajay's got more money than he knows where to put it, so Mom and I are like an investment to him, maybe even a charity. That's what he implied when he insisted on taking care of the remainder of my college tuition that wasn't covered by academic scholarships. *This money is me placing stock in your future.* The crate of jellies would suggest he made a risky investment. He should've put that money toward someone who needed it more. At the very least, donate to a local food bank or shelter.

I pull out a notepad from the kitchen drawer to map out some plans while I'm home, turning over my usual spots, favorite eats, pick-up basketball games at the community center, and friends to catch up with. The pen stops short a few swoops in, stilling on the page. The only thing I can focus on and the only words that manage to get written down are Chelsea Bell. I hadn't heard her name in so long.

The next morning, I show up at the park, knowing there'll be nothing but empty benches and open sky. But on the off-chance she remembered too, I had to go back and find out.

Alone on the concrete, she's sitting cross-legged, wearing overalls and an oversized cherry-red cardigan covered in pom-pom balls. Curly blond hair drapes over her shoulder, and a bright yellow messenger bag rests in her lap.

I exhale as I get closer, shoving my restless hands deep into my jacket pockets. This can't be real. No one randomly finds their friend a decade later over a jar of jam.

She stands on my approach.

"It's you." My shoulders sink.

She looks up from the glistening pavement. Her stormy stare pulls me right into its center. "You came back." She sounds surprised.

Wondering if she thinks this is as incredible as I think it is.

"Have you been waiting long?" I ask.

"Only ten years," she replies with an edge.

I can't tell if she's excited to see me or mad or indifferent. It bothers me that I don't know who she is anymore. "Sorry I bailed yesterday. I thought maybe you didn't remember me."

Her voice treads with caution as it smooths out. "You're sorry about yesterday?"

"I didn't, at first, you know . . . recognize you." She looks around at the fountain in the middle of the square, at the quiet pedestrians taking a Sunday stroll. "But I've never forgotten you."

Chelsea's nose crinkles up as she crosses her arms over her chest. *She has a chest now.* That's new.

My gaze falls to the ground—to our matching hi-top sneakers. "So, you hungry?"

Meryl's is an old lunch car that has withstood the test of time. Skyscrapers shot up around the diner, and she held her ground.

"I love it here." As I settle into the maroon and cream booth, it squawks loud enough to draw Chelsea's cheeks to her eyes. She's got on this yellow choker necklace and cola-colored lip balm.

"These seats aren't shy at all," she observes, pulling off her heart-shaped plastic sunglasses from the top of her head and throwing them on the gray-speckled linoleum tabletop. "What do you suppose this once was made of?" She shifts on her side of the booth.

"Something original to the era. Probably leather."

She runs her short fingernails over the patched cracks in the material. "It amazes me what time does to the surface of things."

"Looks like we both made it north finally."

"How long have you lived here in the city?" she asks.

"Ten years."

Chelsea's eyes widen. My pulse kicks into high gear, and I say anything to keep us talking about now, not then. "It's a different world from L.A. That usually surprises most people."

"I had to buy a jacket."

"You liking it?" What did I just say? I sound ridiculous. What's next? The weather. Sure, Hansen—real smooth.

"It's out of driving distance from my parents. And it's got great hills."

I'm relieved she's engaging, but she hasn't relaxed, and I'm wired from adrenaline and jet lag.

The waitress approaches our table, and Chelsea smiles for the first time today, admiring the woman's blunt blue bob and row of piercings covering every inch of her ears.

Her nude lips smack together while she flips over our rounded coffee mugs. "Coffee? Or something stronger?" she asks, and we both accept the coffee. Black. "You know what you'd like to order, or do you need some time?"

Yes, more than you know. "You cool if I order for both of us?"

"That's fine." Her shoulders settle back against the booth. The morning light shines over her hair in soft waves.

"Great," I say, peeking at the waitress's name tag. *Rachel.* She's directing a red-flag raised brow at Chelsea, signaling a secret code that transpires through eye contact alone, that she'll block my side of the booth if Chels wants to run. I see this kind of shit during parties at school, and usually I don't pay attention to it unless someone needs help. But I want to know what Chelsea's thinking. And I want to tell Rachel that she doesn't know there's history here. I know what I'm ordering for us because it's why I brought her to this exact spot. "Hi, Rachel— we'll have two number nines with fresh-squeezed OJ, please."

"That'll be two nines, gotcha," she echoes, swapping glances between both of us. "Bacon or sausage?"

Chelsea throws her hands in the air, leaving the decision to me.

That makes me smile. Not because it's funny—which it is— but because she either trusts me enough to order for her or she's testing me. If it's the first, I can work with that, and if it's the second, I'll rise to the occasion. Either way, it's progress.

"Bacon, well done."

"Got it." Rachel's sigh is another warning sign, but this one's aimed at me—*hey buddy, you order for her today, and the next thing you know, you're controlling her whole life*—as she slides the notepad back into the pocket of her loosely tied apron, turning toward the counter.

"Rachel."

She twists around. "Yeah."

"Extra butter and powdered sugar, please."

Rachel acknowledges me, and I return to Chelsea. She meets my stare, picking up her coffee. A few moments of strained silence stretch across the table.

"Red or green?"

She clears her throat. "What?"

"It's a question. Red or green?" I repeat.

She looks at her sweater and back at me.

"Point taken. Cats or dogs?"

"That's a trick question."

"True. You still gotta choose."

She nods, accepting the challenge. "Cats to cuddle with. Dogs to walk with."

"Well played. Next—sweet or salty."

"Sweet."

There's no way I can dive into the past on an empty stomach. I'll play this game for however long it takes for her to get comfortable and for me *to build up the nerve to apologize.*

"Sing or dance?"

"Dance." She leans in closer. Her lower lip, full and pouting.

"Laugh until you cry or cry until you laugh?"

"Whichever leaves me smiling."

I squeeze the brim of my hat, concealing the grin tugging at the corner of my mouth. I flip my hat backward, choosing a question I already know the answer to.

6

CHELSEA

"*W*as I right?" he asks.

My jaw slacks open as I inhale the steam coming off the triple stack of buttermilk pancakes on my plate, a pad of butter soaking into the center. "Yeah, definitely pancakes over waffles."

"You once said it's the only thing that got you out of bed early." Seth picks up the syrup and spins the spout around the stack from the outer edge—one, two, three times—working his way into the middle.

"Impressive memory." I tilt my head as he hums along to the music from our table-top jukebox.

He sings the lyrics, adding, "This is Train. 'Drops of Jupiter.' Ever heard it?"

I shake my head.

"Music's my escape," Seth says, grabbing his utensils and slicing right through his stack with the side of his fork. He shoves the heaping hot bite into his mouth. My mind stops making sense as it orbits around this familiar stranger sitting across from me. "You like it?"

"I don't *not* like it."

He flips through the pages. "Do you know any of these bands?"

I shrug. "Maybe. By sound, not by name."

Seth shakes his head, his ears and hair sticking out from his hat. "You gonna eat that before it gets cold?" he asks, chewing— or more like chomping.

Those pancakes are calling my name. I've kept a pretty close eye on my diet while training, and this carb party will come to haunt me later. I blow out a breath. It would be rude to not eat at all. Although, the longer he stares at me, the harder my stomach flips, shrinking my appetite.

I went back this morning hoping he might show up. I had to find out if it was him. And now he's eating breakfast across from me like it's some regular old thing we do.

"It's too pretty to eat," I redirect, checking the dispenser to ensure there are enough paper napkins.

"Food too pretty to eat is a waste."

"Have you seen those baking shows where they paint cakes with actual gold?" I sip my orange juice, clearing the edge in my voice.

"All I watch these days are Dodgers games, when I can catch them on the East Coast, and the occasional show on the Cooking Channel." His words are half-audible as he demolishes his plate while I slowly tear a piece of pancake with my fingers.

"What's happening right now?" Seth asks as I rip off another piece.

"Tastes better this way."

"Do you do that with all your meals?"

"The ones I want to enjoy."

He resumes chewing, his gaze lingering alongside the sugary sweet aroma.

"Quit watching me," I whisper, grabbing my fork and stabbing it into the stack.

"I can't help it." His cheeks warm like freshly spooled cotton candy. "I feel like if I take my eyes off you, you'll disappear."

"I'm not the one who disappears on people."

The color drains from Seth's face, and I immediately regret how I said it. At the fountain, I meant to ask him why he never met me at the playground, but then I couldn't find the right words. They were lost in my own embarrassment. It was obviously a bigger deal to me. I was the one who showed up. I was the one who cried myself to sleep every night for weeks. I've only played this scenario in my mind hundreds of times, and when I actually get the opportunity, I come off bitter. And now I have no idea what to say or do. He keeps staring at me. Is he searching for flaws?

His lips move to speak when Rachel appears by my side. "More coffee?" She reaches her brown pot between our unfinished thoughts.

"Thanks," I say as Rachel turns to leave with an eye roll and Seth picks up his mug. "Rachel, is it possible to get cold butter?"

"Sure thing." She heads into the kitchen.

"That's specific," Seth notes, cocking his head.

"It's gross when it's melted and mushy."

"You feel strongly about your condiments."

I shrug. "Mostly butter."

"Mustard?" He props his elbow on the table.

"Dijon," I reply without hesitation.

Seth's chuckle rattles his fork against the plate.

"It appears I feel strongly about mustard, too."

"You're an odd duck, Chelsea Bell," he says and sighs like he's been holding this confession in for years.

I push around the pancake, waiting for my butter delivery. The flutter brewing in my chest tickles my lungs, and I hold back tears that should've expired the day he bailed. There's no reason for these anymore. I scold myself for not trying harder to hold it together.

He's not saying anything I haven't heard my whole life. The message is clear. I'm different. Too much. Too little. Too direct. Too shy. Writes funny. Dresses strange. Take your pick. Whatever, I'm used to this. We can have breakfast, and he can go back to his coast, and I will waddle back to my pond.

But if that's true, why is he here? Why are his eyes avoiding mine now? And why does that hurt me so much?

Rachel drops a ramekin with three slices of hard butter on the table.

I cough a little, gathering the courage to confront part of the past—the part that's easier to talk about. "I wanted to thank you for helping me that day with my mom when you stuck up for me. It meant a lot."

"Oh." He takes a moment, searching my eyes, waiting for more. "Don't mention it. I don't really remember that part."

"I've been wanting to mention it for a decade, so—"

"Things with your mom, are they still . . ." Seth swallows, "Sensitive?"

"It helps that I'm here and she's there."

"You know that thing I said about you being a duck? I just want to make sure you know that it's a term of endearment."

My lashes lift, and I exhale carefully. "How do you repay kindness, Seth Hansen?"

He pulls a sip from his mug. "I think when someone least expects it."

What does that look like?

"Hey, whatever you don't eat, we'll grab a to-go box for."

"Okay," I agree, fiddling with a loose pom-pom ball on my sleeve.

After he finishes his plate and mine's wrapped up, Seth pays the bill, and we step back outside to the weekend soundtrack of taxis and tourists.

We aimlessly move down the sidewalk, side by side, not vocalizing a clear destination, but I'm also not in any rush to leave now. I have more questions—specific questions—for Seth. I've had too much time to dissect the whys on my own, and nothing ever made sense.

I wrap my hair up in a bun then shove my hands in the pockets of my overalls as we cross the street, kicking through steam in our path.

When we get to the other side, Seth picks up a discarded container, dropping it in a trashcan. He tells me to wait and walks over to a person in layers of random clothes—short-sleeve shirts, long-sleeve shirts, and a sweater—holding a cardboard sign. Her legs are straddling a bag of belongings as she sits on the steps of a convenience store, off to the side so as not to block the door.

Everyone passes her, but Seth stops, squatting by her shoeless feet, dropping something from his pocket into a large Styrofoam cup. I lift my sunglasses, resting them in my hair to be perfectly clear about what I'm seeing. When he returns, empty-handed, to where I'm standing on the corner, I act as though I didn't just witness him give my half-appreciated breakfast to someone who probably hasn't had a good meal in days or weeks. I don't think he wants to bring attention to himself or this person.

Yes, I think that must be the best type of kindness. The kind that doesn't require an audience or applause.

"I'm sorry about disappearing," Seth blurts out, waiting for the light to turn. "It's been on my mind."

My voice raises over engines and busyness. "I thought you were kidnapped. Or in the hospital with a broken bone. I thought you weren't real. That I made you up." The truth slips out before I can catch it.

Seth's palms land on my shoulders, his warm thumbs graze my neck, and he pulls me to face him. Where my eyes narrow from the light, Seth's irises grow distinctly wider in the sun, sincere and bright, as his thumbprints stick to my skin.

"I'm real. Never broken a bone—fingers crossed—and I guess I was sort of taken. I didn't have time to tell you that we were leaving. I'm so sorry." He lowers my sunglasses over my eyes, the arms landing lopsided on top of my ears.

His hands pressing into me sends my pulse spiraling. He was my friend, even if for a week, and a sense of relief unwinds in my gut knowing I didn't imagine it.

I don't always believe in things, but I want to believe *him*. I break away from the intensity of his grip. I pick up the pace, bursting into a walking run, even more confused by the debate my head and heart are having.

SETH

"Hey, wait up, roadrunner." I'm near-sprinting to catch up with Chelsea's stride as her messenger bag bounces off her hip. She's fast. Steadier than I recall on rollerblades—*does she still have a pair?* I'm embarrassed by how winded I am.

"Running habit." She raises a brow, offering a whisper of a smile. "I'm training for the San Francisco Marathon. If I can finish it, I'll qualify for the Boston Marathon."

"No, shit! That's awesome, Chels."

She brings her thumb to her mouth, dropping it when she observes me watching.

"Is it okay that I gave away the rest of your breakfast? I should've asked first."

"I'm glad you did." She presses forward.

"So, you're running and working at the farmers' market. There's so much to catch up on." I'm pretty decent at reading people, but I think I'm striking out here. "I have an idea."

"Does it involve you asking me twenty questions?"

I laugh. Every cell in my body lights up, and I reach for her hand.

"This may be a double standard, but I do have a few more for you."

My hand drops to my side, and I slow my stride. I can't avoid breathing in the subtle scent of warm butter—and traces of sunshine, wet grass, and citrus. She smells like cheerful memories from a long ass time ago, spring and daisies in the rain. I exhale steadily, cautiously stepping in close to listen. "Ask me, Chels. Ask and I'll answer, but first, you wanna come over to my place tonight? We can finally have movie night."

"Is that a good idea?"

"What do you mean?"

"I don't know. It's just that, well, the last time we made a plan, it didn't really work out."

My pulse accelerates. I stop walking. "You're right. It didn't. Here, take it."

She looks at me holding up a slack fist between us with my pinkie sticking out. "What's this?"

"A promise to be there tonight. Go ahead."

She smiles. "Seth, we aren't eleven anymore."

"Speak for yourself."

7

CHELSEA

I checked the address Seth gave me three times, and it's accurate.

Joss Lane is one of the nicest streets in the city. I can't imagine Seth living here, but what do I know about him? Nothing but whispers of memories—doors with chipped paint and broken doorbells. I agreed to come tonight because I want more time—I have new questions—I remind myself.

It's not like before. He said they had to go. He couldn't control that. I can't drag the past around with me everywhere I go.

On my approach, I stare up the drive at rows of glass and oak nestled between two asymmetrical homes. I count each step leading to the front door while I ignore the warning images in my head. What if no one answers? What if someone does and it's not Seth?

I knock once, hand over my chest, begging it to settle, and then Seth appears with wet hair, in hunter green shorts and one of those fancy white cotton T-shirts from a store with blaring music meant to look casual but costs more than I make in a single shift waiting tables. My boss wasn't too happy with me when I called out sick.

It wasn't entirely a lie. I'm not well enough to perform tonight. I wouldn't be able to remember anyone's orders. Not with this freshly showered man on my mind.

When did Seth get fancy?

"You made it," he greets me with a lazy and decadent smile like we didn't just see each other hours ago. "Did you bring the goods?"

"I think I managed."

"This is the most overdue movie date ever."

I pause in the entryway, careful not to slip over the combination of letters—d-a-t-e—that he let loose like an upturned sack of Scrabble tiles.

Seth clears his throat, moving aside, and I walk in, placing my bag on the counter, immediately pulling out the snacks and movies I brought.

He puts his hand over the bag. "Wait."

My whole body stiffens. What are we waiting for? Why am I so nervous?

"I need a few things from the grocery store so I can make us dinner."

I swish around the gulp of air trapped in my mouth. He's friendly and smiley. He didn't mean "date," and he didn't mean to almost hold my hand, either.

"Do you have a favorite meal?" he asks.

"Anything."

"You've gotta have an opinion."

My shoulders shrug to my ears. "I don't. Anything will be great."

He leans over the counter, and I slide onto a white leather barstool. I don't know what to do with my hands. This place looks like it's ripped right from the pages of an *Architectural Digest*. There's no sign of actual life here. No hanging plants or area rugs. No key bowl or bookshelves. *No records.* Do I remember him talking about records?

I catch myself smiling at the crate of jellies.

"Just like you didn't have an opinion about jam or mustard or butter," he teases.

Okay, I give in and laugh. "Food's complicated with me. I usually eat grilled chicken breast. Greens. Water," I answer, digging out my lip balm from my pocket.

"Any marinades or anything?"

"I don't cook much, and all those extra calories mess with my runs."

"What flavor is that?" he asks, watching me smooth a generous layer over my lips.

"Dr. Pepper."

Seth takes a pad of paper and a pen and shoots them across the counter to me. "You scribe. I'm going to brainstorm a list."

"I have terrible handwriting. I can just remember it," I suggest, slipping the tube back into my pocket.

"At school, I'm around chefs all day. I can read anything, Chelsea."

"What and where are you studying?"

"I'm getting my degree in hospitality management at Cornell. During the year, I work at a local restaurant, dishwashing for now. Sometimes I help on the expo line during our rush. But I'm pumped for this summer. A few of us in the program were chosen to open a restaurant with a renowned chef in the city."

"You mean New York? Not here."

"Yeah, exactly." He beams.

"College and everything. Wow." That explains this refined version of Seth. It's hard comparing versions of someone you've known to who they may be now, but the core of a person doesn't change, and beneath all the polish and shine, he's much the same—honest, enthusiastic, and full of ideas.

"It's a solid gig. Pays well and keeps me out of trouble."

He's got a lot to share, and I would too, with all these exciting things happening in his life. I don't know what I expected of the kid who didn't attend school, but now he's got this bright future ahead of him. He didn't run away as planned, but it looks like it worked out for him.

"What about you? What's the world of Chelsea Bell look like these days?"

I'm not in school, and I have no major career plans. *Can't say that.* "Hey, you ever get that motorcycle?" I ask, doodling around the edges of the lined notepad.

Seth nods and pulls his elbows off the counter, straightening his back and tearing his eyes from mine. "Okay, well, we need whatever flaky fish we can find." He flips on the radio and starts to pace. "You eat fish, right? Of course you do."

I chuckle in relief that he didn't press me to answer his question. I could mention my job on the wharf, but he's already full steam ahead onto something else, so I listen and draw flower patterns.

"I haven't saved enough for a bike. Plus, I can't park it in the dorm, and it's not great in winter. Good memory, by the way." He continues with his list, telling me, "Add garlic, thyme, lemon, cayenne." He opens the cabinets and fridge, both bare, then closes them while tapping his fingers against his thigh. "Oh, and don't forget butter. Extra butter." He winks, and his layered dark blond waves fall in front of his eyes. I'm grateful for it because my cheeks pinch into a smile, and I probably look ridiculous smiling at him like we're still eleven and he offered me his lollipop.

Chewing on my bottom lip, I scramble to write down the conveyor belt of words he's spewing. His mind moves at the rate of an intense run, so I use an abbreviation system I picked up at the restaurant to write down what he's saying.

"That should do it," he concludes, invigorated, and I need a nap.

Seth reaches for the list, and I reluctantly pass it to him, bracing myself for the train wreck that will be him interpreting what I've written down. The same way teachers would stumble over my assignments—handing my papers back to me covered in a sea of red ink.

"This looks good. Let's shop," he says, and my jaw drops. *He can read my handwriting?* Seth grabs a light jacket from a closet and offers it to me.

"I'm fine, thanks." But am I?

He has to have noticed the misspelled words. He probably doesn't want to make it awkward. I should be thankful for the favor—and his kindness—but as we walk out the door to head to the store, all that registers is an early evening chill up my arms.

This isn't fine at all.

When we were eleven, even though we had different lives, we wanted the same thing—to be anywhere but where we were. We were going to take on the world together. I related to Seth, and I think I understood him, too. He listened to and understood me. Even though the details have faded, I never forgot the rush or him, and I've never found anything remotely close to it since.

Now I'm looking at him—in pristine packaging—so close I could cradle his elbow in the palm of my hand and guide him back to a time when we were on an even playing field. This Seth is headed lightyears away from where I stand.

This shouldn't bother me, but something does. He drags his fingers through his hair, and I slow my stride, covering my mouth with both hands. *Oh.* It could be as simple as he's visually pleasing—cute and smart and familiar—but it's not just that. It's not like running either—one foot in front of the other —or a simple grilled chicken breast or memorizing someone's grocery list. This is all new. My heart pounds. My vision blurs. My lips crack like dried petals.

This is complicated. Not because I like him—he's easy to get along with. It's how much I like listening to his goals, the way his jacket casually hangs off his shoulders and hugs at his hips, the way he remembers things about me, how his thick hair is always in the way of his almond-shaped eyes—a curtain I want to pull back.

All of this newness has me feeling out of my league here, tripping over my feet on the sidewalk so abruptly that I don't have time to slam my eyes shut as I fall face-first—inches away from hard pavement and stitches and a massively bruised ego —but I never make contact with the ground.

Instead, me and my rapid heartbeats and messy hair land in the arms of a strong and soft cloud.

I mean, Seth. Because he catches me.

8

SETH

*T*he local grocer has everything we need, and Chelsea's list is the cutest thing I've ever held, with her short-hand abbreviations and doodles. The way she writes thyme as "time" and butter as "bdr" has me smiling the entire time we're shopping. And all her drawings—they're playful and detailed.

She's quiet as we stroll along the perimeter of the store and load up our cart. I check with her a few times to make sure she's okay after her near fall on the sidewalk. She assures me she's over the startle of it, but she doesn't say much else about anything.

I don't want to pry. I'm just happy to be hanging out, so I do all the talking, and she listens—the kind of listening that feels like a heavy blanket you wrap yourself in.

When we get back to the house, Chelsea claims a seat at the counter, and I unpack our haul. "I'm making a macadamia nut-crusted mahi-mahi, which is a popular dish at the restaurant. The sauce it's served with is safe—crisp and clean—and my head's been spinning with how to spice it up. If I can combine the savory flavor with something surprising—and then BAM! It hits me at your stand. The jam!" On the counter, I organize the ingredients by steps and pull out the pans and utensils I'll use. "Ready to be my food critic?"

"I won't have anything critical to say."

"How will I learn?"

Chelsea props an elbow on the counter, resting her chin on her palm. "On two conditions. First, I wait until the end to give you my opinion. And second, while you're 'cheffing,' I can ask you a few things."

"Shoot," I reply, tossing a hand towel over my shoulder. "Wait, do I need a Dr. Pepper for this?"

"You might." She giggles, a little flirty.

No, she's not flirting with me. Get out of your head, Hansen.

The sizzling oil in the pan infuses the air with a mild cloud of smoke. That's why her eyes are sparkling and her cheeks are rosy. She's not looking at me like anything other than a familiar face with answers—a time capsule to all the years we've missed.

I grab a soda for each of us, and we crack them open at the same time. The fizzy bubbles tickle my throat.

"Where are we? Whose house is this? What has Seth Hansen been doing for ten years?"

For her silence earlier, I'm taken aback by the sudden line of fire. "How about you start?"

"That wasn't our deal."

I wink and focus on chopping garlic. "Look, my hands are full, and I've gotta concentrate. You wouldn't want me chopping off a finger."

"No, I wouldn't." She chugs her soda. "The replay's short. Nan's getting older. And I like it here. The change of seasons, the museums, the architecture."

"Your mom still performing?"

"She gets the occasional community theater gig, but

nothing like before. She's not traveling for work anymore, either, which I think she misses." Chelsea traces her finger over the aluminum lip of the can. "She wanted us all to move to New York when I graduated so I could follow in her footsteps. I mean, she didn't say it like that, but it was obvious."

I drain the excess oil and transfer the flour-coated filets to the pan. The dusting of cayenne is going to steal the show in this sauce. "We could've been in New York at the same time? How cool."

Her tone sobers. "I would've been miserable there."

I nod, pretending to focus on the sizzling filets, averting my eyes from her. I know she's not talking about me specifically. She means being in the city under her parents' purview, but the grasp in my gut holds tight—she didn't hesitate or consider a scenario in which we would've been together.

In the living room, which is an extension of the kitchen, Chelsea finds one side of the black leather couch while I test out the VCR. This thing hasn't been used. *Wasteful.* All this luxury in the house with no one to enjoy it.

I blow into the open block of the tape deck a couple of times.

"Where are all the pictures?" she asks. "Of your family. Mom, Dad, you?"

I push in *To Catch A Thief* and press play.

The living room is more like a waiting room with a couple of extended two-seaters—enough for the both of us but not big enough for any kind of bubble if she wants to maintain one.

She's been quiet since I put a plate in front of her, and I can't stand to wait any longer. I have to know. "Did you like dinner?"

"You couldn't tell?"

"You've barely spoken two words since, so . . . leaves a mind to wander."

"I was eating. You need me to say it? Seth, it was bomb."

"No, I don't need you to say it, but I like hearing you say it." I plop down next to her.

She crosses her legs, tucking her feet under them, and her wide gaze narrows to her lap. "I don't mean to be so blunt, but I'm curious who you are now. I mean, is this house a rental, or did you win the lottery?"

I sigh, hating this part. Am I gonna tell my sob story to a beautiful girl and ruin a good movie night? *Fuck no.* I pause the tape, which has been rolling opening credits, leaning into the facts. "This is where my mom and her husband, Ajay, live. My dad's gone. Who knows . . . he probably drank his whole life away."

Chelsea turns toward me, her eyes reflecting the screen's light. "What?" she chokes on the word. "He died?"

"Shit, Chels, no. Sorry." I grab her hands in mine. This isn't working. I should've explained this all earlier and clearer instead of causing her to worry. That's the last thing I want to do. "You'd think I'd be better at this."

"You don't have to tell me." She stares at my hands on hers.

I let them go. "I want to try." My pulse gallops in place. I can't imagine she doesn't sense its vibration.

"Sometimes, I can't find the right words—or words at all," she mumbles.

The sunset through the windows begs to convince me the house is cozy. I brush off a biting cool breeze from outside, grabbing a decorative blanket from the arm of the couch and draping it over our legs.

If I've learned anything in the last ten years or ten seconds, it's that some stories are never easy to talk about. Time only softens the details. But I have to be careful because words matter, and everything you say counts for you or against you.

In the static stretch of space between us, Chelsea's gray gaze warms to a mossy green. I take a step out of the shadows, careful to navigate the maze without getting lost in it. "I left you that morning to go back and pack. Just as we planned. When I walked through the door of my house, I expected to sneak in and out like I'd done before. Figured their fight had blown over. When my mom . . ." My throat tightens, and I get out the part that I can, leaving the rest behind. "She'd aged a lifetime in a matter of hours. She took us to San Francisco."

"Oh." Chelsea's brows pinch in the center.

If I could, I'd tell her everything about that day, but it's not my story to tell.

I want to remember the great week we spent together as kids. The swings and blading, discovering the city together, our teeth coated with sugar from penny candy. And it's been a decade. Some things are left for good reason.

"Listen." I clear the stickiness as I swallow. "Some people die and are in the ground, and that's it. Game over. My dad's alive, but he's dead to me."

She scoots closer, and I can't back up. I'm not sure I want to either, and under the pressure of my opening this book, tears roll over Chelsea's quivering upper lip, a glistening trail she licks.

I pull her into my arms, and she wraps hers around my neck. We squeeze in the silence. Maybe for the same reasons—for the missed years—or maybe for different reasons.

We hold on to each other, and I whisper into her soft curls. "Don't feel bad for me, Chelsea Bell, because I'm going to make something of myself. I don't need him to do that. You'll see."

She squares her posture, wiping her eyes with her sleeve. "I know you will. And I'm here to cheer you on." Her supportive smile makes an acrobat out of my heart.

That wasn't so bad. She's okay. I'm okay. Actually, I'm more than okay. I'm grateful and happy she wants to be here, both of us leaning back, our hands cautiously taking turns in the popcorn bowl—salt sticking to our fingers. Our attention moves to the black and white film—to Grace and Cary playing cat and mouse—with the occasional sneaking glance from the corner of our eyes.

9

CHELSEA

I leave Seth with Nan's address and ask him to come by on my birthday. He's heading back to school soon and my mom's flying into town, so our hang-out time has a ticking clock.

My wheels turn as my feet pound the pavement. Even in the wrong sneakers, I run—full of dinner, full of nostalgic junk food, and full of feelings. Of that buoyant boy. And broken families. And ruined birthdays. How could life be so cruel to such a young person?

Ten years ago, I'd gone looking for him, peeking through windows. Probably not the safest idea, but I wasn't thinking about right or wrong. I needed to know what happened, if he needed my help. Being a kid sucks. All this stuff happens around you and to you, and there's nothing you can do about it.

The house is quiet and Nan's asleep when my weary legs pull me through the front door. I gingerly creep down the hall and into my room. It's a compact space with a daybed, dresser, and a small desk by the window. I throw my clothes in the hamper, then crawl between my covers.

When sleep evades me, I reach for my sketch pad under my pillow. I lean against the wrought iron frame, shutting my eyes. The metal rings a hollow melody as my head meets the cool surface. I tap it with my colored pencil, jogging memories.

Think, Chelsea.

Back to that week and the Santa Ana winds.

Back to Seth before his whole world changed.

Rollerblades and rain and scraped knees and swings and daisy chains. Laughter and his smile. Before I realize what's happening, I've sketched the first day we met, exactly as I remember it. I fold the paper into three sections and tuck it under my pillow.

I meant what I said to him. He's got something special to offer and I know he'll make an impact in whatever he chooses to do. He's already doing it. Going on adventures. Attending college. Making a difference in a hungry person's day.

I know there are limitations in this life, and some things aren't meant for everyone. The idea of us running away together, for example. It was silly to believe it would've worked. I had thirty-six dollars and a music box to my name. As unrealistic as our plan was, the dream of it was hard to shake.

What if we had taken that adventure together? Where would we be now?

Some people run away. Some people run in place.

Sleep drags me into its slumber, and I welcome the departure from the what-ifs and wishful thinking. You have to be a certain kind of person to go where Seth's going, and I'm not that.

"Happy birthday," a towering Seth says, standing on the other side of Nan's door.

Did he grow overnight? "Come in, come in." I step out of the way.

He looks around the apartment, ducking his head into the small sitting room across the hall from the black and white tiled kitchen and eating nook. He peeks down the dark hallway in front of him that leads to the bedrooms and a shared bathroom between the two.

"I'm diggin' that herb garden I passed. Yours?" he asks, following me. We separate, sitting on opposite sides of a square coffee table that rests low to the ground.

"It's The Sherries'."

"The who, what, now?"

"The women who live upstairs. Don't worry, I'm sure they'll pop up soon enough." I chuckle, forgetting how strange that must sound to someone who doesn't know them.

Seth is all eyes on the room, its wall-to-wall bookshelves and tchotchkes, all of Nan's memories and mementos. The standing lamp casts an orange glow though it's midday.

"Do you think they'd mind if I cut off some of their herbs? I want to show you something."

"Have at it. They always offer."

I grab scissors for Seth and head into the kitchen while he steps back outside.

"By the way," he calls from the patio, "I love this place—all your books—it reminds me of being in the library late at night. Do you have a favorite?"

"They're Nan's," I project, my throat tightening as I cinch a ruffled cupcake apron around my pale yellow dress. The spatula scrapes the buttercream frosting from the bowl, and I spin the cake while spreading it.

Seth comes inside, herbs in hand. He leans over the bowl. "Nutmeg? Lemon?"

"I'll never tell."

"C'mon. I let you into my magical kitchen process."

I dip my chin to my chest, concealing my smirk. A piece of hair drops in front of my eyes, and I blow on it to get it out of the way, but the curl swings back, making it impossible to see what I'm doing.

"Here, let me." Seth tucks the strand behind my ear. "Nice apron." He plays with the wrinkled ruffles of the neck strap.

My skin erupts in applause down my spine. He's standing beside me now, broad shoulders beneath another tailored-for-him white T-shirt that stretches across his chest. I turn my head, meeting his corded forearm and the smooth curve of his bicep, effectively diminishing my concentration and the breathing capacity between us.

If our silence was a song, this would be the bridge. I'd be singing along about a boy I knew as a kid, who was kind and fascinating and made me want to try new things.

Then the next thing I know, the music would spin in the opposite direction, hooking and reeling me in—just like Seth coming back into my life—having grown up to be this unfairly attractive and charismatic guy. Who likes to stand impossibly close to me, smelling so irresistible that the cake itself can't even compete.

"You got olive oil and a mason jar?" he asks, fixing on my mouth, unaware of how his presence impacts my vital organs.

"Do we have a mason jar?" Nan enters the kitchen, announcing herself. "We've got more mason jars than we know what to do with. Follow me."

"Hello, again, Mrs.—"

"Call me Nan—everyone else does. And you're tall enough, you don't need this step stool. Pick a size," she offers, pointing to the pantry and cabinets, rows full of her canning supplies.

"This is the one." Seth makes his choice easily. "Thanks, Nan."

"Chelsea tells me you two knew each other from the old neighborhood. That's a riot."

"It's true. A pretty lucky coincidence."

I'm smoothing out the second layer of icing like Nan taught me, but the cake is still too warm, so the buttercream isn't sticking.

Nan hands Seth a bottle of olive oil. The kitchen window sends sunlight piercing through the green glass, illuminating the center from a dark forest to a field-of-dreams green.

"Nonsense," Nan's claim startles me. The spatula stills in my grasp. "There's no coincidence in this life. Everything that happens has a purpose."

"Sure, Nan, then why do terrible things happen to innocent people?" I throw my free hand on my hip. Immediately, I understand the error I've made. That statement was so insensitive, especially after everything Seth had told me. I steal a glance at him in a chair too small for his frame, and he's not showing any signs of discomfort, physical or otherwise. I guess I'll experience enough for the both of us.

"You think you know everything, child. You wait. I ain't got these pretty lines across my face for no reason. There's a plan. There's always a plan."

Seth adds, "Makes sense to me."

"It *would* make sense to you."

"Hey, what's that about?"

"Nothing." I return to the cake, forcing a few breath cycles through my lungs. Seth pours the olive oil into the mason jar, and the plop of liquid against glass causes me to open my mouth again. "Okay, since you asked." I circle back, aiming the spatula in his general direction. "You just like to be agreeable." I wave it around, emphasizing my increased desire to prove my case. "I put five dollars on you being too nice to tell Nan that you think this fate stuff's a crock."

"Well, then." He laughs, amused, placing the jar down. When he stands and steps in closer to me, my back meets the counter. *Damn galley kitchen.* "You've got me all figured out. So, tell me, Chels Bells, what's my next move?"

And I don't know his next move, but mine might be to drop to the floor. His aftershave captures all my attention. Orange, cinnamon, something sweet and spicy—yes, I remember this now—warm apple cider on a crisp fall day. He always smelled like fresh starts.

I swallow. "I don't know."

He raises his brows. His hair falls in front of his eyes as he leans over me, swiping frosting from the spatula with his finger, reminding me that I'm pointing the baking utensil at him like a weapon.

Before I can predict his plan of attack, he drops the dollop onto my nose. "I'll take that five bucks now." Nodding triumphantly, he moonwalks back to the table, taking a final spin and bow.

"Oh, honey, that was priceless," Nan remarks to Seth and gives him a high-five. "You should see your face, doll—he got you good."

"You did not just do that, Seth Hansen."

I huff, and then my shock crumbles into a ripple of relief and laughter. I wipe the remainder of the citrus frosting from my nose and finish decorating the cake.

The what-if train arrives once again. Was he about to kiss me before Nan came in? I'm sure he's kissed a lot of people, and my experience can be chalked up to seven sloppy seconds in ninth grade with the captain of the basketball team.

I wipe my hands along the front of my apron.

"Don't think I'll forget about that five bucks, Chels. You owe me." Seth laughs louder than he has to—on purpose.

"I knew it was lemon," Seth says, as we're sitting on the brick stoop outside sharing birthday cake. He taps his fork to loosen a bite. "How much juice did you add?"

I shake my head, shoving a heaping bite into my mouth.

"What aren't you telling me?" He laughs, playful. "Just put me out of my misery."

"You're going to judge me."

"No, I won't."

"Please, after all that fresh produce talk in the market." I give him a second to reconsider his statement.

"It won't change how I feel about you."

How he feels about me? It's not until rose-infused air reaches my lips that I realize I haven't exhaled.

"This what you're lookin' for?" We turn our heads in unison to Nan on the landing, spinning an empty package of lemon pudding mix around her finger.

"Thanks a lot, Nan!" I rush to my own defense.

Seth nods his head, sporting a conquering grin. "Nan, you've made my day. Thank you."

"My pleasure." She closes the door behind her.

"See if she gets seconds." I huff like the one time I dropped my entire allowance on a crane game machine, spending an hour trying to get one stuffed animal. The worst part was going home and telling my parents that I smashed my ceramic piggy bank for nothing. Dad said I broke the bank for a good hard lesson, but I'm not seeing the lesson now.

"You know, for a box of flavored powder, this is really good. Thanks for making us a birthday cake, Chels. I'm grateful to have this time with you."

"Since you'll be back at school on your birthday, I guess I thought . . . well, it's just more fun to share cake."

"It is."

"Can I ask you something?"

"Anything, always."

"How do you do it? Stay so positive all the time? Especially with, you know—"

"You mean the shit with my family? You don't even know the half of it."

"Oh."

"Another story for another time. Not today." He nods, his eyes convincing but his gaze distant. "Life is short. We gotta live it—every second we're given. But it's not like I don't get disappointed, too."

"I envy being able to see the world in color the way you do. You're like a rainbow or something." I stumble over my thoughts. "That sounds pretty cheesy. You're just good, that's all."

"That's the nicest and also, yes, the most random thing anyone has ever said to me." He bumps my leg with his. "Listen, go easy on yourself—I only have me to worry about. I'm not taking care of anyone else."

I know he's referring to me being here with Nan, and he needs to know I'm good, too. I'm not taking care of her—we're looking out for each other. "I want to be here."

"Sure, and I get it, but you also gotta do you at some point, too. What are your dreams? What about school? Who does Chelsea Bell want to be?"

My arm stiffens. The fork bounces off the plate and onto the ground. "I'm already me. My life may not look like how you're living yours, but I'm still me."

"Hey, I'm not criticizing you. That's not what I meant at all."

"What kinda pep-talk is this, then?" I raise my voice.

"It's the I-care-about-you pep-talk, I guess. I don't know. It's me wanting you to be happy."

"I *am* happy." My eyes fight back, threatening to spill. *What does it mean to be happy?*

"You are?"

"I thought we'd never disagree about anything." I distract myself with a patch of dried icing on my hand.

"We're destined to disagree—we're human."

I scratch at the surface.

"But where it counts, we'll always land on our feet."

"You seem sure about this," I reply, barely audible. The flakes easily shake off my hand and fall to the ground.

He turns to face me, leaning against the iron gate. "About you? Yes. I'm sure about you. Final answer."

10

CHELSEA

I pick up my fork, compelled by a pressing desire to spill my guts. Not because I feel like I need to explain myself, but because with Seth, I *am* myself.

"The thing is, I struggle with reading." I place my plate and fork aside. "School was rough. I couldn't get words right—sounds mostly—and when I tried to read or work it out, all the letters would be jumbled."

Seth's expression is contemplative and soft. He tugs on his lower lip with his teeth. "Is that why you're not in college or studying in New York?"

I shrug. "Mom wanted the best for me, but you can't act without being able to read a script."

"Did you even want to act?"

"I wanted to make my parents proud."

"I can't imagine them not being proud of you."

"Maybe that's true. Mom had connections in L.A., and she wanted to use them. It wasn't going to happen, though. She then suggested we all move to New York so I could try drama school. I made a big deal about Nan instead, but we both know why I left. For years, I'd dealt with all the testing. I wasn't going through any more of that. All the reasons I wanted to go with you at eleven were still true at eighteen."

"The testing never stopped?" Seth drew in a long breath, teetering on the edge of pity. He won't take his eyes off me.

My toes tingle, and heat flashes over my chest beneath my dress. "I guess I moved to escape the constant reminders of my failing—and to be with Nan, of course." I try to emphasize how important she is to me.

"They didn't fight you on it?" Seth pushes off the railing.

"I think they wanted to sweep the problem away as much as I wanted to be left alone."

"This makes me so mad. Why didn't someone intervene? Why didn't someone help?"

What could anyone really do or say? The whole thing only brought discomfort to everyone.

"How's it now? Can you read? Did you ever go to that summer camp?"

"The camp wasn't even all that bad. We mostly did stuff like canoeing and crafts, and there was some reading." I chew on my lip, press in my toes, and sigh. "Slowly, I'm getting more comfortable with reading, but writing's still a bit of a disaster. I've picked up tricks and abbreviations to get by. I seriously don't know how I graduated."

Seth nods, blowing out a long exhale—this is new to him, but it's worn and tired for me.

"I don't want you to think of me differently because I took the easy way out."

He runs his hands over his face, revealing a steadfast, gentle smile. "That took a lot of strength, Chelsea. There's nothing easy about what you've been through."

It's impossible to keep looking at him when he's holding my gaze this way—like he sees something I can't see. I search his face for any lines or scars, visual proof that he's not as perfect as he is. "I'm pretty psyched about running, and if I can qualify with timing . . ." I trail off, still on the hunt for any flaw, unsure how to verbalize what I want out of my life when I can't define it.

"Well, hello there." The enthusiastic greeting comes from above our heads.

He jumps up to meet The Sherries before I can warn him they're huggers. "Hi, I'm Seth."

"Seth, pleasure to meet you. Chelsea never brings boys home."

"Oh, is that so?"

And I'm officially mortified.

"Yup," Sherryl confirms, adding, "Apparently she's been hiding the goods."

"Oooookay," I chime in. "Thanks for stopping by."

Seth is out of The Sherries' grasp, and they mercifully take the cue to return to their side of the stairs. Seth's giggle fills my ears, and I know I'm never living this down.

"So, am I 'the goods' in this situation?"

I turn around and run my palms along my dress. I change the subject to the most distracting thing I can think of. "I want to give you your present now."

"Wait, what? It's not my birthday yet, but it *is* yours, and I totally have a present for you, too. Great minds." He smirks. "Okay, on the count of three, we'll each get our gifts and meet back out here. One, two . . ." he leaps up, which causes me to take off to my room, but Seth wraps his fingers around my wrist before I gain an inch.

"Nothing could ever make me think poorly of you. If I'm the rainbow, you're the sun and the rain and all that's essential to make rainbows possible."

The warmth of his hand bursts through me, and as quickly as he grabs me, he lets go. I race faster than I can count to my room and back, high off his words that burrow themselves in the center of my chest. I think I've won, but when my feet skid on the landing, Seth's sitting exactly where I left him, hands clasped together, hanging over his knees. Not a hair out of place—his fancy-fitting shirt clinging to his body like it's been painted on.

"Hey, now. You didn't ask if I already had your gift on me. And I do." He shrugs and smiles like a Cheshire cat, plotting, smugly satisfied with himself.

I pass him the paper in my hands, too impressed to give him a hard time—hoping he assumes I'm panting from the exertion alone.

"What's this?" he mumbles, opening it. His amber eyes land on mine. I'm like fine sand at the mercy of the sun. "No way. You made this? Chels, this is incredible."

"Now you have that moment to go back to, should you ever need or want to."

"The first day we met," he whispers. "Thank you."

"See the spirals?"

"I do. You used them to form clouds. Oh, and the daisy chains and rollerblades. Yes, I go back there often. Do you?"

"I didn't draw one for myself." What do I admit? That yes, Seth, I have gone back to that day and week. Sometimes I'm there, and I'm so happy to see him. Other times I'm scared and devastated.

"And you can draw!"

"Keeps my hands busy."

"Here." He passes me a wrapped package. "It's nothing like your masterpiece, but . . . well, open it, anyway."

I undo the seal and dig into the brown packaging, revealing a mix CD and a cookbook. There's photos and recipes and also blank pages.

"It's a collection of inspiring stories and quotes from personal chefs of athletes and stars. There's a ton of their favorite twists on classic recipes for when their clients are training or getting movie-ready. And, this part here in the back is for you to experiment with your own recipes." He reaches over and turns to the blank pages.

"Thank you, Seth. This is wonderful." I bring the book under my nose and breathe in the crisp smell of ink and vanilla. My eyes close to a memory of our legs whooshing in the air. We're flying on those swings. Smiling on those swings. Blissfully in the moment on those swings.

He snaps his fingers together multiple times. "Shit, Chels. I'm so dense. It's a book. We can return it if you'd rather have something else. Wait, are you smelling it?"

I look at Seth as his eyes search mine, concerned he's done something wrong, when everything he does is always so right. "It's the most thoughtful gift. It will always make me think of you."

He smiles and reaches for my hands. "The CD is for educational purposes and, hopefully, enjoyment. I've put on all my favorite songs from the eighties to now. Your homework is to listen to them and report back." He's excited now, almost beaming. His smile is as warm as his touch.

"What if I hate them all?" I laugh.

"You won't." Confidence curls the corner of his mouth. The same lips that are inches from mine.

"I smell books because when I couldn't read them, it was the only way I could be close to what was inside."

"Books were the only way I could leave my world when I was a kid." Seth squeezes my hands. "You're the most incredible person I've ever met."

I extract my fingers one by one, and swallow hard. My mind refuses to accept his words as they embed themselves in my neurons. "It's like this one part of me doesn't work so the rest of me goes into overdrive. Sometimes, taxing my whole system." I inhale and hold my breath, absorbing a ripple of fatigue.

He must notice because Seth changes the subject, directing us back. "On the kitchen counter, I left you my herb-infused olive oil—a Seth Hansen original. It has healing properties and it's heart-healthy. You can use it to bake or roast anything."

"Does this mean I pass the friendship test again?" Unable to sort through my feelings, I hang onto deflection like a dependency.

Seth rolls his eyes at himself. "You remember that? I was such a dork." He mimics making a dash for the exit with his arms, lifting from his spot on the step, and I know he's kidding, but the thought of him leaving makes me incredibly sad. "Guess I'm going to do the walk of shame home now. Bye, Chels. It was nice knowing you."

My eyes must jump out of their sockets because when he looks at me, his do too.

"I didn't mean it like that—I swear," he insists. "Now you know why I didn't have my first kiss until I was a senior in high school."

"We're all dorks, and my dork liked your dork." Fine. I said it.

Seth turns stop-sign red.

I do not heed that warning. The flutter in my belly now swarms at the mention of kissing, which draws my attention, like a runway, straight to his thoughtful mouth. I circle back to my original question, away from kissing and his full lips and this flutter. "So, is there an expiration date on this friendship or a renewal application?" I swallow hard.

"No way. Ours is a lifetime membership."

I don't know what to say to Seth.

His gaze drops to the stone steps and his feet tap from side to side. "See, Chels, the thing is, my dork now likes you—always have."

The air shifts between us.

"What I'm trying to say is that I like you."

The flutter's now pudding cake tumbling around in my stomach.

"I like you, too." I release the words and swear there's a freak gust of wind that throws us together, a pressure system forcing our bodies closer—a storm building and building, unsure if it's coming from around us or within—as my thoughts are swept away by the stroke of his fingers through my hair, his lemon-scented smile landing on mine, a sweet and gentle exploration over my lips, ending as quickly as it begins.

Seth pulls back, and my head spins and spins. I press my palms into my heated cheeks. His eyes are wide and wild. "You're my favorite person, Chels. And I think I'm up there on your list, too. I'll go back to the East Coast with a great reason to return. I'm on break for a full month during winter." He grabs hold of my hand. "You'll be busy working on training. I'll be at the restaurant. Time will fly. You'll see."

"Does this mean you want to date or something?" I shake my head. One kiss doesn't mean he wants to be my boyfriend. "I'm sorry. I didn't mean to—"

"Yes, Chels. I want to date you or something."

Everything that can go wrong is going wrong in my mind, anxious predictions airing their complaints. No matter how much I want him to stay, it would be unfair to him. I'd never forgive myself if he did. "Kinda hard to do that from the other side of the country, don't you think? Maybe this is just exciting because it's new, and the shine will wear off in a few months."

"No, that's not it." He shoots up and paces the enclosed walkway. He's scraping his sneakers over uneven stone, kicking at dust.

I go to comfort him when he parks himself in front of me, kneeling at my knees.

"Fuck it, Chels. I'll stay. I can transfer and finish school here. There's a shit-ton of restaurants. And you're here. I'm not letting you go again."

My throat tightens along with my fists. "No." I panic. "I can't let you do that." He's lost perspective on the situation. Like he said, it's only a few months. "Your plans and degree—no, just no." I'll never let him give up on himself.

"It's too soon. We haven't had enough time," he demands.

"There's plenty of time, and we'll talk and email and figure it out." Surprising myself at how calm and convincing I sound. "You have a once-in-a-lifetime opportunity at that restaurant." I contemplate some more, glancing over at the songs on the mix CD. Reality sinks in—emails, reading emails, writing emails. "We don't have a computer. But I can go to the library and use theirs. It may take me some time to reply."

"Good thing I'm the patient sort," he says in jest, sitting next to me on the stoop, but I know he's not joking. He *is* patient, probably to his own detriment at times.

He holds up his pinkie between our bodies.

I raise mine, linking it with his.

"Not a day will go by where I'm not thinking of you."

"I'll be waiting." I smile as he leans in, sealing our promise with a kiss.

"You can have my dorm address, but I don't know where I'm staying yet this summer." Seth pulls out a black pen from the pocket of his navy cargo shorts.

My exhale skitters, my lips still tingling.

He positions my right hand on his lap and presses the gel tip of the pen to my skin, angling my ring finger as he needs it until he's done.

"I'm no artist like you, but just because it's not permanent ink doesn't mean it depreciates once you wash it off. I mean it, Chels. What's eight months when it's been ten years? We've got this."

I hold my hand in front of me. It's a simple design, from the heart, and I never want to wash it off.

"You like it?" he asks.

"Daisies are my favorite," I reply softly, wrapping my arms around his neck.

I don't keep Seth from Mom and Dad because I don't want them to meet again. I don't let them cross paths because, self-ishly, I want Seth to myself. It's not a secret or anything, but once Mom finds out about things, it'll be an inquisition and plans to have dinner, and I've never been good at saying no to her.

We spend our final hours together before his flight, walking the city and exploring each other. The way our hands find one another, fingers threading between our bodies, and the small squeeze he gives them every few blocks. We take deep breaths through our laughter, inhaling cool salt air, entranced by a red trolley car dipping below the horizon of residential hills and pink skyline and back up again until it disappears.

"I'll miss these walks," he says.

"I wish I knew how to freeze time." I rest my head on his shoulder in a dream-like state. "You. Me. And two cups of coffee."

"I'll be back before we know it." Seth kisses the top of my head. Fading daylight warms my chin. "Give me your lips, Chels. I'll show you how to freeze time."

And he was right.

PART III

2011

SAN FRANCISCO, CALIFORNIA

"What we have once enjoyed we can never lose. All that we love
deeply becomes a part of us."
— Helen Keller

11

SETH

"*S*eth Hansen's career is taking off. With his steely eyes, signature smile, and quick wit, not to mention his skillful and creative cuisine, he's the perfect face for the Cooking Channel's newest show in the Bay area.*"

I switch off the radio above the stainless steel counter, rolling my eyes and forcing my attention back to the plates in front of me—kicking myself for letting David, my manager, convince me to plaster my face all over the city. Convince me to plaster my face on billboards all over the city. Now these people are talking about me like I'm a fucking tasting menu.

Soaping up my hands under warm water helps me to scrub away that chilling thought as it washes down the drain.

I need to finish the entree presentation, decorating each plate with a balsamic reduction spiral—a three-two-one circle that narrows to a drop of olive oil resting on top.

Tonight's affair is the annual Northwestern Realtors Convention. Every year, they hire a local chef and team for their private events. This isn't my first rodeo with them. Each staff member knows the drill—discreet catering and clean up. Don't be seen or heard.

The ivory plates warm my palms as I carry them from the kitchen to the outdoor patio. The catering staff follows, stepping from tile to stone where the dinner party's in full swing. The sound of crystal clinking and flatware scraping porcelain fills the early spring air.

I'm not one to shy away from a compliment as I come around to collect them one by one, schmoozing with the deep pockets and heavily perfumed plus-ones at the table.

"Seth Hansen, my man. Truly your finest. Here, here, taste this pinot." A glass is shoved in my hand. It's not uncommon for these guys to get close, sometimes closer than I'm comfortable with. They'll slip the waitstaff hundreds to keep the night going.

It's all the same to me when it comes to these real estate moguls, some with their partners tonight, some with their weekend partners. And though they joke and swap stories with me like I'm one of them, they don't know me at all. I'm just the guy that makes them feel okay about the money they blow on dinner in a city with thousands of starving people sleeping on the streets.

I know what's expected of me. I always do. *We all gotta eat.*

"It's edible art, so you enjoy that," I toast. If only they knew that drenching yourself in artificial scent kills the ability to taste the food.

My patience is thinning, and normally, my presence out here would be coming to a close, except I find myself lifting my eyes in mid-conversation, intrigued by the blond in the black dress with a string of pearls draped around her neck. She isn't paying attention to anyone. Instead, she's singularly focused on her plate, methodically chewing and savoring every bite. Was that a moan? She isn't simply tasting her meal—she's devouring the entire thing like it's her last. Her true red lips are unmarred when she dabs the linen napkin to the corners of her mouth.

My jaw drops open, watching this woman eat my food. Putting her lips where my hands had been moments before.

Okay, buddy. She might be a figment of my own ego and imagination. Perhaps, a side-effect of my pre-game ritual shot of whiskey. Tonight, I took two to shake off the apprehension today's date always carries with it. *One more revolution around the sun.*

Each time I look up from the mundane prattling of some suit who sounds the same as the last, I catch her satin-gray stare, her graceful neck, her pulse. There's inspiration in this woman's presence, a cloudy sky minutes before the storm.

My forearms clench, one in my pocket, one choking the stem of this wine glass, imagining what she'd look like with nothing on but those delicate pearls reflecting in the candle-light. I can't keep standing here. I have to distract myself by disassembling the night's planned dessert of espresso and raspberry truffles into something infinitely more complicated. Otherwise, I'll end up pulling her by the pearls into the pantry, inhaling every exposed inch of her body pressed up against shelves of dry goods.

She smiles as if she can hear my thoughts.

This starched chef's collar digs into my throat and—fuck it, maybe her giggle's an invitation. *Let's wager if I'm right.*

"Enjoying my food, miss?" I ask, placing my glass on the table, certain of her answer, phishing for her name.

Silence.

"Would you like to know the dessert options?" I play a little, attempting to break through her cool demeanor with the appeal of something sweet.

But she holds strong, unaffected by charm or my hinting of chocolate, and simply says, "No, thank you."

"Nightcap?" I suggest, overtly flirting now.

She pulls a sip of a dirty martini into her heart-shaped mouth. "Your food is always perfection, Seth." My name lingers on her lips, controlled, confident. A whisper of a smirk that rolls up my spine.

My body remembers. "Chels?" I cough on my exhale, uncertain if I'm hallucinating.

"Hello," she says, drawing in a breath, followed by a less formal, careless "Hi."

Hi. That's what you say after a decade? Just hi?

I slam my eyes shut to sort memory from fantasy.

This is not one of the countless dreams I've had about her since the last time we met. Before everything was different. When our country as we knew it had not completely changed my path. An alternate universe, one where we might have followed through with our promises.

I shove my hands into the pockets of my billowy chef's pants, chewing on my choices.

This is the second time in my life I can remember being shocked so hard, unable to go with the flow or string together something worth saying. And not because I don't have the words—I have an arsenal—but how do you choose one question when it may be the only one you get?

Well, whatever I'm supposed to remember to ask is gone.

"You're a class act, Hansen. Get over here so we can grab a group shot with the man of the hour." Someone's voice behind me hits the back of my neck like hail. I ignore the request until a second one comes.

Chelsea steals two olives from her spear, slowly taking them into her mouth. The black plastic clinks as it lands in the empty martini glass.

It might've been a crush when we were younger—who knows? I try not to think about that time of my life, but the truth is a beast. Beneath that crush was something excruciating to relinquish. I had an unwavering sense of certainty with where things were headed. In an instant, she disappeared.

Chelsea drags her bottom lip between her teeth. Her

searching gaze shifts the ground beneath me. Flashes of that week, the way her knee knocked into mine on Nan's front step. How she smiled when she said she'd wait. Her pinkie finger wrapped around mine.

I've dated casually over the years, but, no one was Chelsea.

Her silence is audible over the flickering candlelight and drop in temperature. She sends me a noncommittal wave, pushing back from the table.

My attention volleys between the guests that have paid for my time and my past. When I bring my eyes back to Chelsea, she slips out of sight. The last glimpse I catch is a tight ball of yellow hair wound at the base of her neck. *Fuck.*

I sweep my damp palms down my whites and tuck my hair behind my ears, plastering on my signature smile. "Let's do this."

The photos turn into post-dinner drinks. Chelsea's not far from my mind, but I have to table my impulse to find her. These people pay, and I'm not here to question their ethics. I'm here to collect that money and make it count. My business only works as well as word of mouth goes. It's never about a single event. All good business comes at a cost—for the lifetime of a relationship.

It's not until the last candle has burned out that the CEO shakes my hand, asks his PA to get me on the books for next year, and hands me a white envelope.

"For the staff," he directs. "Your people did great, as always."

I clear my throat. "Sir, thank you—we're a team."

He nods, not getting what I'm throwing down here, and leaves with his weekend-long plus-one. Hey, I'm not judging. Not my life.

One of the catering staff informs me, "Boss, everything's clear."

I turn around and shake his hand. "Cool, thanks, Cedric.

Split it evenly between you, Rosa, and T," I say, passing him the envelope, unable to shake this restlessness.

He questions my instructions upon seeing the contents of the envelope. I didn't bother looking. Its weight spoke volumes. Cedric's wide eyes confirm what I already know—play money to some is rent for others.

"Have a good night, Boss."

The space is once again unoccupied, so I release the double rows of buttons on my coat, letting it drape open, and untuck my white undershirt from my pants, appreciating the cool night air penetrating the thin fabric. I should probably find some water and walk off the warmth from the wine before calling it a night.

I take a lap through the kitchen, grab my knives, and head down the outside corridor to the hotel's front desk—lonely at this hour except for a kid in his twenties wiggling around in a stiff-fitted, eggplant-colored suit. His alert eyes express an eagerness to engage with someone—with anyone. Maybe a sign?

I change course.

"Hello. How can I help you?" he asks.

"Yes. Thank you. I'm looking for a room number for one of your guests?" I flatten my open palm on the caramel and stone granite. Its surface remains cold despite my elevated body temp.

A giggle slips from his wobbly smile. "Oh, I'm sorry, sir . . ." The kid drops his register to a whisper, which amuses me as we're the only people in earshot or on this floor at midnight. "We can't give out personal information about guests."

I already know this, but I've got to figure out if I completely imagined seeing Chelsea tonight or, if by a stroke of sheer luck, she's somewhere in this hotel, staying in one of these rooms— and if she's here, I'm not leaving without a fucking explanation.

"Ever play the 'yes or no' game?"

"Um, sir, no?" he responds, uncertain and intrigued. "Does it involve seven minutes in heaven with a guy named Victor? Because in college once—"

"Not that version. My spin-the-bottle days are over, sadly."

"I find that hard to believe," his voice carries, calling bullshit.

He's not entirely wrong. I have fun—fun with an expiration date. And that's it. My sole focus is work—working the line, working the crowd. And even that's temporary. Every event I do, every night I cater, each commitment is one step closer. And when I get my restaurant doors open, it will have all been worth it.

I learned a long time ago that the only person and place you can depend on is yourself and your future. It's entirely in my hands. This momentary deviation is an exercise in trust. I can trust myself to confront her after all this time, and I can trust myself to course correct—back on track—when I've collected what I came for.

"My version goes like this. I'm going to ask you a question, and all you have to do is answer yes or no."

"The rules of the hotel state—"

"Listen, I'm not in the habit of putting anyone's job in jeopardy." I glance at his name tag. "Devon." I smile. "Seth. Here's the thing. I'm looking for an old friend, someone I haven't seen in a very long time, and she might be staying here. I'd never forgive myself if I didn't find out."

Devon looks around me and when he seems satisfied, he leans over the counter. "Okay, three questions."

I appreciate his baby face, remembering the days when a clean shave lasted twelve hours.

"But first, when you say 'old friend,' is this some kind of enemies-to-friends-to-lovers romantic comedy? My mom watches *When Harry Met Sally* every New Year's Eve. Are you guys like those two?"

"More like Grant and Kelly."

"Who?"

I shake my head. Doesn't even know what he's missing, but I'm not here for a lesson on classic film. "I need us to focus, Dev."

"Oh, yes, okay, right. First question."

"Have you seen a woman on your property tonight wearing a black dress and pearls with blond hair tied back?"

"Um, maybe." He taps a pen on the counter.

I raise my brows, a reminder of the rules. "She's not someone you'd forget."

"Yes, yes. I mean, yes."

Great. Brilliant. My shoulders drop, my breathing revs up. "What time is check-out tomorrow?" I ask.

"Ten o'clock, sir."

I place a hundred-dollar bill on the counter and turn around.

"Wait, you have two questions left."

"I just needed to know if I was camping out in your lobby tonight. Turns out I am. You've been helpful."

12

SETH

*T*he tile floor squeaks as I drag my disbelief and clogs over to the only reasonable option to pull an all-nighter on—a weathered tan and gold couch with thick cushions that bend to the will of my knees as I collapse into it. *How many Grants have sat right here, waiting on Kellys?*

Bet most of them weren't waiting as long as I've been waiting.

I settle my knives in my lap and hum along to the instrumental jazz coming from large speakers overhead. Upbeat piano keys take a backseat to the seductive and smooth saxophone. Devon has checked on me a few times from behind the counter with a nod and anticipatory smile. All he needs now is a fresh bowl of popcorn and for the show to start.

Maybe she was passing through? Maybe she was as shocked to see me as I was her? Maybe . . . maybe, I'm going to drive myself into a wall with wondering.

The airy drums lull me into a sense of safety. My adrenaline surrenders to the quiet, and a drizzle outside coats the main revolving door.

I'll close my eyes . . . Maybe one eye—okay, two.

Just for a minute.

The faint aroma of fresh herbs and ripe tomatoes from tonight mix with distinct and separate memories I have of Chelsea, amongst fresh cut grass and thick storm clouds, delicate floral and sweet fruit, red cherries and cola, and that sugary lemon.

The swings.

The laughter.

The sun reflecting in her golden hair, as gold as the center of a daisy. The center of my whole world for a time.

"Seth," she whispers.

Not a part of the memory, but it's been so long, sometimes the versions I experience in my head add in their own details, urging me to play the "what if" game.

"Seth." Again, her voice is clear, crisp in my mind. The corners of my mouth rise on both sides. It's us—now we're young adults, but in the field from our childhood. The memories are merging. My chest swells, my knee warms to the touch.

I've been dreaming about Chelsea for so long. Sometimes, we're kids. Sometimes, we bake together in Nan's kitchen. Or share a cup of coffee while people-watching. Sometimes, we lay in each other's arms. Often we don't. I'm always pulled away before it goes to a place we've never been before. A place I thought we'd find our way to.

"Seth Hansen. *Helloooooooo.*" The warmth on my knee twists into a pinching pressure.

My eyes snap open, stealing away my smile. "What the hell?" My vision levels, and it's Chelsea standing above me, heels in her right hand, chills exposed all the way down her bare arms.

"Must have been quite the dream."

"A catnap." I adjust my body, locking my knife case strategically over my lap.

"At midnight? In the lobby of a hotel?"

"Seems as good a place as any. What were you doing . . ." I look at her bare feet and back to her face. "Outside?"

We speak over each other.

"I went for a walk," she says.

"I was waiting for someone."

Her eyes tear away, and she steps back. "I'll leave you to it." She blows a fallen strand of hair from her face, then swings around and starts walking away.

It takes the ding of the elevator reaching the ground floor for me to register that if I want my questions answered, I need to speak up and ask them.

Hey, words—a little pep talk here. I'd like you to get your shit together around this woman. And it occurs to me that's exactly what's tripping me up. She's a woman. Everything about her is "woman." Ten years ago, there were glimpses of that woman, but most of her was still a girl—a lost girl—who gave me hope and then shattered it.

Chelsea steps into the elevator, and something in me springs to life. I take three long strides, my hand catching the closing door. The fraction of light between us flickers on as the door retreats from my palm, making room to get on.

"You, Chelsea," I say, as the elevator door traps us inside. "I was waiting for you."

There's nowhere for either of us to go. And by the warmth in her cheeks and deep arch of her back against the mirrored wall, I think she might be open to my intrusion.

"Oh." Her tired eyes focus on the illuminated numbers until we reach her floor.

"Can I walk you to your room?"

She nods as the elevator opens to a hallway.

"Not worried about cutting yourself on something? City sidewalks aren't always friendly." I note her bare feet again, and she straightens out.

"I managed."

We continue in silence, making it to the fifth room on our left.

She slips her hotel room key into the slot. The green light switches on. "Coming in?" She holds the door open.

I follow her like a starving stray.

"You want a drink or something?" Chelsea tucks her heels under a lounge chair. "That was a long night for you." She makes the observation, sounding like someone who's been around and knows what a long night for me looks like. "There's a mini bar in that cabinet. Help yourself." She heads into the bathroom.

I don't know which part fucks with me most: her composure, her proximity, or her accuracy.

For as many times as I've worked events at The Wharf Hotel, I've never been in one of their rooms. Not for a lack of invitations. I have a rule—I don't mix business with the bedroom.

This room looks like someone plucked a page from a Victorian estate and dropped it in a modern world. Embellished drapes, sturdy wood furniture, brick walls—heavier than I'd expect for a seaside hotel but fitting for a historic city. Shades of burgundy and brown run from carpet to ceiling. A few lights pop from wall sconces, and the electronics are all hidden. Chelsea's silver suitcase, discarded heels, and running water from the bathroom are my anchors to the present.

I scope out the lamp situation for more light. No luck. Thankfully, the mini bar has bottled water. I grab one and move closer to the bathroom door, leaning against the wall and waiting. The last thing I need is more liquid courage. I need to cool off.

The water extinguishes the fire in the pit of my stomach. Cigar smoke and sea air expel from my lungs, the remnants of tonight's socializing.

"So what were you doing out there tonight?" I ask through the crack in the door.

Breathe.

The water turns off, and the door swings open. Chelsea keeps her eyes on me, exiting the bathroom. She bends over to dry her feet. "I like to walk."

Second question. "Do you still run?"

"No." *No hesitation there.* Her tone is a void, so matter-of-fact that I want to get in real close and examine if the Chelsea I know is trapped inside there somewhere. I need that Chelsea before I let her go.

She folds the towel and places it on the bathroom floor.

I peek around the door frame to confirm what I'm witnessing. "You fold your dirty towels?" I don't even try to conceal my amusement.

"You still ask a lot of questions." She smiles.

Those straight teeth and red lips are directed at me, and I like that I'm not the only one who remembers. What I don't like is how she's acting like we're cool.

Chelsea reaches behind her neck and releases her hair from some clip situation. Yellow strands brush the tops of her shoulders. My line of sight hits at her zipper, which extends the length of her spine, stopping between her hips. I'm busy cataloging her body with my eyes when she turns to face me, glass in hand, full of dark liquor.

"Cheers." Chelsea raises her glass and kills her drink in one pull. "When did you get tall?"

"Hit a growth spurt." I step in closer. "I have questions."

She doesn't move.

Woman, woman, woman. I finish the water and crush the bottle.

"Want to make it interesting?" she proposes.

That's my line.

Without warning, Chelsea links her arms around my neck,

pressing into my chest. We slide together like something impossibly slippery. Her mouth lands on mine, and I grip her hips.

She separates the seam of my lips, her determined tongue dissolving any resistance I thought I had. Strong cloves and sweet soaked pears coax my mouth to open, and I inhale deep, dizzy as Chelsea moans, pushing down my coat.

I pull back, my crumbling resolve inches from her heated breath. The rapid rise of her chest pounds in my ears. I can't stop staring at those liquor-soaked, pillowy lips.

I shouldn't do this. Pretend she's just any woman, and I'm just any man. Pretend that we're two consenting adults passing the hour with our bodies.

No.

She doesn't deserve more than she's already taken from me. Years and years . . .

I should stop this right now, demand she give me my answers, and leave, head high and my sanity intact.

I could do that.

"Seth," she whispers my name, longing for something I recognize and need and hate myself for wanting.

Fuck it. I can hate myself later. I bench my questions, rip off my shirt, and lift Chelsea by the thighs. She loops her legs around my waist, and I nearly destroy her dress undoing her damn zipper, spinning us around til her back meets the wall.

My hands in her hair, teeth nipping her jaw, her neck, her collarbone. Her kiss glides along my stubble, teeth scraping over my skin.

I'm not thinking about answers anymore. I'm not thinking clearly at all, too busy committing her to memory. I'm lost in the throes of time—how one minute it robs you, and the next, rewards you.

I'm convinced that at any moment, I'm going to wake up to find this is the most real dream I've ever had about us. If I just keep her close, I can prolong the way her shiny hair wrapped in my fingers soothes my sore hands and the lilting rhythm of her voice as she exhales every syllable of my name.

But the pressure in my ears from a blaring sound matches the force on my chest, splitting us apart. Chelsea sneaks under my arm, diving for the bed. She's answering a call, and there better be a fucking fire on the other end to walk away from a kiss like that.

My forehead flops to the wall, to the warm spot where her back was seconds ago. I much prefer that view over the hound and boy with a musket I'm greeted by now.

My chest rapidly rises and falls.

Chelsea clears her throat, steadies her voice, which grabs my attention to her bending over, pressing the receiver between her ear and shoulder, while reaching her zipper, fastening her dress.

"Hi . . . Okay . . . Sure, well, make sure Jonah goes to the bathroom before bed. It's been rough the past few nights. He's been waking up."

This is caretaking Chelsea. Nurturing Chelsea. This is hot.

She takes a brief inhale, and starts talking faster. "And the eye drops are on the counter. That Dr. Gillman prescribed. Give them a kiss goodnight for me. I'll see you in the morning."

Wait. See *you* in the morning? Kiss? Them?

She ends her call, looks up at me, and the blank expression makes the picture crystal clear. Movement in the corner of my vision snakes my attention. She's rubbing a spot on her left hand with her right hand. I break through the static space between us and grab it, zeroing in, remembering the last time I held this hand, an idealistic fool with a pen and a promise.

I swallow hard, straining to adjust my vision. Through the antique filtered light of the room, a faint tan line circles around the base of Chelsea's ring finger. *No.* I can't even entertain the possibility that my—that she—*this woman* is—"Chels, do you have a family?"

She holds eye contact and her answer is an unwavering "Yes."

I drop her hand and step away.

"It's not—"

"Stop." I sigh.

"You don't understand. I'm not—" Her cheeks pale. Her red lips are smears of pink to her chin.

I drag the inside of my wrist across my mouth before the evidence of betrayal stains my skin.

"Whatever bullshit you're about to spin, I'm all set with excuses." Words shoot out like weapons. "I don't do drama. I'm. Not. A. Homewrecker." I grab my shirt from the floor. "Happy *fucking* birthday, Seth." My voice scratches as the door closes behind me.

I bump into Devon as I leave with all my unanswered questions and defeat.

"Did you find your friend after all?"

"I was mistaken. I don't know that woman."

13

CHELSEA

I missed my bed. Almost as much as I miss kissing.

Seth stormed out, and I decided that staying the night in that hotel room would be torture. Since Paul was crashing in the guest room at the house, I snuck in, and unlike a teenager living her best life, I crawled under my covers and cried.

He didn't let me explain.

I want to be angry about that, but I don't blame him. It looked bad. Worse than the truth. But who wants the truth, anyway? Especially when it hurts.

Five hours later, I'm back to being mom—flipping blueberry pancakes and squeezing oranges by hand.

"Mom, you're home," Jonah squeals as he crashes into my side, and I release a guttural oomph, stepping us both to safety, away from the sizzling griddle.

"His hugs are fiercer than yours," Paul announces, trailing behind the kids.

"One night as promised." I kiss the top of his wiry bedhead and breathe in last night's shampoo. There's been so much growth this year from ages five to six. He began Kindergarten and simultaneously stopped calling me Mommy. All that's left of my baby are the weight of his hugs and the way his hair smells of fresh air and sunshine.

"Good morning," Paul adds while Paige settles in at the table.

"They do okay?"

"Everything was great. I can take care of my own kids," he reminds me kindly.

I'm not used to this. Any of it.

I turn to Paige. "How did you sleep?" My daughter, who's nine going on nineteen, yawns and shrugs.

Force of habit when we're all together in the morning, I lift two coffee cups from the mug tree on the counter and slowly fill one for myself. I return the other.

Paige sips OJ, and I smile at her through the rising steam. "Jonah snuck into my bed last night."

"I had a bad dream," he admits under his breath, releasing his gaze from me to the floor.

"Why didn't anyone get me?" Paul interjects, pulling out his phone.

"Your snoring is probably what woke him up." Paige giggles.

"Hey, now, it's a medical condition." Paul walks around me, grabbing a small glass and pouring himself a shot of juice. "Since you're here, I'm gonna head out." He places the glass in the sink.

"You sure you don't want breakfast?" I offer, twirling the spatula in the aroma of melting butter and bubbling blueberries. "It's okay if you stay."

"Please, Dad—it's your favorite," Jonah begs.

"You promised you'd have meals here sometimes," Paige points out.

He contemplates their requests, but I catch it, the settled stare which means his decision is already made.

"I won't make a habit of missing pancakes, but not today."

This part is hard—adjusting to new normals. I paint on an encouraging front and make good on my end of the deal. "You had a bonus night with Dad. He has to go now. You'll see him in two days."

Paul kisses the kids, then comes around the counter and sticks out his hand. "One for the road?"

I place a pancake on a paper towel, slap on a slice of butter, and fold it like a taco.

He pauses before heading to the front door. "So how was your big night out?"

The rest of the pancakes stack in a perfect tower as I load them onto a plate.

"Fine." I could go into detail. A woman I volunteer with at the kids' school invited me to this work party of her husband's, so she'd have someone to talk to. I stayed a courteous amount of time. I didn't want to be rude. But I had to bail after dessert because I couldn't sit in a room full of strangers anymore. I couldn't sit in my own skin anymore, either. Not with Seth tracking my every move.

Paul smiles. He's always accepted *fine*. And though that was part of the problem, I guess I should be grateful now. It's a kind gesture, one I'm not required to respond to and one he isn't obligated to offer.

"Kids, I'll pick you up from school on Tuesday. Love you."

"Love you, Dad." They sigh in unison.

He sends me a wave and locks the door on his way out.

"All right, PB and J, who wants to go surprise Nan?"

"Mom, I'm not a sandwich," Paige objects.

"Excuse me—Paige Beatrice." I flatten my tone to match her serious one. "Will you be joining us?"

Six months ago, my life veered off track. It's taken me thirty-one trips around the sun to realize that life changes, and when it does, it messes with our internal GPS, altering our stories until they're something unrecognizable.

Today's date has been creeping up on the calendar like an uninvited guest. A date that had significance for nine years worth of memories, nine bouquets of red roses, nine toasts with whatever sparkling wine was offered by the glass—even when we could afford more, we kept the tradition. Tomorrow, its significance will simply become a shadow, an empty vase, a single flute.

I answer my phone on the first ring. "Maria."

"You get the papers?"

"Holding them as we speak."

I fill half a flute with Moët and top it off with a splash of pomegranate juice, carrying the proof—hot off the press—of the dissolution of my marriage, and my bruised pride, into my bedroom. The cherrywood vanity is cool and smooth as I brush my arm over its rounded edges, staring into the oval mirror, carved out in smooth floral patterns. The piece was a wedding gift from my mom—her dreams of fancy dinners, galas, performances.

It will last longer than my marriage. *Cheers to the end of a chapter.*

"Have you had a chance to think about what's next?"

My silence should speak volumes. But Maria bills by the hour, so I start talking. "I signed up for a class. To get my feet wet. Begins next week."

"You're going to be okay," she assures me.

My fingers shake as I run my nails over the signature lines. Our names, side by side, his swooping letters and my chicken scratches, ending the way we began, in agreement.

"Quick and—" I pause, because it hasn't been exactly pain-less, but it hasn't been as painful as it would've been had we kept going. "Thanks for everything, Maria." I hang up, tossing the papers in the drawer, next to the one photo from our wedding and my wedding band—a simple gold circle that barely fits anymore. *I'll save it for Paige.* My lungs burn, my hand remembers.

It was a casual affair at the San Francisco courthouse despite Mom's input. She wanted a synagogue and ketubah. We compromised with stomping on the glass and a moment of silence. Nan hosted dinner at the pier for our small party afterward. I wore an eyelet babydoll dress in ivory that fell off my bony shoulders and covered my growing abdomen. We barely knew ourselves, never mind one another. We were young, embracing our uncertain future, hopeful smiles on display, committing to forever.

The way forever became too fragile to hold.

I don't know if love is meant to fade or die the way ours had. Paul and I had shared something greater, more valuable than romantic ideals of growing old together. We had shared a purpose before our promises. First with Paige, who surprised us all, and then with Jonah, who planned his arrival precisely, arriving on his due date. Something the doctor said rarely happened. And I knew from the start he'd be a force in the world.

It wasn't their fault. It wasn't any of our faults. We made sure they understood that when we sat them down and told them Dad was going to live somewhere else.

Some people, well, they grow so much that they grow apart.

Paul and I, we grew apart when we grew up.

I give the drawer a wiggle, pushing the warped wood back into place. I apply a fresh coat of red lipstick and blot twice, checking my makeup in the mirror. When I've blended beneath my jaw and around my brows, I secure my hair in a tight bun at the base of my neck.

The oven timer going off in the kitchen startles me. I pinch my cheeks for color and release a breath, standing tall.

This batch of muffins is a flop, ranging in size and shape, and some of the steaming tops slide into one another like novice dance partners. There's only so much trying I can take. On my reach for a container to store the muffins in, the Sunday paper comes into view, casually waiting for someone to notice it. *For me to notice it.* Tethered to curiosity, I abandon my task and instead engage in an internal debate of should I or shouldn't I look at his photo *one more time* before recycling it.

I lick my finger and flip through the *SF Daily*, passing the finance and real estate pages until I reach the entertainment section, stopping at Seth, unable to shake away the memory of two nights ago, how easily I slipped into the me I was before I am now.

The me who was running somewhere all the time.

The me who was kissing him.

I was in shock, us randomly colliding in the world like that —picking up where we left off, like the universe bent time, and our bodies fell under some nostalgic spell where nothing else mattered.

For that one moment in possibly my entire adult life, I gave myself permission to just be.

Technically, the ink dried on my divorce papers Friday afternoon, but it wasn't until today that I had the final copy in my possession.

My lips tingle as the newspaper ink marks my thumbs.

He's exactly as I remember him, but now he's taking up half the ad space of the Sunday paper, on billboards, and plastered all over television as the city's homegrown and hottest up-and-coming talent. So much to show for himself. As I knew he would.

It's all laughable at this point anyway. I shove Seth's smirking face into the recycling bin, then switch on the first station, loud enough to drown out the image of him stepping away, his face twisted in disappointment, his eyes clouded by judgment and disgust. *I would've assumed I was married too.*

My eyes press together as the hotel door slams shut behind him. The blank space intensifies the succession of flashes—his soft mouth against my skin, hands tugging my hair. My panting, burning lips and slick palms.

I couldn't find my words to explain. Time ran out.

Familiar lyrics land in my ears. I force my lids open. "You've got to be kidding me," I bark in my empty kitchen, throwing my hands in the air. It's the music that he placed over my ears and injected into my head at eleven years old.

I need to learn my lesson and avoid classic rock stations altogether.

Better yet . . . Forget music. Forget my failings. Forget Seth Hansen.

Rage clean it is. I aim my bottle of Clorox and switch on public radio.

The last time I sat in a classroom, I still lived with my parents, sporting braces and counting down the days until graduation— freedom. I'd about forgotten how small it could feel being in a room that wasn't meant for you. Back then, school was a nightmare. Everything but art class was a chore. Mom had me seeing so many tutors that when I moved to San Francisco, I vowed never to subject myself to testing ever again.

But this time's different because I'm here in this chair— made for a toddler—because I want to be. I've spent the past decade pouring myself into my family and, somewhere along the way, lost all sense of direction. I'm finally taking a step toward figuring out what to do with my life.

The Bay Community Center is geared toward all ages, but

we're all adults squeezing like sausages into these desks. My knees bump the bottom of the table. I'm also actively ignoring the warning sound the plastic chair makes every time I shift in my seat.

"Hello, everyone," the man in the brown tweed coat and baggy dress shirt welcomes the class. His navy pants are loose, too. The guy looks barely out of school himself. He's unreadable, which sends my dangling-by-a-thread confidence plummeting to the ground.

"Remember, this is not a pass-or-fail course." At some point, the instructor writes his name on the board: Foster. "Show up, do the homework, and you'll get your money and time's worth."

I pull my pen from my bag and begin sketching vines as Foster opens up intros. In the time the circle gets to me, I've learned about the guy who wants to work with animals but can't stand the sight of blood, the woman Nan's age who wants to take this course to figure out what career best matches with her astrological sign, and the person next to me who's decided on a career change after two years, leaving their personal assistant gig behind.

My heel taps the faux tile floor, one, two, three...

Foster flips through the papers in his hands. "Chelsea Bell," he says, startling me. He pauses, honing in on the sound effects coming from my direction. "You're up."

I drag my bottom lip between my teeth and cross my ankles, dropping the pen in my lap. It quickly takes off down the smooth fabric of my pencil skirt. I slam my sweaty hand on the rolling cylinder, placing the problem-maker vertically on the desk. I clear my throat. "Hi. I'm Chelsea, and you already know that," I fumble. "I'm hoping to figure out what kind of job might be a good fit for me."

"Thanks, Chelsea. What did you do for work before?"

"I take care of my kids and sell jam. Once waited tables, odd jobs here and there. I mean, this is a career class. I'm here to find a career."

"So you're a stay-at-home mom?" Foster clarifies.

"Yes." I shouldn't be ashamed of it. I wanted to be home with my kids—we made that decision—but my stomach sinks as I admit it. Stay. At. Home. A reminder that there's choice and sacrifice and a fine line between the two.

"You know," my neighboring classmate chimes in, "moms at home work like one-hundred-hour weeks, and when you think about those hours, all unpaid, bravo to you. I couldn't do it. Nope. Not for anything."

I nod my head, surprised that anyone notices the invisible load.

"Thank you, Joss. And yes, Chelsea, to your point, our objective is to expose you to as many tools and resources as possible to get you to your goal. So, you're in the right place."

Foster takes a seat on the top of the wide desk at the front of the room, and I attempt to conceal a giggle when I notice he's wearing bright blue, yellow, and red Superman socks. His loafers knock into the wood frame of the desk. The fluorescent light overhead bleaches out his complexion. "So, I'm going to have all of you take home a career interests assessment, just as a starting point."

"I don't take tests," I inform him.

"Oh, this isn't a test."

"Does it ask questions and then proceed to offer multiple choice or short answers?"

Foster slides to his feet. "Well, yes." He walks over, depositing a blue booklet on my desk.

When the class ends, I hurry to leave.

"Coming back next week?" he asks as I pass his desk. "I think you should. If you don't, I'll have no one else around to appreciate my socks."

My lashes stick to my eyelids. I hadn't meant to laugh at

him. "I was surprised. That's all." My confession fills the empty hallway of open doors. Immediately, my throat tightens and runs dry at the sight of the image before me. A mirage? No. Still daydreaming? Definitely not. *If I can see him . . .* I dive back into the room . . . *he might've seen me.*

I wish there was any other option here, but there's no time —I return to my fun-sized desk and hide underneath it, securing my arms over my head. *He saw me. No, he didn't. Yes, he did. No, he didn't.*

If only Foster could keep his cool, but no, that's not happening. "Chelsea, are you all right?"

"I think there may be an earthquake. I'll just wait it out here." My breath staggers.

"There's no earthquake. Are you sure I can't help you?"

I should absolutely crawl out from under this desk before Foster looks up my emergency contact on my application. All I need to do is wait out this very real catastrophe which would be running into Seth Hansen right now.

Footsteps in my direction warn me that Plan A has expired.

"Chelsea, I see you. Under that child's desk."

Scooping up my final shred of dignity, I pull myself to a standing position, straightening out my skirt.

"I dropped my pen," I say, meeting his hardened stare head-on.

"Well, where is it?" he accuses.

I shake my head and slink around him, leaving the room as fast as my unsteady legs and minor fib about the pen will carry me. I'm two feet from the door when Seth catches up.

"Hey, wait up."

I keep walking.

He opens the door for us and I step into the night air, which hits acute and cool, a jolt of compression to my lungs. I instinctively tip my head to the sky. The city lights stretch for miles.

"Hey, I want to apologize for storming off the other night. You're an old friend, I should've—"

I sigh, continuing to my car.

He keeps on. "You didn't have a ring on. You were solo at dinner."

My keys jingle as I dig them out from my bag.

"I assumed you weren't . . . married."

I unlock the door and open it, tossing my bag inside. I could leave it at this and drive away, but before I never see him again, I want him to know as much of the truth as I can possibly share. "My divorce was finalized last week."

"What?"

My hands are hanging on the doorframe as I face Seth under a streetlamp glow. "That night at The Wharf Hotel was the first time I'd been out in—well—a long time. I booked the room as a safety measure in case I had too much to drink to drive. Not that I need to tell you that part." I can't see past my own disappointment to recognize whatever he may be thinking.

"I'm an ass." Seth's hand lands on mine, trapping my fingers beneath his.

My voice treads cautiously with each word. "I could've tried harder to explain." My eyes dart to his pulse point, tapping over my skin as he rips away his hand, clearing his throat.

"What are you doing here?"

I drop my hand to my side, stretching my fingers, shaking off the tingling remnants of his touch. "Taking a class." What's he doing here at seven o'clock on a Tuesday night? "And you?"

"Teaching a class."

I accept his answer. It seems neither of us wants to push this conversation past politeness.

"There are things—we need to talk. Have time for a coffee?" His stare pours over my chilled complexion, earnest and inviting like melted butterscotch over a scoop of vanilla. I may like ice cream—it's tempting to look at behind glass casing, *sure.* It even smells like a great idea. My mouth waters, my tongue swipes over my lips in anticipation of that first taste. But it hurts to digest.

The last thing I can handle tonight is going down that road with Seth. The talking road that will only lead to him hating me.

I'm wiped out from the last ninety minutes—and nine years.

"I can't," I reply.

He accepts my excuse for a raincheck, holding my door open. I buckle my seatbelt, and he lowers his head into the driver's side, his face close enough to mine that his minty breath lands on the tip of my nose.

"About the other night," he says, hesitating, "I'm sorry."

As I drive past Seth on the sidewalk, hands in his pockets, I realize neither of us said goodbye. I yank on the steering wheel, pulling the car over, and park on Bay View—a residential strip a few miles away from my house.

I walk the rest of the way, churning over Seth's final two words, wondering how much distance sorry can cover. How many miles regret travels before it stops.

14

SETH

*M*y phone buzzes in my pocket. It's from my manager. He doesn't love the idea of me sinking paychecks to float dreams, but he's always been supportive of my goals. I'm not in the mood tonight to field work questions or socialize. I ignore the call.

Clear nights are best for the bike, but I've been on foot this week, using the added time to keep my head in the game—scoping out real estate and the restaurant scene. I pull my hunter-green coat up to my ears, popping the collar, shielding my neck from the breeze kicking off the water. The eateries on my walk are full of people waiting their turn, pouring out onto the wide, welcoming sidewalks.

Every corner of this city is alive with neighborhoods offering a robust range of cuisine, a chorus of flavors I can catalog in the air. Some people know a city by its sights and sounds, even the climate. For me, it's all about the taste.

I duck in to grab a couple of slices from Pop's—my favorite pizza shop—folding each in a paper plate, taking dinner to go.

"*Buon appetito*, Seth!" Fabrizio, the owner, salutes me behind the brick counter with an air kiss against his fingertips.

"Always. See you next time."

I'm moving slower than I do with hot plates, my sneakers dragging along the concrete. My thoughts weigh more than they're worth right now.

I haven't seen Chelsea in years, and the first thing I do is accuse her, like I have any clue or right. I know better than anyone that things aren't always what they seem on the surface. And the minute I laid eyes on her, I let that stormy stare and red satin pout get under my skin.

Would've made my night, and life, a hell of a lot easier if she'd been any other woman—breathless in a hotel room, an unremarkable exchange neither of us would remember.

But then she said my name under the night sky, like I was a star she was wishing on, and my perspective, along with my resolve, crumbled. Where did I go wrong?

A simple tan line, and I fucked up—my outburst, fueled by tunnel vision and a prickling heat behind my neck—a full body awareness that something's coming to devour you, and you're not even going to try and stop it.

My chest was half twenty-one again, hopeful and anticipatory, and half rattling-cage-of-questions, prepared for battle—to finally get some fucking answers and relief.

Chelsea had always been that to me. My personal brand of kryptonite.

The pizza slice permeates the paper plate, reminding me to pick up my pace. The tomato sauce at Pop's is perfection, sweet enough that it begs for one more bite. Hints of basil and oregano, thin crispy crust, charred artichoke hearts, and roasted garlic.

New York had great pizza, but San Francisco is my number one.

It takes no less than five paces for me to be back in my head tearing that night in the hotel room apart, piece by piece. There's nothing I like less than making a complete fool of myself, but killing possibly the only chance I'll get for answers, that was just piss poor management on my part. I played my hand and lost. *She wasn't married.* Fuck me.

Chelsea couldn't get out of my presence fast enough after her class. *"You. Me. And two cups of coffee."* I mutter under my breath. The memory stings, hissing through my teeth.

I remember when those words used to mean something.

How easy it's been for her to forget.

My jaw tightens, and I tuck the plates into my chest, speeding up toward my apartment before they cool completely. Chilled air grazes my face.

This entire week has been a nightmare of intrusive thoughts. You'd think after all this time, I'd have forgotten the details. Nope. They've been waiting for me to peel back the protective layer that I've funneled my feelings into. Work. It's been me building my dream one meal at a time since moving back from New York. It was a mess at first, but I didn't let anything hold me back.

My friends in the program begged me to stay at Cornell since I only had a year left to finish, but San Francisco had the one thing New York didn't.

Up until recently, there wasn't much about San Francisco's laid-back pace that resembled New York, especially with the restaurant scene. Now, chefs want to come here and make a name for themselves. We've got access to the freshest ingredients and the competition is getting fierce.

Commercial property has been the largest hurdle for me, but when the timing is right, it will happen. I'm going to finish what I set out to do ten years ago. And once I break ground, the television gig and the catering business will have to take a back seat.

The dream of this restaurant has been the one constant in my life. It's held me accountable. Kept me moving forward.

I pass by a painted brick wall with a pair of silver eyes in the center, one winking, the woman's permanent smile on display. I fight the following image as it appears in mind, Chelsea's cautious smile, reminding me that she was also once a part of my plan.

Unlike the image in this mural, Chelsea's smiles have to be earned. I liked that she never masked her feelings with me. Tonight I learned, as she turned away from me, that being embarrassed paled in comparison to being shut out.

I keep sliding into the past, to all of the happy minutes we spent together. Why does a mind torture you with the highlight reel of a person, even at their worst? Since my thoughts can't be trusted, my eyes need to stay on the prize, on these streets, especially its people. It may be competitive and hard to own a restaurant, but I've never shied away from work, and there's work to be done here.

There's space for second chances.

I can feel it, as true as I feel the woodfire oven heat seep into my pores. I make it to my apartment just as my fingers stop registering the scalding slices. The front doorman nods as he pushes the iron and glass door open, following in behind me. Once we're both inside the building, he greets me with stead-fast deference.

"Good evening, Mr. Hansen."

I shake the evening air off my shoulders, adjusting to the elevated temperature of the small lobby, and hand him his slice. "Freddy."

He breathes in the steam on his way to the U-shaped desk where the doormen sit during their shift. His tailored mocha suit matches his mustache. "Aw, thank you," he says, then hides his plate out of sight. He won't take a single bite until I've left and the coast is clear.

"Any deliveries?" I toss the plate, shoving the folded triangle into my mouth.

This is our standard routine—swapping baseball stats over

slices, checking in on our lives—his wife, Flora, and their three children. I don't have much to share on my end aside from business, though the papers would suggest otherwise. Every time I have a dinner engagement or show up at an event with a colleague, rumors fly. At first it pissed me off, losing my privacy to false narratives, but I work the media attention to my advantage, talking about causes that matter, bringing the focus back to the food and the city.

Freddy asks after my mom, how life across the pond is treating her, and I'm minimally engaged, which is unlike me. My ears perk up. "Sorry about that. Did you say there was a package?" *Maybe the set of blade sharpeners I ordered.*

"Yes, sir, from London," he says, passing me a cream square envelope addressed with Mom's rushed handwriting on it. Probably her annual birthday card.

I thank him and head to my floor. Koufax greets me with a couple hungry meows as I drop my keys on the entryway's glass table and switch on the lights. I scoop her up and chuck the envelope on the kitchen island.

A few pets and head kisses later, and I'm prepping fresh food for her. While Koufax eats, I shower, washing the sticky remnants of garlic and cod from tonight's lesson off my hands and hair. I close my eyes, head hitting the cool tile.

Let it go. Let her fucking go.

I scrape my nails over my scalp, recalling her hands in my hair, body flush against my chest, tasting her teasing mouth, intoxicating adrenaline rushing along the exposed parts of her neck, her pulse point vibrating on my tongue. The way her hair fell to her shoulders and brushed my cheeks. Her lips like poetry over mine.

It shouldn't feel like a personal rejection when a simple coffee invite's turned down, but with our history, it's a major blow.

The higher the stakes, the harder the fall.

I've spent years trying to convince myself that she was this terrible person, that when faced with her, that's all I could see.

And now I have questions stacking to their tipping point. That woman who sat silently stroking her martini glass stem, surrounded by strangers, didn't seem okay to me.

Water dumps over my face and aching body. I hate that I don't know how she's feeling.

My shower's less of a reprieve than my walk. I dry off with a single mission in mind—catch the end of tonight's game—one thing that will guarantee a break from thinking. I swipe the card from Mom on my way.

I remember my parents' marriage. Most notably, the way there were no survivors. Who we each were before "we" ceased to exist. My knuckles knock into one another as I turn on the television and tear open the envelope.

Happy Birthday, my darling son.
Don't spend this all in one place.
Love, Mom

Enclosed is a check. I toss the card on the table where my feet are propped up. Looking back has never gotten me anywhere.

My phone goes off, vibrating in my pocket. I dig my hand in and turn it off.

There's a man on second. It's the bottom of the eighth, two outs, and the Dodgers are up to bat. *Focus, Seth.* Just like the player. Keep my stance steady, eyes on my dream—I can't let a curveball like Chelsea Bell have me chasing outside the zone.

15

CHELSEA

"Mom. Mom," I repeat, my voice dusty from being pulled out of sleep. "Yes, I'm awake," I add, squinting at the clock. Illuminated red numbers read six forty-five a.m. "Why in the world are you calling me this early today?"

"Chels Bells, it's a day without the kids. I wanted to make sure you were getting a move on the morning. In fact, I checked the weather. Clear skies."

If my only options were to wake up to a rooster's cock-a-doodle-doo in my face or my mom over the phone, I'd choose the cock, every single time.

"Seriously." I sit up and face my matted-down hair in the vanity mirror, the roots beginning to frizz. "I'm up, I'm up." That's a half-truth. Technically, I'm vertical, but I haven't moved an inch on the day. Usually, I'd be deep in school prep at this time.

"What are your plans?"

"Six forty-nine a.m. And you've reached your question quota for the hour. Love you. Talk later. Bye." I hang up as she attempts to sneak one more in.

I thought I'd be used to these split weeks by now. It's been six months of sharing—schedules, Sunday breakfasts, phone bills—and I'm still walking to the fridge right now on auto-pilot to pack lunches.

Even considered moving or, at the very least, a major demolition job to switch up my routine, to break the habits that become a life, but there's been enough change for Paige and Jonah. It's as simple as that.

What's less simple, is the shadow I'm hauling around. It doesn't matter that the divorce was amicable. It doesn't matter that little has changed in the way of inconveniencing our routines. Paul and I get along. On paper, this is an ideal situation, but even when wrapped up nicely, failure still weighs.

The kitchen tile floor chills my toes, and I regret leaving my slippers behind. I secure my silk robe, then pull out a coffee pod to place in the machine. One popping sound and two button pushes later, the mug's full, and the steam coaxes a genuine smile.

Until we decided to separate, I hadn't missed a breath, a meltdown, a scratch. With Paige, it was me and her for so long, and then with Jonah, he needed extra attention early on, and the nights grew longer. Sleep was sacrificed. Though the family dynamic had shifted with Jonah, we were together, and I always knew what was happening with my kids.

Everything's split now. Split days. Split houses. And my memories-to-be-made are split down the middle, too, halved like a watermelon—and a broken heart.

I carry my coffee in a daze over the creaky wood floor in the hallway to the kids' bedroom. Paul found this place through a friend when we first got together, and it ended up being within walking distance of the closest private school. So no matter how tight of a squeeze it had gotten over the years, we were creative and spent as much time as we could outdoors.

The beds are made, and I place my mug down, slipping into

Jonah's. The blue and white sailboats ride the waves my legs make shuffling under the covers. I pull his weighted blanket up to my waist and bury my face in the pillow, breathing in the smell of sunshine and dirt, bath soap and maple syrup, smiling at the model cars on his side, built from popsicle sticks and craft glue.

The shelving wraps around the room, and I focus my attention on Paige's wall of art, displaying flowers and families holding hands, and the playbills from her favorite shows. Paige is a butterfly. She's social to Jonah's shy. Easily liked, like my mom.

My world's centered around being "mom" and this newly acquired abundance of time is suffocating. I'm told I should be rejoicing, reclaiming the hours any way I can. But I don't know what to do. I miss them. When they come home from their dad's, I hold them tighter, longer. And they'll whine, "*Moooooom*. It's only been a couple of days." They count the days—I count the seconds.

The first few months were the hardest. Silence gave me too much opportunity to think. And thinking led to overthinking. So, though I give her grief, Mom's daily check-ins are something I look forward to.

I understand now better than ever that change doesn't announce its arrival. People you think you know—they change, too, and routines change like pick-ups and drop-offs . . . *oh shit,* my fingers pinch the bridge of my nose as I remember where I left my car last night.

I slip on joggers and a sweater, smudge my fingers under my eyes, rubbing away the remnants of mascara stains while dialing Nan for a ride.

"Are you gonna take me up on my offer?" Nan asks as I latch my seatbelt. "Think of all the money you could save living rent-free. And with me? Eggies every morning," she says, playing dirty. Nan makes the best breakfast—a simple plate of fried eggs and buttered toast.

"Paul's covering the mortgage for now, and we need to keep things stable for the kids. We love you, but they're going to need their own rooms soon and with school, and Paige's drama club, it's too much."

"All excuses." Nan cracks her window and unwinds a strand of red licorice from the center console of her car, where her candy stash replaced her ashtray when Mom did the same.

Years ago, Mom made a bet with Nan about lasting thirty days. At her moodiest, I'd laugh with Dad that the competition alone between the pair would guarantee Mom would never take up smoking again. Pretty sure Nan knew that, too.

"What do you mean you ran home last night?" She chuckles as she chews, turning off Commercial Street and hugging the curb.

I lower the volume of her crime podcast. She can't get enough of collecting the clues, and right about now, I'm feeling like one of her unsolved mysteries.

"Well, whatever it is, I'm not judging. Amused as all hell, yes." She rips off another cord.

My stomach drops, unsteady from Nan's depth of perception limitations. I steal a strand and chomp hard, grinding artificial cherry between my teeth. My shoulders fall, and I lay my head against the headrest. We're driving by rows of homes, each with a staircase of similarities, their painted wood and Victorian-style triangle roofs. I whisper a wish under my breath for Nan to quit driving altogether. Whenever I offer, she won't hear of it.

"Spill," Nan commands, her hand on my arm.

"Nan!" I shout. "Hands on the wheel. Both of them. You can't steer with your knee." My voice squeaks.

"Well, well. Who pooped in your cereal this morning?"

"Gross."

"Figure of speech, dollface. Your choice. But you've got T-minus two minutes before we roll up on the evidence that something's on your mind. Then I'm dropping you like a bad habit, because I've got a date with my hairdresser."

I smirk. She grins. We both laugh, melting away any tension I brought with me.

"Your hair looks great, Nan." Loose curls frame her face, and the sun highlights the silver layers around her temples.

"That's true—it always does." Her assuredness draws you in and demands you show up. She can't help but tease out your most authentic self, at times reluctantly. "I don't go twice a month because I need to. I go because it makes me feel good, and the gossip's gold."

I nod my head, realizing for the first time how alone Nan has been for decades, and I always assumed she was completely content in her solitude. Maybe I wasn't looking close enough or listening clearly. She jumped at the chance to ask us to move in, and seeing her stylist so frequently, keeping the jam stand . . . she's always kept busy. And until now, so have I.

"Hey, want me to make you an appointment with Majorie?" she offers, patting down my morning bedhead, my roots sprouting like alfalfa from my scalp. "She's great with curly hair. Would be nice to see it make an appearance. It's been so long."

"No, thanks." I flatten my hair with the palm of my hand, dragging it to the base of my neck and twisting the mess into a low bun. *When's the last time I wore my hair curly?* The thought blends into wondering where I was the last time my heart sparked with curiosity and desire.

When I had that incredible week at twenty-one and—
My imagination cuts directly to the hotel.
With Seth.

The way he stared at me when I let my hair down, devouring me with his intense silence—he took up that entire room, his strong shoulders and commanding mouth. The interaction still has my body on edge, like a cruel cliffhanger.

Thinking about Seth in this way is an unproductive use of my time. Talking about it with Nan is not an option, either. The Seth I dream about is in the past—an alternate dimension. The Seth he is now is successful Seth, face-in-the-paper Seth, big-everything-from-his-wallet-to-his-ego Seth. I need to bury this spark of nostalgia and the sound of the hotel door slamming shut. The effort to extinguish Seth from my system mixes with the waves of nausea from Nan's wide turns.

As if she's caught me and can hear my thoughts anyway, Nan pulls her car up next to mine, stopping abruptly. My chest thrusts forward, the belt pressing into my sternum. Her face is as serious as it is soft. "We're all still figuring it out. If the puzzle was obvious, what would the fun be in that?"

"Love you, Nan." I kiss her rouged cheek, then hop out of her vintage convertible beetle.

She speeds off. "Menace." I shake my head at her driving, but mostly at myself.

When I step out of class the next week, Seth's leaning against the wall in the hallway, his ankles crossed, hands tucked in the pockets of his black chef's pants. Something about his relaxed stance in this long corridor sweeps me back to high school, sixteen and fueled by lyrics and anticipation, the way everything seemed larger. It was easy for me to tuck myself away from rituals and rites of passage that my peers wanted to participate in. This is different now. There are no lockers to hide behind and he's staring directly at me.

My heartbeats blare in my ears. The sheet of paper I'm holding drops to the floor.

"What's this?" he asks, bending over and picking it up.

"Homework."

"Ah," he mumbles, scanning the page. "Not bad. This looks sorta fun."

"Fun," I belt out, almost snorting. "Maybe if you know what you want to do with your life."

"You have to decide by today?" he whispers. "I think you've got a solid fifty years left to work it out."

"I don't have to figure it out this minute." I refuse to blink or breathe or take the bait.

"Oh great. Now that we've freed up some time for you, I was thinking we could grab a slice and split a pitcher," he says, disarming me.

I've spent the past week cementing angry-eyes Seth into my mainframe. I never wanted our story to end with him despising me, but when it arrived, I accepted my consequence.

Seth must read the confusion in my eyes, because he quickly adds, "If you're going to make any life decisions, I'm a chef, and I can't, in good conscience, let you do that on an empty stomach."

There's a million reasons to reject this offer, but I'm running out of ways to express something I don't entirely understand. He's being kind, but kindness is a tricky beast, as it mimics other kinds of emotions. "The thing is, um, you see . . ." My shoulders curve in, and I shake my head, releasing the tension from my face, lowering my voice. "I don't have the space in my life right now for—"

Seth kicks off the wall and towers above me, causing my throat to run dry.

"We all gotta eat."

My stomach growls, and Seth smirks. His brows lift slowly as I meet his line of sight. "I don't drink beer."

"Then you'll love what I'm about to show you."

This Seth is reminiscent of a place I don't dare traverse.

Uneven terrain.

Easy to slip and fall.

"Stop looking at me like I'm about to eat you for dinner. I'll return you in one piece." He rolls his eyes and starts walking, pauses, then glances over his shoulder. "We're on your clock, Chelsea. Let's go."

Does he hate me for what I've done?

He should.

The pizza shop's more like a to-go counter supporting six small round tables inside with wall-to-wall Giants memorabilia and city history. Seth takes off his messenger bag and unbuttons his chef's coat, revealing a simple—transparent—white cotton T-shirt. He claims a free table in the center of the room, removing two used glasses, dropping them in a dish bin by the soda fountain. And that's when I understand why he brought me here.

"I haven't had this stuff in years."

He nods, handing me a glass. "You trust me to order for us?"

"Not at all." I deadpan, masking the truth with sarcasm. It's never been him I can't trust—*it's always been me.*

The fruity bubbles fizz on my tongue as Seth returns, placing plain cheese slices overflowing on paper plates.

He remembers.

I swallow as he stares at me, deflecting to the grape soda. "Tastes like Fun Dip."

Seth nods, smiles, and folds his slice in half, shoving an unshy bite into his mouth. Everything about him is confronting. I suppose that comes with the territory and luxury of not caring what other people think. The melty cheese slides off the edge of his crust. His eyes dance over my face as he chews, grease painting his lips.

"Don't you like all the meats on yours?"

"What?" he asks.

"Nevermind. Just enjoying the view."

He stops chewing, and I realize I've said the wrong thing.

"Of the city," I clarify. "The photographs behind you depicting San Francisco's neighborhoods are incredible."

He peers over his shoulder and resumes polishing off his slice. "Right, Chels—the photography."

My jaw drops slightly, and I quickly shut it, pressing my lips together. "How's that ego of yours treating you these days?"

His laughter rattles the base of our table. "Well, thank you. And I still like meat on my pizza, but I come here regularly, so I don't mind switching it up—for the sake of saving time, of course."

This guy is actually giggling to himself. Clearly, he's fully entertained at my expense. And yeah, that ego thing, I bet it's good and healthy. In the brief time we've been in this shop, he's checked his phone twice and attracted the attention of the three guys behind the line, two whispering women at the counter, and countless pairs of eyes glancing over at our table.

Some people simply stand out.

I test my slice against my lips, refusing to play whatever game this is. It's cooled, so I fold the crust in like Seth did and take a bite. Warm and light on the sauce.

He doesn't take his eyes off me.

"It's perfect."

Seth nods, satisfied, like he's keeping score or something.

I count the floor tiles, stretching my neck, passing my gaze over his feet, up the length of his legs as they extend out like mature tree roots. If I were to stand up and not pay attention,

I'd easily end up on the floor. *Note to self: Don't break your face in the pizza shop.*

"I love these black and white images and their composition. You can see the impact the last ten years has had on the city."

Seth's smug stare falters, his brows drawing in, voice sobering, sliding under my skin as he wipes the shine from his lips. "Yeah, well, a lot happens in a decade."

The crumb of playful energy between us has hardened tight like the chords running up his arms. He flips his wrist over, looking at a watch, the leather band worn-in and soft, a large round pewter face telling the time. "I've got to get going." He grabs his jacket and bag, collecting our paper plates with one hand, and walks back up to the counter again.

"Hit the spot." I straighten out my cardigan and skirt, and push my chair under the table. My pulse quickens. I'm not sure if it's the idea of going home to a silent house or suddenly ending the night that's causing me to chew my inner cheek. I finish the last of my soda.

The faint music in the background is drowned out by kitchen commotion and conversation as the man behind the counter hands Seth another slice between two paper plates. Seth thanks him and adjusts his bag over his shoulder. "Chelsea?"

"Yes." I glance at him under the restaurant's white light, and before my eyes, the room transforms into a field—Seth on his back, lying in the grass, smiling under the sun. He knows something, his eyes spilling secrets.

"So?"

I shake away the vision. "Can you repeat that?"

Seth exhales—his voice warms as it wraps around me, nestling under my skin. "Come with me."

16

CHELSEA

"My place isn't far and I'd like to show you something."

I try to ignore his charm and focus on all the reasons this isn't a great idea. These feelings and flashbacks keep waging war in my head. So I'm shocked when I reply, "I could use a walk."

Our steps align as we move down a busy sidewalk, arms swaying past the other like opposing hands on a clock—fingers whisking through the air, electricity pinching my skin.

Seth's lapels are propped up to his ears, and every time I glance over at him, he glances over to me, causing me to look up at the night sky.

"Watch your step." He grasps my hand, pulling me into his body as we pass by floating trash stuck to dog—or human—feces. He grips my ribcage as he holds our hands together, firm and careful, the placement not too high or low.

My lungs register his touch, gatekeeping my breath until he lets go. When he does, my legs wobble, so I hang behind to steady myself.

Catching up to his stride isn't what's holding me back.

He notices and walks back to me.

"Did you know there are six thousand homeless people in this city and there's more than enough space to shelter them? We live in one of the largest centers of innovation in this country, and we can't take care of our own. More people move here every year for the promise of jobs, acceptance in our communities . . . hell, for the weather, and then they can't afford to live . . . Basic shit, Chels, like a roof over their head and three meals a day. We're not even talking anything fancy." His voice booms, stealing my breath.

With nothing profound to offer, I kick at the air, and listen.

"And then what happens? They lose a job because a start-up got absorbed, or they can't find something that makes enough, or they have to leave a dangerous home situation, and where do they end up? Right here, on the streets, without access to anything but drugs and survival. I love this city. It guts me to see something I love suffering like this."

Whether he's reading an ingredient list or taking on the struggles of humanity, when Seth gets a thing in his heart, it pours into everything. *That hasn't changed.*

He's the guy who points out the cracks in any foundation or person because he sees what can make it better, from missing amounts of flour or water or salt, to the devaluation of a society's moral compass, and even a hurting heart.

My tongue scrapes the roof of my mouth, hyper-aware of my immediate surroundings, of a city I've been ignoring for a decade. There's always an excuse—because it's easier, because I'm exhausted, because I can. He's out here trying to make a difference in the world and—I shake my head to relieve an acute pressure between my eyes.

I'm a part of the problem.

"You have so much passion. I can't imagine having that kind of deliberate energy for anything . . . well, aside from Paige and Jonah. But that's grilled cheese with the crusts cut off, not tackling social change." I'm one person to two people. Not *the* person for everyone.

"I don't usually go off like that."

He has no clue what it feels like standing in the shadow his light casts.

Absent-mindedly, I grind the soles of my heels. It feels good, which might be the only thing holding me up. "It's been ages since I've walked the neighborhoods. I go from the same points A and B to C and D every day. I live here, but I don't know the city anymore."

Seth stops at a corner in front of the tallest building on the block. Comprised of glass and steel, polished gold-lined double doors, splotches of flashing brake lights reflecting on the thick handles. My head's sprinting in the silence, the hum of street traffic and footsteps around us.

"Welcome home, Mr. Hansen," a man's voice cuts through the road noise as he pushes the door open.

Seth extends his arm for me to walk through. And all I can think is the boy in beat-up rollerblade who wanted to run away has finally found a place to call home.

Not just any place.

"Freddy, this is Chelsea . . ." Seth narrows his gaze to confirm what name I'm going by since my divorce.

"It's Bell." I reach to shake the Freddy's hand. "It's nice to meet you."

"Pleasure's all mine, Ms. Bell." Freddy walks behind a large desk, and Seth hands him the folded-up paper plates. While they speak quietly, I crane my neck, stretching the width of the ceiling, staring at the floral glass sculpture hanging from it.

"No two pieces are the same," Seth whispers beside me. His breath on my neck and the chime of the elevator straightens my spine.

"Beautiful," I tell Seth. "The art."

Freddy holds the sliding door, so I move toward it, and we both step on.

"Goodnight, sir."

"Goodnight," Seth replies to Freddy, smiling as the doors close. He pushes number eighteen out of forty floors. Eighteen inhales. Eighteen illuminated knobs. Eighteen opportunities to say *I'm sorry.*

We enter into a well-lit hall with three apartment doors. Seth walks straight ahead to the one in the middle. I pause in the doorway. "I never changed my name. It's always been Bell."

He swallows and nods—not in approval, but with understanding, confirmation, a mutual awareness settling in—as his brows smooth out and my shoulders relax. Though everything in our lives seems to have changed, there may be a few things that have stubbornly, and coincidently, stayed the same.

Seth switches on the lights and locks the door behind us. I'm greeted by a cackly hello.

"Well, hi there." My tone elevates like it did when my kids were babies. "Animals and babies activate the squeaky part of my voice." I pet a soft coat. It occurs to me that my voice isn't the only part of me that assimilates in any given situation.

"This is Koufax." He picks up the white cotton ball of fluff and kisses the top of its head.

"You named your cat after a baseball player?"

"Not just any player. One of the greatest pitchers to have ever lived."

"So, this is why you had to get back?" I smile at the sparkle in his eyes.

"She's gotta eat, too. And Freddy."

"It's thoughtful to bring him dinner. I'm sure most people wouldn't do that."

"Like I said, we all gotta eat." He slips out of his coat and offers to take mine. I notice he removes his shoes, so I do, too. The pads of my bare feet roll against the shiny wood floor.

Seth peeks at my toes. "Red."

"What?"

"It's your color."

I shouldn't let that comment rush my head, but it's already halfway through me before I can bury my reaction. Behind my eyes is the memory of his coarse stubble scraping my chin, red lipstick on his collarbone and jaw. The way I could've mapped out the path from his mouth to the places I kissed, connecting all the spots I marked as mine.

Seth's cracking open a can of something potent when my vision restores. It's incredibly bright inside. Every light in the place is on, which makes snooping unavoidable. A brown leather couch and matching loveseat fill up the open-concept living space. The kitchen area is off the living room, custom-built with butcher block counters, chrome, and reflective surfaces. A flatscreen television is mounted on an exposed brick wall, and I suppose he kicks up his feet on that coffee table, the wrought iron legs spiraling like braided spaghetti.

If there wasn't a bookshelf with photos, culinary awards, and Dodgers memorabilia, I'd have guessed he was house-sitting. I didn't picture Seth domesticated, a guy with a hefty lamp collection or a matching furniture set. I expected something entirely less lived-in because, in my mind, he was always adventuring in the world.

I rub the pointed edge of a black frame holding an image of Seth—the Seth I last knew—standing beside an older man in front of a restaurant. Their arms are crossed, their adjacent grins wider than the breadth of their puffed-up chests. I glide my fingers over to the next frame—a faded Polaroid—of a woman with summer-bright hair on the back of a motorcycle. Her long legs are stretched across the faded black leather. She's got a helmet in her hands and excitement in her eyes.

"Here." Seth's beside me, handing me a glass of white wine. I inhale grapefruit and fresh-cut grass, something else too, soapy and strong. I take a sip, letting the peppery citrus warm my veins and overpower breathing in Seth.

"Is this your mom?" I ask, picking up the framed photo.

"Before she had me. Some place in Nevada, I think."

She's young? I take a long pull from my glass. "Did she ever have more kids?"

"People do what they want," he states without room for discussion.

"Do they?" He's standing so close, my throat swells and my fingers run frigid, gripping the stem. "You look like her."

"Like my mom?"

"Spitting image."

"She'll love to hear that. Do your kids look like you?"

I think about it. Paige looks like Paul, and Jonah does resemble me, but in his own way. "My son has my eyes and way of navigating the world. He's kind and bright and always trying his best. I don't know how to describe it. It's like your kids are woven into every piece of you in some way, so it's hard not to see yourself in them." I smile. "Paige was running laps around us all the minute she was born. I'm just along for the ride with her. With Jonah, it's different." He and I are similar. *I get him. And he gets me.* "When Jonah was a toddler, he'd crawl over in his diaper, always in a diaper because he'd wail if I put clothes on him . . . Anyway, he'd lay his curls in my lap and rest his eyes, and our breathing would sync up. Like I wasn't really breathing until he got there."

I'm hesitant to look at Seth. Hesitant to move at all. I completely lost myself recalling those early years.

He takes the frame from my hand and puts it down. "Boys and their moms."

"My conversational skills have centered around mealtimes and bathroom breaks for the last decade. I'm a little rusty."

"Not as rusty as you think. He has your hair then? Your natural hair."

I nod. "And my laugh."

Seth does that irritating and appealing reciprocal nod that I can't decode—where his chin dips slightly, and I want to swim in his thoughts. I haven't slept through the night in years—subtlety loses its meaning.

"Where's this one from?" I point to the other photo, shifting my weight to my hip, sliding my fingers up and down the fragile glass.

"My last summer in New York. Before I moved back.

Helped the owner open his first restaurant, remember?" he asks, a biting bitterness in his tone.

I close my eyes. *Remembering.* My gut sinks.

They shoot open. I don't want to remember. Not here. Not now.

Seth draws his lower lip between his teeth, looking at the photograph, and I want to be there with him, too. I'm not ready to talk about what happened, but I'm aching to hear about the things I missed. Like pressing play after a pause. A very long pause.

"I never really wanted a degree. Didn't see how it would serve me back then. What was college like?" I tread softly.

He runs a stiff hand over his trimmed coppery beard. "Adrenaline and exhaustion. Long days. Nights, too. Magic."

"Sounds incredible." I sigh in the glow of his memory. But that can't be right—he said *moved back* after the summer of 2001. "Wait. You didn't stay in New York?"

A round of inhales and exhales loop between us. My eyes tear from his gaze to the Seth on these shelves and walls. The guy I promised to wait for.

"Plans changed." He dismisses it as nothing. "I needed to get back to claim what was mine—build something with my own two hands. On my terms."

"You didn't graduate, Seth?" I swallow hard. "Why?" My voice shakes.

"Doesn't matter. Like you said, didn't end up serving me."

I turn my back to the wall, shielding Seth from the inferno of shame crawling up my neck. That whole life was so important to him. It was everything. None of this makes any sense. I do the math quickly, my head spinning from the outcome. He didn't stay in New York. Seth came back before winter break.

He came back.

My hands tremble as I spin around, knocking into Seth's arm, dropping my drink to the ground. It shatters on impact.

Shards of crystal fly across the hardwood and over my feet.

"Don't move," Seth's demand raises the hair on my arms.

"I'm so—"

He presses his pointer to my lips. "I'm going to throw you over my shoulder now."

My pulse races and before I can object, he lifts me in his arms, cradling my back, linking an arm under my knees. Seth holds me like a feather, and I'm stiff as a board as he lays me safely on the broken-in leather couch.

He kneels by my feet, holding them gently. His touch tickles. "Stay still. I'm checking for strays." After he's satisfied with his examination, he stands.

"Seth, please let me—"

"I'm going to clean this and then I'm going to show you something. Try not to get into any trouble for like five minutes."

He disappears down the hallway, and I sink into the cushions, scooting to the edge. This place reminds me of those winter clothing catalogs staged at some mountain resort. There's a chenille throw I use to cover my exposed legs and feet. My pulse is returning to something manageable, and I'm grateful for the moment of solitude to slow down from being swept off my feet and knocked on my ass at the same time.

Being in Seth's arms didn't feel like disgust or disappointment, and someone who can't stand you doesn't spot-check for embedded glass. But he's also not letting me speak, and that's not like him. I want to scream. Confused doesn't even begin to cover it. This is exactly the kind of complicated I don't have space for. We're dancing around each other, our bodies teasing and testing, *remembering*. I'm sweating through my clothes as I smooth my palms over my hair, tucking the ends back into my bun.

Koufax hops up onto the couch and curls behind my knees. "No fog tonight." I smile at the skyline, its resolve and history and originality. She's purring when Seth returns with a bunch of maps in hand, tossing them on the table in front of me.

"Karl's saving up for June."

"Who?" I ask.

He snorts in disbelief, shaking his head.

I laugh a little, still riddled with heat. "Should I know him?"

"Do you use Twitter?"

"I use a toaster—does that count?" I playfully nudge his knee, and my gut twists at the familiar gesture. *Stop it, Chelsea. You're past indulging in weak knees and memories. You can't. Not with him.* I need to apologize, at least for breaking his wine glass. And then I'll leave.

Seth drops down next to me. "That absolutely doesn't count. Karl's the name of the fog. There was this anonymous Twitter account last year that started as a way to be playful with all of the bad weather we were having. It's become the place for all things 'fog,' like random tweets about the weather."

"We call the fog Karl?"

"We do," he answers, smiling.

I'm relieved that Seth has returned in a lighter mood. He must have equally needed a breather.

"Are you taking a trip?" I ask, signaling to the maps.

"*We* are."

I momentarily giggle at the absurdity, and cough, tasting the exhaust fumes of a bus we never rode together. Clearing the tackiness in my voice as I lick dryness from my lips. "Um, there's no way. I can't go anywhere."

"Not an overnighter. Day trips." He shifts his body, and I tuck my salvaged feet in further under me. Seth notices my legs folded into a triangle, and doesn't move an inch to give me some slack.

My toes curl. "Your place is nice. Homey."

Seth pets Koufax.

First, I run my mouth about my riveting life as a mom, and now I'm telling him his house is homey. Could I be the most obviously boring person on planet earth? And this proximity thing isn't doing me any favors either. Seth rests his forearm over my legs as he slides his fingers through his cat's fur.

I breathe deep, trying to block the invisible magnet that's apparently in this room, pulling my full attention directly to Seth's mouth. I thought it was just kissing I missed. I think my body misses other things too.

Like how natural it feels, leaning back with another person, sharing a couch cushion. I allow myself to relax in the moment. Seth drags my legs over his thighs and gently runs his hands over them, back and forth, back and forth. The friction his palm makes over my legs might as well be directly on my skin.

If he knew my core temperature right now, he'd consider giving me his sweating ice cubes so I could dump them down my shirt. "Can I have one?"

He digs a cube out and hands it to me, the melting water coating our exchange. The ice cracks in my mouth as I chomp away. Seth places two fingers in his mouth, pulling the moisture from their surface. The pressure between my teeth barely relieves the throbbing between my thighs.

"Chelsea?" Seth repeats my name. "So, what do you think?"

It takes me a beat for my brain to send important messages and blood flow to my vital organs. "Yes, right, well . . ." I scan the large lettering on the maps looking for dates. "Are these local maps?" I question, curious, not following anything he said. He's got my legs trapped, and I can't run. Not sure I would if given the chance.

"If you want to figure out what kind of career you should go after, you might need to start at places that inspire you. That's where these come in."

I scratch behind my ear, careful not to disturb my hair, contemplating his plan.

"Let's get you reacquainted with the city. It's evident by your footwear tonight and the timid two steps you tried to trail behind me the entire walk to my place that you haven't spent any real time here in a while."

He's right. I haven't had time—*made time*, I internally correct myself.

"You're supposed to try new things to see what might stick. And these lists suggest the best places to explore—museums, restaurants, coffee shops, parks, and of course, you'll have the best guide in town to show you the hidden gems you can't find on any map."

I'm focusing on every word he's saying. "You want to show me around the city?" But when? How?

"Yep." He sips from his glass, sucking a drop of melting ice from his lower lip.

I flex my toes and stretch my neck, not much different from Koufax beside me.

"You in?"

The idea of more time with Seth tugs like taffy warming in my hands—unforgiving at first, then softening, taking on a different shape. Maybe spending more time with Seth is exactly what I need to figure out my future, and maybe, if I'm lucky, I can repair our friendship, too. I don't need to rush my apology, and he doesn't seem in any hurry to seek it.

I know we can never be restored in the same way, but maybe it can be something new. And it would be nice to have a guide, someone who knows the city inside and out. "I guess with the kids being with their dad half the week . . ." I'm rolling their schedule around in my mind. "I'll need to check with Paul, but it should work."

"You run your decisions by your ex-husband?"

I'm not looking for Paul's stamp of approval, but we're raising our kids together—it's the courteous thing to do.

"Don't answer that."

My head pounds. "I wasn't planning on it."

"Good. You in or what?"

"Are you sure? I don't want to put you out. I can take the maps and walk around myself."

He swipes the pages from my hands. "Did you check out number thirteen on the hot spots?" he asks, opening up the maroon and white pages, leaning over me and holding my legs in place. "Right there." He shows me. "That's our first stop tomorrow."

"Tomorrow!" I wasn't prepared to start so soon.

"Got a thing against breakfast, too?"

I could look at this list and feel sad, but instead, I roll my eyes at his playful comment and do a mental mini-cartwheel when I see where we're headed.

17

CHELSEA

eryl's is exactly the same—even better because of that fact. The air's sweet and heavy with pancake batter and sizzling butter and the clang of stainless steel stirring milkshakes in their containers. The booth announces my arrival as I slide in, and it makes me laugh.

"Do you have a quarter?"

"I might've brought a couple," Seth says, laying a stack on the counter. "Don't pick a shitty song." He winks.

"I'll let the universe decide." I'm sure the music selection has been rotated out since we were twenty-one, but I don't care enough to look before I drop in a quarter and squeeze my eyes shut, pressing two random cream and black tiles below the glass casing. I lean back into the booth, the warm sun kissing my cheek through the windows. My fingers tap along to the opening beat of drums and lyrics.

"Excellent choice. Do you remember this song?"

My gaze falls on Seth, his stare shooting through me. "I remember everything." And I hold my breath, waiting for it. The moment when Seth asks—where he rips open the time capsule, turns the bottle upside down, and I'm forced to watch as the past shakes out in front of us.

He's got his lower lip between his teeth, hands wrapped around his mug, poker face in place, and he lets it be. We simply sit as the song carries on speaking for us.

When I used to run, I'd be on mile ten, beginning to choke from the pressure in my lungs. That time to myself, the movement alone, offered me protection from myself. Pushing through miles meant pushing past invasive thoughts. I haven't run in years. Not the kind that gets you across finish lines.

But I'm not her, I tell myself. *I can do better.* I'm not someone who stumbles reading anymore and I'm not someone who stays in a dead marriage. *I know how to lose.*

I press my thighs into the booth, trapping my palms beneath, bracing for the impact that everything around me makes, the noises, the smells, the uncertainty. And I do it with a smile. I absorb the shock. Hit after hit. I lock them up. I do it because I have to. I have Paige and Jonah. I do it to make sure everyone else is okay.

The song ends and Seth looks over his shoulder, grabbing the server's attention.

My sneakers tap the base of the booth. I turn to the window, exhaling through my nose, fogging up a small circle where my bare lips meet the glass with their imprint.

On the pavement, words didn't trip me—the voices hushed. Once I stopped running, it was as if I sailed through the last decade. I kinda wish one thing had tripped me hard enough to notice what had become of my own desires and dreams.

"No lipstick today," he notes as the server approaches the table.

I touch my mouth, realizing I forgot to apply it.

Seth orders our usual. It's peculiar to think we have a usual, and I wonder if something happening twice in the same place warrants a lifetime of comfort.

"What cuisine are you planning to serve at your restaurant?"

He stops mid-sip and jumps right in. "American bistro. Clean ingredients. Local. Fresh. A twist on the classics. Think pot pies and meatloaf and grilled fish. Affordable, of course." He pushes up the sleeves of his hoodie to his elbows as his smile lights up the entire dining cart, competing with a level of brightness from outside.

I rest my chin in my palm and slide my sunglasses on.

"Headache?"

"A little. I'll be fine. It sounds exciting, Seth, like all the food you'd eat as a kid, but actually edible."

He laughs. "We're the TV dinner generation. Only so much of that institutionalized crap you can ingest."

"My mom would've duct taped my mouth before letting me eat anything in plastic."

"Well, your mom's always been a different story."

"Truer words have never been spoken." I chuckle. He does too.

"But that's it, right? Like my mom and dad were always working. Those microwavable meals meant I didn't starve, cool, but they were full of garbage. And in school, working with chefs who live to cook, I learned that keeping it simple is always best." He pauses, then leans forward, his enthusiasm rolling across the table and up my arms. "I want people to come into my restaurant as they are—strangers, hungry, maybe they had a rough day or year . . . I want them to not worry about a thing, enjoy a great meal, and leave full and as friends—leave better than when they walked in. And of course, I want them to come back." He runs a hand through his disheveled morning hair and what I thought was comfort before pales in comparison to what it feels like to sit in the basking warmth of Seth Hansen's dream.

"That's incredible. All of it. I can't wait to go."

"It's got a bit of time left to marinate, but it's close. There's this Cooking Channel show I'm a part of next month, and I'm banking on it helping me get that final financial backing to purchase property and hire an opening staff."

He's got this plan. Knows what he wants. It's intoxicating.

"So, how is Summer?" he asks, throwing me off guard.

"She's threatening to visit soon." I laugh at my troubled sense of humor, throwing up jazz hands. Seth laughs too, which is as equally appreciated as it is annoying. I need being around him to be less effortless. "My parents are really good. She loves L.A. I don't think she'll ever leave now. No reason to. There's too many stomping grounds to hold onto. She occasionally gets recognized around town. She likes that."

"It's tough to be in the spotlight. I imagine it's even harder to step away from it." Seth's smile sobers and he pushes the stack of quarters toward me without breaking eye contact.

I slip another quarter into the jukebox as the pancakes are placed in front of us. "Your choice."

Without hesitation, he flips through the case and makes a selection. Classic rock. Classic Seth.

I raise my hands to plug my ears before the banging and clashing succeeds in worsening my headache, but Seth catches them mid-air in his grasp. "Wait. Listen. It might grow on you." And by the spirited grin he's sporting, I know he's going to be right this time.

There isn't a single thing I recognize about it. There isn't a single thing I despise about it, either. I think I could like the sound of new things almost as much as I like the feel of someone old. *Do I tell him? Or do I keep it to myself?*

My hands withdraw, stinging, as I ball them into a fist on my lap out of view.

This music may not be familiar, but the voices interrogating me are—back to when the decisions I made and the price we paid cost more than a song.

18

SETH

The bathroom at Meryl's is some kind of torture chamber for anyone taller than a toddler. Elbow to elbow, you're bumping into greasy walls. I hunch to take a hard look at myself in the narrow mirror, splotched with dry spots and smeared disinfectant. I splash some water over my face in hopes of pulling it together before I spend the day with my long-lost . . . I don't know what to call her.

She's a friend. Sure. We'll go with that.

But I don't kiss friends, or anyone, the way I kissed her.

She kept trying to apologize last night over the glass breaking, and I refused to let her. Sorry isn't something I take lightly, and there's only one apology I've ever wanted from her. I resign to not worry about labeling Chelsea anyway. The last time I thought we would define what was between us, she disappeared.

Last night, when I invited her over, I told myself it was innocent enough, but then she rifled through memories and curled up on the couch, stretching her neck, exposing that pulse point that shoots adrenaline straight through me. I sat as close as I could get without actual friction, taking in the details, counting every time she breathed in my direction. I suppose I didn't need to gather her legs on my lap like a greedy squirrel on the cusp of winter, but she was cold and tired, and that's what magnets do in the presence of one another—they catch.

Her thighs trembled at my touch, strained beneath my palms.

I did nothing. Asked nothing. And in return, learned nothing.

The problem is, when I'm around Chelsea, I'm distracted by what I still want to know. And when I'm not with her, all I want is more time to get to know who she has become. Either way, I'm fucked, so I might as well choose the path of least resistance.

My skin tightens at a fist thumping on the bathroom door. The thin walls shake, as do the mirror and my reflection. I run my hands through my hair. "In a minute," my startled voice projects over the pounding. I unhook my hat from my belt loop and adjust it over my bedhead.

Her laughter swept across the diner, all compelling and melodic, and it occurred to me that Chelsea's like a bird, always caged and dying to break free. She's been refined and serious in every situation since that night at the hotel, but here at the diner, she's tearing apart pancakes with her fingers and leaving lip prints on windows.

Maybe this adventure around the city might help her reconnect with the girl beneath the tight bun and tired eyes and pleasantries. The one with opinions and fire and answers to my questions.

I'm trying to reconcile all of the versions of Chelsea I know. The diner was our first stop. I needed to test out if I could handle this brilliant plan of mine because helping her means revisiting the past, and I haven't stepped foot in Meryl's since the last time we were here together.

To make this work, I have to avoid reminding myself of who else she's been in my life.

Chelsea's waiting by the entrance as I make my way to the front of the diner car. She's dressed in a pair of black skinny jeans, a red flannel shirt with gold thread, holding a disposable camera in her hands. Her sunglasses are on top of her head now, the corners of her eyes smiling.

"I see you came prepared." I whistle at her polka dot sneakers, snagging mints at the register before closing the door behind us.

Karl's heavy, the sun completely out of sight. I pop open my hand, letting Chelsea choose first.

"Which one do you want?" she asks.

"Take a guess."

"I don't like guessing."

"What if I told you, you can't lose."

She smiles—a faint whisper of a shared moment—as she leans in to inspect her options. She picks up the pink mint, brings it to her nose, and then pops it in her mouth. "Thanks. I probably have bacon breath."

Do I tell her bacon is my favorite thing? "Well, I didn't want to alarm you, but I can smell it for miles."

"What? Are you serious?" She looks around me and back to herself, cupping her free hand around her mouth. "Is it offensive? Should I go home and change?"

"Chelsea. I'm kidding. You smell good. I mean, like you." I narrow in on her mouth. "No one is offended by how you smell. I promise."

"Dick move, Seth Hansen." She shoves my shoulder. It doesn't budge against the mighty force that is carefree Chelsea. It leans in.

"Worth it. And no one escapes Meryl's without diner smell." I smirk, my thumb resting against the residual confectioner's powder on her flushed cheek. I peel my finger away for proof.

"Oh." She relaxes on a sigh, blowing sugary dust into the air. Her minty breath lingers on my skin. I rip my hand away and shake it out by my side.

She looks at me, her eyes clouding over from their limpid gray to a squall—glistening bits of hail striking through their center like glass.

The swings. The storm. A torrent in my life.

The only option I've ever had is to hold on.

"I'm a mess, aren't I?"

"You wear it well, Chels."

"Dialing up the charm." She brushes off my compliment. "Don't worry, you don't have to pretend." She reveals her perception of me.

A hand taps my shoulder from behind. "Are you him?"

I turn around and see a man and woman bundled up in scarves and winter coats like it's February on the East Coast—giddiness tugging at the sides of their mouths.

"Did I cater an event for you?" I ask, tipping up the brim of my hat.

"No," the woman screeches. "You're Chef Handsome . . . I mean, Hansen. We saw your billboard on the way in from the airport and then on the bus. I knew it was you. I was telling my husband. We're visiting from Tampa. Huge foodies. We can't wait for your show, right honey?" She whispers something in his ear, which, thankfully, I can't hear.

"Yup, my wife loves ya. Can I grab a picture of you two?"

"Sure thing." I locate Chelsea, and she's moved away from the interaction, off to the side, with a gentle smile. Her perfectly straight teeth sparkle as she holds up both of her thumbs and that ridiculous camera made of paper and plastic. My chest squeezes.

I take the picture and wish the Tampa tourists well, offering a few restaurant recommendations in the area.

"Just to be clear, I'm never letting Chef Handsome go,"

Chelsea says when they're out of earshot. "Why didn't you smile?"

"I didn't smile?"

"Not the real one."

"It's weird when people recognize me when I'm in street clothes."

"Does that happen to you a lot?"

"Hold that thought." I dig out my cell and put it on silent. "It's probably going to get worse once the show airs."

"Yeah." She looks around me, over me, under me, but not directly at me.

I'm not sure she understands. I want her to see how important this is to me. "When something really matters, we do what we have to, even if it's at odds with what we want."

"You mean for your restaurant?"

"The restaurant's the manifestation of what I want—the tangible thing I can hang my hat on."

"I've never doubted your place in the world. You'll make a difference with your food. I know it."

She says shit like this, and I'm twenty-one and eleven and all the ages in between, falling under a spell of euphoric recall. After she left last night, I stupidly went through some things I saved, thinking they would help me understand what I'm doing here with her and why I'm doing it.

Wrong call. Didn't help at all. Instead, it reminded me she's the one person who always gets me going—my ideas are drawn toward her curious mind. She has this special way of accepting people as they are. We have these little things in common that seem meaningless until you put them all together, decade after decade.

From the moment we met, I was myself with Chelsea. I knew it—my heart knew it—and being safe in that way sent me flying into a future I envisioned. With my head in the clouds, my feet left the ground, and they never landed the same again.

She's not only the last person I let in but also the person who let go.

"Anyway, Chef Hand—"

"Chelsea," I warn, stepping in close.

She laughs. "All right, all right. Where to next?" She spins around, uncertain of the direction we're headed.

I pull heavy cool air through my teeth and tuck my head beneath my hoodie.

"The beginning, of course."

She looks at me, bewildered, the corners of her mouth curling like a question mark.

I let her stew. A little mystery is good for the imagination and for her.

We walk a few blocks and hop on the BART. It takes us to the farmers' market and the fountain.

Chelsea peers over the edge, dragging her fingers along the stone. "This isn't exactly the beginning."

I'm by her side, staring at the tumbling water and its recycled patterns. "You're right—it's not, technically." I open my bag and pull out two sample-size packets of blackberry jelly, handing one to Chelsea.

"We've had so many stops and starts, it's like we circle back each time," she says, peeling back the flimsy lid, dropping the jelly on her tongue.

"I figured this was the beginning at one point."

She swallows and smiles. "What do you remember from that week?" Chelsea probes at a distance, smoothing a palm over her hair.

I stick to the facts. "I remember being on break, disappointed my mom couldn't stick around, also excited at the prospect of working on recipes without interference. I remember Rainy Days and Nan's spark." I lift my empty packet and toast hers then take both and stick them back in my bag. "The rest of that week, well, you were there. The music we listened to, the things we shared, sitting on your stoop with that lemon birthday cake. I've never been able to recreate one as good."

"You've tried?" She clears her throat, bringing the viewfinder of her camera to her eye. She starts snapping away, twisting the angles of her hands, winding the film after each shot.

"Why are you using that?" I'm not ignoring the question, merely dodging it.

"Why not?"

"Because it sucks."

"It's a starter."

"That's your starter," I exclaim.

"Not exactly." She laughs at my overreaction. "They were left over from a birthday party the other weekend, and I'm still trying to justify investing in a good camera when I have to save for things like braces and college. Let's keep moving."

We walk around the fountain. Chelsea scratches the space beneath her bun.

"I spent a week once trying to perfect the cake recipe without using jello."

"Ah, well therein lies the issue. It's not like cooking. You've got to follow the rules." She leans in closer, her arm brushing mine.

I whisper by her cheek. "I'm a rule bender."

"Eight minutes and ten seconds," Chelsea says as I slide into the cab.

"Timed me, really?"

Her shrug and smile rub at the sore spots. "Here ya go." I pass her my camera, the strap catching between our fingers. "Sixteenth Avenue and Moraga, please," I say to the driver.

"No." Chelsea's voice mixes in with my directions.

The cab halts. My arm shoots out in front of Chelsea.

"Sorry, man. She was talking to me. Still Sixteenth—thanks." The driver grips the wheel and pulls into the street. "What do you mean, no?" My knees are cramped in the backseat of the sedan.

"I'm not taking that fancy-ass camera. You saw what I did with your wine glass. I'll drop it in a puddle and break it or something."

"That's what this trusty strap is for." I drop it over her neck, and my knuckles skim the soft dip of her collarbone. "Listen, where we're going, you'll want it. My mom gave me this camera last year, and it's collecting dust in my closet."

"I can't accept this."

"It'll be a loaner to replace that party favor in your hands, and when you upgrade to your own, you can give this one back to me."

"This is a lot for me."

"The camera?"

"All of it," she emphasizes, and I think I understand her meaning as Chelsea's eyes glisten and the faded rose color on her cheeks brightens.

"How about for the rest of the day we keep it light? We can just be Seth and Chelsea, who've been paired together on a group project to complete this assignment, and we've only met for the first time. Deal?"

"Deal." She sticks out her hand, and we shake on it.

The cab stops at the corner and we hop out at the stairway. Chelsea's face lights up as the sun breaks through in scattered cyan patches, illuminating the murals on each of the 163 steps tucked away between homes and grass. Somehow, the steps blend into the mix of plants and grass surrounding both sides. I like to think it was built to blend in on purpose.

"I have to bring the kids here."

I adore being an observer of Chelsea as a mother. I'm also enjoying the way her enthusiasm slowly erodes the fortress she's built around her feelings.

"Paige loves art and Jonah loves anything to do with the solar system. Look at these spirals, Seth."

I bend down to see it from her vantage point. The yellow and green designs, daisies wrapped around stars, pieces of stone and glass placed with precision—an explosion of color bouncing off the slate canvas in her eyes.

"This was all done by the hands of the community. Three hundred people collaborated on the project. Can you imagine what it took to come together in this way, the attention to detail, the communication, patience, and problem-solving? Our neighborhoods," I add, shoving my hands in my pockets, exhaling hard through my thoughts, "this is what the city is built on. Trust, creativity, diversity. Right here in front of our eyes, all around us, this is what it means to be in the arms of San Francisco."

"It's beautiful."

"On a given day, think of how many people pass over these steps. I wonder what they see?"

"The bright colors, an uphill climb, maybe nothing at all," she says.

"It's like falling in love, over and over again, discovering new ways to treasure the same place." I'm overpowered by another memory, *a wet field of weeds and wishes.*

"Stay right there. Just like that." Chelsea takes a few steps down, cradling her new camera like a newborn.

I'd be lying if I said seeing her smile while holding it didn't make me happy.

She peeks past the side of her grip. "Seth."

"Chels."

"I love it here, too," she says, eyes on me, fingers firing away.

19

CHELSEA

*W*e arrive at The Square with two coffees and artisan sandwiches, walking the perimeter of the park, passing restaurants and taverns and the massive church on our left, before finding an open section of grass for our impromptu picnic.

The area's saturated with river birch trees and people taking a rest under their eighty-foot shadows. Scattered laughter is carried in the air: kids playing frisbee, singers with guitars, and a group of girls handing out pamphlets.

"We've covered a lot of ground so far," I acknowledge, taking a bite of fresh mozzarella, basil, and tomato drenched in olive oil and balsamic vinegar.

"Is it all coming back yet?" he asks, propped up on his elbows, sipping his coffee. The curve of his bicep peeks through his white scoop-neck shirt—coarse blond hair covers his forearms.

Ache sparks in my chest. "Sort of." I lay my arms over my knees and zoom in on the view in front of us, not sure if I'm paying attention to it as I slip into some kind of nostalgic cocktail—a blend of joy and guilt, realization and suppression.

Captivated by what hasn't changed even though it has. Like the city. Like Seth. Like me.

Spending the day reacquainting myself with the neighborhoods has been a pleasant surprise. I'm aware that with everything on Seth's plate, this must be eating into his time. He's doing me a big favor, and I'm trying to rein in my thoughts from lingering on what happened when he went back to college that spring.

Past. Present. Past. Present. Past.

I bite into hints of salt and savory olive oil. "Eating this is ecstasy," I say, moaning.

Seth's thick lashes lift and his tawny eyes expand, transitioning to mahogany.

"This sourdough's unreal. You have a radar for hidden gems."

"Was there any doubt? Local eats are my jam." His smile is full of pride. He wears it well because I know it comes from goodness—caring about people and his passion.

I wipe my mouth with a paper napkin. "Since Paul's gone, cooking has become pretty tedious. We used to tackle mealtimes as a team. He'd make our food, and I'd make Jonah's. But now I'm eating Jonah's discard pile—cartoon-shaped noodles and chicken nuggets every day. Not that there's anything wrong with nugs, but I'm realizing I've been disconnected from everything, even something as simple as the food I like."

Seth stretches, landing his arms over his knees, mirroring my body position. "Why are you making his food separate from yours? Seems like a serious waste of resources."

"It probably is—I know it is—but his doctor once told me that eating is eating, and as long as he's eating, I need to prioritize that over the *what*."

"He's picky?"

"I don't know anymore. He has a real aversion to certain textures and smells. Anyway, it's kid stuff. I'm sure he'll grow out of it." I'm ready to change the subject when it occurs to me that I was also particular about the foods I ate. "My mom forced me—literally made me try new foods. She called it a no-thank-you helping. Can't tell you how many times I swallowed without chewing because I felt like I had to. I won't do that to Jonah."

"Definitely not. Incredible what parents thought were solid strategies when we were growing up." He rolls his eyes as he teases the tips of the grass.

My skin tingles as he pinches the blades, threading his fingers through.

Incredible is not how I would describe it. Invasive, maybe. Life-altering. "I failed him, you know. It's my job to make sure he's nourished and healthy, and every time I put dinner in front of him, all it contains is white. They say to eat the rainbow, and my kid will only eat clouds."

Seth faces me. "I get it. You want what's best for Jonah. But you're also being hard on yourself. It can't always be perfect, Chels. Not even you. Though you're about the closest thing I've ever seen."

"Please." I flick the brim of his hat. "You need to get that vision of yours checked out." If he only knew how perfection has never been the end goal for me or in reach. It's always been about the path. And I battle it every step of the way.

"I've got twenty-twenty. Test me." He moves his face in, staring-contest close.

I think about it—acting on his dare—quizzing him on every detail, but I don't know if I'm ready for those answers.

His knee grazes mine. Our eyes hold steady and clear. Like a funnel, we see straight through each other to a granular level. After a lifetime of separation, there's still nothing that compares to being next to Seth.

I can't think in complete sentences when I'm inhaling his scent and being subjected to his sincerity. Why does he have to be so "him" all the time? Even when he's stern, he's sincere, and I don't really know a better form of kindness in this world.

My hands hurry to wrap up the rest of my sandwich and messy feelings as air rushes from my lungs. My skin itches beneath my bra.

Droplets of rain hit my nose and chin, coaxing my mouth open like slow wet kisses. I kick off my shoes and shoot up, turning back to Seth—his expression perplexed, patient. I wink because I can't trust my mouth to not betray me by blurting out all the ways I've imagined him. So I take off running down the hill, arms flailing in the wind.

The sky cracks open, drenching everything, including me. My head tips, and I catch the cool moisture as it lands on my tongue. My hands wave through the air. My hips swerve to that new song from this morning—its lyrics about letting go are stuck in my head. For the first time in ages, I'm in the moment, dancing away threatening, self-deprecating thoughts—the earth at my feet, the song in my head, and Seth's smile behind my eyes.

"You're getting soaked." He raises his voice over the weather.

I open my eyes to Seth, very wet, carrying the camera he lent me under his hoodie. The concern in his eyes is mostly concealed by the brim of his baseball cap.

"I don't care," I shout to be heard.

"I can see that." He laughs, licking his shining lips.

"Dance, Seth. Do it!"

"I'll end up on my ass."

"I've missed you," I admit, matching his smile with my own, almost missing the moment his lips flatten into a hard line.

Seth tears his gaze from me and stalks up the hill, the distance between us stretching tight.

I try to piece together the gravity of what just happened. My words were honest but unfair, reminding us both of what a disappointment I've been to him.

With my mom, it was school and performing.

With Paul, I stopped marriage counseling.

My kid eats from one food group.

My sense of worth has always been tied to shame, the ways I have failed everyone around me—including myself.

By the time my limbs move, and I make it up the hill, stepping my soaked-through sneakers onto the sidewalk, Seth's hailing another cab. "I can jog home."

"You're not jogging anywhere. Look at yourself."

He's right. I don't want him to be right. "Seth, I'm sorry. We were having fun. I didn't mean to bring up the past."

"You didn't do anything wrong." He's looking over my head, refusing to make eye contact. "It's been a great day. I lost track of time, that's all. I have a catering gig tonight."

He's lying. Equal parts direct and avoidant—a master architect when it comes to talking about his feelings, but this isn't that at all. He's putting a wall between us, maybe because beneath all this helping, he knows I'm the same girl who breaks things.

I'm not going to push the subject. We said we'd hang out to get my project done, and that's what we agreed to, and clearly he can keep to his end of the agreement. It's not his fault that I can't filter with him. I never could.

We ride in silence. In the musty cab. Our respective gazes out opposing windows.

Someone used to smoke in here, and I crack the window even though my jeans are plastered to my skin and my hair's a mop on my head. I need this circulation more than I need comfort right now. I need to focus on the outside of me—the parts that only hurt temporarily.

Spending time with Seth is risky, and I know that. Did I assume that starting from the beginning meant starting over?

My place comes into view, and I want to thank him before I go.

The fare monitor stabilizes at thirty-six dollars.

"I've got it."

"Let me take care of my part," I offer.

He refuses.

"Okay, well, thank you," I say, averting my eyes. My hair pulls heavy at the base of my neck, drawing my shoulders in. "I also wanted to thank you . . . for today." Regret rolls thick down my throat. "It's the most fun I've had in a long time."

Seth remains silent and acute embarrassment crawls up my neck.

"Bye, then." I assert myself, flinging open the passenger door.

Six steps to the door. That's all it will take. That's all I have left in me right now.

"Chels." Seth's voice wraps around me, then so do his arms. Seth's hugging me. He's holding me, his head resting next to mine. His breath hits behind my ear. "It's me. It's not you."

I drag my teeth over my bottom lip and bite down the urge to bring my mouth to his.

He gently kisses my temple and spins me to meet him at eye level. My eyes dart all around his face. He was mad and disappointed with me, wasn't he?

"If you're free next Tuesday, come with me to the community center."

Seth's invitation gives me whiplash. "To your class?" The question comes out twisted in uncertainty.

He lifts his arms, and I wait for the impact of another hug, which might be the end of my resolve. I'm not sure how much more I can take in his presence without closure.

He hands me the camera. The clunky weight hangs over my neck. He takes three steps down to the landing, his hands finding his pockets, casually rocking back on his heels, waiting for my answer. *Exactly as I remember. He'd show up at my house when we were kids, knock on the door three times, and wait for me to come out and play.*

"Tuesday," he says, encouraging me to confirm. "And Chels."

"Yeah?"

"Dress to get messy."

"Mommy!" Jonah screams at bedtime. "I hate brushing my teeth. The toothpaste at your house is gross."

"This is your house too." I pick him up and lug his body like dead weight into the bathroom. My chest tightens as he wiggles in my arms, his feet kicking my knees. Is this the battle I want to choose with him today? *Breathe.* Be the calm for both of us. "The flavor isn't your favorite, but we still need to brush your teeth to keep them strong. Would you like to brush them now or after jammies?"

"No," he demands. "I don't want to." He cries and squirms in my arms, too hard for me to keep him safe, so I kneel on the ground. He curls up in my lap, his hands over his mouth. I sing to him, holding his back against my chest.

Paige appears in the door under dim light, ready for bed in her tie-dye pajama set.

"How about if I get you a rinse glass?" I ask Jonah.

"Then you can swish and spit. We can race. It'll be fun. I'll show you," Paige adds.

He nods, wiping his eyes.

I turn to Paigey and whisper, "Thank you."

The stress of switching up routines has taken a toll. Though Paul and I keep most things consistent between our homes, it isn't always feasible. Sometimes, something as simple as bubblegum toothpaste derails an entire night.

I switch beds and lay down next to Paige, combing my fingers through her hair. "Thanks for your help."

"I love you, Mom, and we need the toothpaste Dad has."

"You're telling me," I whisper. "Love you to the moon and back." I tuck wavy strands behind her ears. "How was Dad's?"

"The usual. We played board games and ordered pizza and breadsticks for J. What did you do?"

"I had pizza too."

Paige yawns and turns over. I pull the covers to her chin and tuck her in, kissing her on the forehead. I nuzzle into her ear and repeat our nighttime ritual. "Snug as a bug in a rug."

I swap lamp lights for a row of hanging stars and moons that help when Jonah wakes at night, ensuring he doesn't trip over his bed. Usually, he'll crawl into bed with his sister, and I'll find them together in the morning, conspiring over whatever their secret brother-sister language is.

"Mom." I peek my head into the room. "He loves you too." Then she turns over, and I close the door.

Lunches get made, clothes are set out, and the kitchen is wiped down. I call Paul while I'm settling in with a glass of white.

"Hey, Chelsea, what's up?"

I push through my apprehension, bringing this up—again. "Jonah had an epic meltdown tonight over the toothpaste. The same toothpaste we've always used, but I guess you have the new flavor, and earlier today, I was talking with a friend about his eating, and it occurred to me—"

"A friend?" Paul interjects.

I sometimes forget that Paul's been my only real friend for a decade. There's Mom and Nan, of course, but I never made time for close relationships outside my family. I didn't find the effort worth it—maintaining relationships with other moms I had nothing in common with. Only so far diaper talk can go, and I learned that those groups of women were often smiles on the surface, false advertising underneath.

"Yes, a friend." I'm sure he's curious, as I would be if he said those words. Especially if that friend was spending time with my kids. "That wasn't my point, though."

"No, I didn't mean it like that. I'm a little surprised but glad. Did you meet through that career class?"

"I canceled that class today." I drink the wine—crisp pears and pineapple.

"Why?"

"Me in a classroom? Recipe for disaster."

"We've gone over this . . . you don't have to work. I'll help as much as I can while the kids are in school."

"But then what? I'll have no way to support myself or contribute to their college fund?" I focus on my toenails—there's a chip in the polish. *Did that happen during my dance party in the rain?* "Paul, I want to work. To make something that's mine." Seth's voice rings in my declaration.

"I want that for you, too, but it's a lot with the kids. There's only twenty-four hours in the day. Your mom would help if you let her."

"No." I dig in, shoving my feet into the crack of the cushion, hitting a metal object. "Can we not talk about this anymore?" I pull out a toy truck, shaking my head. We've had this conversation many times, and my position remains unchanged. "I'm going to figure my life out. But that's not going to happen by me sitting in some class taking assessments. I need to get out there."

"Okay, so then what about Jonah?"

"I'm concerned that what we brushed off as baby preferences are becoming rigid habits now. Have you noticed anything?"

He clears his throat, and I know that sound—he's mulling it over. "He's a feeling kid with conviction."

"Is it just that, though? It wouldn't hurt to talk to his teacher."

"Worth a shot. The school might have additional insight and resources."

I finish my glass, swallowing the pins and needles I experience when I think about what school resources were like for me—hours inside while kids got to play. Constant isolation.

The shrill of Jonah's screams this evening cut through all my reserves. His outbursts are increasing in volume and frequency. Every day, I navigate every detail, from the clothes he wears to the flavor of toothpaste. "Thanks, Paul."

"Goodnight, Chelsea."

My bed's calling, but once I'm sitting down, it's impossible to move. My mind catalogs the day's events. I'm wiped out.

The closer I look at my life, the fuzzier the picture gets. I've been fading in front of my own eyes. And today, Seth helped me see past that.

It's not until I notice a wet spot spreading on the armrest of the loveseat that I consider I'm crying. I can't remember the last time I cried. Maybe when Jonah learned how to ride a bike. I touch my fingers to my cheeks and inspect to make sure it's coming from me, then I try to scrub away the mark on the loveseat. *Shit.* I'm rubbing my mascara into the cream-colored, unforgiving fabric. *What removes tear stains?*

I run to the cleaning cabinet under the sink, rifling through the bottles and brushes and go with a white eraser sponge. Shockingly, it works.

There's been so much change, and change is like having the earth shift beneath you. This is Jonah's way of protesting and expressing feelings he doesn't have words for. We all do that—I run, Nan makes jam, Paige sings and dances, and Seth . . . he works.

I meant what I said when I told Seth I missed him. I didn't recognize how much I missed having a friend outside of my home life who isn't connected to the chaos. It was more than that too. Being in Seth's company, laughing at his jokes, getting frustrated by his stubbornness—it's as close as I've gotten to spending time with myself.

The me I was. The me he sees. The me I might still possibly be.

How can I make this work and preserve our friendship?

At first, I thought telling him what happened back then was important, but that's selfish of me, a desperate attempt at lessening my guilt. I don't know what to do or how to proceed. I wonder if knowing the answers is always a good thing anyhow.

Once you have them, you can't unknow them, and no matter what Seth learns, I'll never be able to make up for what's been lost.

20

SETH

I crashed on a random dude's couch that summer, a block away from the restaurant—too spent to notice much about the place other than its size, with four of us kitchen staffers there. No one cared. It served as a spot to lay our heads for six hours if we were lucky.

Opening the restaurant was our priority, and for most of us, we felt lucky to have any part in it.

The other option would've been to head back to San Francisco until school resumed in the fall, and I'd shared with strangers before when Mom and I had nowhere to live—I knew what I was capable of. But being on the line, working with the greatest chef, I'd never had those experiences.

So, yeah, at that point, I had no intention of going back until winter break.

A month into summer, I stopped hearing from Chelsea.

Not my best idea hanging onto her last postcard, but it was all I had left, and I never could shake her from my thoughts anyway.

The handwriting was quintessential Chels, and she didn't

write much, but I knew the words were hard for her to put down. Knowing she wrote them for me had to mean she cared.

Pancakes are not the same.
The city misses you.
I miss you. —C

On the reverse side, there's a grayed-out image of a trolley cart heading up Market Street. The image is raised from the coarse paper beneath. I had picked at the edge to discover it was one of her photos glued on top of a stock image.

Chelsea had doodled daisies around the corners of the postcard, similar to the ones I had drawn on her finger. She kissed the back with a cola-colored lip balm that lost its waxy shine by the time it made it across the country.

I slide my thumb over the phantom outline of her lips, bringing it under my nose. The smell is long gone. I've taken it out a few times since Chelsea and I started hanging out again. I don't know why, maybe looking for clues, a way to understand how she got here and why she left to begin with.

We study the past to better understand the present and to prepare for the future. Am I now seeking or preparing?

When she said she missed me, something inside me slammed on the brakes. Of course I wanted her to say it, imagining in my mind the day she would, but the minute she did, I wasn't the helpful friend standing in the rain, shielding her camera from damage—I was some pathetic guy following breadcrumbs around our city from a girl who ghosted me.

Once she stepped out of the cab, I decided something had to give, and that something was going to be me. We were young. Young kids do young shit like declaring their favorite band by following a trend or rollerblading without a helmet or quitting school for a girl.

They make vague promises and think it's set in stone.

They think they're in love after spending one week together.

They swear they know it all—that it's possible to meet your soulmate at eleven. A cosmic collision. Two people who move through life like stars. Occasionally crashing into one another, but always on separate paths.

No question, I want to help Chelsea, and she needs it, so here I am for a reason that has nothing to do with tending to an old wound but, instead, in moving forward.

She's on her way to starting her own career, and in a few months, the show kicks off for me.

———

Chelsea arrives a few minutes early, which gives us time to orient her to the kitchen before class starts.

There's spare chef coats for volunteers, and normally, I pay no attention to the fit of the starched fabric when someone else is wearing it. Chelsea's another story—she always is.

The material stretches snug across her chest as she fastens the buttons. My eyes travel up her neck and follow the straight path of her jawline. Tonight, her hair's down, ironed flat, razor-sharp past her shoulders. My fingers want to rummage through her sophisticated exterior, anxious to tease out the colorful person inside. The girl who makes art from flowers and wears polka dots and doesn't worry about ironing her hair or hiding her heart. The girl who dances barefoot in the rain.

"You need to pull your hair back." I point to her loose ends as she straightens her posture.

"Oh, right. I have something in my purse." She walks toward the table in front of us where her things are, and a twinge of remorse pinches my throat.

It's my kitchen for the next ninety minutes, and it's not like the health department's going to show up for an unscheduled inspection check, but I'd know. And once I know something, I can't make any other decision but the right one.

"So, what's your plan for me?" Chelsea's hair's secured in a sheltered low bun, not a glossy strand out of place. The man in me chastises the chef in me who made her do it.

I prep the counter with mixing bowls and rolling pins, counting to make sure we'll have enough to share in groups of two.

Her shy smile and glazed-over look as she watches me means she's found a memory—and I can see it clearly, each decade, where her smile has meant something different to me. "How old are we?"

"Eleven."

"And?" I encourage her to share it because I think remembering is the key.

"Just something you said about my smile."

"What did I say?"

Chelsea's face warms—pink, honest, and irresistible. She stumbles over her words as she gathers them, and I may want to hear her answer, but I know I don't need the distraction.

"You said you liked it." She shrugs.

I meet her eyes head-on. "When something matters to me, I pay attention. Like a recipe I know by heart. Through and through. Maybe even a little obsessively." There's a lot of shit I forget, but her smile will never be one of them.

Eleven, an immediate friend.

Twenty-one, a hopeful runner, confused girl, eager-to-be-independent woman.

Right now, she's someone I want to get as close as possible to without breaking. Close enough to pause the years that came between us.

No. You don't want that. You want to help her get back on track. Once you do that, you can both move on.

One step closer won't hurt. "I still do."

"Still what?" Chelsea's voice cracks.

"Still like your—" Before the thought concludes, my feet press forward, eyes on their target, the sliver of space between her parted lips as they surrender to their natural resting place.

"Seth, what are we—"

Footsteps and chairs dragging along the tile floors, pierce the bubble, shredding the insulation—the entire space is illuminated like a petri dish, and we're under a microscopic lens.

I rip myself away from Chelsea's pouting red mouth.

"Chef Seth!" Steph announces herself, projecting over the raucous. "I see you brought a tasty snack." She gives my sous chef a solid once over.

Steph probably registers Chelsea's lack of response as shock, but I know better. Once again, she slips beneath her mask into this person I can't get to. Steph waves her hand in the air, laughing with her classmates as they settle into their seats.

"I'm playing. Nice necklace," she observes, eyes on Chels. "David Yurman?"

I lean over and whisper, "Jewelry needs to go too." *An oversight on my part.*

Chelsea places her hand over her collarbone.

"All right, all right. Class, this is my friend, Chelsea Bell. She's going to be joining us tonight, and hopefully she'll be back because we're awesome. Right?"

"Here, here, Chef," the group cheers.

"Like you, Chelsea wants to make nourishing meals at home. Now we're all in this kitchen for the same reason. Say it with me." I pick up a rolling pin and point it like a mic toward a concert crowd. We all project and speak in unison, "Real Food. Simple Steps. No Scraps."

I lay the rolling pin down and turn to Chelsea, who's tucking her necklace into her pocket. "Let's partner up with the same person from last week." I turn around and write the word on the whiteboard.

Jackie calls out from the back. "Chef."

"Yes, Jackie."

"How am I gonna make something I can't pronounce?" she stirs the class up, causing everyone, including Chelsea, to chuckle as conversation crosses the aisle.

"Tonight we're making a kitchen-sink quiche with whatever ingredients you have in your fridge. If you can pronounce pie, you'll be good. Because that's what quiche is. It's a savory pie that can be served at any meal and is under five steps. Come grab your baskets and get your stations prepped."

One person from each pair steps up to the table and grabs the ingredients and tools they need.

"What should I do?" Chelsea's at my side.

There's no chance I'll remember my name, much less this recipe, if I'm breathing her in all class. "I want you to work with Steph."

"I don't know if that's a good idea. I don't want to hold anyone back."

"My kitchen. My rules, Chels." I load up her arms—rolling pin, basket, and the recipe card. My brows raise in anticipation, waiting to see how well she takes direction or if she'll push back. I know I'm hedging my bets, but there's a fine line between hard enough and over the edge.

Her chest rises beneath the stiff coat, her nostrils flare. She pivots on her heel, walking to the back table where Steph sits, grinning like I just served Chelsea up on a silver platter.

21

CHELSEA

"*H*i, again," I say abruptly.

"Hey."

This woman's dressed like she stepped out of a magazine— ripped denim at the knees, an off-the-shoulder fishnet sweater with a magenta tank underneath. And I'm looking clueless in this bulky starched coat, wincing in embarrassment at the gold clinking around in my pocket.

"I don't bite," she responds. "Well not unless you want me to." She winks, and I sit down, placing the basket of ingredients between us like a wall. Even if she bites, I doubt I'd feel it. My skin buzzes, every atom charged from the almost-kiss Seth and I *almost* had.

"I'm Chelsea."

The next thing I notice about my new partner is that she talks with her hands. I track them, trying to keep up with what she's saying.

"Chef covered that. I'm Stephanie Howard. Steph to everybody. How old are your kids?"

This I can talk about easily. "My daughter's eight and my son's five. Yours?"

"Cece's four and a firecracker. Which apparently builds up an appetite. Last week, I found two empty granola bar wrappers and a half-eaten apple under her pillow. Do you know what happens to an apple after a couple of days?"

I giggle at the idea of moldy buried treasure. As horrifying as that smell must be, if my kid was eating fruit, it would be a win. "My kid squirrels away last year's Halloween candy."

Steph surveys the basket. "Cece comes home from daycare and all she talks about until bedtime are snacks."

"You have a snack monster on your hands—that's what my Nan calls it. Kids come home with a full lunch box, then spend the entire afternoon raiding the cabinets."

"Smart lady."

"I'd kill for my kid to eat an apple. I wasn't always the most adventurous with food, and I think that's rubbed off on him."

"The mac and cheese diet. Tough break."

"Worse. He rinses the cheese off."

"Won't eat the cheese? What about the powdered stuff?" Her eyes widen. "Here, you need this more than me." She passes me the recipe card.

"Seems pretty straightforward."

"That's Chef's motto in class. 'Five Steps or Less.' Most of us are working and on a limited budget every month, so we need to keep it simple."

It's expensive living here, and I forget about money sometimes. I'm aware money is finite, but since I've been technically unemployed for most of my adult life, I haven't paid much attention to the dollars and cents of our daily living. In that way, Paul has taken care of me. I didn't mean for it to pan out like this, to hand over full control to another person. It wasn't dramatic either. Paul didn't demand to be in charge of our finances. One day, I managed my money—the next, I didn't.

One day, I was planning for a certain future—the next, I was living another.

If I ask my parents for help, they'll just pick up where Paul left off. Nan's off-limits, too. Anyway, she pulls money out of thin air. *Five bucks here. Five bucks there.*

"What's going on?" Steph circles her hands around in the air, directing them at me.

"I'm sorry, what?"

"You're looking into outer space or something? All starry."

I blink hard and adjust the rigid sleeves of this coat, rolling the cuffs up to my wrists. I've been disappearing into my imagination lately. "Unless it's a recipe I know, I'm a terrible cook. I can't keep track of all the steps."

"Well, I'm no Barefoot Contessa, but follow me—we'll get you set up."

There's sixteen women in here, and with it comes a consistent hum of voices. Seth's at ease, used to the grins and batting eyelashes. It all blends together into static noise, making it difficult to concentrate on Steph's lead. I close my eyes to listen better.

"Chef doesn't mess around about cleanliness."

My eyes snap open.

Steph walks us to a wall and grabs one of the communal coats available. She secures the fit and brings us over to the sink. "Step one—and we never forget this one—wash hands. I swear, the first few weeks of class, he timed us, so make sure, twenty seconds, warm soapy water. Sorry, it's the industrial pink stuff. Smells like a hospital. Paper towels are on the wall, and the trash bin is by the door."

"Thank you," I say, grateful for her guidance. "You don't have to answer this, and I'm sorry if it comes off as intrusive, but I'd love to know how you get your hair to stay curly and look so beautiful? Mine always frizzes up. I think I damaged it using a flat iron for years."

"Just like what we're doing here, less is more. That's the most important thing to remember. Got any hair masks?"

We sit back at our table and Steph's about to hook me up with tips when Seth's shadow hovers over our basket.

"Ready to get messy?"

My pulse pounds, warming my palms as I look up at him.

He's towering over our table, and it happens again, like it happens every time our eyes lock—the room melts into nothingness and it's only us, eleven and swinging on the playground, twenty-something and wrapped up in each other, weeks ago and pressed into a wall. I strain my neck to trace every curve and corner of his body. His words are commands that demand a person's attention—my attention—and every cell in my body responds and obeys.

"You don't trust me?" He's singling me out, and it's obvious.

Steph shoots me a side-eye. I know she can sense the tension because his stare is cutting through it.

When he smirks, my heart leaps headfirst into the shallow end. Not much different than my attempt at making a quiche will be—a probable catastrophe.

Seth gets in close, leaning over the table, tilting the recipe card.

"Chef, I've got your girl covered." Steph sends Seth back around to where he was standing, her fingers flicking in midair, sweeping him away.

He nods, slides his hands into his coat pockets, and moves on to the next pair of partners.

He doesn't correct Steph.

Neither do I.

As predicted, the center of the quiche was undercooked and the crust was burnt. Might've been the pan placement in the oven. Might've been how distracted I was chatting with Steph during class. I'm holding a small plate of evidence I'll microwave later when I get home.

Everyone wraps up cleaning their stations, and Seth takes a minute longer to gather his gear. On her way out, Steph's still cackling at Seth's dropped jar, a drawbridge of disbelief. She also gave me her number so we can talk hair.

"Can I carry these knives for you?" I offer.

"I think you've had enough excitement for one night. You can switch off the light on the way out."

"You're never going to let me live this down, Chef Handsome?"

His chin sways side to side. "Never going to let you near an oven unsupervised, that's for sure."

I peek into the career class and see it's empty. The rush of adrenaline evens out. I didn't want to bump into Foster after dumping the class.

"I talked to the instructor. He's a nice guy."

"You did what?" I bark.

"I told him I was helping you with the homework, like an independent study, since you dropped the class, which I still think was hasty."

"Seth."

"I didn't want anything getting in the way of you coming back to my class because you didn't want to hurt that guy's feelings. Which you are coming back, right?"

My sigh's audible. "I'm not some fragile creature who can't take care of her own stuff." *Or am I?*

Seth holds the door open for me.

"My car's this way." I nod to the right.

"Pizza?"

Saying no to pizza hurts a little. The thought of attempting to salvage this quiche hurts more. "I smell like soggy eggs and defeat." I laugh. "And I have these leftovers."

He leans forward. "I promise you, you don't, and that—" he points to my to-go container "—is inedible."

I step to the side, sucking on my bottom lip.

"I've got some great spots for us to check out tomorrow, and I don't want to eat alone. You'd be doing me a solid."

"You have Freddy."

Seth takes the burnt quiche from my hand and tosses it in the trashcan. "Freddy's off tonight. It's his wife's birthday."

He wins. He always wins.

Shoulder to shoulder, we walk and talk, swapping inhales and exhales. Our breath comes out in tiny puffs under the streetlamps.

"How'd you get on with Steph?"

"I like her." It didn't take long for us to find common ground.

"She's great. Everyone in class is. Strong women doing what's necessary for their families."

"Necessary?"

"Everyone in class comes from the DV system."

"What?"

"Domestic violence. Abusive homes, partners. First, they go to a shelter. Once they get set up with jobs and are out of safe housing, they opt in for a life-skills program at the community center. For a lot of them, this isn't their first round, but for some, this is the first time they're on their own. My class helps with cooking skills and confidence in the kitchen. Everyone deserves to eat well."

"I didn't realize."

"They're single moms, like you, who want what's best for their kids. To take care of others, you gotta take care of yourself first. Starting with the basics—shelter, sleep, food. Good food doesn't have to break the bank."

I get it now, why Steph mentioned her limited budget.

"Steph liked you too," he tells me, unprompted.

"She was just being nice."

"No, it's not like that. Steph doesn't conceal her feelings. Probably my favorite thing about her, even when she calls me out."

"So you do this pro bono?" I run my hands up and down my arms.

"I donate my time because I can and because it's important."

Our feet scuff along the concrete, sticking close to each other.

"It's incredible, Seth."

"Does that mean you'll be there next week?"

"I did fail the assignment and have no idea what I'm doing, but the instructor keeps inviting me back, so that's promising."

Seth winks. Then pulls me in for a side hug.

That feels good. Everything around him does.

22

SETH

*G*iants fans in our section have been pre-gaming. A tacky substance peels from the soles of Chelsea's canvas sneakers as she sinks into her seat.

I plop down next to her, appreciating her ballpark-friendly attire, including a worn-in royal-blue Dodgers hat that now has a suspicious electric red smirk tucked beneath it.

Late spring mornings are generally cool, but by mid-day, the sun is a halo over us—an isolated haven of diehard hope, hops, and fresh hot dogs. They are by no means Dodger Dogs, but with enough ketchup and mustard, I can swallow any fantasy and digest it as reality.

"What?" I ask.

"Nothing." She reaches across my lap to scoop up a handful of peanuts.

"No answer, no peanuts." I hold the paper sack hostage two feet above her head.

She gives me a full smile that can be seen across Oracle Park. "It's seriously nothing, Seth. I just didn't picture you as a bleacher guy."

"What did you picture?" I crack a peanut between my teeth.

"Payment." She holds out her hand.

Top-Forty playing and escalating voices in the air make it hard to hear. "What?" I lean in.

"You want answers, you're gonna have to fork up a peanut."

Chelsea brought her A-game with her today, and spending time with her in this way is like fueling up at empty.

She breaks open another peanut and pops one in her mouth. "Figured your manager would score box seats, something fancy for the 'fresh face' of the network's newest cooking show."

Is she flirting? "You've seen the articles." My phone buzzes in my pocket. If I was with another woman, I'd be prepared for a little harmless flirting, but I'm not Chef Seth with her. With Chelsea, everything has consequences. "You know I don't desire all of the attention that comes with this business? I chose to be behind the line for a reason. My relationship is with the food first. This 'fresh face' label comes with the territory, but here in this section, no one cares who I am. All we care about is the game."

"You've always had sky-high goals and dreams, and now look at you—you're making it happen." She nudges my shoulder. "I figured all that buzz came with some perks, too."

"C'mon, these are the best seats in the house. The action doesn't get any sweeter than this. Can't beat the energy or the breeze on the back of your neck. Not to mention there's an unlimited supply of cold beer."

"When I was in eighth grade. . ." Chelsea pauses, her tone settling soft, followed by a sigh. "There was this annual art show. It was kind of a big deal. Every year, the teachers chose their favorite pieces from graduating students. The school hosted a small event and decorated the cafeteria like a gallery. One of my projects was picked."

"Chels, that's amazing."

"The thing is, once my mom showed up, no one cared. I felt

so bad for the other kids. It didn't matter what we did or where we went, everything always turned into a red-carpet affair."

I reach to hold her hand, but Chelsea shifts her focus to the field.

"The seats are great, especially for people-watching." She gestures to the camera hanging off her neck.

I tuck her story into a safe place, nibbling on the corner of my salty thumb in search of the closest beer vendor. He's three rows up.

Being a Dodgers fan is one of the few things in my life that resembles longevity, and today they're playing their rival team. I have a rare weekend off from work and a surprise planned for Chelsea later. "It's my one real tradition."

"Who'd you go with as a kid?"

I scope out the field being prepared, a last minute polish, and the pitchers on both teams are warming up. "Mom worked most weekends, so my dad would take me." The corners of my mouth tug at the memory as I follow the pitch into the catcher's mitt. "On the drive over, he'd belt 'Take Me Out to the Ball Game.' His range was pretty impressive for a guy who didn't ever say much." I catch Chelsea smiling. "Unless you got him talking about baseball. He had some pipes on him hidden behind his mustache and austerity. I think he may have taken me once to a concert there, too. It was so late when we got home, he carried me into bed."

"Those are nice memories."

"Haven't thought about them in a long time." I clear the pinch in my throat and rub my palms into the tops of my jeans.

"Do you get season tickets?"

"For the Giants? No. I only come when the Dodgers are in town. Their rivalry is one for the ages."

"Um, I'm afraid to know," Chelsea titters, shifting in her seat.

"CliffNotes version: they played each other a lot when both

teams were New York-based. One from Brooklyn, the other, Manhattan."

"And the other answer?"

"Well, there's history and history's layered. Picture this shit —nineteen fifty-one, bottom of the ninth, four to one, and the Giants take the whole thing off a pitcher's change, which leads to a three-run homerun, known as The Shot Heard Round the World."

"Are you still recovering?" She bends her lower lip into an exaggerated pout.

I press my lips together and shake my head. "Put that away." My thighs tense, and the vendor's out of sight.

Chelsea's pout rolls into an infectious smile. "Wait, I thought that had something to do with the American Revolution."

I sulk a little, adjusting my hat. "Didn't peg you as a history buff."

"Oh, I'm not. My dad is. He goes to those reenactment conventions or whatever they are. I don't ask. All I know is a couple times a year, he dresses the part and meets up with a bunch of history enthusiasts. And the week leading up to it, he gets all method, shouting lines and pacing the house. My mom encourages it, as you can imagine."

I can't hold it in. My amusement thunders from my belly, loud and bold, shaking our shared armrest.

"So, what happened after that devastating loss?" she asks.

"Eventually the franchises moved west, and thankfully, put a little distance between the two teams. But you can feel it, right? All Giants' eyes on us."

Chelsea's jaw slacks as it hits her that we're sitting ducks in enemy territory. She's peeking around at the seats, taking in the wave of orange and black, an occasional royal blue and white buried in the stands like bait.

Chelsea goes from scanning to shooting up from her seat. I

follow her line of sight. There they are—in their sparkling whites—the players taking the field.

The bag of peanuts shakes in my hand as I cheer for our team, stomping my feet. "Let's go, Blue Crew!"

A shrieking whistle somersaults out of Chelsea, two fingers jammed into her smile.

As the players take their positions, we take our seats. A sharp click in my ear draws my eyes to the camera in front of my friend's face. She snaps another picture. This time I'm ready and stick out my tongue, making a silly face. She tilts her head and plays along, her brows and lips twisting up to her nose, tongue hanging out of the corner of her mouth.

Being here with someone else isn't entirely my tradition anymore. Usually, I take in the game solo, but I'm happy I invited Chelsea. It's been a great day.

The first home run has the roar of the crowd vibrating our seats. The people around us leap up each time the bat makes contact. We stay seated for half of them. And the game goes on like this under the intermittent clouds and high sun, inning after inning, hit for hit, run for run.

By the seventh inning stretch, my legs need movement and my cheering throat seeks lubrication. "I've got something to show you."

"You say that a lot," she points out.

"Is that a complaint?"

"Just an observation."

Chelsea takes my hand, and I close my fingers around her palm as we navigate the rush of bodies moving in the opposite direction. I walk her through the seats and up the stairs, crossing rows until we make it to the last row behind right field.

I put my hands on her shoulders and bring my head beside hers so we're facing forward together. "Look."

It takes her a moment, and then, on artist's instinct, she raises the camera.

Do I nod triumphantly? Yes, I do.

She snaps a few shots and turns the camera on me, elation erupting over rosy cheeks, and her gray eyes reflecting daylight bouncing off metal beams. "It's all here. The fishing boats. The skyline and bridge. And do you see those clouds? They're evenly spaced. If I wasn't standing in this exact spot, I'd think it was a paint-by-number canvas."

"I like the view too—the way the field still holds hope when no one's occupying it."

Chelsea's pleasure is a reward in itself, her lips disappearing behind the brim of my hat as she flicks the beat-up material. "How many of these have you been through?"

I take it off and shake it out. My mop of hair drops in front of my eyes and I push it back to examine the hat's well-worn state. "I keep things until I can't. I'm not great at letting go."

"I know," she states, and a shiver crawls down my neck.

Chelsea pulls me in front of her camera. She flips the lens around so it's facing us. Before I know it, she's rapid firing, *click, click, click.*

"Way to give a guy warning."

"Candids are the best."

"How do you know if our faces made it in?"

"I don't," she sings, taking off down the steps.

This view is better—carefree Chelsea. Being at the game, somewhere new, and touring the city, replacing her routine with remembering. I want this for her. And I'd be lying if I didn't admit I like the way it feels, knowing I have something to do with it.

But as her hips and ponytail sway, I'm more turned on than a friend should be. I'm yanked back into our history where complication is our tradition.

The tug in my chest won't quit, and after the game ends, it leads us walking at dusk toward our final destination. I'm distracted by the Dodgers loss and the rise in the city's homelessness crisis. The composition of the streets enrages me as we pass by works of art on building walls and human beings sleeping beneath them in a row of trash bag tents and cardboard beds. This city, a love of my life, is decaying before my eyes as it fails to prioritize taking care of its beating heart.

I stop walking because Chelsea stops, facing a few boutiques and a café.

She asks me a question, and I don't hear her the first time. "Can you repeat that?"

"Have you ever seen these door posters?" she asks, pointing to a storefront window. "They're from all over the world. Different colors and styles. Doors are the face of a structure—they say so much about what's inside. And I love how welcoming the yellow one is. Doesn't it remind you of the center of a daisy?"

Tightness drags across my jaw. I try to breathe through the flashback, but when I exhale, the opposite of what I intend happens—I'm like a sieve around Chelsea, my disjointed thoughts pouring out at once from all angles. I shake my head, summoning the memory. A typical residential street with trimmed lawns and clear sidewalks and so many doors. "The thing about doors—you never know what's behind them."

Chelsea crosses her arms over her chest.

I step in closer to breathe her in. "I don't know how you do it. Raising kids. Sometimes, I still feel like I'm a kid." A kid stuck in the same revolving door, trying to grab my things and get away from that house.

Her cool fingers press into my arm. "It's not like it comes with a manual. And it's not always easy for me. I'd hear of this mythical intuition you're supposed to get when you have a baby, but it wasn't like that. It's trial and error. Requires an unlimited supply of patience. I mean, I was young when I had Paige."

"Chelsea, I'm not criticizing your choices—that's not what I meant. I meant I admire the fuck out of you. How much you give to others. I'm me. One person. One role. You're so many wonderful things. I don't know if I could manage all that." My head is heavy from overthinking about the streets and all the children who call them home—kids like me who raise themselves.

"I don't know if I'm good at that, either." Chelsea removes her hand and rubs both her palms together. "You just do what you have to. There's me the mom, and then me the person. I love my children, but that's not all I am, right? I'm not just one thing. It'd be nice if all of the parts of a person could coexist."

She unknowingly taps into my thoughts from earlier, and I switch gears, unloading what's on my mind. "Do you think joy and suffering have to occupy the same space for them to truly hold value? Do they need each other like a pitcher needs a catcher? Or flour needs water? Or a band needs a guitarist and bassist? Does the worth of a person only get noticed when they're sleeping under wall art?"

"In art, we capture sadness in beauty all the time."

"I don't know what I believe anymore. I used to understand things clearer. Life felt pretty black and white for a time."

"Well for me, it's like developing film. You need darkness to expose light." She tilts her head, questioning if I follow, as crease lines form over the bridge of her nose. "Why are we doing all this exploring for me? Did I upset you?"

It isn't about her, *not entirely.* I don't want to ruin the great day we've had, but curiosity pushes me to ask her what I've never been able to ask my own mom about. "What do you think it means, or tells a kid about their place in the world, when the two people put on this earth to care for them care more about themselves?"

Chelsea's sigh deflates the center of my chest. She's not even trying to mask her sympathy because she has a sense of what I'm getting at.

She closes her eyelids and drops her chin before releasing her arms and stepping closer. Each breath clears a path, past thirty-one and twenty-one, to the last recognizable moment of my childhood, spending a week together, plotting our escape, sedated by blissful ignorance and innocence—before I stepped into that house on my birthday.

Chelsea opens her eyes.

The periwinkle sky fades like a bruise.

The wind picks up, pushing our bodies into each other.

I bury the haunting image away in an attempt to salvage my dignity.

Foot traffic around us is an imperceptible scuffle. Nothing matters at this moment but Chelsea. Her dilated pupils and serious mouth. Her proximity.

"I remember your door."

My throat pinches like her words are fingers wrapped around it.

"It was a peachy sort of yellow," she tells me. The fingers tighten. "I remember all of the doors. I knocked on every single one."

"What?" I ask, clearing my airway, disoriented, my chest pumping hard.

"When you didn't show up like we planned, I called. When the number was disconnected, I went to your street . . . but I didn't know which house."

I close my eyes and the phantom fingers release their squeezing grip on my neck.

"I met your neighbors. On both sides," she continues. "No one knew a thing."

"You looked for me?" I ask, slowly lifting my gaze to Chelsea, flipping my hat backward. My curiosity is weary, my veins wired, and my voice cracks.

She nods. "My knuckles were raw when I bladed back home."

I reach between us, turning her ball cap backward. "Chels." I breathe her name and lean in, taking her jaw in my hands, drawing her mouth toward mine. Her eyelashes shimmer under the orange glow of the street lamps and shop lights.

And then, right there, in the middle of the sidewalk, in front of a random door poster, I kiss Chelsea Bell like she's mine. So tender at first, it sweeps across her lips in a whisper. I deepen our kiss, and she pulls me into her arms.

Together, we banish our fears and burn our excuses.

No longer can we hide. No longer will I pretend.

My thumbs tremble as they press into her heated cheeks. Nerves and excitement riot throughout my body, indistinguishable from one another. The way they leap from the heart at the same time and flood like a raging river, there's no containing it.

Kissing her is the catalyst. Things like plans and perspective fly out the window. Goals get swept into the street. All I'm certain of after tasting Chelsea is the lingering hint of tart cherries on my tongue and the realization that her kiss is riding a high I'd chase forever.

23

CHELSEA

*S*eth tugs on my lower lip, drawing his face back and holding my gaze. Nothing has or will ever come close to the way my body responds to his touch.

"I've wanted to do that since the last time."

"I've wanted you to do that since the last time," I admit.

"Correct answer." He smiles, teasing my jawline with his lips, burning his stubble into my skin.

My lungs freeze when his cell rings, but he ignores the call.

"Aren't you going to answer that?" I ask, breathless, lost in scattered thoughts.

"No."

It keeps ringing. I'm trying to stay in the moment. "What a luxury."

Seth cocks his head in confusion, stepping back.

I take in the semi-deserted street, wondering how long it's been since I've kissed in public. "Mom duty. We're never off the clock. We never silence our ringer. We never ignore a call."

Seth digs into his pocket, answering, low and throaty, "Seth Hansen." His full smile has simmered into a subtle grin. "Hey, David."

I slide my tongue over my throbbing lower lip.

"Actually, I have plans," he adds. "I know the studio's time costs money. Fine, I'll make it work." He waves his phone in the air. "See why I shouldn't answer? I'm going to need to postpone our morning adventure. I have show stuff to take care of first thing."

"I didn't know we had plans tomorrow," I say with a twinge of disappointment now that it's canceled.

"Don't do that."

"What?"

"Run your tongue over your lip like that when I'm trying to concentrate."

"Oh. You mean like this?" I demonstrate.

"Give me your mouth," Seth growls, wrapping his arms around my waist. He plants a firm and tender kiss on my lips, then buries his face into my neck, planting soft kisses up to my ear. His tongue, wet and warm, drags my earlobe between his teeth. He releases it into the cool night air, then whispers, "All I want to do is spend the day kissing you. That was my grand plan."

"I was thinking of checking out the MOMA. I can do things solo now." I attempt to exude a can-do attitude, my breathing labored once again. Standing in moderate darkness conceals some of the flush I feel spreading across my chest and warming my cheeks.

"How about in the afternoon?" he suggests softly, an inch of space between our swollen lips.

I clear my throat. "I get my kids back tomorrow, and I was thinking of going for a run in the morning."

"Okay," he accepts without protest, stepping back, creating a column of space now.

"I want to spend more time together, but we're on a clock that revolves around our established lives."

Where do we fit?

"Yeah, I understand. A run sounds good, though—we can run together if you want." His eyes are searching the same way mine are searching—for a simple solution. When I neglect to respond to his suggestion because I'm out of practice, he adds, "Class on Tuesday?"

I exhale. "I'll be there."

Seth offers me his arm to the corner of the street. He waves his hand in the air for a taxi, and one slows at the corner and flips on his meter. When Seth opens the door for me, I step into the cab, sticking to the cracked leather seat. The mix of street soil and spices traps my senses. Seth settles in next to me, his fingers splayed over my thigh. "During class, I won't be able to be Seth. I have to be, you know—"

"Chef Handsome." I wink.

He presses his lips to mine.

"Where to?" the driver asks, rolling down his window.

"Alamo Square Park, please," Seth replies.

"I ran a mile this morning and walked two." The phone's on speaker as I wrestle with my wet hair in front of the mirror.

"Way to go, Chels. How'd it feel?" Mom asks.

"Slow but good." My cheeks are still pink from the exercise and hot shower. "Maybe I'll try again tomorrow."

"Excellent. You know what else would be perfect for you? There's got to be some kind of running club you can join to meet other people. Make it social."

"By social, are you referring to singles specifically?"

"If there happens to be a nice and cute divorcée, even better."

She means a nice Jewish boy to marry like all the women in our family have. "I tried that. Remember Paul?"

"Oy vey, Chelsea. I'm going to get a headache if you keep this up."

If I can't joke about my failed marriage, I won't survive the shame of it failing.

"The club might have a game night, too," she says, pushing harder. "You never know when a charming and eligible man might waltz right into your sauna, or better yet, a stretching routine. You can ask him for pointers."

"*Okay*, the train has left the station. There will be no matchmaking, Mom. Paul and I belong to the same club, and we never go. The minute you took my Bat Mitzvah off the table, you lost your voting rights in my dating decisions, thank you."

"Don't you start with me. That was a difficult choice your dad and I made. Reading in Hebrew. How was that going to work?"

The brush slips from my palm and dents the wood of the vanity. *Shit.* I rub my thumb across the prominent dip on its surface. Her words still hold so much power over the child I see staring back at me in the mirror.

Oblivious to what she's said, she keeps talking. "Well, you let me know when you meet a special somebody, okay?"

"Sure, I'll send out the bat signal."

"I want you to be happy. That's all we want."

"I am happy-ish. I don't need a running club or Scrabble partner to make me happy. I need a local wine and . . ." I almost slip and say, chef.

"Don't you want to have someone to share your life with? A *beshert*, your person. That's sacred."

I shake my head, pushing away the image of Seth's smile. Seth's lips. Seth's kiss. "Mom," I groan. "I'm not looking for my soulmate."

"Promise me you'll let us know when you do find the one, so we can celebrate. And so your dad can sleep at night again."

"For the love of—okay, I promise I'll say 'the word' when I

meet someone worth saying the word for." I walk to the closet and mindlessly sift through rows of black, tan, and white, choosing a khaki skirt and sheer button-down shirt. I'll need my snow-colored lace camisole, too.

"Maybe I can call the kids before bedtime for a chat and song—"

"Nan will be here. The cooking class with Seth is tonight."

"Well, that's nice for her." Her tone isn't lost on me. I slip into my clothes quickly, checking for wrinkles.

"How about we call you and Dad before dinner," I suggest. I know it's hard for my mom to be far away and for someone else to get "grandma" time with the kids. She makes the decision to stay in L.A., and I think overall, the distance has been best for our relationship. Breaking free from my parents has made it so I can raise my kids in my own way.

"So, Chels, do you think spending time with Seth is the best idea? You've been seeing a lot of him lately."

"Not *a lot*-a lot. A little." I comb my fingers through my hair once more and resign to quit fussing with it.

"What does a little mean?"

"It's just a class and a couple of coffees." I opt to omit the word date.

"I see." She exhales slow and deliberate, like she did the one time I impulsively stole a pack of gum from a convenience store. She knew it was only a matter of time before I confessed —the guilt was immediate and swift.

This silent stretch is as tight as Mom's grip was marching me back into that store. Made me apologize right then and there. Never took a single thing again that didn't belong to me without asking. Not even a french fry off someone's plate.

I apply my lipstick, blotting the edges where it bleeds slightly into newly acquired fine lines, as I over explain everything. "We had breakfast once. Went to a Dodgers game, and last night after the game, he took me to see *Vertigo* at an outdoor theater. It was fun. This park plays classic movies all year long, and can you believe this spring it's Hitchcock? They also hosted a trivia session. Did you know you can take a spooky tour in the city of all the locations where the movie was filmed?" Wait, I'm not a kid—I don't need to tell her any of this.

"I don't know, sweetheart. Given your history, this is, well, I just don't want to see anyone get hurt."

"He's not going to hurt me, Mom." My heart hammers in my chest. I haven't forgotten her propensity to caution me about my decisions.

"It's not him I'm worried about."

"Mom." I steady myself, fingers locked on the phone. "Don't get involved this time."

"What's that supposed to mean?" she demands in a high-pitched tone that pierces my ears.

I hold the device from my face, in shock that she's making me spell it out. "You know what it means."

"I did not get involved before."

The floorboards creak as my feet press into the wood. I'm taking tiny pacing steps across the length of my room, gathering strength, finding a way to talk to her about the impact she made on me at an impressionable age. I don't blame her. I'm responsible for myself, but her opinion mattered. It really mattered.

"You told me not to rush. That we were too young. That he was too far away and long distance didn't work."

"Of course I did. You had your whole life ahead of you and you were acting like that boy was your final destination."

"You're not hearing me. It wasn't what you said but what it *meant*. You put doubt in my head, and then I . . ." My chin lowers, and I cover the receiver, wiping my cheeks.

"I'm your mother. It's my job to help you."

"Mom," my voice dies. "I'd like to go."

"Before you hang up, I'm thrilled you're running, and if

Seth's helping you with this eating nonsense with Jonah and his inflexibility, I'm glad for it. You didn't love everything I made, but look at you now . . . you're not picky. I'll email you some of my green smoothie recipes. What kid doesn't like a smoothie? Tell him it's a milkshake. Or better yet, I have protein ice cream you can use."

"Paul's at the door with the kids. I'm hanging up."

"Wait. What's the word? For when you find your happily ever after."

The front door swings open and the kids zoom past me with a quick "Hi, Mom." Jonah turns around and squeezes his arms around my waist. My mom is in the background telling the kids hello even though they can't hear her.

Paul hangs on the front step, handing me their backpacks.

"Bye, Mom." I hang up.

It's hard to imagine being in a relationship ever again, never mind the variety of fantasyland my mom's trying to pitch me. The reality is I don't have experience with romantic relationships. I dated two people in my life and married one.

Does my time with Seth even count? Can you count something that never had a chance? When Seth kissed me last night, a flash of possibility crept in—and today, I realize it's time. If I want to keep kissing Seth, we need to talk.

My parents may have always thought they were doing what was best for me, but I wonder how they could know what that was when I've never seen it for myself.

24

CHELSEA

"How'd their day go?"

"All good," he assures me.

It's always smooth sailing reports from Paul. I try not to get annoyed that he doesn't seem to experience the same hurdles I do. We agreed to share everything about the kids. I want to ask him about it, but we also agreed to trust one another in raising our kids together.

"Hey, I've been meaning to check with you—do you want the key to the house back?"

My fingers tap against the frame, holding the door open. "I think it's wise for you to have one in case of an emergency."

"I don't want you to feel like this place isn't fully yours."

"I don't feel that way. I may not have financially contributed, but I made it a home."

"But it's a lot to keep up with. Have you considered downsizing? Apartment living has its perks. No lawn to take care of."

"I wouldn't call the back patio a lawn." I laugh.

"There's plants." He's not being sarcastic.

"We'll see you later this week. Thanks for everything, Paul."

"You never need to thank me. They're mine, too." Paul

heads down the front steps, stops, and cocks his head over his shoulder. "Chelsea, don't take this the wrong way, but I haven't seen your natural hair since we had Paige. Looks good."

I thank Paul for the compliment and close the door.

The unmistakable plink of plastic pieces making contact with the living room floor reaches down the hall, letting me know Paige and Jonah are setting up a game of checkers.

My profile catches in the hall mirror—frazzled blond strands falling to my shoulders.

Paul's right. I was different when we met. He was too.

His now salt-and-pepper stubble and hair used to be jet black. His face has always been consistent and steady, reflecting his personality—focused, serious, provider, punctual.

When I met him, his twenty-eight was somehow grown-up to me. He was a problem-solver, and I was like a complicated math equation without a clear solution. He did solve other people's financial problems—just not our marriage problems. I suppose those weren't his to solve anyway. Marriage is a team sport, and neither of us had what it took to play anymore. We tried, though, for Jonah and Paige mostly, believing we might find a way to connect outside of parenting.

We decided to take a time-out, give each other space, maybe too much, and when we came together to try again, I knew we were better apart. Once I tasted that kind of peace, I had to fiercely protect it.

I'm grateful I get to raise my kids with Paul. And that he eventually forgave me for asking for a divorce. When I see him now, my chest aches with longing. Not for Paul but for the family I had. I crave and long to comfort the girl I was back then. All the insecurity I carried around that detrimentally informed my decisions—rushing forward with my life as fast as I could without awareness of the consequences.

In many ways, Paul began as a bandage, covering childhood

scratches and scrapes, and of course from everything that happened with Seth that summer.

By everything, I mean everything we left open. When Seth returned to school that spring, I sent a couple of short emails, and occasionally we caught each other on the phone. Then summer swept in, and he started working at the restaurant—weeks went by in silence.

Silence had always been my companion—as an only child and as a retreat from all the noise. I didn't know what would happen when I was receiving it from a person I cared about. How the separation compounded by my mom's disapproval would infect my thoughts.

To escape the physical distance, Seth's absence had me playing out imaginary scenarios in my mind, too scared to ask for clarity, to face the inevitable rejection I was so sure was coming.

Seth was in New York, making a name for himself. He was going places.

I was convinced he'd forgotten about me.

The night I met Paul, I was having a rough day. He came into the restaurant for a client dinner, and his attention was gentle and kind, even waiting for me until the end of my shift to ask me for coffee. Perhaps I was craving connection, anything to fill the void of the miles between me and Seth. And when Paul showed up in my life, I accepted my time with Seth for what it was—temporary.

It all happened so fast.

"Mom," Paige shouts from the living room. "Mom! Jonah, stop!"

My eyes dry as I race into the living room. The checkers board is flipped over, and Jonah's rolled into a ball on the floor. My knees ache as I bend to sit on the hardwood. "Paige, grab a cup of crushed ice for me, please."

"He was going to lose and—"

"Paige. Ice." At this point, it doesn't matter what happened. She's frustrated as she stands up.

It's hard. For everyone. But especially for my baby boy, who can't always find his way. I never know if my approach will help or hurt him more. But I try. I try it all and keep trying.

I sit down by Jonah, placing one hand on his heaving back. His skin's pulled so tight his ribcage is visible beneath his toddler-sized T-shirt. Because of his limited diet, he's on the smaller side. And every time I hug him, I'm worried he'll shatter.

"Hey, J. You're safe. I'm here." I steady my palm in even circles over his ragged breathing. "One, two, three, four . . . five, six, seven, eight."

During the hyper-testing period of my life, I taught myself to count. The rhythm of counting kept me calm. I'd count anything. In school, I'd count the seconds until the bell rang. In waiting rooms, I'd count the tiles in the ceiling. I'd count cracks in the pavement as I hopped over them.

So as Jonah sits here curled up, I count. "One, two, three, four . . . five, six, seven, eight."

With each revolution, his lungs fill slower and exhale lighter. Paige returns, handing me a cup of crushed ice because Jonah likes crunchy things. As his body unlocks and unwinds, his entire face flushes, tears saturating his red cheeks.

"Here," I whisper, encouraging him to take a bite.

Tension eventually melts from his jaw, and when his eyes open wide and are clear, I know the storm has passed. I know he's found his way back.

Paige collects the black and red scattered circles from around the living room.

"Jonah, I see some of the pieces under the couch. Do you think your hands can fit under there, and we can help Paigey put away the game?"

"I can make it a challenge!" he exclaims. Before the cup of ice goes flying, I secure it from his grasp.

And just like that, everything returns to . . . well, not normal, but our normal.

I pull an elastic tie off my wrist and twist my hair into a low bun.

I skip Seth's class, wiped out from another mealtime battle with Jonah where I gave in—cereal and toast—so he'd eat something. I put enough pads of butter on the slices. He enjoyed digging through the tops with his fingers.

Nan hears defeat in my voice when I call her to cancel, and she shows up anyway with a sleeping bag under her arm and a bowl of homemade chicken soup for me.

She uncorks a bottle of wine before disappearing with the kids to their rooms, where I know magic is about to be spun in the way of storytime. The ways she always did when she'd visit me in Los Angeles.

On paper, Paige and Jonah might be great at Paul's, but when they come back home, there's always feelings to untangle. This is part of the process our co-parenting counselor assured us was common. We have to be patient. *These things take time.*

I settle into the living room lounge chair and flip on the Classic Movie Channel. My legs stretch, and I sink into the cushions. The soup goes down like hot stones over my throat. I'm enjoying a glass of wine and powering down. I need this.

When my phone goes off, I seriously consider ignoring it. It can probably wait. With each ring, I shift my eyes from the television to my bag hanging in the hallway. The shrill of the ringtone has me shooting up to answer. "Hello. Seth?" I bring us back to my comfy spot.

"Are you hurt?"

"No, what?" I lower the volume with the remote.

"You didn't show up."

"It's been a long day. I'm sorry I missed class. Was Steph without a partner?"

He exhales. "She asked for you."

"I didn't mean to let anyone down."

"I'm glad you're okay. And though I'm a fan of late-night, raspy-voice-over-the-phone Chelsea, I was worried."

"Thank you for checking on me." Rehashing my exhausting afternoon is pointless.

"We lost Jackie from class. She went back to her boyfriend, left the program—the possibility of the new life she was building for herself and her kids is gone."

"I can't begin to imagine what life must be like for her. To get to a place where you go back. It must be horrible."

"Yes, it's unimaginable and still, it happens all the time. Sometimes they return, but often, they don't. So, yeah," he says, his voice landing flat, "that sucked today."

"Can I help in any way?" I offer. A few seconds of contemplation simmer between us. "Swimming pool or beach?"

He laughs, and I lean my head back into the lounge chair.

"Beach for the sand. Pool for the swim."

"Farm or city?"

"City with a farmer's market." His smile's audible.

I take another sip. "How many Hitchcock movies have been filmed here?"

"Please, woman. Three. What's playing in the background?" he asks.

"I'm watching *Dial M for Murder*."

"Again?"

"Watching the same thing is comforting, even when it's a thriller."

"Cuisine operates under a similar premise. With comfort

foods, it never fails because you anticipate the flavor and texture of ingredients, and it recalls good memories."

"Exactly," I agree, adjusting my position to take another spoonful of soup.

"Driver or passenger?" he asks, circling back, taking the wheel.

"In this city?" I playfully point out. "Definitely driver."

"Okay, let me do better."

"Time's-a-ticking, Chef Handsome."

"Soft or hard." He raises the stakes.

I did not expect that.

"Chels?" His voice stokes something inside me.

"Seth?" I pant.

"It was cheese," he explains, followed by a deep twist in his tone that reaches my core, "but now I want to know what you're wearing."

My chest heats and the cool stem of the glass rattles in my fingers. I rest it on the table. "It's real exciting over here— flannel pants and my daughter's musical theater tee."

"Want company? I hear the popcorn at your place comes with extra butter. Or come over here if that's better for you."

"Hold, please." I get up and pad over to the kids' bedroom, cracking open the door to find Nan.

She peeks up from Jonah's bed. He's sleeping cuddled in her arms.

"I was thinking of going to Seth's to watch a movie. Are you okay staying a while longer?"

"I'm not driving home tonight," she says, sending me eyes.

"Okay, I'll be back soon."

"Go have fun." Nan winks.

"Just a movie, Nan."

"Pretty sure the kids these days call it Netflix and Chill." She chuckles and returns to reading her book under artificial starlight.

My cheeks flush with warmth and I'm grateful for the curtain of darkness in the hall. I close the door, bleaching Nan's last words from my brain, and put the phone up to my ear. "I need to change and I'll be right over."

"Do not change a single thing. And I'll come get you."

25

CHELSEA

"*H*ave you eaten anything substantial?"

"Some of Nan's soup. What gave me away?" I ask, under the white light of the kitchen, which feels more like a spotlight every second that passes. I lean against the counter, mesmerized by Seth's shoulder muscles as they expand and contract under his white shirt.

He pops up from the fridge, laying out ingredients— chicken, spinach, garlic, mushrooms, lemon, parmesan cheese —then steps directly in front of me. The sharp edge of the counter cuts into my palms.

"Your mouth's stained purple and your stomach's growling." He presses his thumb to my lips, brushing the pad across. "Want to boil water?"

"I can do that."

He hands me a stainless steel pot. "You must have a great teacher." He smiles as he works.

"The best," I admit, my lungs pulling in air, greedy to inhale Seth too—citrus and clove, key limes and cinnamon. He smells like a vacation I desperately want to take.

One shared meal and two glasses of red later, and I'm

trailing Seth into his bedroom, dreaming of a hammock under the sun.

I dissolve into a teenager there. Curious about everything. Cautious about nothing.

Dark wood flooring extends from the rest of the apartment into this space. The walls are painted in burgundy, covered by framed art and the front-page edition of *L.A. Times* when the Dodgers won the World Series in 1981.

A single floating shelf displays a collection of hourglasses. My head tilts as my neck bends, my eyes roaming over their range of shapes and designs, some pocket-sized, some plastic, others made of wood and glass.

"You have so many," I remark, getting a front-and-center view.

Seth stands beside me. "Whenever I see one, I buy it. Started when I was a kid. I find them calming, watching the particles of sand slide back and forth. I didn't get serious about collecting them until after college, I guess."

"They're beautiful."

"Do you have a favorite?" he asks.

I point to the only one lying on its side, perfectly smooth like two teardrops embracing each other.

"Interesting choice." Seth's arm brushes by my cheek cautiously reaching for the all-glass design. "I made it."

My pulse speeds up. "You did what? How? Why is it on its side?" I ask, noticing two sand colors, black and white, buried together like one wave protecting the other.

His smile curves in amusement as he holds his creation. I watch his profile as he speaks, wetting his lips once before continuing. "If you can believe it, it's from a kit. Simple enough instructions. After I finished pouring in the sand, I was struck by how the two colors merged together while remaining independent of one another."

His spicy scent invades my inhale, spreading inside my

lungs. I force my eyes to remain open when all I want is to close them while listening to his voice wash over me.

"It reminded me of life, how sometimes when you don't want something to end, you pause." He clears his throat, turning to face me. "Ever rewind the bridge of a song, just to listen to it over and over?" Seth nods as I shake my head, not following. "Okay, maybe you stop and smell the roses. You hold that inhale until you can't."

"Yes, I've done that."

His gaze lands hard, my skin tingles from our closeness.

"There are some things that you can't bear to see end," he says, placing the keepsake back in its original placement. The fragile surface rocks as it settles on the shelf.

"Don't you want to see what happens when they become one?"

Seth smiles, evading the question.

"Well, have you ever wanted to stand it upright?"

"Never," he says, exhaling from his chest, bumping my shoulder with his bicep.

I scold myself, talking like I've got any right to tell him what to do with his stuff. "It's pretty random that I chose the one that you made."

"Is it, though?" he asks, and I'm uncertain if he's looking for an answer. His gaze narrows to my throat, burning into me as I swallow.

"Lately, I've tried to work out why things happen the way they do and also why they don't."

Seth takes my hand, lacing his long fingers through mine. "I try not to borrow trouble, Chels, because I've always believed our thoughts have minds of their own. If you think about something enough, you breathe life into it. Let me show you something." I squeeze my now empty hand into a fist.

Seth returns from his closet with a box. "This may make us laugh. I saved some stuff."

We walk to his bed, and I sit cross-legged on top of his indigo-blue comforter. The box is square and wooden with Seth's initials burned into the top. He lifts the latch and the gold hinge creaks as it opens.

The lamp's glow in the far corner of the room bounces off a piece of plastic. There's some aged paper that's yellowed over time, but that's all I can see.

Seth reveals each item, handing them over one at a time.

"What are these?" I inspect what I think are books on cassette.

"Things I'd picked up for you when I was in New York."

I hold them in front of me, reading the titles. "You bought me books on tape?"

His arm is flush with mine, the touch transferring heat from my shoulder to his, my forearm to his, our thighs, and knees, and every atom we cannot see. "Back then, you shared how tough reading had been for you. I found them and thought you might—" he pauses, affection curling the corner of his mouth. "It's nothing. The lady at the record store said they were under-rated. She gave me a great deal."

"Seth, I don't know what to say."

"You don't have to say anything."

Hasn't that been part of the problem? I never say anything. Even when invited, being in his room registers as this massive invasion of privacy. Sitting on his bed, comforted among his memories, surrounded by the ghosts of the years that I passed on. It's like traipsing over a graveyard and disturbing a final resting place.

"What's this?" I'm referring to the next item he places in my hand. It's a pale-yellow rectangle that has a hoop drilled into its center. As I examine it, I gasp . . . "It's butter."

"Not just butter. A butter keychain."

"Are you kidding me? This is the best thing I've ever seen."

"I planned to bring it home with me on winter break."

My momentary enthusiasm collapses. My heart's breaking. "Seth, this is—"

"When I saw it in a shop near the restaurant, I had to get it for my little butter queen." He keeps his head high while my chin drops.

I smile at the sentiment, though the gesture's not lost on me.

He flips the rectangle to the opposite side. "It has a crown." His voice drops low, and his throat bobs as he swallows. "The thing is, if I hadn't met you, I would've walked by that window and never given it a second thought. That stick of plastic would've meant nothing to me. But it did mean something to me because it reminded me of you, and you were the world to me."

I can't . . . I won't beg for his forgiveness. I don't get to cry over keychains.

Seth closes the lid.

"Wait, what's that?" I point to flashes of white, blinking to focus.

There's hesitation in Seth, deepening his gaze from a rich bourbon to something thick and impenetrable like mud. He uses his pincer grasp and lifts the strand from the bottom of the box. My skin tickles against the dry leaves grazing my hand. "It's fragile."

"Dried flowers." *Daisies. A chain.* "No," I whisper, adrenaline catching in my throat.

Yes, he confirms with his stare.

"Seth, this isn't what I think it is?"

He nods.

"You kept it . . . all this time?" I touch the stiff petals—once round and flexible. Bright bulbs have withered into hardened marigold. "I'm afraid they'll crumble to dust."

"Possible."

This. Is. Impossible. Impossible to contain. "Time wears things down, doesn't it?"

"Sometimes. And sometimes, it preserves things, too."

"Thank you," I whisper. "For sharing this with me." I hand the daisy chain back.

"He places the box in my lap. You hang onto it," he says, like it's taken a lot to hold onto these things, and he's ready to let them go.

I accept the box. He deserves to be free from all of this. I peek inside again, adjusting its weight on my lap, when I see something I recognize immediately—a folded-up postcard.

"I sent this to you." My fingers trace the daisy doodles, remembering borrowing Nan's glue gun to make sure the photo would stick.

"Chels, I want you to know why I kept all this."

"I think I understand," I reassure him, staring at my hands, into the past—what it all might have meant had time worked for us and not against us.

"Now that you're here, I don't need it anymore," he says softly, pressing his lips into my hair.

I'm suddenly desperately sad—and mad at myself—for being so damn restless back then. For my impatience and insecurity. And him—I'm more confused than I've ever been.

He has this box of stuff when he was the one who lost interest. Who stopped calling. Thought it was okay to go weeks without speaking.

I get he was in an exciting and new environment and I was doing the same things every day. I get that Seth has always been like a wave that visits the shore and retreats back to the sea, where adventure awaits. I get that I was like wet sand that stays exactly where I land.

But what I don't get, what I've never understood is *why*.

"When you got back to town, you didn't call."

"Are you serious?" Seth rolls his shoulders back, his gaze

severe, pushing on the edge of the bed, forming a ravine between us. "You cut off all communication with me. Not the other way around. I was supposed to track you down?"

My eyes fill. "That's not what I meant to say."

His voice shakes—each calculated word dipped in anger and aimed at me. "For the fucking record, I went to Nan's. The Sherries said you moved in with a guy in fancy pleated pants. We had a plan. You and me, Chels. We made promises."

"I thought we *did* have a plan."

"Never once did I deviate from that plan. It was a real blow to the ego, how replaceable we were to you."

"To me?" I snap. Not believing my ears. "You're the one who fell off the map."

"Me?" He throws his hands in the air. "I thought you were in the hospital or an accident or worse. I couldn't reach you when I tried."

"I don't recall you trying that hard. I waited for you. To call. To write. For weeks. Nothing." My words fall out in hammering blows. *One, two, three.* Wine turns rancid in my stomach.

"The phone works both ways," he challenges. "Do you know what that kind of silence does to a person's head?"

The memory of that summer swoops in with acute accuracy like it was yesterday.

"I do." I loosen my grip on the box, exhaling the final traces of steam I have left to argue. My voice rebounds gently. "At first, I thought you were busy. You didn't have a phone hooked up at that place you were living, and I didn't want to be that girl who called your work."

"Busy doesn't mean dead, Chels. I would've known you cared." Seth runs his hands over his thighs.

"My caring was never the issue."

"Then what was?" He stands up, pacing to the window and back.

"I don't know."

"Yes, you do. Just own it."

"I have no problem admitting when I'm wrong." My veins hum.

"Then what was it? What happened?"

"I don't think I was ready for all that distance." My throat throbs. "We had no concrete plan. Not hearing from you had me convinced that I was far from your mind." I rub at the center of my chest, and I do the one thing I promised I wouldn't do—I cry. "I didn't realize how fragile I'd be."

Seth kneels in front of me, his hands grip my hips. "You've only ever been strong to me, the bravest person I know. I was working eighteen-hour days. I needed to prove myself, to suck everything I could out of that gig, so I could come back here, and to you." He tucks a loose curl behind my ear, gently cradling my head.

I shake my head. *No, this can't be right.* "It wasn't clear to me that that's what was happening on your end. We left it all so up in the air. And then . . ." My chest squeezes, tormented by the decisions we make based on the assumptions we create.

Paul. Right place. Right time.

Seth's warmth vanishes from his face as he slides his fingers to my knees.

I count the revolutions of the ceiling fan above us until my face dries. And then I tell him what happened, because he asked and deserves to know. I tell him because he called me brave and I want to be. "I explained to Paul that I was pregnant."

Seth sits on the floor and rests his arms over his knees. "What was his reaction?"

"He proposed."

Seth drops his head between his arms, scratching his hands through his hair. "It was eight months. You couldn't wait eight months?" he pleads.

"My entire world flipped over. What was going to happen?

You'd come back, I'd say surprise, and we'd raise someone else's baby together?"

"You could've called. Answered my calls. I could've been there for you. We would've figured it out."

"Sometimes, I feel like an observer of my own life. My mind detaches from things that hurt and retreats to a safe corner to wait out the storm. It's been a decade and talking about that time of my life feels like I'm telling someone else's story." I bury my head in my hands. "I didn't call you because I couldn't say goodbye."

Seth pulls me off the bed and into his arms, kissing the top of my hair. The box tumbles to the floor.

"I hurt you," I confess. "I'm sorry. Not a day goes by where I'm not."

"It's done, my butter queen," he gently whispers into my ear.

"You're making a joke right now." I laugh through my tears.

"It circles back to what I was saying earlier—that all of this had to go down this way so we could be here right now. It's not how I would've scripted it ten years ago, but it doesn't matter anymore. Our time is here—finally. I've been waiting for these answers, and as much as they tear me apart, I want to know it all."

"Are you sure?"

"Everything," he repeats and kisses me.

His kisses are wishes. Mine are confessions. Together they're an apology. A shared effort to release the past.

I don't regret my children or my life. I regret the inability I had to trust Seth and myself.

I catch my breath, my skin on fire with urgency. But I have to pause, even if it physically hurts. "At first, I didn't dwell on how I mismanaged things. Mom flew into town and helped me prepare. She knew about you. Nan knew, too. They acted like it was a closed chapter, and maybe they acted that way out of love for me—focusing on my future—but it felt like someone had dog-eared a page in our book, and I was forced to put it down. I guess I got used to pretending too, since there was nothing to say and no one to talk to about it. All my energy went into being a mom. If I had spoken about it, it probably would've broken me. I couldn't be broken for my child."

"You did what was right for your family. I would've done the same."

"That's generous." I raise my eyebrows, then stand up and move to his bedroom window. Chills rush from my wrists to my shoulders. The street lamps illuminate each water droplet collecting on the diamond-shaped glass.

"Why do you help all those women?" I ask.

"I want to help them."

"Yes, and also, I wondered if you're helping them because they're single mothers, like the way you're helping me."

Seth breathes, the vibration like a symphony orchestra swooping through the room. I move back to the bed, the rain pattering behind me. I reach out my hand to him. "Look at me."

His hair blocks his eyes as his gaze drops to the floor.

"Look. At. Me," I beg, choking on desperation to understand better. "Please."

Seth's chin tips up, his heavy eyes land soft as he takes my hand. He's eleven. He's twenty-one. He's everything in between. "No one sees me like you do," he says, pulling up, guiding me into his lap on the bed. I slide down his thighs as my thighs settle over his waist. He cradles my head in his hands, bringing our mouths closer, his searching lips lock on mine, coaxing them apart.

Our tongues dance slowly as he lifts me into his arms, teasing his fingers through my hair, holding our bodies flushed together. My back meets the wall, snapping me from the tranquil trance of our embrace. Seth's kiss steals my breath, his thumbs digging into my hips, his length pinning me in place.

"I need you to see yourself as I do." He releases my legs to the floor, taking my hand, turning us toward a full-length mirror. Our reflections are showered in light from the standing lamp in the corner of his room.

There's a stadium crowd's worth of chaos cheering in my chest.

Seth rubs his fingers into the tops of my shoulders, relieving pressure as our eyes stare back at us. He smirks behind me, his intentions pressing into my lower back. "Ready for the rules?"

26

CHELSEA

"*P*robably not." My slick palms slide together in front of me.

He lowers his mouth to my ear, whispering. "Trust me."

I nod. *I do.*

"Answer the question right, keep a layer. Answer wrong, lose a layer."

My eyes dart between us. *He's serious.*

"How do I win?"

Seth marks a kiss on the side of my neck, licking the paper-thin skin over my pulse.

"If you haven't noticed, Chels," he says, blowing over the cool path he left behind, "you can only win if you play."

My knees lock, supporting the rest of my body. I try to lean on him, to melt into his sturdy chest. Seth gently sinks his teeth into my neck, a warning nip that straightens my spine.

He draws his tongue over the sensitive spot behind my ear. "Ready?"

For what exactly, I want to scream into the void. I can barely breathe, my throat's raw in suspense. Something feral in Seth's eyes strips me as I stand fully dressed. I don't think I'll ever be "ready" for Seth Hansen, though the ache I'm caging would firmly disagree.

Unable to rely on my voice, I grab his hand and hold it in front of my waist, spreading it wide so I can write a message. My finger locks as I draw swooping letters *y-e-s* over his prominent creases and pillowy palm.

He kisses my hairline, nails skimming under my shirt, his smile reaching his eyes. My heavy lids close as his fingers caress my stomach.

"Open them, baby. This only works if you watch."

"Try me." He has no idea what my imagination's capable of, but I follow his lead. I'd follow him anywhere.

"What's my favorite song?"

I pause, racking my brain. "Something I can't stand," I tease, half-serious.

Seth releases a *tsk-tsk* that filters out through his teeth. He drags my shirt over my head, tossing the loose fabric on the bed.

His knuckle scrapes down my spine, over the clasp of my bra, tracing shapes around my sides and along the bones in my back. Chills shoot through my arms and chest. My thighs slack at the sensation. Fragmented exhales escape, releasing hostages of heat huddled in my lungs.

"What's my favorite memory of us?"

"Seth, how can I know something you've never told me?" I argue. "Do I get a clue?"

He laughs in glorious victory. My body shivers.

I can only respond with my favorite memory, but that's not possible either, because there isn't one that stands out—there's a treasure trove of minutes and hours. "The first time we went to Meryl's?" I know it's wrong by the tilt of his head . . . wait, the image dawns on me—it's the day we met. The day both of our lives were changed forever. "I want a redo."

"Sorry, Chels, we don't get those."

"You're making the rules up as you go." I blow out a frustrated breath, mixed in with inescapable arousal. He touches me. I respond.

Seth lowers into a squat and rolls my elastic waist to my ankles.

Perspiration pools behind my neck and knees. I freeze, my skin prickling with needles.

He lifts his gaze, requesting my compliance.

I step out of my pants and rest my feet flat on the hardwood, crossing my arms over my chilled chest. Seth guides each arm to my side with care.

"Almost there. Two more questions."

"I have no more answers," I manage, my pores tightening with every graze of contact we make. His body heat radiates at my back.

"Oh, I think you do." He smiles and commands, "Eyes forward."

Looking at myself isn't easy. I see things distorted, like holding an image upside down or zooming in on a shot too close. I can't bear to confront what he will see too. My focus is everywhere but where he wants, following the curve of the mirror, its sleek oval frame.

"Chin up, Chels. Look at me."

I inhale as my eyes rise to meet him, painfully surveying the landscape of my body. Someone who's carried babies and ripped her knees to shreds. Who slowly replaced her sense of style and color with monochrome and bleachable attire, straightened her hair and stretched her skin—a shape that changed without her permission.

"What's one thing you love about yourself?" His question strikes.

"I'm a good mom." I remind myself, *that's what matters.*

"Being a mom is something you do for others. One thing

you love about yourself that has nothing to do with anyone else."

"It's an unfair question."

"Just one."

I mentally carve holes in my exterior flaws, willing the force alone to shatter the mirror before there's nothing left to excavate.

My freckles have moved from where they once stood.

My breasts have lost their spring.

My hair dried out. My lips thinned.

My feet are wider. My eyes are tired.

There's a roll of skin over my knees.

This is my mocking reflection, laughing at me.

"Sometimes, I see glimpses of myself. Pieces that depend on other people. You know, the things that stop you in your tracks. With my parents, I was a dimming soul in a city of lights. Once I had kids, I became theirs. They became me. The person you're looking for, Seth, is maybe buried somewhere in between, if she's there at all."

He seizes my hips in his hands.

The jolt of his stern voice snaps me from my spiraling thoughts. "I make a mean stack of pancakes and organize the jam at Nan's, and I can fold a fitted sheet better than anybody. Halloween costumes are my thing, and my kids get an original one every year."

"Chels. Stop thinking about what you do. Look at who you are. What do you see that you love?" His playfulness darkens, battling to win a war. He flicks the clasp holding my bra together. The black straps slip down my shoulders and the clasp releases. With his tongue, Seth warms the spot where metal hooks imbed in the center of my back, gathering the lace into a black ball, tossing it to the pile on his bed.

My legs lose their fight and my eyes surrender. "Seth." I

release his name. It hurts to speak it out loud. The game's over. I forfeit.

He remains diligently on task, bearing my weight against his chest as he removes his clothes in silence. Each second twisting like a coil connecting us.

I open my eyes. We're even on the surface, each with one layer left.

Seth's defined arms and strong legs are hidden behind me, a glimpse of suntanned shoulders scattered with strawberry-tinted freckles.

His fingers slip through my hair, pulling it free from the clip. He rests his head on my shoulder. "Can't you see what I see? How fucking special you are? How bright and beautiful and significant?" His hands caress the vertical lines stretching below my abdomen. "It's not one thing I'm looking for. I see just fine—always have—and what I see is a woman who limits access to herself. Whether you're scared, out of practice, or digging in your heels, you're not believing in you the way I do. Until you can be that person for yourself—anytime, in any place—find me. Find me, and I'll remind you."

"I don't know if it's possible to see myself the way you see me."

"Then you'll be missing out on all the reasons—" Seth spins me around, his mouth on mine. "Clearly, I need to try harder."

I want to believe in what Seth does. That there's a purpose in everything. But there's too much I barely understand about myself to believe in someone else's version. The only evidence I have that he's right is how it feels to be with him.

Inevitable.

A story that's already been written.

Something I can't explain in any rational way. Two souls who promised to always find each other.

We kiss harder, our breaths ragged with desire.

Seth stills my needy hips, lowering to his knees.

My pulse grows wild in my chest. I anchor my hands in his hair. My moans drown out the echoes of doubt. *For now.*

27

SETH

$\mathcal{C}$helsea's breath quickens as weightless air skims between her teeth. She tastes better than any dream I've ever had. Her fingers tug through my hair as my tongue meets her quaking body in thick, deliberate sweeps.

She grips my shoulder, humming in a euphoric state. Eyes glassy. Lips pouting, parted, panting. *She's real. This is real.*

"Seth," she whimpers again, stretching beneath me.

"Yes, baby." My lips drift like floating kisses back and forth over her stomach.

Her nails dig into my skin.

Years and years of saving this part of myself for this one person. Sex never came with strings, a means to an end. It wasn't intimacy. But with Chelsea, with her . . . everything is . . . my thoughts scatter as she arches her back.

"I need you." Her chest heaves, rapid inhales and exhales, her command unapologetic, brave, and sexy as hell.

"What do you need?" I refuse to contain my satisfaction or deny a fucking thing I feel with this woman.

"You're going to make me say it," she rages, highlighting the red streaks across her chest and every place on her body I've claimed. "I can't," she whimpers.

I will always want her, want the world for her, but she has to want it for herself. She has to ask for what she wants. "This is a team sport, Chels. So, tell me what you need."

A few beats of silence expand between us. The rain outside hits like hail, tapping against the dark glass, threatening to break through.

"I want you to finish what you started against that wall until I can't remember my name or yours or why we're—"

I scoop Chelsea up and pin her between me and the wall, burying my face in her neck. "Hold on," I growl, and she wraps her arms around me tight, her legs clenching my waist.

My boxers are around my ankles, and I'm losing my mind as she drips sweet anticipation down my stomach.

I reach for the condom, managing to pull one from the top dresser drawer. As I rip the foil with my teeth and roll it over me, Chelsea's lips land like little explosions over my skin. I had planned to take my time—fantasized about it—but waiting was something we had done enough of. It was pure torture.

"You smell like me." She smiles.

I meet her eyes and she's whispering my name over and over again, like an act of prayer, as we become one. She's never appeared more stunning than she does in the reflection of my affection.

All I want is to drag us back in time.

To have met her at the right time, *the first time.*

To have given us a chance, sparing all the disappointment and disconnection. *Just because it didn't work before, doesn't mean it can't work now.*

She's everything I've always adored about her—a tangled beautiful mess. As she rocks her hips into me, I thread my fingers through her blond waves, weaving them together like wet vines.

The more I think about a past I so desperately want to forget, the stronger we crash into each other. The thought of her disappearing once again—never tasting her or holding her again—destroys me. I crash into her body with reckless abandon until tears spring from her smoky eyes, drowning out the screaming ones in my heart.

I carry her over to the bed. We melt in the sheets, a pile of sated sweat and soft kisses.

As we lie in each other's arms, the intermittent raindrops run horizontally across the windows in their own race. I count our breaths. She counts the pace of our fading pulses. We hold up our hands together, counting our fingers. We count everything we can, except for the years we've spent apart, because after today, I'm done counting backward.

"I didn't know sex could feel like that." Chelsea rests her head on my chest as it cools down.

"Is that a good thing?"

"Good doesn't exactly cover it." She laughs.

"Are you critiquing my technique or something? Are you challenging me?" I breathe in her buttery hair.

"It's something about the pressure. The way you touch me is like having all the tension in my body unravel."

"That's what happens to me when you're close. I feel like there's air beneath my feet."

"Sometimes, I want to literally peel my skin off. But your hands are magicians or something. All it wants is more and more, and I don't know how I'm going to get out of this bed."

"I don't see the problem here."

"It's getting late." Chelsea smiles, bringing to my attention the one thing I've avoided thinking about since she came over.

"A few more minutes?"

"It's a school night."

"I know," I add, kissing the top of her head.

"What's the time?"

I look at my clock over her shoulder. "It's 3:15."

Her shoulders vibrate as she giggles.

I'm missing something. "What's with 3:15?"

"It's the exact time I was born. Do you remember asking me that question?" She lifts her head and meets my gaze.

I roll on top of her, propping up my weight. "You're incredible. Your mind and memory." I lower my head, planting a kiss on her rosy lips. "Thank you for remembering . . . for both of us."

She squeezes her eyes tight. "This is hard for me."

"Hearing compliments? Or sex? Because you know I wouldn't say it if—"

"Being with you is—" She brings a thumb between her teeth. "I'm still figuring out what this is."

I take hold of her hand, gently pulling it away from her nervous nibbling. "We've got time to figure it out, Chels."

"I can take a compliment. I just don't know how to let it in and believe it. Asking for what I want. I'm not good at that, either."

My fingers cradle her flushed face, the tips of our noses brushing. "Guess that means we'll need to practice. Lots and lots of practice."

Before the sun's high enough to reach from the window to the pillows, my phone blares in my ears. Which can only mean one thing—Mom.

"Everything okay?" My voice trips over the gravel, stumbling out.

"Sure, honey." Her wobbly tone suggests otherwise. I sit up, the wall against my back, and scrub my hands over my face. The bed's colder without Chelsea.

"What is it?"

"I don't know how to say it."

"Are you dying?"

"Seth, no."

"Okay then, who is?"

"No one's dying. It's your dad. I found him."

I swing my legs over the side of the bed and reach for a fresh shirt. "Cool. So, you're raising the dead."

"I need closure."

"The minute that piece of shit walked out the door with his janky suitcase and obnoxious cologne, that was closure. You can't be serious with this." Something grazes my foot. I pinch the fabric and pull up Chelsea's misplaced lace, the scent of her fresh in my mind.

"It's not your choice what I do with my life."

How can a space that was absolute ecstasy hours ago be suffocating now? "I'm fully aware that's the case."

"He'd like to know you."

I squeeze my fist, pressing it into the mattress. "You do whatever you want. But that man made his choice. And I've gotta go. Love you." I toss my phone. Cupping my hands over my face, I close my eyes and breathe in Chelsea.

We agree to meet at Rainy Days on Saturday.

"Aren't you a sight for sore eyes," Nan remarks as I approach the booth with a bag of compost. "Where ya been there, Mr. Hottest-Chef-In-Town? You know, I read the papers."

"Looking great, Nan." I lean in and kiss her on the cheek. Her platinum hair has silvered around her temple, framing the effulgent glow in her smile.

"I eat my fruits and veggies." She directs her focus on Chelsea. "Unlike this one."

"What? I eat tomato sauce and olives on pizza." Chelsea straightens out the jams, facing all the labels forward.

"Hey," I greet Chelsea, kissing her on the cheek. She hands me a paper cup. "What's this?"

"Coffee from our favorite place, Café Blue Eyes. Nan's been going there forever. She loves the music—"

"You brought me coffee?"

She shrugs like it's no big deal.

"I know Café Blue Eyes. Great scones. Thank you." The gesture warms my heart.

"What's all this?" Nan asks, opening the reusable bag.

"Ah, well, Nan, I wanted you to have a bunch of fresh compost for your garden."

"Well, aren't you an absolute gem! Thank you, dear." Her eyes find a blushing Chelsea. "What are my great-grandbabies up to this fine Saturday?"

"Science museum."

"They'll love that."

"I suggested that they skip the 3-D movie, though. I don't know if that would be too much for Jonah."

I join the conversation. "Man, I loved those. The rush. You're right in the action—it's like flying."

"Or falling," she counters.

"Is there a difference between the two?"

"Well, well." Nan cackles.

Chelsea clears her throat, hands on her hips, squaring off to face me.

I drag my victory smile between my teeth, narrowing in on the placement of her sprawled fingers, the exact spot my mouth was conquering a few days ago.

"It's hotter than a scorched tamale out here right now."

"Nan," Chelsea scolds, but her smiling eyes are traitors.

"What are you two kids doing today, then?"

I brush off the edge in my voice as I dance around the truth, uncertain I know what that is anymore. "We've been touring the city, making up for lost time."

"That's lovely. Speaking of lost time," she pipes up, glancing at a thin gold watch on her wrist. "Will you head back to my place and grab a case of caramels and chocolate-covered cherries by the door? I've unpacked everything, and I can't find them anywhere. I might've left them in the cupboard, but I swear I had The Sherries pull them for me."

"Sure thing, Nan." Chelsea looks to me. "Did you walk?"

"I rode the hog."

"Well, that won't work for jars." Chelsea contemplates.

"If it's too much trouble—" Nan interjects.

"No trouble at all," I reply. "I'll ride us to your house and we'll grab a cab back."

"Me. On your bike. What about a helmet?"

I laugh, two steps ahead of her. "How'd I know that would be your first question?"

"Because I'm predictable."

My stare suggests otherwise, and by the flush in the dip of her V-neck shirt, I'm confident she catches my meaning. We may have lived separate lives before the other night, but in that moment, all of that ceased to exist for me. We're together right now, and that's what matters. As it should be, should've always been. I don't need a definition or declaration. I just need her.

I secure the second helmet I have under Chelsea's chin. The buckle clicks, and I steal a kiss before stepping to the side to put mine on. Chelsea straddles the leather seat, her long legs and bright smile will be my undoing. I exhale and kick the engine on.

She wraps her arms around my waist, gripping tight. The vibration of the motor purrs beneath us.

"You carry this spare for all the groupies?" she shouts over the road noise.

That makes me snort. "All those restaurant groupies," I tease. "I work with greens, not guitars."

She squeezes tighter, and I take off. Chelsea's excitement blares in the wind and in my ears. It's my new favorite sound.

The cherries and caramels were still in their aqua mason jars on a shelf in the kitchen. When we dropped them off, Nan sent us away again, saying the market was slow, and the day was too beautiful to waste. She demanded, "You kids have fun."

When I thought about having fun with Chelsea, my mind wandered to indoor activities only. I couldn't wait to be close to her again. To wash away the edge of my mom's news. And by the spark in her eyes when we made it to the perimeter of the park, we were on the same page.

———

Knowing Chelsea has to leave to meet her kids later means we're making the most of our day, under the covers. The daylight warms her bare shoulder and her hair shines in gold spirals. "I'm burning every inch of you into my brain."

Chelsea buries her smile into my chest.

"No more hiding," I tell her, pushing back her curtain of sunshine spirals, tucking them behind her ear.

"I developed some film. Wanna see?"

"Does it mean you have to leave this bed?"

"I can make it quick." Her brows lift along with her flushed cheeks. She leaps naked out of the bed, surprising me.

"I'd say hurry, but this view I can work with."

Chelsea returns with a handful of black and white photographs she's taken on our adventures over the past few weeks. I don't know much about photography, but I know what it means to create something from a lens of love. "If I could, I'd give you a Michelin star, especially this one right here," I tease, holding up an image of us at the game.

She swats my chest, and I make an exaggerated "umph" to play along.

"I think that might have startled me more than you." She flexes her hand.

I bring her wrist to my mouth, brushing my lips against her pulse. "There were days where all I could think about was you. Wondering where you were in the same moments, if we were sharing thoughts. If somehow we were doing the same thing at the same time. When you don't have photographs, you have to use your imagination."

Her eyes track my mouth, hanging on to every word. "I used to fear you'd be my waking thought for the rest of my life," she admits, and I kiss her.

"You don't have to be afraid anymore, Chels." I abandon the photos on the bed and pull her into my arms. "I can't believe I've been missing out on these all this time."

"They're just boobs."

When I recover from a gut-piercing laugh, I clarify what I meant. "Listen, I'm all about your body. But on this rare occasion, I was referring to your hugs."

"Oh," she says, biting down on her lip. "I'm also a great hugger."

"You're great at a lot of things." I slide my finger along her jaw. "I can think of my newest favorite thing you're great at right about—"

She grins. "You going to answer that?"

"Answer what?" Fantasizing about Chelsea's thighs wrapped around me.

"Your phone." She reaches her arm over to point at the ringing device on my dresser.

"It can wait." It takes two seconds before her expression sends me grabbing it. I answer without looking at the number, standing up now in a power pose, giving Chelsea the same view she gave me. She covers her mouth to conceal a rumbling laugh.

"Seth Hansen," I answer.

"Seth, son." A deep, tired voice rushes to my gut.

I drop the superhero act. My blood boils. "Don't ever call this number again." I power off my phone.

I swipe my pants from the floor and yank them on. I retire at the edge of my bed, scraping my nails through my hair, resting my head in my hands.

Chelsea's cool fingers run over the muscles in my back and shoulders as she leans her warm cheek against my skin. "Want to talk about it?"

"Not really," I mumble.

She stays close. "When you're ready, I'm here."

My thundering heart reverberates in my ears. I'm not supposed to feel this way anymore. It's been too long to let him affect me. Why now? When things were good. Knowing that man's around, talking to Mom, calling me, is a tidal wave crashing down on the life I worked so hard to build.

And what am I going to tell Chelsea, this woman I love? I'd tear myself to shreds to preserve and protect what's mine. I hate him. *I hate that man.* But the boy in my heart, who's only present when I'm with Chelsea, whispers until he screams.

Help me.

28

CHELSEA

"*I*'m going to get dressed," I say, kissing Seth's shoulder, Koufax at his feet.

"I'll grab a quick shower."

"Okay."

"Okay." We're painfully aware of each other's presence.

I wait for Seth in the kitchen. Ten minutes later, his feet shuffle across the wood floor. I twist in the barstool seat, turning it from side to side as Seth starts making coffee.

My eyes track his sequenced movements—coffee grounds, sprinkling salt, steps to the sink, pouring water into the machine. He doesn't say a word.

Each swift motion winds tight in my gut until I'm primed to implode. I rub my thumb along the granite bartop, regretting the smudge I've left behind.

It might be a crime to disturb his ritual here, but the bitter shift in his demeanor is not something I can let linger or blatantly ignore. Ignoring problems doesn't make them go away. It leads to ignoring each other. I don't want that. Never again.

He catches my prying gaze and waits. Usually, Seth's the one who manages to describe things way better than I believe I can. If he only knew how much I needed him to try. If he's not willing to tell me what's going on . . . my thoughts churn into words that register as they leave their mark. "Do you think this will work between us?" I ask, gathering my hair into a low bun, my heart somersaulting in my chest.

He spreads his palms over the counter, gripping the edge— the veins on his forearms bulging. "Do you want it to work, Chelsea?" His question shoots straight through me.

"I want to understand you."

"You don't?" he questions, his mouth returning to a hard line.

"I think I know snapshots of you mixed in with the version I've created in my mind over the years." My words trickle away.

"Do I know you?" he redirects, edging his face closer.

"I was sure of it." I perk up, bracing the impact of his close-ness, captivated by the range of reddish blond and brown that covers his chin and cheeks and upper lip. Age has darkened his features and carved sharper angles along his jaw. I've tried to draw him from memory and dreams. Nothing compares to the original.

"The last hour has changed that, Chels? Really?"

"Do you remember what I said about the distance with-drawal creates? The truth is, I'm often wrong, especially when I think I'm right."

"What happened to, 'I'm here when you're ready?'" He wets his lips, pushing back from the counter.

The coffee percolates and I'm grateful for the moment it takes for Seth to fill our mugs, so I can gather my thoughts. He places mine in front of me.

"With Paul, it was different. We had time to learn about each other, and even then, we were more about our partnership and respect." I'm stumbling trying to explain. "With you," I sigh, "it's the opposite. I feel everything all of the time like this compression in my chest I need to survive. I don't know how to care about you the way you need. But I'm afraid if we don't talk about what is on your mind, this thing between us, you will start to hide until I can't find you anymore."

"That's not what's happening here." Seth straightens his stance.

The hazelnut aroma clings to the air. I pick up my mug and press the porcelain lip against mine. "It's hard enough for me to share my feelings."

Seth comes around the counter and sits across from me on the other barstool. He rests one hand on my knee while pushing hair out of his eyes with the other. "My mom called earlier, telling me she wants closure with my dad and that he's seeking some kind of relationship with me. She neglected to also add that she gave him my phone number." Seth squeezes the top of my thigh. "I haven't heard that man's voice since I last saw him. And he said my name with ease, like I belonged to him, like he'd just stepped out for a pack of smokes and was on his way home." Seth's eyes cloud. I cradle his tense jaw, bringing him in close, and kiss his downturned mouth.

"Maybe he's trying," I offer as a possible comfort.

Seth's body runs rigid, pushing back from me. "Fuck that guy."

I reach for his hand.

"That man dropped us like a bad habit. Why are you defending him?" Seth's voice shakes as ripples of his anger roll over my body. I slide my fingers from his grasp.

"I'm not defending what he did. It was a terrible, unimaginable betrayal, but I know that our parents are also people, and sometimes they make mistakes. I'm Team Seth. I always have been and always will be. You don't forgive them for them—you do that for yourself."

Seth remains silent, and I force the invisible door between us to stay open, with my eyes on him and my knee between his legs.

Though it's hard to talk about, impossible to package in any palatable way, being honest about my experience is the only choice. "When Paul and I split up, it threatened to destroy me. I had failed. Hurt someone I cared for. Hurt myself and my kids. I couldn't stand up some days without holding onto anything. Paul could've let me suffer through those early days of separation—he had every right to despise me. We could've made it solely about our own needs, his pain or mine. But he didn't, and we didn't. We chose our children's well-being. We knew if we treated our divorce with compassion, we'd teach Paige and Jonah that people can grow apart without breaking. We wanted to do better for them. But not every parent has that chance or choice."

"We all make choices. He can live with his."

Seth is a man, but I know there's also a little boy, like Jonah, who's got the mic right now. I want to help him help himself. I want him to see how his dad leaving is not a measure of his worth. But I also recognize the exhaustion in his eyes. "I know you can't believe that. All the women in your class, Seth? They did what they had to."

"This isn't the same thing."

"Okay, so what is it then?"

Seth gets off the barstool and shakes his head, disappointed in me, perhaps.

"I'm asking questions because I want to understand. Help me understand." I want to scream. I swallow it.

He stops at the wall of windows that overlook a narrow side street, pushing his hair back from his forehead once again. Golden light brushes his frame, and standing in the shadow of brick and stone, he resembles a chiseled ice sculpture on a summer day—commanding everyone's attention before he melts away.

"On my birthday, after I left you . . ." Seth's voice sticks. His gaze fixes out the window.

From across the room, my sharp inhale syncs with the rise in his chest.

"I went home like I said I was going to. You know that part." He pauses, chewing on his lower lip, sliding his hands into his pockets.

I gingerly step in closer. When he resumes speaking, I hold my breath so I don't miss a word.

Seth glances at his bare feet. "I ditched my rollerblades on the front stoop and stepped into the house," he recalls, returning his attention in front of him, to somewhere else entirely. "It was dark. Like the sun had given up on us before the day had even made headway. The darkness was doing me a favor because I didn't notice my dad right away, slouched in the recliner, staring at the television. A western was on, but the volume was off. I had left when they were screaming, and I returned to silence.

"I asked him where Mom was, repeating myself, escalating with each attempt. Something broke inside me as I ran through that house, calling her name, flicking on every light. I remember that, using her name—Caroline—and I don't know why I did that. Maybe it was easier."

Seth's shoulders sag. He transforms behind my eyes, his spine curving like a wilting flower starved for water. *A head of strawberry-blond hair sticking out from his hat. The dusting of freckles sprinkled across the bridge of his nose, like he'd just got done rolling down a hill and didn't bother washing up. The crooked smile,* now weary, laced with hesitation, like it can't quite make the distance.

It occurs to me that it's not simply Seth's personality that's bright. It is physically bright wherever he is. He always keeps the lights on. And now I understand why. He can't stand to be in the dark. He sees his father there.

One step closer, I press my thigh into the cushioned arm of the leather couch, maintaining enough space to not disturb his memory. My pulse has steadied as I inhale gentle swoops that catch in my chest.

Seth runs a hand through his hair and rests his shoulder slightly against the window. He holds his hand out in front of him, examining each side. I inch my body once more, close enough that his freshly showered citrus and soap scent tickles the back of my throat.

"I thought she finally had enough of their fighting and was leaving him for good. I imagined she was waiting for me with our bags packed. But her half-full perfume bottles were still on the dresser and her book was on her bedside table and her pink slippers were tucked under the right side of the bed. She would've taken those."

My chin trembles, thinking of his mother's belongings, the simple things that become our identity. *She was a reader. She was organized. She appreciated nice smells, like I do.* She could be any mother, any woman in trouble.

She could be Steph. She could be me.

The sunlight reaches my eyes, pixelating my vision.

"The void in my dad's voice when he told me that she was in the hospital and would be back in a few days is something that lives with me. It was like he was talking to me, but he wasn't there mentally. Off the reflection of the television, I caught a glimpse of a small round cake on the kitchen table, set with plates, party napkins, decorated with blue candles. I asked him —no—I *accused* him of doing something to her when I saw the suitcase at his feet. People without a plan don't pack."

As Seth's voice climbs, it grows cloudy and thick, like the

story has been jammed inside for so long that his larynx is struggling to release it.

"He ordered me to sit. I refused. He reminded me it wasn't a request. So I sat out of exhaustion, not out of obedience. It was then that he said he was leaving, that Mom needed help, and he couldn't be the one to provide it." Seth looks at me now, breaking his trance. "So much for vows and shit," he spits out, mocking his grief.

I've never thought of Seth as someone attached to the institution of marriage. He's always been a man living life on his own terms. But this isn't that at all. I thought he didn't settle into a long-term commitment as a personal choice born from a disdain for rules and conformity, not because someone he trusted broke his faith in it.

His brows lift, noticing the shrinking proximity between us. "I wanted the cake. It was royal blue and smelled of vanilla bean. Now that I say it out loud, it's a weird thing to want at a time like that."

"You were a kid. A kid with a birthday." *With wishes to make.*

Seth shrugs his shoulders. "He said there were frozen meals in the freezer, and I needed to lay low until she came back." Seth blows a breath through his nose. The exhale is hard and tired. "I mean, I knew they were unhappy, but I guess as a kid, my mind figured that fighting led to forgiveness, as it had done before."

There isn't a single thing he's sharing that isn't cracking my chest open. Each piece of the puzzle has me examining any possible scenario where a parent chooses to leave their child. Trying to understand why and how, and I have so many questions, but Seth's not done talking.

"I think I was crying at this point. I didn't want to be alone at night. I could get through the day—I'd done that plenty—but night was a different beast entirely. My imagination was wild with fears. But I couldn't face what was happening, that he was choosing to leave—and his leaving Mom meant leaving me, too."

"Seth," I say, unable to maintain my distance a second longer. I step in and freeze as his tone turns icy, warning every instinct I have not to touch him. My mind responds, telling me to pause. My heart spars back, telling me to run to him.

"Then he stood up to leave and I lost it, begged for him to stay. *Don't go. Please don't go.* Repeating those words until my voice disappeared." Seth's expression hardens, and his words end in a splintered whisper, excruciating to dig out. "How pathetic was I? Too big to wrap my arms around his leg and hold on. But I was trying—with my words—I was trying to slow down time."

He presses his palms into his eyes and holds them over the pain.

Koufax nudges my fingers as she hops off the couch, weaving between Seth's legs, rubbing the top of her head at his ankles. The nurturing rumble vibrates in the air. Seth reaches, tenderly brushing his thumb over her fur.

"Remember that channel that played all the black-and-white sitcoms?" He chuckles through bloodshot eyes. "*I Love Lucy, The Munsters, Happy Days.* They kept me company that night."

"Sure." I did remember those, and I smile because he needs me to remember the bright spots that exist when we're suffering. Out of all the people I've known in my life, Seth has shown me that. I just didn't understand how hard he had to work for it.

"And he was right, and he was wrong." Seth levels his stare, returning to the story. "She did haul her lethargic body through the front door, her paper blue hospital gown shoved into her skirt, but it wasn't days later. She came back the next morning, gauze wrapped around her wrists."

My knees wobble. I circle my thumb over the fragile skin

protecting my veins, one woman's choice between options and none.

"Mom said we had to leave. That people wanted to send her away—they'd take me from her, too, and she wouldn't let that happen. She was in a hurry, dragging her feet around the house. She grabbed a bag, her slippers, her book, and her perfume bottles."

My thoughts are racing at the speed I imagine Caroline to be moving, collecting what she needed—or thought they needed—to survive.

I ask. "Seth, where were you?"

He looks back to me under swollen lids and soaked lashes.

I repeat my question with urgency and apprehension—my palms as slick as skating rinks. "What were you doing, Seth, while she was packing?"

He shakes his head.

"Seth. Please."

"I was in the bathroom with a bucket and a bottle of bleach."

The details don't matter. I fill in the blanks. I won't hear another word without holding him. I leap forward, closing the gap, wrapping my arms around his waist, my ear pressed into his thin cotton shirt. His muscles tighten at my initial touch, then soften as I squeeze harder. He slides his hands to my lower back, dropping his chin, breathing into my hair.

We hold each other this way, daylight consecrating our embrace.

Then he takes my face in his hands, brushing his thumb along my jaw. We cast shadows over the floorboards as the haunting in his eyes dissolves—the dying embers of a fire.

The weight of my body rests on his forearms. I lift on my toes. "No child should go through what you did."

"No, they shouldn't." His forehead meets mine. "But they do, all the time."

My fingers dig into his shirt, unable to accept this truth. "Did you ever talk to someone about what happened? A counselor? A friend?"

"We never spoke of it again."

"No." *He never told anyone.* Furious fists form in my gut. This can't be. A stream of bile shoots from my stomach, falling short of my mouth. "But how?" My eyes flood.

"We got off the bus on Fourth Street that day and didn't look back—that's how. We rotated shelters for a few months until Mom went back to the airline. It took time to make our situation better, but we made a deal—I wouldn't give up as long as she didn't. She kept to her end, eventually meeting Ajay. So you see?" he demands, pulling me flush to his body. Seth cradles my head in his hands, his fingertips applying deep pressure to my scalp. My skin erupts in electricity as his terse lips and tired eyes work over my face. His hungry stare keeps me afloat. "It's nothing like you and Paul."

This is what he cares about, me and Paul? My spine strains from his desperate tone, the ends of my hair tug in his grasp. The lines of his forehead hunch together, devising a plan. The same way they do when he's watching an important play on the field or inspecting a plate for perfection.

And then Seth's mouth is inches from mine, warming my lips. They part as he whispers, "You can't compare me to him. You just can't, Chels." His words coat my throat. I swallow them whole.

I want to explain how I made that error in judgment, but regret is a poor excuse and has no place here. "I shouldn't have —" my voice quits when Seth surprises me again, his tongue entering my mouth, claiming my apology.

My heart thrashes, my core tightens, my focus shifts to his enveloping arms and consuming kiss, his morning scruff scraping my chin, the pulse in his neck, and the hint of hot coffee and heartbreak on his breath.

I'm spinning when he steps away, my entire body stoked with need.

"Chels, I told you this not for your pity, but because I want you to understand why everything I've ever done has to have meaning," he implores. "Without purpose, what else is left of a life?" He pries my hand off his arm, kissing the translucent space where my blood is pumping hard. He stares at my wrist, savoring it once more. "You're going to be late," he reminds me, taking my hand in his, leading me to the door. "We'll talk more later."

When the elevator doors connect, I count each pearl and black number down to the garage.

When I make it to my car, I switch on talk radio.

When I get to my kids' school, I buckle them in. Jonah requests a rock station.

When I arrive home, I empty two lunch boxes.

I navigate the following hours in a haze. I make dinner, I clean the counters, I bathe my babies, read a story, turn on the nightlight, and tuck them in.

The house quiets. I crawl into bed.

Don't go, please don't go. I can't escape Seth's pleas—the anguish as he relayed the scene, begging his father to stay.

As if I'm peering in the window, cupping my eyes, trying to see inside, banging on the glass, screaming out to save him.

I don't know what age I am anymore. Collective images of Seth and me, they're all plucked into a million floating petals above my bed. *He loves me. He loves me not.*

Gut-wrenching sobs rush from my gut. I slam my eyes shut, pressing my sorrow into my pillowcase.

I cry for Seth, my friend.

I cry for that boy who rescued a stranger on her birthday and planned to escape with her.

I cry for that same child who bladed home as my hero, only to be stripped of his armor.

While a street over, a little girl slept safe and sound in her cozy twin bed, dreaming of daisies and wishes and the brown-eyed boy who made her brave.

29

CHELSEA

Steph drops a reusable bag full of groceries on my kitchen counter in another stand-out Steph outfit that matches her flamingo-pink lipstick—denim and satin, head to toe. "I like your place." She slips off her jacket. I take it from her and hang it on a wall hook above the entryway bench.

"It's cleaner when the kids are with their dad." I return to the kitchen. "Would you like something to drink? Water, coffee?" I can't remember the last time I had someone over to hang out and cook that wasn't related to me.

"I'm good, thanks. I've given up on clean as long as Cece is having fun."

"You should bring her over to play with Paige. She'd love it." I peek into the purple mesh bag. "Speaking of fun, thanks for coming over."

"Do you like truffle oil? I brought a special flavor." Steph makes herself at home. I like that about her. It puts me at ease how comfortable she is all the time.

"I can take truffle oil in small doses. The smell is strong."

She throws a hand on her hip. "I have something for you that smells heavenly."

I follow her with my eyes as she reaches into the bag and hands me a small plastic jar with thick ivory cream in it. I unseal the lid and bring the jar to my nose. "Floral. Smells great. What's this?"

"My favorite hair mask. Give it a spin and see if you like it."

"I don't know how to use it."

"You got a comb?"

I nod.

"Apply it in the shower. Leave it on for twenty minutes."

I nod again, chewing on my bottom lip. It's been a decade since I took care of my natural hair. "Would you mind showing me?"

"Where's your bathroom?"

I point to my bedroom. "Through there."

"C'mon." Steph lifts the jar from my hands and leads the way.

She does a once over of the tile and chrome design, lined with one wall-to-wall horizontal mirror adjacent to a glass shower. "We need a hair towel, shower cap, and a chair."

I return with everything.

Steph glides the chair by the sink. "Sit here so we can get your hair damp."

Once I sit down, Steph drapes a towel over my shoulders and leans my head back. "Your kids are delicious by the way," she comments. "Those newborn portraits in your bedroom are beautiful. You take those?"

"I did."

"They're treasures."

"Did you have newborn photos taken of Cece?" The warm water runs over my scalp. Steph twists out the excess and straightens my posture.

"Sure. I got them somewhere. You coming back to class next week? Chef stuck me with Poppy, and that lady never shuts up about conspiracy theories. Us moms have no time for that shit."

"Oh, wow. That sounds pretty awful."

"Don't get me wrong. Everyone's got their thing, but we've got snack monsters and bills to pay and gotta stick together, Chelsea."

"I thought I might've been too quiet, coming off snobbish or something." I wonder if she knows I'm a pro at concealing my thoughts—I suppose it's a symptom of growing up with an actress. Summer performing to her audience of one. She always asked for feedback. Was her monologue believable, bold, big enough? She'd hand me her cosmetic bag of lipsticks and eyeshadow palettes and tell me to go to town as I watched her transform.

"I've got a peopling limit, but that hasn't applied to you."

Maybe I was misled by first impressions. Maybe there's still so much to learn about people beneath their expressed exteriors. And maybe we have things in common aside from our weekly cooking class, like an appreciation for bold lipstick colors and protecting the people we love at all costs.

"I've never had girl friends," I admit.

"Well, girl, you've got me now."

My eyes don't resist closing as Steph combs through my hair, using her nails to separate it into sections. It's such a kindness, Steph coming here, and I'm still sore from things with Seth. I pull in diaphragm breaths to suppress tears—of sadness, relief, and even gratitude.

"When I married Paul, I started straightening my hair. I don't know why. I just needed a change or something. He never asked me to do it, but I was home with kids all day, and it was like if I changed the outside of myself, I could conceal the things inside I didn't want to see."

"We all have parts of ourselves hidden away."

As Steph works through my thick curls, I reconsider the first day we met. How certain I was that she couldn't stand the sight of me and my carelessness in disregarding safety protocols in a kitchen. "You knew my necklace was David Yurman."

"Is that a question?"

"I assumed everyone going through the program would be—"

"That we'd all be poor?"

"I assumed that. I'm sorry."

She twists two sections up, clipping them to my scalp. She works in a conditioning treatment through the section she's holding. "You're not entirely wrong. If we aren't poor before we leave, most of us are usually strapped after. When I got out of my situation, I couldn't get to the bank in time. It wasn't planned. I had a moment. That's it. I grabbed the cash in the safe and my kid's piggy bank. I knew I'd never have access to my money or my things again."

My fingers tremble in my lap. "I'm glad you made it out."

"Leaving all that behind was worth the cost. But sometimes, I see a fine necklace draping from the neck of a woman or baby portraits on the wall, and I miss my stuff." Steph's gaze goes distant. *"But,"* she says, staring at her flawless brown reflection in the mirror under the heat of incandescent light. "I like my bones intact more."

I reach my hand to hers, and she squeezes it. "There must be laws. Something that can protect you."

"Sure. But then I'd have to show my face in court. And I'm not willing to do that. I've got my Cece to think about."

"Howard probably isn't your name."

"Neither is Stephanie." She winks.

Of course.

Steph finishes each section and covers my head with a shower cap. "Okay, keep this on for twenty minutes. Don't ever fall asleep with one on or it will be unpleasant, and I don't do middle-of-the-night calls."

"Noted." I smile.

"You have beautiful hair—be proud of it."

On our way to the kitchen, Steph peeks over her shoulder back into the bedroom. "Change your pillowcases to silk."

"That's better for curly hair?"

She takes my chin in her hand and smiles. "Better for everything."

"How can I thank you or pay you for the masks?"

She waves me off, ready to make dinner while my mask sets.

"My kitchen is your kitchen."

"Grab tomatoes and garlic and a cutting board." Steph pulls out the bottle of truffle oil and leafy greens.

As she's washing her hands, I organize the ingredients on the counter. "So, I was thinking about finding a finance class, something that can help me with budgeting and business."

"The community center has all that. Ask your boy. He's gotta have someone managing his money for him. See if he can hook you up."

"You like being in his class?" Seth isn't far from my mind, ever.

"Yeah. Chef's a good one. Not many of those readily available. He really cares about the community."

"And people," I add.

"I noticed some people in particular." Her brow lifts in my direction. "He's pretty taken with you." She dries her hands on the towel I pass to her.

"No," I gasp. "We've been friends since we were kids. With some stretches of not talking between."

I grab my phone and record a voice note, reminding myself to check out the business and finance courses offered at our local community college. Relying on someone else is how I got here in the first place.

Steph laughs, leaning on her hip. "Oh, so you mean to tell me in all of the classes we had before, I just missed him marking his territory with those intense eyes he was giving you that whole night."

There's nothing I can do, so I laugh, too.

Steph picks up the truffle oil. "Thought so."

After Steph leaves, I'm sitting at my vanity, reuniting with my post-shower reflection. "Well, hello there old friend." Tropical aromas of plumeria and hazelnut release as I easily comb through my soft hair. "It's been a long time."

A droplet of water lands on my collarbone. I reach for it, awakening the memory of Seth's lips right where my nail grazes flesh, sending chills over my chest. He wanted me to look at myself without looking away.

I should've pushed harder the last time we were together and not left at his insistence. He thinks my compassion is pity because I didn't or couldn't express myself clearly.

"Seth, Seth," I whisper.

My phone chimes, alerting me I have a text. It's from Seth. My eyes retreat, and I glance over my bare shoulder. Then I open the message to read it.

> Hey. I handled our last conversation poorly. I don't know how to talk about some things.

My fingers find the ends of my hair, twirling strands tightly into coils. I breathe and read the message again before responding.

> I get it. I'm not great at things I've never done before, either.

> You always seem to get me. Thanks for being you.

> How are you feeling?

I'm better. Missing you.

My cheeks turn from peach to pink.

> Miss you, too.

You know that running list in my head of all the things you're great at?

> Sure.

Add listening to the line-up.

And boobs. You added those from earlier, right? ;)

His joke surprises me, and I'm laughing, elbows on the vanity, the phone in my hands.

> I'm great at boobs?

It's an all-encompassing "greatness" list. Wish I could hold you right now.

> You mean hold my boobs? ;)

Always.

Throbbing fear and desire rush through my veins, sparking an idea. I reach for the knot tucked between my cleavage, releasing my towel. It falls around my hips. The phone sways in my grasp as I steady my breath.

Pushing through dizziness, I lock my spine, stilling my hand. I position the phone close to my face, my hair settling at my collarbone.

Taking the photo is the easy part. Snap and done.

My words are the challenge, but I manage to type a message that's playful and true.

> So you don't have to burn your brain.

I refuse to let myself count the seconds of vulnerability fatigue after sending the image. Instead, I smile, counting each soft, defined curl as it dries and takes shape.

My message notification chimes again, once, twice, three times, like Seth's peppering kisses.

> CHELSEA!!!!
>
> I don't know what I did to deserve this.
>
> If this is what making up with you looks like, let's spend forever fighting.

I wish he were here to swap laughter and crawl into bed with. I secure the towel around my chilled skin, bringing my phone with me. I sink into the mattress.

A minute later, a final text comes through.

> Meet me in our dreams.

———

The next day, Seth takes me to Billy Goat Hill for a breathtaking panoramic view of the skyline—industry and flat-roofed residences, neighborhoods built on sloped streets and blooming hills, all surrounded by mountains and an ombre of blue.

"This is my favorite hidden gem, and the final stop on our 'Seth and Chels take the city' tour," he says on our approach. A single swing hangs from a eucalyptus tree.

I gesture toward the flat wooden seat. "Should I?"

"You should."

I run my hands over the braided rope to find my best grip as I lower into the seat. The tree gives a sturdy tug when I push off. Seth's palm connects with my back, gently joining in the effort.

The afternoon's dry and warm. "I've never been up here before."

"What if we had met like this instead of on the playground?"

"Would've been tricky on rollerblades." My words hum as I lean into his open hand, enjoying the fondness of a memory and the new one we're making. The air's still except for the artificial breeze from swinging.

Seth asks, "I've always wanted to know what else was happening that day. What was on your mind? It took you a few minutes to notice me—face toward the storm, catching raindrops, swinging. You had thrown your helmet to the ground."

The rope scratches my skin as I grip tighter, skidding my sneakers along the dusty ground, slowing my swing to a stop.

"It's really silly. I'm embarrassed to tell you."

"Tell me anyway." Seth holds the rope, steadying its sway.

"My parents hadn't listened when I picked out the exact helmet I wanted for my birthday. It was this very nineties New Kids On The Block-themed helmet. Had a white background with neon shapes and the band members' faces on it. It was all I had asked for."

"You were disappointed." Our eyes connect.

"It wasn't really about the helmet or the books or threatening to send me away. That basic helmet meant she was refusing to accept me. I convinced myself that if I put on the helmet she gave me, I'd become more invisible than I already was."

"So, it wasn't just about the summer camp thing." He sighs.

"Your appearance. The bright colors and clothes you used to wear. I get it. You wanted to express yourself."

"I suppose I wanted to be seen as *me*. Not a reflection of someone else's idea of me."

Seth takes hold of the swing and twists the ropes so I'm facing him. "Even in that simple helmet, you stood out. I saw you. I couldn't take my eyes off you then, or now, or ever."

30

CHELSEA

*W*e go back to Seth's place carrying cartons of Chinese takeout, swapping dishes and battling chopsticks for the last spring roll. When he cracks open his fortune cookie and asks me to stay the night, I crawl into his lap and take a bite.

Seeing the sun rise at Seth's means watching the sky lift from purple clouds to orange and gold layers while squeezing juice into two glasses. I dance along to a soundtrack of show tunes in my mind while making breakfast.

"I can't believe you're up this early, and you made burritos." Seth snakes his arms around my waist, nuzzling his nose into my neck.

"I've been getting up this early for years—doesn't mean I'll ever like it."

"You cooked for me."

"Thought I'd give you a little break. You wore yourself out last night."

"Never," he boasts. "I can get used to this, you know," he adds, snatching a slice of bacon.

"Unless you're okay with eating breakfast for every meal, you'll be sorely disappointed."

"Oh, I wasn't referring to the food. I was talking about this masterpiece." He steps back to the counter, and his well-rested eyes lazily travel the length of my body. "You. In my shirt, barefoot in the kitchen, sipping fresh orange juice. You're fucking beautiful, and I'm one lucky man."

"You sure got your sweet-talking mouth on." I look up to locate the plates on a shelf, too high for me to reach. Seth's arms slide along mine to take them down.

He whispers in my ear, "If the heels of your feet leave this floor, and I get a peek at what's hiding beneath my shirt, we'll be microwaving these burritos." He places two plates in front of me.

"As if you'd ever use a microwave." I laugh, my wide gaze fixed on Seth's joggers and white tee—the same one he always wears under his chef's coat—a layer he only lets a few see. The sight of Seth at ease in his safe space lights a fire within me. So do his lips, as they curl like they're doing now. "You're ridiculous."

"Maybe." He smirks. "But you secretly love it. As much as I —" Seth's stare sobers as he takes my chin in his hands, "—as much as I love you."

My back arches against the fridge, the handle digging into my side. I open my mouth, certain some sentiment will make itself known. My pulse jams in my throat, sending my jaw snapping shut.

"I said it. Deal with it." He plants a kiss on my forehead.

It's one thing to have Seth touch me, to show me how much he cares, and quite another when he says he loves me casually in conversation, like it's something he's always done, like "Hey, Chels, pass me the butter" or "Great job on that BJ, Chels." I'm working myself up in his kitchen under the scrutiny of his sincerity.

"Dance with me?"

"Dance with you?" I restrain a nervous laugh that slips out anyway.

"Give me your hand, Chels." He reaches for me.

Seth's warm fingers pull me into his chest. He presses a hand into my lower back, dipping his chin into my neck, and I lean into him, resting my forehead just beneath his collarbone. Breathing him in is a luxury that defies all rules of logic. My head swirls as we spin in slow circles over the kitchen floor.

"I love you, Chels," he tells me again. "I love your naked body in my clothes. And your bacon—damn, that's stellar bacon. I love the way you're fighting telling me you love me." His hand maneuvers under the shirt I'm wearing, up my thigh, landing on my hip. "I'm scared too, but I'm done waiting for our lives to catch up to us. It's our time. It's finally our time." He claims my eyes, my heartbeats, and finally, my kiss—diving in hard and uncompromising. Our lips slide easily, slippery from bacon grease and unchoreographed dancing.

I throw my arms around his neck and part my lips, deepening our embrace. My foot's on the gas pedal, accelerating down coastal Route One, top-down, open road. Bursts of heat strip my senses, one by one. I close my eyes. Taste, smell, touch, his voice whispering over my skin. I'd crawl inside his mouth just to get closer.

Does he understand what this kiss means to me? What *he* means to me? If I keep kissing, my hands in his hair, and continue to mold my body perfectly against his, he'll know this means more than words. Like all the songs on the playlist he gave me when we were young. He knew I'd memorize every one of them and absorb those lyrics as his words.

Yes. We can do this. We can begin again.

My balance falters, and the gap between us widens as he rips himself away. Sharp blasts of overhead light penetrate my eyes as I attempt to orient myself. My organs riot. My skin screams. My aroused body aches for his return. "Come back," I whisper, breathless.

"You gonna answer that?"

"What?" I ask, our chests rising and collapsing.

"Your phone's ringing." He points out with eyes as hazy as mine. "We need new ringtones."

"Shit." I blink and run my hand down Seth's shirt. *Where's my phone? Who's calling me at nine in the morning?* My hands begin to shake. *Something's wrong.* I locate the source of the sound in my bag on the couch. My fingers slip against the plastic, and the phone rattles against my ear.

"Hello." I find a spot on his couch and tuck my knees into his shirt. "Paul."

"Hey. I'm heading to the school. The principal called me when they couldn't reach you," he explains, his voice rushing, tone clipped.

"Wait, slow down. Is this about the kids?"

"Jonah's been in some kind of altercation. A kid wouldn't stop pulling J by the hood of his sweatshirt. He asked him to stop. There were other students around. He punched the kid in the face."

"What do you mean, a fight? Why didn't the school call me?"

"They did call you. Can you meet me there, please?"

My throat burns. "Yes. I'm leaving now." I slam my phone shut and grab my bag through blurry vision, turning back when I realize I have no pants on. I crash into Seth's chest, the pile of my clothes already in his hands.

"Thank you," I manage.

"Let me help you." He slips my sweater over my head.

I rest my weight on his shoulders and step into my leggings.

"Can you tell me what's happening?"

"Jonah hit another kid. A boy who wouldn't stop touching him. There were other kids around egging it on, or doing nothing—I don't know." I'm struggling to put on my sneakers. "And the school tried to call me, but my phone was in my bag, and we were in the bedroom last night, and then I was cooking and singing, and we were dancing . . . and I missed the call," I yell.

"Chels, anyone could miss any call. They got a hold of Paul. And he reached you. It'll be okay. And fuck that other kid."

"I have to go."

"I know," Seth says softly, exhaling into my hair. He kisses me. I barely feel it.

We keep Jonah home from school the following morning. The principal and school counselor suggested we bring him to see a therapist that specializes in similar profiles as his. Apparently, as she put it over the phone, *kids who are bright but have issues with self-regulation.*

"Chelsea." Paul asks for my attention. "We won't do anything you're not comfortable with. Let's first see what this lady has to say."

We're sitting in the waiting room of San Francisco Children's Hospital, and I'm chewing the inside of my cheek, waiting. Waiting is the worst. The facility has an entire neurological disorders wing with people waiting. Paul keeps reminding me that it's our best option, known for its network of therapists and doctors, and is ranked the top facility in the Bay area.

Jonah's playing with Molly, the therapist, in a colorful room, with toys and games, small tables and chairs—all kid-sized. He's smiling and engaged and in his element. There's a garden scene painted on the walls, giving the illusion that there's fresh air to breathe and vitamin D to absorb. I count the clouds through the observation window.

"Mr. Jacobs and Ms. Bell? We're ready for you," Molly announces calmly through the cracked door.

I shoot up, and Paul follows.

"Hi, honey." I approach Jonah. "Are you having fun?"

"They have all the dinosaurs. The carnivores, omnivores, and herbivores."

"That's amazing, buddy," Paul replies.

"Jonah lined up the dinosaurs by classification and the time period they existed in," Molly informs us, kneeling down, meeting him at eye level. "Jonah, I'm going to talk with your mom and dad. You can keep playing with dinosaurs or the red buckets on those shelves. Okay?"

"Okay."

Molly directs us to a tall round table in the corner of the room, out of earshot from where Jonah's safely in his imagination.

"So, first, let me assure you, Jonah's a wonderful kid who's a pleasure to talk to."

My shoulders drop, and I look for comfort in Paul. He puts his hand over mine and I'm grateful for the support.

"So, Molly, what are we talking about here, then?" He takes the lead.

"Between your intake forms and the school paperwork, I believe Jonah would benefit from some further evaluation."

"You mean testing?" I ask, my throat constricting.

"Thanks for asking. Jonah's showing some initial signs of Sensory Processing Disorder. Have you heard this term before?"

I shake my head "no" as my vision blurs the paint on the walls into muted shades of springtime roses, peach, lemon, moss, lake, and plum. Over the sky, white airy clouds float aimlessly. No, not clouds—petals, like the ones I saw in my room the night Seth told me what happened to him as a child. I straighten my vision, blinking back my disbelief. "Okay, okay, what do we do?"

Paul adds, "So, what does this mean?"

Molly smiles, and her tortoise-shell frames skip down the bridge of her nose. "Well, it means a lot of different things depending on what we learn. First, assessment, then diagnosis would be the next step. And from there, we might be talking about multiple types of therapies—a combination of things like change in diet and new routines, and of course, lots of patience for everyone—Mom and Dad included."

"What's Sensory Processing Disorder?" Paul circles back.

"First, there's Sensory Processing, which is the ability to take in, sort out, and give meaning to information from the world around us. It's the neurological process of taking sensory input—think textures of clothes, smells of foods, temperature of a room, sounds. The disorder component is when the child has difficulty detecting, sorting out, or assigning meaning to sensory input around them. We all have sensory differences, but when it causes significant difficulties in a child's daily life, development, or social interactions, that's when we consider interventions and therapies."

My hands are back in my lap, twirling the sheer yellow thread at the end of my scarf.

"You noted in your paperwork that Jonah has an aversion to textures in food, often has outbursts out of nowhere, and still night wakes. We need more information. I can spend more time with Jonah here in the clinic."

"He's doing okay in school, though," I add. "This is the first time we've had a physical incident like this."

"And that makes sense to me. Are there any other stressors or shifts in his life that could be at play here? We take a holistic approach. It's not simply one thing."

"And what happens if we skip the tests and decide to keep a closer eye on him at home?" I ask.

"Every year our brains grow and solidify, becoming more rigid to change. Jonah's at an ideal age where occupational therapy can make a lasting impact on his development. I'm not telling you what to do, but I want you to have all the information before proceeding."

"What kind of impact are we talking?" Paul presses.

"Confidence, for one. Auditory processing challenges are common in SPD. This can impact both reading and writing development."

"I'm sorry, did you say reading?" I ask, on the verge of vomiting. I shuffle through my brain, searching, panicking, trying to recall what it felt like to be six.

Is that why my parents kept me under such close watch?

Why food made me gag?

Why smells reached me before anyone else in a room?

Why it hurt to read?

"When a child has accommodations at home and in the classroom, they can meet their full potential, greatly influencing their confidence and relationship with learning. You have an exceptionally bright child who, I believe, with the right support, will continue to thrive."

These realizations bleed into the present.

Why all my clothes need to be soft.

Why I hug so hard.

If I experienced these things, it means . . . I flatten my hands over the brick in my abdomen, bracing myself, but having to ask. "How does a child develop this?"

"We also always recommend counseling support for parents, to help navigate the process of diagnosis and intervention."

"Is it hereditary?" I clarify with urgency, my skin crawling out of itself.

"I'm hesitant to answer this question because the research isn't definitive, and parents often blame themselves. So please hear me when I say that we don't entirely know. There can be unknown prenatal complications, or during birth there can be environmental causes—"

"So yes, this can be inherited?" my voice raises.

"Yes, ma'am, the initial research suggests it's inherited."

"Thank you." The words disintegrate on my tongue. There's a permanent ink stain in the wood grain of the table.

"Why are we just seeing this now?" Paul interjects. "Surely, his teachers would've picked up on this."

"SPD is hard to diagnose until there's more development. It takes the shape of a lot of other spectrum disorders."

Paul straightens in his seat, his voice projecting like we're in a tunnel. "How soon can we get these tests scheduled?"

I've heard enough. He can handle logistics. I get up, making my way to Jonah.

"Hi, Mommy."

"Hi, my sweet boy." I pull him toward me, breathing in sunshine and citrus, and kiss the top of his head. An obstinate tear escapes and disappears in his unruly blond hair—he got that from me, too.

31

SETH

a knock at the door startles Koufax, who leaps off my lap. I switch off Sportscenter, dropping my feet from the coffee table to the chilled floor.

I peek in the peephole, practically ripping the door off its hinges when I see her. Backlit by the hallway's sconces, Chelsea's sunken cheekbones come into view, streaked with mascara. Her eyes are bloodshot. Her spirit broken.

She's in my arms before the door latches shut.

My eyes are everywhere, searching for physical wounds. "What's happening? Chels, baby."

She squeezes my neck, and I lift her up, carrying her to the couch. I hold her until her flooded gasping steadies into clear breathing.

"I've made a mess of your shirt." She wipes the residual moisture from her cheeks.

"I've got another one." I brush the stuck wisps of hair from her face. "Can you tell me what's going on? Do you want a glass of wine?"

She shakes her head.

It's been days since we've spoken, aside from a few sparse

text messages. She said she was busy. I've been busy, too. I didn't read between the lines.

"They think my son has this sensory disorder." Defeat registers in her eyes. A purple hue settles beneath her lashes.

"Is it okay if I ask questions?"

"I might not have answers."

"Is it Autism? I don't know much about that, but I hear about it from the moms in class."

"No, it's not. Though it would help in some ways if it was."

"I don't get what you mean."

"Autism is a recognized disorder under this one diagnostic manual and is supported under federal law. Our useless insurance won't recognize Jonah's diagnosis, which means it's not coverable. None of it. We have to pay out of pocket for all these therapies he now needs. And here's the best part . . ." She laughs, sarcastic, tired, chewing on chapped lips. "The accommodations at his school aren't even guaranteed because of this. He's not protected. The school doesn't have to do anything to help him."

Heat rises up my neck. "How could anyone afford that?"

"They scrounge, they sacrifice, move money around, steal. Or else they can't."

"What about kids who don't have access?"

The heart shape of her mouth flattens into a line. "Well," she bites back unintentionally, but I get it—her reserves are depleted. "I guess they don't get the help they need. They get lost in the system."

"This is criminal." I stand up.

"We have a meeting with his teacher and a team at the school. There are some options, but they require additional testing. Between his new eating plans and therapy schedules and visual routines at home, I haven't had any time. I'm sorry I haven't called. I'm so tired at night, I pass out." She buries her face in her hands, revealing an array of marker stripes on her arms.

I roll my shoulders and lower back down next to her. "This is new, Chels—stop being so hard on yourself. You have nothing to apologize for. Do you hear me?"

She nods, pulling her face from her palms, tears streaking through the mascara stains.

"I should've seen the signs. Paid closer attention. That's my job."

"Chelsea, you're not an expert on this. How could you have known?"

The finest points in her eyes harden like compressed charcoal. "Because it's me, Seth. Jonah is me!" Her despair escalates, vibrating from her throat. I pull her onto my lap, her thighs falling over mine. "I mean—hello—the trouble with reading, aversion to certain foods and textures and smells—that was all me as a kid. Why I can't listen to certain types of music because the instruments are too loud for me. They pushed me back then, my parents and teachers, everyone pushed. I was left feeling different with no reason why. I ended up hating myself, and now there's a reason that explains it all—I don't want Jonah to ever think this is his fault. I can't let him go through what I did."

I run my fingers through her hair.

"Seth, he needs me right now, and that's all that matters."

"Of course, he needs you. You're his mom."

She pulls back and takes a deep inhale.

"What aren't you saying, Chels? Why do I want to throw up right now?"

More silence. "My son needs me."

"Yeah, you said that."

She slides off my lap and sits on the coffee table in front of me, our knees touching. Her tone softens and steadies. "If I hadn't been distracted recently, I might've had a clearer head. I would've noticed what was happening to my son before a teacher had to bring it to my attention. Like you said, I'm his mom. I'm responsible."

"Whoa, whoa. I'm not even sure I know what point I want to make here, so I'm just going to say everything, because this is bullshit. Let's be clear—your plan in the last thirty-six hours under extreme stress is to shelve your dreams . . . again? What the hell have we been doing? You think you'll go back to being 'mom' Chelsea all day, every day, and everything will be fixed?" My chest cracks as it expands. There's a fucking hammer in my head. I can't bring myself to face that this grand plan of hers means we'll be shelved, too.

Chelsea shoots up and paces the room. "You don't get to psychoanalyze me. I'm not some problem for you to solve, Seth. You're not going to fix yourself by rescuing me."

I tighten my grip on my thighs, closing my eyes, methodically breathing, bracing the blow.

Please don't go. Don't let her go. Not when I just found her, again.

"I wasn't trying to rescue or fix you," I say, raw and weary.

"It's my life." She's back in front of me. "Right now, I barely get a moment to shower or sleep, nevermind find my life's purpose, oh, and also be in a serious relationship with someone who also happens to be on the cusp of the busiest time of his career. Who didn't ask for kids. What is this? Are we dating, trying to date? We never talked about it, and I don't know if I'm even ready for that."

"I'm sorry. Pause right the fuck there. I get to decide what I can and can't handle. I won't justify any of my life's choices to anyone. I won't apologize for them either. And I most definitely will not allow anyone else to define them for me. I'm choosing you and my career. Plain and simple. Your kids are a part of your package. I can have both. I *want* both."

"When would we even see each other? Be realistic. We've known each other for years, but only in small increments.

We've missed more than we've been present for. How can we risk everything for something we don't even understand?"

"Like this. Just like this." I stand up and take her face in my hands. "By staying. By talking through it. By being us. That's how we figure it out. We went decades without answers, and now we can figure those out, together."

Her face twists in agony. She whispers, her lips grazing my chin, "All I want—need—is for this to be a different time in my life."

"Chels—"

"Our timing is never right," she murmurs, defeated. Chelsea's being honest, and it hurts.

It hurts deep in my lungs, and I drop my hands, turning toward the window. The black sky is a blank slate and welcome reprieve from the recurring pattern in my life—the women I love leave. "I don't have to explain why you're worth it to me. I'd choose you every time," I confess, dropping my head, kicking at empty air.

"I'm not *not* choosing you, Seth," she says from behind me. "It's messy and complicated, and I have to figure things out. The same way all those women have to figure their own lives out. I get it, why you want to help everyone, especially me, but you can't. You can't save her by saving us."

"I told you about my deepest . . ." Bile burns the back of my throat. "Scars."

"Please, Seth, I don't want to leave like this."

"Then don't."

"Maybe we can try and just be friends?"

"No."

"But—"

"This is your signature move. Walking away when anything presents an ounce of a challenge or possibility." I cut her off because I'm done with excuses. I refuse to let her dig at this wound ever again.

"That's unbelievably mean, and you know it. It's my kid."

"Lie to yourself, but don't lie to me." I turn around, my back to the city I love. "You don't have hard conversations. Instead, you make decisions for everybody before you know the truth about anything. You won't ever risk what it takes to have anything of your own."

She's fidgeting with the sleeves of her sweater, shaking her head. "You don't understand because you're not a parent."

"You have no idea what you're talking about." The walls are crumbling, barricading my resolve.

Controlling every muscle I have, unable to find the strength to say goodbye to her . . . to the life I began to imagine with her. Everything I love about this woman is evaporating in a cloud of smoke. In front of my eyes—repressed rage and predestined grief—we both become someone I don't recognize.

"I've already been a parent, Chelsea." My chin trembles in disbelief. I aim my pain, unloading with precision. "While you got to eat birthday cake and make your wishes at eleven, I was wiping my mother's life off the bathroom tile. Do you know how hard it is to get blood off grout? What it takes to erase the scent of bleach from your memory? For years, I was up all night, doing checks on her. You think that no one can possibly understand what it means to be confined by our choices. If no one knows you, Chels, it's because you don't let them. And fuck me, I've spent most of my adult life trying to find a way—a way back to you. Compared you to every woman. No one held a candle to this vigil of you I kept hostage in my head—this paralyzing panic that rips me to shreds when we're apart."

I don't notice the way she gets in close. So close, the radiation from her body raises the hair on my arms.

"Relationships, all of them, take time and effort, Seth. Love takes time."

"The way you're treating us doesn't feel like love at all."

"I've always loved you." She places my resistant jaw in her

cold hands, the tips of our noses brushing. "Hoping I'd see you again was the only thing that kept my head above water some days. But love without action is simply an emotion, a fleeting image that's been exposed through a single-layered process. To love someone," she stumbles over a shaky breath, "is being there to love them, and no matter what part of my heart wants you—the part that's always been yours—I don't have the time to give to anyone but my children and myself. For once," she emphasizes, pressing her forehead into mine, "I'm seeing how badly I've neglected myself. I'm not who I want to be, not yet." She releases her fingers from my face. "You've given me a glimpse of that person and giving you my scraps is not any way to thank you."

My jaw locks. "I don't want you to thank me. I want you to make this work."

She presses her eyelids closed, tailoring her tears, one drop at a time. Excruciatingly slow like this moment. "We both know you have so much coming down the pipeline. The show, a restaurant, your commitment to our community. Seth, our lives are heading in different directions. I don't want to be in the shadow of anyone's success ever again, and I'm never going to stand in the way of it either."

"It doesn't have to be like that."

"I lived with someone I love in the spotlight my entire childhood. It's not good for me." Chelsea presses her salt-stained lips into my shivering ones. Her tongue dissolves the seam of my mouth.

Chelsea's air fills my lungs as I grasp the material of her sweater. If we keep this pace, I'll keep breathing. If we don't let go, I can hold onto this spring like it'll last forever.

My eyes sting. "Why would the universe bring us together only to tear us apart? We aren't my parents; we'd handle this better . . . we wouldn't abandon your kids or our careers. We won't make the same mistakes." I pause, catching my breath as my muscles atrophy at the hands of her resolve. "Don't you get it? Even knowing you were in the world brought me infinite comfort." I press in closer, my voice scratching like a broken record. "Knowing you, someone who understands me. I've loved you for as long as I can remember, and I'd never discard what we have. To not even try . . ."

Chelsea's eyes widen, and she turns from me. She brings her thumb to her mouth and chews on the corner, her cheeks flushed, her shoulders slumped.

"We've always had terrible timing. How long is it going to take us to accept this?"

"There's no such thing as good or bad or right or wrong timing. Time waits for no one, Chels. There's only right now. The choices we make. And I'd choose it all, again and again, because that's what you mean to me. You see this as an obstacle —I see it as an opportunity. Stop selling yourself stories that aren't true. Stop acting like what we share isn't worth it to you."

Chelseas's bottom lip quivers as she fights herself. It's killing me to witness. "I'm so proud to know you," she says. "You're changing the world—leaving it better than you found it."

"So are you. One child at a time, with Jonah and Paige." I exhale, my anger too heavy to carry.

Chelsea struggles to accept what I'm saying. Her gray eyes fog over. She's not debating me on this. If it were up to me, I'd retrace our steps to the beginning and find a way for it all to make sense. To understand why the women I care for most in this world would rather leave me than be with me.

So, this is what surrender feels like.

I center my thoughts, imagining a future different from this present moment. *Chelsea waking up, her morning hair on the pillow, sleepy eyes lifting to greet the light. I'm already awake— always awake before her—coffee rousing her from a dream, stretching her legs under the covers.*

With each detail I add to the vision, my mind loosens its

chokehold on my heart. I inhale, forcing my forearms to relax over my thighs as I sink back into the couch. In this scenario I'm creating, *Chelsea's grinning. Her smile funnels from my brain to my bare feet. Her lips, still stained from the red lipstick she wore the night before when we dressed up and went dancing.*

People do what they want to do. She's telling me that this is what she wants. I've been so caught up in my own desire and vision. I know she's going to go. Part of me accepts that she's never entirely been here. Whatever remaining time we have, I want to spend it with her in this imaginary alternate future, where tomorrow is tomorrow, but tonight is ours.

"Do you have to go back home tonight?" I ask softly, preparing myself to say goodbye.

"No," she says, surprising me. "The kids are with their dad until the morning."

Our weapons retired. My gaze settles on hers. "Stay with me. For the next nine hours, can we simply be us?"

She steps into my open arms.

32

CHELSEA

*W*e spend those late-night hours together, dreaming that somewhere in time, a version of us is happily waking up tomorrow to morning kisses and love notes Seth hides around the house, in our life together, tangled in the sheets, surrounded by memories hanging on the walls, children crawling into bed before the sun rises, our toothbrushes side by side . . . years of laughter, lazy Sundays, summer nights watching the Dodgers, Seth's cooking, pancake dates, city walks, kitchen counter escapades, road trips, bickering over music, foggy walks, sharing birthday cake, and swinging in the rain.

Nostalgia and adventuring, childhood healing and peace.

Where I lay my head on Seth's chest, listening to the rhythm of his heart during heavy spring thunderstorms. He strokes my hair and wraps his arms around me like he's always done. And maybe for two people who could never get our timing right, the dream of it was all we'd have.

PART IV

2011

SAN FRANCISCO, CALIFORNIA

"To see a World in a Grain of Sand
And a Heaven in a Wild Flower
Hold Infinity in the palm of your hand
And Eternity in an hour."
— William Blake

33

SETH

*T*he show producer signals that we're ready to go on, dropping his fingers in three, two, one.

"This is Spence Ellis, The Best in the Bay Area for your Top-Forty dance parties—and it's time again for Friday's Five-Questions-In-The-Hot-Seat-At-Five, and listen up here—we've got a special guest today. Homegrown culinary royalty," the radio host announces into the mic. "We have with us in the studio San Francisco's hottest man behind the line and in front of the camera, his new show on the Cooking Channel kicking off this summer. Let's all honk our horns in gridlock for the one and the only Master Chef Seth Hansen." He drags out the final consonant of my name for a few beats. The dramatic effect blares through the booth.

I'm sitting across from Spence, who's well past his prime with his flat-brimmed station cap cocked to the side, chugging an energy drink like he's got spare lives. I could educate him on the ingredients or hospitalization statistics with that crap, but I'm not in the saving-people business anymore.

Okay, I'm not saving *her* anymore.

"Welcome, man. How are you doing these days? Getting geared up for the show?"

I tighten the lid to my water canteen, my foot bouncing off my knee. "Does that count as a question?"

"Ha, that's a warm-up." He leans into his mic.

I need to pull my shit together and see through this heavy fog I dragged in here with me.

"Yeah, yeah, I'm fine, getting pumped for the show to air—recently wrapped up a class I teach at my neighborhood community center."

"Great, man, happy to hear—we're all stoked for it, too. What has it felt like being the one dude they picked for this show? I mean, the city has become foodie central—there are so many chefs to choose from. And you're the guy."

I clear my throat. This is awkward. "I feel good about it—having the opportunity to showcase the freshest ingredients and get into so many kitchens at one time. We'll reach more people than I can in a single event or tradeshow or whatever."

Spence nods the entire time I'm speaking. I can't tell if he's digging what I'm throwing down or the energy drink is kicking in.

"Do you know what dishes you'll be focusing on this first season?"

"What I can tell you is that we'll only be sourcing locally, but specific recipes are under lock. As long as we're giving the public access to real food at a reasonable cost, everything else will take care of itself, right?"

"Definitely, cool, cool. So let's get to the questions from our listeners."

I clap my hands, warming them together. "Let's do it."

The standard regulars get thrown my way. Half are about the show, the other half are about my personal life, mainly my dating situation. I say enough while dodging the details. Entertainment is part of the job, but I'm not in the mood to be generous about life outside the kitchen.

When the show's producer waves through the glass that we're clear, I place my headset down and signal to Spence with a thumbs up. I sip my water and prepare to leave. I'm used to speaking to a crowd. These radio gigs are a part of the promo and publicity tour. They're tedious, but anything to get good ratings. Good ratings equals good business. Good business guarantees I'll be restaurant-ready as soon as possible.

Rehearsals began this week, and we've completed test runs on the dishes slated for episodes one to three. I like the people I'm working with, and the hours are in and out in the morning. It's a sweet setup, and it gives me a much-needed distraction from the empty apartment that awaits me every night.

Spence reaches across the desk to shake my hand before I can stand up. "Thanks for coming in. Let's have you on again once the show is live."

"Thank you." I tilt my head back along the swivel chair. I mull over the words I spewed across the airwaves . . . one blatant lie stands out—fine. I think I said it ten times. Sure, menus still got made. Network execs are happy. But the minute I step out these doors, I'm facing that it's been anything but fine.

But I've come to a conclusion on my night walks around the city that this is what *fine* does to a person. It convinces you that everything is as it should be. As *she* decided it would be. And once a decision is made, you have to swim in its fineness, whether you're drowning or not.

Sometimes you don't realize how not fine you are until you're consumed by something or someone. That's what happened when I met Chelsea for the third time, which turned out to be our last. I know her well enough to believe she wouldn't call—she'd keep to her word—but that didn't stop me from reaching for the phone every day, or staring at the hourglass, still on its side, waiting patiently, not ready to give up. Some days, I walk to the park where she danced in the rain. I was so annoyed with myself for not being able to keep my head on straight in that moment.

She said she missed me, and every ounce of anger I had melted away. There was this flooding sense of desire to own that I had missed her too. I had missed her more than I could bear at times. I wanted to take her in my arms and never let go. And then I did the exact opposite of what I was feeling, overwhelmed by how easily I could forgive the past, and determined to not let her back into my life again.

None of that holds a candle to how much I miss her now.

She kept convincing herself that time wasn't on our side. And she never once wanted to come up with a plan. Pissed that I'd convinced myself that if she fell in love with the city again, she'd fall in love with herself in the process. I'd be lying if that plan on some subconscious level didn't include falling in love with me, too.

I'd never known anyone as scared as Chelsea. Afraid of herself and what others thought.

When she left my apartment the next morning, I wrecked my knuckles boxing. I tried to function doing what I always do, but my usual routine overwhelms me now. Everything reminds me of her—her shampoo, her fingerprints, the extra butter in the damn fridge. She's all over this city. It's suffocating.

Intellectually, I understand her choice, even if I don't agree with it.

I even respect her choice, though it splits me in half.

So, I don't call. I don't look for her. I carry on.

My fist slams into the swinging doors of the station, bruising on the way out, barely denting the ache in my head. The gym, work, and even time temporarily scratches the itch. These months have forced me to admit something to myself—

that *fine* is not fine at all, and no small effort is going to change that.

"It's a joy to see you, Seth," Mom says, cupping my face with warm hands. "Was the flight turbulent? You look tired."

"The flight was . . ." I stop myself from using my default word. I promised myself mid-air that I'm dumping the word *fine*. If I can't be honest by thirty-one, I'm headed in the wrong direction. "Hello, miss." I grab the server's attention. She acknowledges Mom with a smile, and then it fades when she looks at me, probably due to the scowling crease between my brows that has taken up permanent residence on my face. I attempt to rub it out with my thumb. "I'd like an Earl Grey with lemon and sugar, a splash of milk, and . . ." I pause, quickly glancing over the limited breakfast menu, "a waffle benedict, please."

"Sure, thing. And for you, ma'am?" she asks.

"The pancakes with berries for me, thank you, Summer," Mom replies, checking the sleeves of her heather-gray sweater.

I glance up at the server's emerald green name tag with gold lettering, and my shoulders tighten as she writes down our order. *You've gotta be fucking joking.*

"Haven't been back to this city since I left," I gripe, staring out the window at New York. I don't hate it here, but the pit in my stomach reminds me of what this place once meant in my life and who I left it for.

"It's been too long since we've done this. Thanks for meeting me on my layover, sweetie. How's home? Fog lifted yet? We miss having the house there."

"How's Ajay?" I ask, circumventing anything to do with where I'm coming from and why.

As if I could even forget for a second.

"Is this jet lag?" Mom's expression sours. "You never miss a name, and you barely spoke to our waitress like she was a person."

You mean the innocent bystander who has the same name as Chelsea's mother?

I lean into the table, uncertain what's about to fall out of my mouth, when Summer, helpful but with horrible timing, appears by our side, placing our drinks on the table.

My chin angles in her direction, and I push my hair away from my face. "Thank you, Summer."

She walks away smiling.

I stir my tea.

"Ajay's enjoying retirement." Mom carries the conversation. "Building model airplanes. Getting glue everywhere." She beams, lines curling around her eyes and along her cheeks. She's wearing the same mauve lipstick she's always worn, but now it sticks a little to the front of her teeth, and I have to remind her it's there.

She laughs quietly behind a paper napkin as she blots the enamel. "I've seen these new lip stains at Macy's. They're supposed to last twelve hours. I should try them for longer flights."

"You look lovely, Mom. You always do." Her short hair curves around her face, brushing the top of her light blue blouse underneath her sweater.

"Thank you, darling. Oh, here we are," she says as Summer delivers our orders.

I scan the table for syrup for Mom's pancakes and to dip my waffle in.

"Excuse me, do you have any maple syrup?"

"No sir, not today. We have jam. Would you like me to bring you that?"

"No syrup?" I can't fathom that condiment not being a staple and someone jacking up the dry goods order.

"We also have powdered sugar. Would you like that as a substitute?"

"No. I do not want jam or powdered sugar." I drop my head into my hands.

"Seth, are you all right? I'm sorry," she whispers to Summer.

Why can't this woman have any other name?

Summer's not taking the hint. "Powdered sugar is sweet and light. A great option—a favorite, actually. It might sound like an odd choice for a benedict, but I assure you, lots of butter and powdered sugar will do the trick."

"No fucking butter and powdered sugar, Summer," I grit through clenched teeth.

"Sir?"

"Seth," Mom scolds.

"I'm so sorry." I rebound as quickly as I can. *What's happening to me?* "I'll have a BLT. Can I have that instead?"

"Should I take the waffle benedict back?"

"No, I'll pay for that, too. Actually, forget the BLT. This is enough. Jam is fine. I'm fine. It's fine."

Summer backs up slowly, and I return to my window gazing, cursing my plan to meet Mom like this. I thought the gridded streets and great food would help. But Chelsea's everywhere because she's a part of me.

"Seth, should I be worried?" I focus on the narrow lines above her lip—they're more pronounced with age. "Do you want to share something?"

I sigh, cracking my knuckles under the table.

All of Chelsea's words haunt me, but the one thing I can't get out of my head is the comparison she made. That my helping other women was motivated by some kind of need to fix the past, because the eleven year-old version of me couldn't save my mom from herself. My teeth tap together as I gather the strength to ask the one question I'm most terrified to learn the answer to, but whatever it is, I'm not a scared kid anymore —I'll handle it. "Did you want to die that day?"

She brings her hands across the table, reaching for mine. I meet her halfway across the grainy wood surface. "Oh, Seth." Her shoulders fall on her exhale. "I don't think I was in a state of mind to know what I wanted. My depression had been worsening. There were good days and bad days, but I didn't know how serious it had gotten. I remember decorating your cake, licking blue frosting off my thumb, and then the center of my chest caves in, like a meteor shot right through me, and it was too big, and I was too fragile, and everything suddenly went dark. I don't know if I'll ever have a clear story to explain what I was thinking, but on that bathroom floor . . . all that mattered, all I wanted, was for the pain to stop."

"I just don't get how you can't remember every detail." I say that, but I'm jealous. I could use some forgetting right about now. One exhale that doesn't include Chelsea Bell.

Mom clears her throat. "I recalled later that he'd told me he wasn't happy and didn't see a future with me anymore."

That sounds familiar. I scrape my upper lip between my teeth. My eyes fill.

She squeezes my fingers in her brittle grasp, her apologetic eyes are transparent and remorseful. "I'm so sorry I couldn't talk about it. And when I finally could, you seemed okay to me. You were at college, had a social life, making headway with your goals. Parenting doesn't come with a manual."

Doesn't come with a manual . . . Chelsea's exact words. I shove the memory into a locked compartment, understanding now what Chelsea had meant about helping other women—that the woman sitting across from me had hurt me long before she ever did. "My birthday was the first time I thought I lost you. Then, when the towers went down, I was on-campus, and the entire quad was flooded in silence. All I could think of was losing you—again. You remember the rest—six hours straight of me calling you, Ajay, and the airline, reaching voicemails and busy signals."

"It was horrible. Flights were grounded. Airlines and staff were managing the chaos and consoling passengers. But you didn't need to worry about me. I was safe."

"You say that as if I had a choice. I wasn't just any college student on September eleventh. I was a kid paralyzed with fear because I always felt responsible for your life. How I could've told you not to work that day. How I could've been there to stop you from flying." Overdue tears make their way down my cheeks, losing traction in my beard. "If only I had never left that afternoon to meet Chelsea. You wouldn't have hurt yourself. I would've stopped it. I could've saved you."

She nods her head, still brave enough to face me. "No, Seth. You wouldn't have been able to save me. I could only do that for myself." Her eyes are swollen from a grief that's old and heavy. "Can you do that for yourself now, Seth? Can you see a therapist to talk about it?"

"I don't know." Once I knew Mom was safe in New York, I quit school and packed it all up for my city and my girl. To travel across the country and find out only one had waited for me. "That time of my life, I was so sure about getting back to my roots. I didn't want to manage a hotel—I wanted to cook real food, make it accessible, help people from the inside, you know? I really believed food could heal, and I wanted to do it my way." And for Chelsea. She had stopped returning my calls, went silent on email. Something had happened, and I had to come home. I wasn't going to let her slip away.

"So let me ask you—knowing what you know now, how things have turned out, do you regret your choices and your experiences? Not what happened to you, we have little control ever in that, but the life you've lived because of it."

I'd like to pretend this is solely about our history, but everything my mom is saying has Chelsea written all over it. Chelsea said she couldn't love me because loving someone must exist in the act. So for me, the greatest act of love I could give her was letting go. "I don't regret any of it. Not for a second."

She leans back. We both do.

"Does the pain of losing the person you love ever quit?" I ask.

"Over time, the sharpness dulls, and the longing doesn't stick to your lungs. Eventually, I replaced the emptiness from your father's absence, and it faded altogether." She lets my hands slip from hers.

I bring them under the table, pressing my palms over my pants.

"Replaced it with what?" I ask, confused, desperate to follow any yellow brick road if it makes me feel less shitty than I do right now.

Coffee splashes over the edge of her cup onto her saucer. Mom removes her shaky hand from the handle and unzips her purse. "He asks about you." She passes me a piece of floral stationery with a Nevada address scribbled on it. "If what you're saying is true, that you don't regret your life, consider that as good as any place to begin."

"Begin what?"

"Forgiveness. We aren't here on this earth forever, Seth. You should give your dad a call."

34

CHELSEA

"*N*eed anything before I head out?" Steph asks me, gathering her purse and coat. We've been meeting weekly to hang out. Sometimes with our kids, and others, like today, it's moms' night-in, working on recipes together, attempting the ones they'll be less resistant to. Steph's a shark in the kitchen when it comes to improvising, and I'm managing to burn things less and less.

"Call you later." I give a wave and a smile.

"Hey, are these yours?"

I close the cabinet, tossing a floral dish towel over my shoulder. A sheltered chuckle escapes as I meet Steph in the front hallway. "I was playing around with depth perception in these."

"They're beautiful," she insists. "I love the colors." She picks up one of the images I developed this week. "I remember having one of these sand-things, but never seen one with multiple colors, and these swirl patterns are fire. Why can't I remember their name?"

"Hourglass." I brush my thumb over the film, remembering the way Seth would trace figure-eights over my body. "Sometimes, I try to count the grains of sand."

"To torture yourself?" A low rumble reverberates through Steph as her shoulders bounce. "Some things are impossible to measure." She holds the photo into the light. "What's the fascination here?"

"Well, they're timeless." I sigh, my vision clouding. "Anyway, I've tried needlepoint, rehabbing vintage radios—nothing's sticking. But this keeps me busy, and it's been fun scouring antique stores outside of town, like treasure hunting."

"You have a gift, girl."

"They're just me playing around. And it's yours. Keep it." I smile at being able to offer Steph something. She's the most selfless person I know, and her friendship has kept my head up.

"I know exactly where I'm putting it in my office." She wraps her scarf around her neck and slips on her jacket, crossing the landing to the front steps. "Hey, you know we can talk about it. You just let me know."

The outside light illuminates the path to her car. "I don't know what you mean."

"What's behind all this newfound hobbying you're doing?"

I shrug and lean against the door frame. The night air nips at my toes.

"You can call him. He'll answer."

I blow a kiss and hold myself as a chilly breeze passes by. "Text when you make it home."

"Always do. Night, babe."

The sky's foggy—not a star in sight—and I take a moment, breathing in the promise of fall.

There's a lot in life I haven't mastered yet, in addition to these random crafts I've tinkered with. Like how to lose a best friend.

Not a day passes without reminders. I pick up the phone to tell him a funny story or ask a question. I squeeze my pillow tighter. I lose time staring at nothing.

He knew the parts of me I had forgotten. I knew him, too.

It's a large city and a small world. And there aren't many places to hide.

I made the rules. I should be able to follow them.

A drop of water lands on my cheek, mixing in with the evidence that thinking about Seth still hurts. There are no words to measure his absence in my life. I keep trying. Trying hurts, too.

Saturday's rush is winding down, and I'm packing up the remaining jars while Nan keeps on me about my future. As if I'm not running circles around the same orange cones in my head, I don't need a referee, especially one wearing floor-length faux fur in broad daylight.

"Those kids deserve a mom who's happy," she mentions for the third time in under an hour.

"I'm not unhappy, Nan. I'm in flux."

"You need to fall in love." She clears her throat for emphasis.

"Real subtle. I've already been in love."

"You think after Papa died that I stopped falling in love? Put down that jar and come here."

I squat down to meet her at eye level, running my fingers through the silver synthetic fibers of her coat. Nan takes my chin in her soft hands, and the malleable pads of her fingertips conform along my jawbone. I lift my gaze, meeting salon-styled curls and sincerity in her eyes.

"The minute you stop falling in love, with plants, places . . . with people and with yourself, you might as well shrivel up. This attitude is mediocre—it's settling—and it's not a good look on you."

"My children make me happy. It's what I do well." My knees

can't support the weight of my body when the internal foundation is faltering.

"Motherhood's *one piece*. You're a whole person. If I truly believed you were happy, I wouldn't say anything. But I know you better than that. I remember everything. I remember who you were before marriage and kids. I remember you with him. Do you remember?"

My fingers freeze in her coat.

"Time waits for no one, Chels."

"What did you just say?" *Seth had said those words the last night we were together.*

"I don't care what you have to do—go thrift shopping, take a class, *capture it all*, but do something. I love you, more than my own heartbeats, but don't come back here next weekend. Don't show up and settle anymore for the same old story. Go out there, take some damn risks, and fall in love."

"Nan," I object. "I know you want what's best for me."

"Good. Then the question you have left to ask yourself is, do you want what's best for you? Now, go get yourself a cup of coffee and a cherry scone." She hands me two five-dollar bills and waits for me to stick out my tongue for a cherry drop.

I accept the gesture because I have no other choice and nothing left to say. Gathering my bag and camera, I head a few blocks over to Café Blue Eyes.

Capture it all.

The two afternoons we spend with Molly have become some of my favorite hours of the week. She's incredibly patient with Jonah, and he's thriving. Breakdowns that used to tear us to shreds are becoming manageable. As Jonah learns about himself and develops his coping strategies, I learn more about my strengths.

Molly bridges a gap I didn't know existed between my son and myself. We're communicating from a place of connection, and as the weeks progress, I step further away from the blame I was inflicting on myself—that my failures were making my children's lives harder.

"Chelsea." Molly approaches me at the end of today's session. "Jonah, five minutes to play while I chat with your mom."

"How'd it go?" I ask.

"Great. I know he's still having a hard time when things seem unfair in his routine. It's okay to give him some buy-in and flexibility with the list."

"Brushing teeth is still a battle." I tuck my hair behind my ear.

"There may be too many steps. Have you considered doing it at a different time? He's probably tired right before bed."

I hadn't thought of deviating from our planned routine. In part out of fear. The routine's what keeps me anchored. "It can be overwhelming, all that fury coming from such a small person. I sometimes have to put myself in time-out so I can respond versus react in the heat of the moment."

She looks at Jonah with a nurturing smile and returns her attention to me. "I wish more adults would put themselves in time-out. You're ahead of the game by modeling to Jonah how to take space when you need it. It helps us to remind ourselves that anger's a secondary emotion."

"Sorry, what does that mean?" I shift in my chair, finding the material unbearably itchy.

"You ever hear someone say, 'I didn't mean what I said when I was angry'? Anger often surfaces when we're sad, masking the primary emotion. If you remain curious enough to find out how that person was feeling, usually, not always, you'll learn they were feeling hurt. When kids are taught over and over again that their feelings are too unmanageable or not accepted, they adopt other strategies to express themselves—to cope."

"You're saying that pain is behind anger?"

"Exactly. Jonah needs you to listen and help him feel safe. Sometimes that will look like providing space, but only if he asks for it. Otherwise, I recommend sitting with him until the feelings pass. Jonah's not meant to go through these confusing emotions alone."

I chew on the inside of my cheek, shifting again, peeking over at the block tower Jonah's building. "That helps so much, Molly. Really, thank you."

When we enter the car, Jonah asks for the music before his seatbelt's secured. He loves music, and some of the ways we now build our relationship are on these drives home—rocking out to my old CDs. He plays imaginary guitar. Sometimes I sing. He'll ask me about the bands.

"Louder, Mom."

I flip on my turn signal, pulling out of the hospital garage. My heart trips over a beat when the piano keys seep through the speakers.

Drums roll in and the melody fills the car. The lead singer's gritty voice settles in my ears and fills my limbs with helium. My hands slip down the steering wheel. I'm weightless, letting the strings of the guitar lift me up, tapping my foot gently over the accelerator. I don't fight the wave of words, as if he's speaking them to me himself. They enter and compress my chest in their longing plea and exit achingly slow. As the vocals increase in speed and volume, I pretend I'm strong enough to survive listening to this song.

He passes me the CD, slipping from his fingers to mine, undeniable electricity in the exchange. Swinging in the warm rain, dancing to silent lyrics, barefoot in the park.

I'm blinking to see through the fog in front of me, blinking at the red octagon . . . appearing out of nowhere. I slam on the breaks, shooting pain crashes into my knee, and my torso thrashes against my buckle. I bash my shaking fingers over the CD player, hitting buttons until the music stops. I need it to stop.

I whip around to check on Jonah. "Are you okay?" I say through shallow breathing.

He gives me a perplexed look, perfectly unharmed, not a hair out of place. "I like that song. Put it back."

"I can't," I tell him, cracking the window. A rush of air fills my lungs. Someone lays on their horn behind us, and I exhale enough to steady my fingers, wrapping them around the leather once again and cautiously accelerate across the lane. Maybe even a little slower.

Music has always been a gateway to Seth.

Where there's music, there's memories.

Where there's memories, there's missing him.

During the time I was married to Paul, of course Seth crossed my mind, but I was immersed in my life, and Paul preferred talk radio. Music collected dust during those years.

I never wanted to be with Seth while I was married to Paul, but things with Seth had always been different. Whenever we crossed paths, it was like reuniting with a missing piece of myself.

It's been months and months, but since that door opened, I haven't been able to shut it, and I've tried.

When we pull up to our house, Jonah runs inside to play a video game my dad bought him, and I stay in the car to collect myself, to assess if there's any damage to the radio, and to rewind the bridge.

The flow of adrenaline has steadied, and flashes of the past year with Seth play like visions in my rearview mirror.

His smile finding me under that child's desk.

His touch slipping me out of my own discomfort.

His mouth encouraging me to try. To just try.

The soft blend of piano keys releases, and it occurs to me as light rain trickles down the windshield, you have to want something. It's not enough to be talented if you don't want it—aren't committed to it.

Seth helped me see that it isn't solely one thing I love about life—it's all the details. Everything we see and experience funnels through both light and dark. The process exposes what makes the world shine.

He was giving me a chance to discover the city. Beneath that, he was hoping it would lead me back to what inspired me. He had us chasing all over town, but it wasn't about where we went that mattered. It was how I captured it.

I'm not like my mom. I don't want to be in front of the camera. I want to be behind it.

"There's no use in hiding it," Foster remarks.

I snort-laugh at another pair of mismatched socks.

"So, you're back," he greets me as I snag a seat up front. "I wondered if that was the same Chelsea Bell on my roster."

"It's me." I flash a smile and pull out my new notebook and pencil bag. Last night, Steph gave me embossed pencils, each containing an encouraging message, as a "set yourself up for success" gift. However, I'm thinking she wasn't completely transparent with me as I read the messages.

Orange: "salty and sweet."

Green: "naughty vibes."

Yellow: "courageous cougar."

I mask a gasp, coughing into my elbow. She knew I'd be nervous.

"Festive pencils."

I angle their messages from prying eyes, then look up. "I didn't realize you were teaching this class."

"It pays the bills." He winks, chuckling at himself for making a finance joke, which I catch. "Does your taking this class mean you know what career you want to go into?"

I choose the yellow pencil and flip open the notebook to a fresh page. "It does."

35

CHELSEA

2015

*L*ast night, Paige brought up attending drama school. The idea of my kiddo on this stage triggers painful childhood memories. But I maintained composure, listening with an encouraging smile as she went through the application materials. She's ready to take life by the reins—and while I'm her biggest cheerleader, I'm also chewing my inner cheek to shreds, simply unprepared for time to be so swift.

Spring in the city is my happy place. The pavement at my feet, mile by mile, to the top of the hill. My stride's steadily improving, training to run the marathon in July.

I had to accept the changes in my body as it aged, learning how to work with it, not against it. Running was never really about qualifying. It was about forcing a goal—to prove to my parents that I could accomplish something for them to be proud of. In my twenties, that decision was the first real step I made in taking a chance on myself, even if the motivation was misguided. But as a parent, I get it—sometimes, we make choices to survive the here and now.

Luxuries, like reflection and acceptance, come with perspective, and perspective takes experience. I made a lot of life decisions without experience, but like someone wise once told me, *it all had to happen exactly as it did* so I can be where I am now—that's perspective, and it always comes at a cost.

Answering a muse has made for an interesting few years. I'm lucky that my creative outlet found a home in photography, which has given me financial independence.

Once I embraced the thing I was passionate about, my career bloomed, and that satisfaction trickled into every part of my world, including running, and time for myself outside of home and work. I don't need a medal or ribbon. I don't have to be the best at it, either. I'm having fun, waking up before my alarm clock and my mom's morning calls—excited to be back on these slanting sidewalks and winding roads.

Movement is an exercise in letting my shadow tag along. On foggy days, I barely notice her, but today, with the sun directly above, she's right beside me.

We all have pasts, places in ourselves that follow us. For so long I tried to dodge my shadow, staying out of the light as often as I could. I looked in the mirror only to cover up my failures and flaws.

I push far right so a couple in their matching maroon tracksuits can pass.

My shadow isn't so scary anymore.

I've kinda gotten used to her, like with so many things I've little to no control over—my brisket that always comes out as dry as my hair in winter, and my kids growing up. I definitely couldn't control diagnoses, or my own brain as a child.

There's power in adjusting your lens.

As the breeze chills my damp skin, I chug water and wipe my sleeve across my forehead. I answer my phone on the first ring when I see it's the gallery calling.

"Are you sitting down, Chelsea?" Hattie, the owner, asks in a whispered register. She's quiet enough that classical music from the gallery floor is audible in the background.

"I'm never sitting down." I bend at the hip, stretching after my run.

Her nails tap on her desk. The clicking sound is unmistakable from the first night we met for drinks two years ago when she tapped her martini glass with onyx-painted nails. Hattie's a generation older than me and a pro at two things: art and people. She's married to a client of Paul's, and when I told him I was serious about selling my photography, he set us up. We've been working together ever since. I manage my art. Hattie manages me.

"You may want to find something to hang onto because what I'm about to say is fall on your ass—get ready for it—big news."

My pulse climbs back to racing. "Tell me before I stop breathing."

"*Memory Lane* sold."

"What do you mean, it sold?" I clear my throat, suddenly bone dry in denial.

"I mean every single print sold," she shrieks, enunciating each word like dropping individual sandbags off the pier one at a time, each splash louder than the last.

"That's impossible. Sold. Like sold, sold?" My thoughts speed up. "I mean, how many times can I say 'sold' in a sentence? They've only been up for a week. Wait, we haven't even had the show yet, and we've been prepping for months. Are you sure?" I take a breather, resting my shivering body on a nearby bench. The metal's surface seeps through the thin material of my leggings. I split my sweaty bangs in half, brushing them away from my forehead.

"I've never seen anything like this." She's talking quickly, rushing me off the call. "Not that your work isn't divine, and people like local artists, but in this amount of time, even before your debut event . . ."

"Why are you acting so strange?"

"I'm not. Chelsea, you okay?"

"I'm in shock, honestly." I exhale hard. "What happens next?"

A quick and heavy laugh expels from her scratchy voice. "You celebrate. Gotta run. The buyer's here, and I need to wrap up the sale. We'll talk soon." The line goes dead.

I've got more questions. Like a million.

"Is the blindfold necessary? Not that I don't appreciate a well-planned accessory, but this may be excessive. How about I promise to keep my eyes closed."

"How else can we surprise you," Paige says.

"It's necessary," Paul adds, supporting Paige.

"I don't like surprises." I remind them.

"The kids wanted to do this for you."

"We're close," Paul's fiancée, Hannah, guides me into a space with a gentle hand on my back. My other hand's being squeezed in Jonah's grasp.

Paul and Hannah have been living together for two years, and she's been an important addition to Paul's life and the kids'. We get along well and she's a yoga instructor, which has given Jonah lots of opportunity for movement.

The unmistakable clash of glass colliding with ceramic fills my ears. Upbeat rock plays low enough I can't make out the song, but it gives this place a welcoming feel. Reminds me of the natural hum of a baseball park before the main event. Inviting light teases the material around my eyes.

My smile melts as my nose makes contact with the aromas in the air. Garlic, butter, something acidic and sweet. I'm chasing the scent to wherever it's coming from because I'm suddenly starving. "We're definitely in a restaurant, and if we aren't, we need to leave immediately and find one."

"Watch your step, Chelsea," Paul says from behind me.

Legs of a chair scrape as Jonah helps me settle into a soft cushion. Nan's cackle breaks through the mix of unknown voices, scents, and conversations.

"Can I take this thing off now, please?"

"Nan?" Jonah asks.

"Do as you like, dear."

I yank the silk tie away from my eyes, blinking to adjust my vision. My smile returns as each face in my family comes into view around the table. Jonah to my left, and Paige on my right. Hannah's sitting with perfect posture between Jonah and Paul, and Nan's leaning triumphantly in the chair next to Paige, across from me.

There's a tabletop spread of balloons and roses and daisies. Quite the scene for us. Usually we stay home for celebrations. Menus are tricky for Jonah, and I spend most of the day in the city for work, so I like being home with the kids at night.

"You orchestrate all this?" I'm jealous of Nan's sweating Manhattan.

Her rosy cheeks lift and she sips her drink, ignoring my question.

Hannah waves and hands me a small blue bag with a gold ribbon. "Happy Birthday, Chelsea."

"You didn't have to."

Hannah's face falls.

I rebound quickly because the gesture's thoughtful, and I'm learning how to accept attention and gifts. "This is lovely. Thank you."

Paul reaches around Hannah, ruffling Jonah's hair.

"Dad, I styled it," he groans, flattening his wiry locks with the palm of his hand.

The space is cozy and bright, upscale but welcoming like a diner—soft earth-tone seating, glossy oak tables, and natural light from large windows. Greenery in colorful ceramic pots hang from a muraled ceiling. "Have you been to this place before?" I ask, looking out the windows at the front of the restaurant with a clear shot of the street.

"Not yet, but it's been hyped up in my foodie Facebook group, and I'm shocked Nan got us reservations." Hannah's auburn hair shines against the sunset behind her.

"Seems I've got a few tricks up my sleeve left." Nan teases me with her cocktail.

"Can you magically get us a round of drinks?" I wink.

She glances over my shoulder, probably trying to grab our server's attention.

"Seriously, everyone, thank you for making my birthday extra special and going to all this trouble."

"It's not every day we get to celebrate your birthday and your show selling out," Paige squeals, with more energy than exists in my entire body.

"A first, for sure," I acknowledge.

"Definitely not the last. It's an incredible accomplishment." Paul raises his water glass. "Cheers!"

"We need real drinks to toast this occasion." Hannah lifts her brow like a turn signal, catching the eye of someone behind me—hopefully with a drink tray.

Nan's smirking into her glass, fishing out the maraschino cherry, noticeably avoiding looking at me.

"Hi, there. We're ready for celebratory beverages, please," Hannah boasts.

"You came to the right place," the server greets us. "Welcome to The Playground."

My fingertips tingle on the water glass as my eyes dart to the nearest emergency exit. It's behind me. Of course it's behind me.

I refuse to look, even though I can now clearly inhale who's behind me. I'm staring hard at Nan, willing her to fess up, but she's all starry pupils right above my messy bun—that I threw on top of my head because no one informed me where we were going.

You can do this, Chels. Just breathe.

I want to slide under this newly polished tabletop and disappear, but there's no time. This is happening, and not how I imagined it would. In my daydreams, I was prepared. In my imagination, I was calm and collected, and my heart and sweat glands weren't betraying me. I did my hair and wore a better bra.

My tingling fingers go numb, and the rest of my organs freeze. *Traitors.*

His body heat at my back runs up my spine, a static swell of energy, as my gaze rolls from the cream-colored napkin on my lap to a pair of familiar black shoes, then slacks, mounting the distance up a starched chef's coat . . . following each rounded button as they reach an exposed tan neck, a close-shaven face, solid-as-rock jaw, landing on a pair of determined eyes.

"Happy Birthday, Chels."

I cross my legs under the table. Thankfully my stomach's empty or else the contents of it would be coating his custom-made shoes. "This is yours?"

Modest joy beams from his chest and stance, and his hands slide into his pants pocket. "All mine."

The corners of my mouth play tug-of-war between elation and self-preservation. "You did it." *Of course he did.* It's one thing to believe he would and another to see he did. That it was all worth it.

"Mom, who's that?" Jonah asks, tugging my denim jacket.

"An old friend," I reply, then remember what's just gone down and shoot daggers across the table at the woman responsible for my now visible perspiration-above-my-upper-lip situation. "You knew this was Seth's place?" I accuse.

"Oh, Chef Seth! It's such an honor to meet you. I loved your show a few years ago." Hannah reaches out her hand. "Hi, I'm Hannah Katz, and this is my fiancé, Paul."

Nan's guilty grin is louder than this restaurant full of people. She chews on the cherry. "Maybe at one point," she admits casually, responding to my question. "Or perhaps, a stroke of luck," she feeds the group a line of crap, and everyone but me and, obviously, Seth, eats it up.

What would possess her to think Seth would ever want to see me again? "Which point would that be? A week ago when you made the reservation?" What must he think of me? That I'd carelessly show up and barge in on his dream like this. I mouth to Nan, "You're grounded." Then tune in to what Hannah's saying now.

"We're celebrating Chelsea tonight, but you seem to already know that. Wait, how do you two know each other?"

"Actually, Chelsea and I lived in the same neighborhood when we were kids," Seth shares.

"How wild is that?" she exclaims, her gold bangles chiming together against the table.

"Wild," I mutter under my breath.

"Chelsea, how did you not know this place was here? It's been all over socials," Hannah presses, not taking a hint.

"I guess I didn't—"

"We actually met on Chelsea's birthday," Seth interjects, rescuing me from Hannah's inquisition, and I can't begin to imagine why. Doesn't he have a kitchen to be in? Anywhere to be, other than in front of me, my eyes at his waist level, sucking all of the much-needed oxygen out of my lungs.

I laugh inwardly at how utterly ridiculous timing can be. We're at this restaurant in part to celebrate *Memory Lane* selling, and now the inspiration for that collection is here too, looking as irresistible as the cheesecake I spot at the table next to ours.

"I'll send your server over," he replies, backing away from me, his steps syncing with my counting. Seth walks over to Nan, planting a gentle kiss on her cheek—my face warms as if his lips were on me.

A woman in a fitted black spaghetti strap dress appears at Seth's side. She places her hand on his arm, squeezing slightly. His eyes drift to her wrist and up to her shoulder, passing the length of the black and gray mandala sleeve tattoo covering her arm.

She's leaning into him, knee bent, her nude lips moving slowly in his ear.

His lips curve and curl into a—he's smiling. Smiling at her. And now she's smiling at him.

My fingers gather the napkin in my lap into a tight ball. "So that drink?" I throw out, smacking my dry lips together, interrupting their little embrace and this freight train of feelings crashing the party.

The woman nods at something Seth says and turns around, grabbing two empty drink glasses off a table she walks by.

Seth addresses our group. "Drinks are on the house tonight. Enjoy your dinner, and let me know if there's anything you need," he adds, his eyes on mine.

"You and I will be speaking later," I tell Nan, with Seth out of earshot.

I release the napkin from a choking grip, wetting my lips, swallowing hard.

He's moved on. He should. I want him to be happy. Even if that can't be with—

"Chelsea, what a secret! You didn't tell us you knew a famous chef."

Paige looks down at her phone.

"Put it away," I say, shorter fused than I mean to be.

Jonah's holding the menu upside down. "Mom, can I eat anything here?"

Paul already knows his order, probably selected it online before we got here, and is waiting for the rest of us to catch up.

Just like that, drinks are delivered and everything's back to its regularly scheduled programming. Except I'm sitting in Seth's restaurant, overwhelmed by how much it feels like home.

The five bites of my meal I can stomach is everything I remember his cooking to be like—made with care. Jonah's enjoying Seth's take on chicken and waffles. Paul's eating most of the chicken. I don't think Hannah has stopped for one second to breathe and Nan leans back in her Manhattan haze.

I try to focus on my family, but I'm like a match seeking its spark. Any chance I get, I swipe my attention from the table to find Seth.

Our entrees are cleared by the same woman—hostess, I guess; girlfriend, I cringe—and she comes back to the table, relaying a message that Seth wants to give the kids a tour of the kitchen. He sends Paige and Jonah back with wide grins, paper chef's hats, and a stack of mini-pancakes on a stick. They're served with a side of warmed maple syrup, powdered sugar, and a bowl of hard butter. A simple candle stuck in the butter is placed in front of me.

He doesn't deliver dessert with the kids, and he doesn't join in as everyone sings, and he doesn't linger until I make a wish. Seth doesn't stick around at all. Not to see us resist when the server tells us the bill has been taken care of or to say goodbye.

I don't know what I expected him to do in front of all these people. Did he know I was coming? Or was he ambushed like me?

We're leaving, but my feet drag. The server thanks us for the additional tip, and Jonah grabs my hand as we walk back through the restaurant.

"Mommy, those look like your pictures." He points to a red wall we must have passed on our way in.

I follow Jonah's line of sight to the photos, tipping my head to catch the images inside the frames. I squeeze his little fingers.

"Too tight," he whimpers.

"Oh gosh, I'm sorry." I put his knuckles to my lips and kiss them, then release his hand.

Nan appears by my side. "Well, how do ya like that?"

Paul stops too. "Chelsea, you're pale."

The park. The stadium. Billy Goat Hill. Our adventures together. The hourglasses. All of it. *Every. Single. One.*

I blot the corner crease of my eyes with my sleeve.

"Mom, these are your photographs!" Paige announces to the restaurant. The full house goes silent, then erupts in applause. Jonah hugs my side. Nan rubs gentle circles on my back. I rest my head on her shoulder.

"Yes, they are."

It's not until we're out of the restaurant with the spring city air blowing our stride a few paces ahead that I take a final glance over my shoulder at Seth's dream come true—exactly as he wanted it, full of nourishment and people who leave feeling like friends. A flash of color pops into view as the door swings open and closed once more, like the sun peeking out from a cloud, a smile appearing from a frown.

He painted it yellow.

Butter yellow.

PART V

2021

SAN FRANCISCO, CALIFORNIA

"Synchronicity is an ever-present reality
for those who have eyes to see."
— C.G. Jung

36

CHELSEA

$\mathcal{I}$ leap out of my shared ride and from the blasting air-conditioning onto the sidewalk. Debris crunches under my boots, and my ankle rolls as I peel a discarded wrapper off my heel, unable to avoid a swift tunnel of dry wind that blows my hair in every direction. I push thick waves behind my ears and adjust my flannel scarf, straightening the ends.

Fall has been a welcome shift after an unbearably hot summer indoors. I've never regretted moving the kids up north out of the congestion to live in Marin, under a canopy of majestic trees, but it's good to be in the city.

When the silver sedan inches away from the curb, I remove my disposable mask, fold it in half, and slip the stiff material into my coat pocket. State restrictions are lifting here, but overall, people remain conscientious about public health.

It's been a while since I've been back, partly for this reason. I come when there's an exhibit or invitation to an event or when I need to check on Nan's. She finally agreed to live with my parents in Los Angeles—a year ago—when the world and her memory shut down, farmers' markets closed, and the Sherries had moved east to be close to their grandkids. Nan's single stipulation to moving—keep her condo exactly as she left it until the time was right.

My playlist continues to hum low in my right ear as I remove the left bud. The streets have always carried their own soundtrack, collective conversations of citizens. It's a low rumble mixed in with movement—and the cadence always takes me places.

The city isn't the same. Neither am I. Nothing ever is what it once was. But no matter how much things change, there are constants, like Karl lifting to the promise of sun. I tilt my face to absorb the gentle rays, skipping briskly along as I head to the studio.

First, I'm stopping to Café Blue Eyes for warm cherry scones. They freeze well and ship easily to L.A.

The sidewalk narrows as the sturdy maroon and white awning comes into view, the green metal tables sprawled to the curb to accommodate outdoor seating. My mouth waters in anticipation, the distinct aroma of strong coffee thick in the air.

I chose something more sophisticated for my meeting today—a woven red skirt paired with my pink blouse that Mom insists brings luck. The alternating textures of wool and silk brush against my skin, rough and cool, scraping and soothing. My hip knocks into the corner of a table as I tug at the hem of the skirt. Its unstable leg slants with ease like it's made of wet clay, and though I reach to steady the base and break my fall, the lattice metal still digs sharply into my skin, drawing blood.

"Shit," I mutter, sticking my finger in my mouth to combat the sting, removing it quickly to assess, and blow a cool breath over the tip of my pointer.

"Chelsea . . . Bell," a distinct voice runs up my arms.

It can't be. After so many years. My chest fills with air, and I lift my gaze, sliding my sunglasses down the bridge of my nose, then from my face completely, buying myself another round of inhales and exhales as his amber eyes land on mine.

"You look good," he adds, his tone scratching over every surface of my body. Not flirtatious or friendly, just a simple, matter-of-fact observation, a conclusion drawn from a hypothesis after data collection.

And from the data I'm collecting, it may be an accusation and not a compliment. His strawberry-blond stubble has morphed into a full beard, coarse and unkempt, with iridescent strands of gray peppered throughout. Equally thick hair gathers behind his ears, exposing tanned cheekbones and faded freckles. Everything about him is longer—nails, outstretched legs, lines at the corners of his mouth.

I drop into the seat across from him, my disbelief too heavy to hold, and take out my right earbud. "What are you doing here?"

His attention is laser sharp on me, and his eyelids hang over fatigued irises. "What are we ever doing anywhere?" he replies elusively.

"There's this work meeting. That's why I'm here." And I don't mean to come off so obvious. I cross my ankles and rub my palms over the ridges of my skirt.

He picks up his double espresso. "Life sure likes to bring us together." He laughs low into the steam. "Congrats on your business." He perks up. "I see your work around . . . online," he corrects himself. "It's stunning, really, Chels. You're doing the thing. As I knew you could."

My hands still. "You looked me up?"

"Yes." Another statement of fact coming from the hard line of his wet lips.

"You're not online. I've looked, too, from time to time."

"Never served me well."

The porcelain cup rattles as he places it back on the café table. The memory is old, from a time when the man sitting across from me wasn't a stranger. I have the scars on my heart to prove it. His eyes have aged, too, reflecting a hollowness I don't recall. I wonder what's put it there—what's become of the boy I once borrowed time with? *Some things haven't changed.* The pull between us is the same, strong and magnetic, like a stifled spark that finally caught enough air to go up in flames.

"I read about The Playground."

Seth's brows draw together, and I can read the resistance on his face. My mentioning his restaurant closing is unbearable to hear.

"Lockdown killed so many businesses in the neighborhood." He pulls a chrome flask from his jacket pocket and tips a brown liquid into his espresso cup.

"It's been horrible for so many people. Maybe there might be some—"

"We've always had bad timing, haven't we?" he interjects, stopping my "fix-it" train from continuing.

His words are sore reminders of my own from years ago.

All the promises I broke.

How we can't always take back the things we say.

"How's your timing now, Chels? Can you stay for a coffee?"

My fingers twist together in my lap. "I can't be late for my meeting. Rain check?"

Seth smirks into his hunter-green peacoat, covering his mouth and chin. "Sure thing," he replies, then drinks from his cup. "You still got my number?"

"You still have mine?" We both could have called but chose not to. That means something.

When my legs feel strong enough to support me, I push back the chair—the feet catching on swollen concrete. I force it back to get out. "I'll see ya," I say, pausing for courage. This is harder than I imagined, when I'd allow myself to believe it might happen, practicing in the mirror all the things I'd say and share and explain. Which amounted to what? Me losing all my words when a simple *I'm sorry* would've sufficed.

I'm unprepared for this version of Seth. He's always been a pillar for me, and this man before me is crumbling. My hands beg to reach out and collect all the pieces, to start gluing them back together.

The wind picks up again behind me, nudging my legs forward. As I walk by his shoulder, Seth's fingers wrap around my wrist, pressing into my pulse. First, I glance at his grip, his touch, tight around my bones, and then I fall down the spiral to the center of his eyes, searching for any variable of light, for the idealist I've always known.

Seth uses my wrist to pull himself to his feet.

The city takes little notice of our exchange, busying itself around our stunned faces and familiarity—our bodies a breath away from one another—the pedestrians striding past us like ghosts.

"I've got nothing left, so let me say this final thing. You could've handed me the match, Chels, told me you were going to hurt me, and I would've lit myself on fire anyway. It was my choice too. All of it. I know you. I know you'll blame yourself for something along the way. Don't do it. Live your life." He lets me go, returning to his solitude.

I arrive at my destination completely unaware of how I got there or why I'm there— forgetting all about the cherry scones.

Two weeks later, I duck out of a full house, desperate for a quiet corner. The front stoop is the one spot I find that isn't occupied by Mom and Dad, neighbors, and cousins. The overcast day has melted into an oppressive pressure of light with sparse leaves to filter out the brightness. I inhale the lingering scent of roses on my sweater.

It's all loud. The voices, the sun, the buttons on the phone as I touch them.

I straighten out my corduroy skirt and hold myself close. The receiver's ice against my ear.

He picks up on the second ring. "Chels." His tone lands tired, a sound that breaks my heart.

"Seth." I can barely utter the words. "It's Nan."

Nan's expressed wishes were to not make a fuss, which was near impossible for Mom. Though Nan and Mom were oil and water, they were also each other's kites and rocks. Nan's tenacity was Mom's tenacity. Nan's optimism was Mom's ability to chase her dreams.

"She would've loved these," Mom says, pushing past a clogged throat.

"Sterling was her favorite." I lean back against the firm white plastic chair.

"The more silver, the better." She smiles at me behind her oversized black framed sunglasses and one of Nan's wide-brimmed hats. She squeezes my hand as we each adjust our positions, settling in our seats—as best we can. Colma, known as "Cemetery City," is a few miles outside of downtown. Colma was Nan's choice.

As in life, Nan was a feisty contender until the end. She didn't let Alzheimer's steal her fuschia smile or her connection to the natural world. She spent her final months in Los Angeles with Mom, gardenside, nurturing the earth.

The Rabbi stands before us in what once must have been a stiff black suit, now well-worn—its color resembling the stub of a cigar, coated in charcoal gray like his long beard, faded at the corners and edges.

Rows of full seats hold still behind our family. I haven't

turned to see, but by the collective nerves of mourners crawling up my neck, I know she was loved.

The service will be short and simple—I've anticipated that. It's the seven days to follow that I've been preparing myself for. It will take endurance to sit shiva. The eye contact, silence, covered mirrors, the formality of death, the finality of life, the forever path of a soul.

Nan's name coming from the solemn man in front of me is comforting, his voice steady, and I hang on to every word. We've spent the past twenty-four hours answering questions, sharing who Nan was. His somber tone projects sincerity, convincing me that as little as he knew Nan, he's still present in our grief.

"Rose Leah Hahn, also known to those who loved her most as 'Nan,' shared her life with her beloved Myron for forty beautiful years, raising their daughter, Summer Bell, and is survived by her granddaughter Chelsea Bell, and her great-grandchildren, Paige and Jonah Jacobs. Nan made friends wherever she went, and aside from her family, her greatest joy was her garden. You'd always find Nan's hands busy. Her daughter tells us that Rose would say, 'Busy hands, clear head.' This motto in life led to a second career for Rose with her company Rainy Days, which she successfully ran with the help of Chelsea. Chelsea is going to share a few words."

I release Mom's gloved hand, smiling at Paige and catching Jonah's eye. Paul nods in support, next to Hannah, both of their arms wrapped around their three-year-old twin boys. My legs wobble as I rise. My dad stands with me, offering me his arm, walking me over to Nan's pine casket.

Dizziness seeps from my head to my chest, standing in front of Nan and not beside her.

The paper in my hand shakes, and the notes I wrote blend into one large black hole. I crumple the page and hold it tight in my grasp.

"Hello." I clear my throat, swallowing the stickiness. "I'm at a loss for words seeing so many wonderful friends of Nan's here to honor her life. What a testament to the way she lived. Whether you knew her as a friend or family or the jam lady, I promise Nan knew you. And she'd be tickled you're here and also aggravated that we aren't already back at the house eating. But that was Nan. If you were in her company, you were fed, usually with something sweet. Which is fitting for Nan, as she was the sweetest person I knew—never a harsh word for anyone." I sigh, considering the connection we all have here today, our stories crossing because of this one person.

My swollen voice evens out as I continue. "It wasn't just about the sweets for Nan—she savored. She'd sit with the same Manhattan until the ice melted fully. In a world that seems to be chasing shiny new objects, Nan knew the importance of holding on to what you've got. Didn't matter what it was: jars, leftovers, letters, books, these little tins she always kept around —nothing went to waste. Maybe that's because she was raised in the Great Depression. Maybe that's why she went into the preserves business . . . in the long life she lived, she witnessed so much change, she wanted to preserve what mattered most. And when she wasn't able to remember, all those things she somehow knew to hold onto, they helped us to remember for her. No one, and I mean no one, was as lucky as I was to have had so much time with someone I love, respect, and treasure. She taught me . . ." I scan the rows of people, collecting my thoughts, slipping into sadness as particles of dust and moisture fill the sky.

Behind the rows of chairs, my gaze lands on Seth leaning against a tree, out of view, in black slacks, a black-button down, and a leather jacket. A bouquet of daisies hangs upside down in his hand. His sunglasses are propped on top of his thick hair. A faint smile attempts to break through, quickly dissolving.

He's here. *He's here.* My heart.

Seth's words from so long ago surface. *Find me, any time, in any place. Find me, and I'll remind you.*

I straighten my spine, adjusting my voice to break through my stuffy nose.

"She taught me," I return my gaze to Seth, letting warm tears fall, "that we never say goodbye to the people we love. That the world carries on with or without us, and we have a duty to capture the time we're given and grow something from it. She taught me about sacrifice and forgiveness. To never leave home without five dollars. And you always have time for a cup of coffee. That no matter how much time passes, if there's still time, there's still hope. We were so lucky to have her rose-colored lens on life, and there won't be a day moving forward where she'll not be in our hearts and in our memories." I place my hand on my chest. "Nan, you gave me the courage to hold fiercely to this one precious life. I already ache for your laughter and miss your buttered toast and salon gossip. I promise to keep my hands in the dirt and my head in the clouds. Well, I promise I'll try." My voice collapses.

We observe a moment of silence. A collective exhale rises, and when Seth closes his eyes, I give him his privacy, dropping my chin, struck by the dew sticking to the front of my shoes. I walk back to my empty seat.

A breeze picks up across our laps as Nan's casket is lowered into the ground. The Mourner's Kaddish prayer is being recited in Hebrew. Jonah fiddles with the torn black ribbon pinned to his suit jacket and fumbles over the words. Paige has her hands locked in her lap, trembling chin lifting to the clouds. Mom and Dad's voices stand out from mine, *the few lines I memorized from childhood.*

The Rabbi invites the immediate family up first to honor Nan at the close of the service. My parents step up to the pile of soft soil. Dad leaves the shovel upright where he found it, and I lift the wood handle, still warm from his turn.

I fight closing my eyes. I know we will be okay without Nan, but it doesn't mean I want to be okay without her. *One, two, three, four . . .*

It never feels like enough time. Not when there's love still left to be shared.

The tip of the metal breaks through the tiny mountain of dirt. I level the shovel with the ground and twist my wrist. *Five, six, seven . . .* three scoops and three twists . . . *eight.*

Seth hangs back as everyone disperses. His hair is combed and tucked behind his ears. On my approach, I notice the dark hue under his eyes. I stop at the tree, the thud of dirt as it made contact with the casket echoing in my ears. "Thank you for coming."

Seth hands me the flowers. "You have her laugh." He smiles.

I nod and smile back, thinking of Nan's infamous cackle. "She adored you."

"Feeling's mutual."

"Have you got any leads on a new restaurant?"

Seth kicks at the grass beneath him. "I don't have the capacity to start again."

"There must be a way," I quietly object.

Calm and resolute, Seth responds, "That dream's done, Chelsea. I've let it go. Accepted it."

It can't be done. I can't accept this, even if his eyes are begging me to. "Do you want to come back to the house? There's more food than we know what to do with."

"I don't think that's a good idea."

Grief is an unreliable companion. I should only be thinking about Nan, not about the woman from his restaurant all those years ago, wondering what came of that chapter. I don't ask about where he's living now either, even though that's my following thought.

"Oh. Of course. I didn't mean to assume—"

Seth's attention shifts to my right. "Hello."

"Chef, good to see you, apart from the circumstances," Steph says, appearing at my side. "Are you ready?" The car keys jingle in her hand. She wraps her arm around my waist and drops her head on my shoulder. "I'll be in the car."

"Bye, Steph," he replies, his deep voice embedding in my heart.

"Thank you for being here. It means the world to us."

He reaches for my hand, interlacing our fingers. He leans into me. His soap and citrus scent stings the back of my throat. Seth's minty breath tickles my cheek. He holds his lips there, right against my heated skin. It takes all of my strength not to root my limbs in place.

"Be well, Chels Bells," he whispers and turns away from me, striding across the lawn.

A week later, I find myself in Seth's lobby, asking Freddy for a favor—to let me up even though Seth ignored my last phone call and text.

I'm not trying to pretend like I'm a part of his life like an ex-girlfriend who can't let go, but there's no way I can exist in a world where Seth's suffering and not help in some way.

Just because our relationship ended, it doesn't mean I won't always care about him. Some friendships and people are non-refundable.

He told me to live my life and he came to Nan's and said goodbye, and he meant it. I haven't been able to rest, not knowing if he's okay.

So, yeah, I don't entirely have a plan here as I ring the bell and knock.

Seth answers barefoot, peeking his head through the slit in the door. "Go home, Chels."

My face tightens, and I push through a pestering urge to

obey his request. "I'm here for that rain check coffee." I tread softly. "One cup."

He rakes his hand through his hair and opens the gap for me to enter. Seth shoves his hands in his pockets and walks ahead of me, his classic cotton T-shirt loosely hanging on his shoulders.

I follow the sound of his thundering steps in the dark hallway, behind his shadow, moving toward the kitchen, departing from our intended path when a flickering glow in Seth's room catches in my periphery. Squinting, trying to make sense of what's pulling my spine straight as I walk into his room, dimly lit by a single bedside lamp.

My fingertips numb at the sight. I take a full sweep with my eyes, confirming what I'm seeing. The basics are here—bed, dresser, nightstand, lamp.

Everything else—gone.

The walls are bare. Memorabilia. Books. Floor lamp in the corner. All gone, but the hourglass he had made, positioned on its side, alone on an empty shelf—light disappearing over its surface like the final moments of a sunset, where a deep orange sky burns into a black horizon.

He's here. The hairs on my neck inform me as Seth's exhale grazes my cheek.

"Snooping. A new hobby you've picked up?" He passes me a glass of water. "I'm out of coffee."

"Are you moving?" My stomach drops. *Please tell me you're moving.*

"This is the only home I have. I'm not leaving." He adjusts the hourglass.

"So you sold everything else just to keep it? That doesn't make sense to me."

Seth laughs, not tender or satisfied. This laugh is cynical and shredded. A sound I've never heard from him before. "Well, my business was going to shut down, so I sold everything

I could to buy myself as much time as I could. And it wasn't enough. Okay, Chelsea." Defeat, like hot steam, rises in his eyes. "Why are you here?"

I pause to gather my thoughts. "I want to be here if you need a friend." I barely get the words out, but there they are. "No matter what, we've always been friends."

Another harsh sound mirroring mockery shoots from his throat. "I'm all set."

I move in closer to Seth. On my approach, he glances at my hand as if I'm a stranger, sharply pivoting his body out of reach.

"Why are you shutting me out this way? So much time has passed. We can be—"

"You can't be here. I can't let you see me like this."

"Seth—"

"You have to go. There's nothing left for you here." His eyes plead, hard and clouding over.

I ignore every rational thought to respect this man's space, and step toward him. *Try harder.* Mom's voice rings in my ear. Chelsea at eleven pushes me off the swing and yells, GO HELP HIM. FIND HIM. Chelsea at twenty-one begs me to get on that damn plane and go see him in New York before brutal self-doubt makes it impossible to distinguish fact from fiction.

I lift my shoulders and tilt my head, eyeing the hourglass. "Somewhere, in another place in time. You and me. Remember?" I ask fondly, remembering the night we spent dreaming together.

When he doesn't respond, I add, "I can't leave you." Putting my water glass down on the shelf, wiping the corner of my eye with my thumb.

"You already made that choice. Twice. I don't have it in me anymore. Our story is over." He swipes the hourglass from the shelf and stands it straight up. "The end."

"Seth, no." My voice cracks as decades of hope disappear in front of my eyes. The tiny grains of sand quickly rush down the center of the hourglass, slipping through the present, into the past, to their final resting place.

My pulse riots.

My eyes burn as I breathe him in.

One last time.

37

CHELSEA

*N*an's is a sea of artifacts, and eight weeks after the service, Mom and I psych each other up, summoning the courage to dive in.

We knew Nan was going to leave the condo to me. My parents didn't need it, and years ago, Nan gave Mom everything she wanted her to have, including her emerald wedding ring which Mom never takes off.

"I feel like an executioner," I say, labeling laundry baskets, one for save, one for donate, one for recycling. "Should we start?" Unable to reconcile how anyone rummages through a life once someone is gone.

Mom stands over my organization system in the kitchen, boxes of recipe cards at my feet. "I haven't cried since this morning. I'm due for another round." She laughs at herself, fresh tears lining her lashes as she opens a cabinet. "You take the high shelves. I'll attack these." She points to the pots and pans. For a woman who's trained to emote and suppress on cue, she hasn't attempted to hide her grief at all.

"When's the last time you think Nan used these?" I hold up two bottles of her specialty spices.

"By the looks of that handwriting, probably when The Police were number one on the charts."

I blow out an exaggerated breath—*that* band will never not make me think of Seth.

"I know, pretty gross." She misses the meaning behind my reaction.

"It's not that."

"Okay, then, what?"

"Forget it."

"No, Chelsea. Something is clearly bothering you."

Out of all bands, this is the reference she makes. *Of course it is.* A memory surfaces. He removed the headphones with gentle hands, and the world swayed even after we'd stopped swinging. "Seth."

"Oh." She places the pot in her hand into the donate bin.

"You see him at Nan's?"

"No," she replies. "It was kind of him to come."

I rub my eyes. "He was here, too, in our twenties. Came over for my birthday. Nan helped him gang up on me about something. It was the lemon cake. We had our first kiss on the terrace steps." I realize I've stopped speaking, my fingers touching my lips.

"A nice kid, Chels, though he was a perpetual bachelor as an adult, if I recall reading that somewhere. He never did have a family, did he?"

I shake my head. "What does the media know about a person? You should get that better than anyone."

"I'm not implying—"

The tips of my ears grow hot. I'm so irritated that she's judging him. That anyone judges a person without getting to know them first. "It's entirely unfair of you. He's the best person. Always puts others before himself. You know, when we were eleven, we planned to run away to San Fransisco together. To this house, in fact."

Mom's eyes widen, and she crosses her arms. "You're kidding."

"I'm not," I reply, relieved to tell her after all this time. "Seth had it bad at home. And I was so mad about that ridiculous reading camp."

"What," she hesitates, arms unfolding, "stopped you from doing it?"

I look her in the eye. "His mom needed him more."

"Well," she clears her throat. "I was wrong to say that. And for what it's worth, I'm glad you stayed."

"I didn't want to hurt you." I move on, untwisting a cap from a bottle. My eyes water from the whiff of pungent dried herbs and the pinch in the center of my chest. "Yup, that's hazardous," I report, coughing from the stench, dumping out the contents, and tossing the glass bottle into the recycling basket.

Mom's timid giggle turns my head in her direction. She's half-laughing, half-crying. "This is the pan she'd make my favorite fried eggs in."

I inhale an imaginary aroma of bubbling butter. "She made the best eggs and toast."

"Butter delivery devices."

"Exactly."

"You were such a pain in the ass, though."

My brows pinch. "Generally or specifically?" I slink down from the step stool and rest for a moment.

"In order for you to eat, the conditions had to be perfect. Toast, cut in triangles, with butter on half, strawberry jelly on the other. Your eggs couldn't touch the toast, so Nan always gave you separate plates. You have no idea what I'm talking about?"

Sounds a lot like Jonah, and the realization settles deep, somewhere between guilt and acceptance. "Being particular isn't being a pain. It's knowing yourself in the most assured way."

"If I don't tell you this enough, I want you to know you're a better mother than I ever was."

"Stop it." My skin tightens. I scratch an itch under my braid.

"I'm serious. I was young when I had you, and I didn't try to figure out what it meant to be a mom. I dragged you along to whatever I was doing—auditions, late dinners, cast parties. I folded you into my life. I wasn't intentional. Not like how you are with your kids."

"It was a different time. There are more resources for parents these days."

"Well, you still make the choice to put your kids' happiness first, and that's not something I ever did. I pushed you when I should've been holding you. And I'm sorry. It took me too long to realize all you needed was the space and permission to be yourself. I wanted a life for you that came from having options, and since I never got a degree, it became so important to me that you did."

Hot tears jam the back of my throat. "I thought you wanted to be an actress."

"I love my life, don't get me wrong, but I fell into that career. I had the right face at the right time in a restaurant once, and the right person noticed. And that career had an expiration date."

"Why are you saying all this now?"

"When someone you love is gone forever, it makes things real clear. I don't ever want you to wonder if I'm proud of you. You're the joy of your father's and my life. The disco ball at the dance party. The best mom. And look at you now—your career and success. I've watched you your entire life give to everyone else, making things easier for the people you care about, and I've never been more proud when you pursued something for yourself. And look, Chels, it paid off in spades. Look what happens when you love yourself as much as the rest of us love you."

"Or fake it until I make it." Now I'm laughing with a wet face and snotty nose.

"A great performer doesn't wait for the stage—she takes it."

It's true. For the first time in my life, I feel like I belong in my own story. I see how Seth knew I belonged there the whole time. Our life paths may have been opposite in every way, but we weren't so different from one another.

"I can't remember the last time I saw you without makeup." I note my mom's fresh skin and silver hair.

"I can't remember the last time I let anybody see me without my face."

"You're the most beautiful woman I know. Always have been."

"Thank you, Chels. And I want you to understand, had I known about Seth, how much he meant to you . . . I'm sorry I didn't see it and support you better. I thought it was young infatuation, attachment to a charismatic kid with a great smile."

My throat is sore talking about Seth to anyone, but especially to Mom. She didn't mean to discourage me from having a relationship with him, but her critical voice took up space in my head. "I could always be myself with him. How often do we receive that kind of acceptance in this world? I wasn't attached to Seth—I was in love with him."

She nods and smiles at me. "If you don't have any regrets by my age, you probably haven't tried hard enough." Her eyes glance over my shoulder. "Chels, we should repurpose the mason jars. There's a woman on YouTube who recycles glass into mosaic frames." This has been a lot for Summer. She'll need to take time to process everything we've shared.

"I think I'd like to keep the blue glass. Maybe I'll use them as planters or something." There are rows of mixed mason jars, different colors and sizes, some with their original tin lids and others with white plastic lids.

"Nan would love that," she says. "Where are the jams?"

I lift an empty medium-sized jar with both my hands and hold it up to the window. "They should be in the bottom cabinet."

"What's in there?" Mom's phone rings and she picks it up, lowering her finger and pointing at the blue jar in my grasp. By the hello, I know it's my dad. "Chels and I are getting the kitchen worked on."

I shake the jar to jostle whatever's in there. "If it's an insect, I'll lose it," I whisper.

Mom waves me away with her hand while wrapping up her conversation with Dad.

"Mom, it could be alive. Get a pan."

"Chelsea Bell, you think I'm gonna smash some beetle with Nan's copper pans, you're nuts. Whatever it is, it's not alive. Alive things scatter."

"I felt that in the pit of my soul." I grip the lid, preparing for the sight of insect carcasses. "I should wait for backup," I mutter over Mom hanging up with Dad.

"Honey, I've got to go. Our daughter's running her active imagination into overdrive. See you tonight. Love you." Mom hangs up and pivots to me with playfully stern eyes. One brow lifted up. One brow slanted down.

"What?"

"Open the damn jar."

"If something in here has a heartbeat, I'm leaving, never coming back, and you'll have to pack up this entire house by yourself."

"And I'm the one with a career in the dramatic arts." A loud bellow escapes from her frame, making her puffy eyes seem a bit less weary.

"Something's definitely stuck at the bottom." I force the lid, twisting it off, and hold my breath as I dump the contents in my hand. A cylinder rolls in my hand. I yelp a little in anticipation, and Mom continues her hearty cackling at my expense. I rest the mason jar back on the counter and remove the thin rubber band.

"Mom, what in the . . ." Crisp green and ivory papers curl in my palm. I separate them, counting . . . five, ten, fifteen, twenty.

She dries her eyes on her sleeve and comes in close, taking the pile of cash in her hands. She flips through it. "That's five hundred dollars, Chels."

"What?" I giggle. "Nan hid money in a mason jar? Why would she do that?"

Mom steps on the stool and pulls down another jar. She turns it upside down and another roll of five-dollar bills hits the floor. We both look up to the shelves at all the mason jars, and Mom's smirk unhinges into a dropped jaw like the kid who cracks open the pinata, knowing they're about to be showered with candy. "I guess she was saving for a rainy day."

Turns out, it wasn't just the mason jars—it was books and shampoo bottles and shoe boxes and those little red and white tins that retained their distinct scent of menthol and sweet cherry after decades—it was two hundred and fifty thousand rainy days.

38

SETH

"These booths are noisy little suckers," the man says, his weathered knuckles gripping the aluminum border of the table as he adjusts his weight on the cushion.

"They've seen some life," I respond, leaning back as far as I can get.

"This place reminds me of that one diner in L.A. Do ya remember it? We'd go for Reubens sometimes."

"Nope." *I only remember your cowardice.*

"They had seats as red and headstrong as these." He lets out a reminiscent chuckle.

I roll my eyes, stirring my black coffee with a metal spoon. I narrow in on the clink of soft aluminum against porcelain, his thick salt-and-pepper mustache, his tired brown eyes that mirror my own.

"Son, look at these old bands. Brings me back. I've got a quarter. Got a favorite?"

Heat rises from my gut to my neck, much like the steam coaxing my lips to curl in amusement. This guy's gotta be joking. "You don't get to do that," I spit out.

The packet of sugar shakes in his hand. He pours half of it

into his mug and rolls down the top, securing the white crystals inside. "The son or the song part?"

"All of it." I rest my elbows on the table and get in close. "You don't get any of me. You made that choice."

He returns his attention to the tabletop jukebox, flipping the metal pages inside the glass casing. His smile returns, too, and I'm unclear how anyone can smile at anything right now.

I lost my life's work. One day I had a restaurant and the next, I was under water, selling everything I owned not attached to the walls to keep The Playground afloat. I couldn't bear to sell Chelsea's art or my apartment, probably for the same reasons—they were all I had left.

Mom offered to help me, but that was unacceptable.

Then Chelsea storms into my apartment, kicking through the debris that's left of my life, and wants to help me too. I'm not some fucking charity case.

I was harsh with her, but it was the only way to guarantee she wouldn't return.

It was my dream—it was all my responsibility. No effort was enough to keep the doors open. Just like how his efforts will never be enough. But I set this meeting, so I might as well get it over with.

"You still driving trucks?" I break the silence.

"Nah, my eyesight is shit for night driving."

"So, how do you live?"

He rubs at the corner of a paper napkin on the table with his yellowing nails. "Ya look so much like your mother. I'm real happy for her." He abandons the napkin and takes a sip from his mug. "I'm working part-time at a tire shop. I've got some savings. I don't need much."

"No wife?" I ask.

"Not good at marriage. Ya like living in this foggy city?" he redirects.

"It's home," I answer him.

"Why'd ya ask me here, Seth?"

I've been badgering myself with the same question since I made the call. I never threw out the balled-up piece of paper with his number on it. And well, I know why I called. I just don't know what purpose it will serve. "A woman died."

"Sorry to hear that." He sucks in his upper lip, rubbing the bristles of his mustache over his lower lip.

"Don't be. She lived an incredible life. She was a grand-mother, a mother, and my friend."

"Lucky lady."

A flash of bright red whisks by the window, and I strain my neck to see it. A little girl with an apple-colored beret holds a woman's hand, a teddy bear tucked under her arm. I watch them blur down the street until they disappear.

"She had this gift of finding fruit right before it was about to spoil and would spin it into the sweetest jam." I smile, thinking about kindness and how people we aren't even related to, who owe us nothing, end up changing our lives. Nan's infectious smile—her granddaughter's too. How the lines around Chelsea's eyes turned upward, compared to my father's slanting on a slope.

Whether we like it or not, we're made up of the parts and pieces of the people we come from. Sometimes we get lucky in this life, tripping over stars and landing directly in the orbit of someone special—who doesn't resemble us in any way or carry our DNA—but we know them instantly. We know their heart and their light. And we can't help but be drawn to them.

"Seth, I was glad ya called," he says, pulling me back to our conversation.

"I'm not interested in your feelings." I wave the server over. Her hair's purple, and I think she's saying something behind her cloth mask even though she doesn't have to wear one anymore.

She fills our cups and scopes out the man across from me

with warm eyes. It awakens a memory of being in this exact booth twenty years ago, and that server—what was her name—who shot me daggers with her eyes all morning? Who knew that Chelsea was too good for me before I accepted it.

My dad smiles at the server and thanks her. He's refusing to engage with any of my resentment.

This anger's heavy, and I feel its resolve slipping from my grasp. "You ever have to laugh at how ridiculous everything is? Life. Love. The Dodgers this season." I can't even contain it anymore. And so I don't. "What's the actual point? I don't know. I thought I had it all figured out." I pull a gulp into my mouth and let it burn on the way down. "I was wrong. I don't have any answers, but I know I tried. I gave it all a shot."

"Gave what a shot?" he asks, eyes on me, hands still.

"My restaurant, my community, a woman. And you, you packed it in when it got hard. You turned your back on a frightened kid—a sick wife. So yeah, I'm laughing because I don't know a damn thing other than I'm not you, and that's enough."

I slap cash on the counter and rush to remove myself from this situation, but the unyielding material's sticking to the sweat behind my thighs and I can't make my escape.

My father places his hand over mine, trapping it against the weathered linoleum. I stare into the static. Air expels from my chest in hard bursts. My pulse kicks in my veins, my head throbs, my eyes sting. He won't let go.

I was left alone to process what happened that day. Why Mom tried to end her life. Why he left me with someone who couldn't take care of herself. I never got those answers, but would they have done me more harm anyway? I found ways to funnel it all into something good. Food and service, establishing myself in a city I love, working in the community to create access to healthy eating. I took the shit I was given and used it to grow things.

It didn't erase my past, but it gave me my future—for a time.

"You're right—it was my fault. I was young with a big ego. I'd never dealt with caring for someone with depression before. I didn't know how to handle it." He gathers strength to continue. The pads of his fingers are rough over my hand, and they match. Same shape, same size. "There are no excuses for what I did, and if ya leave and never speak to me again, I'll accept that. All I'm asking is to listen to me before ya go. Can ya do your old—*me*—a favor? Five minutes of your time. Can you stay for one cup of coffee and one song?"

Chelsea's words at the funeral echo throughout the diner. *No matter how much time passes, if there's still time, there's still hope.*

It's unreal to me, how I can be sitting across from a man I barely know—who I resemble in appearance—meanwhile, Chelsea is all I see in that booth across from me, light dancing over her red sweater, her lips pressed to the glass, her nervous fingers tearing at the paper napkins. All the things she never knew I noticed. How incredibly easy it was to fall in love with her.

This is the first point in my life where I have no sense of what lies ahead. All I've got is time on my hands.

Maybe I don't need these answers as much as he needs to get them off his chest. To think I'm older now than he was then. If he had a friend or someone to talk to. If Mom did, too. If they could've found a way to talk to each other.

Their story isn't mine.

Suddenly, the urge to own the consequences of things I couldn't control as a child dissolves like granules of sugar into a steaming mug. With no one left to blame, I say, "One song."

My father drops a quarter into the machine and selects two tiles.

No one would believe me if I told them which song he chose.

There's no sense in torturing myself, so I leave the barber shop and take the long way to the community center, avoiding the block where my restaurant used to be. To most pedestrians passing by, it's four walls and a roof, but to me, it's a gutting blade.

The night air is shocking against my trimmed beard. I rub my hands over the short hair, feeling my cheekbones for the first time in ages.

In time I'll be able to walk by the location, and it won't hurt the way it does now. I know this because when you first lose something or someone you love, you seem to find them every-where—on menus, in bleacher seats, at the park . . . and if you've let that love into your home, you also find their scent on your pillow and laughter in your shower . . . even Koufax curls up in Chelsea's old spot on the couch.

I pop into the main office on my way to class. Once on-campus activity resumed, I was able to return to teaching in the program. Volunteering at the center was the one thing I missed the most when I opened The Playground.

Tonight, there's a security guard in the office I haven't met yet.

"Hey, man." He nods.

"Nice to meet you, Hector." I extend my hand, peeking at the scripted letters on his name badge. "I'm Seth. I instruct—"

"I know who you are, Mr. Hansen. In fact, my wife loved your cooking show back in the day. She watches the replays. Would it be any trouble to grab an autograph? She's got your cookbook and swears by it."

"I'm here Tuesdays and Thursdays. Bring it in, and I'll sign it."

"Thank you. She's going to flip."

"Sure thing." I leave to prep for class.

I have a lot to be grateful for—my community and this center. It gives me purpose, and purpose keeps me going.

39

CHELSEA

Six Months Later

The man looks good standing in front of his food truck. As good as a filtered Instagram picture gets when zoomed in at the level I'm doing right now.

I fill my glass to the top and decide to carry it and the bottle with me back into the explosion down memory lane, which has taken over the living room.

It's been raining for a week straight—unheard of in this area. I start the fire and grab a flannel blanket to cover my legs. Why I decided to spring clean today is beyond me.

Maybe the rain?

Maybe the launch of his new business, serving San Francisco the same affordable comfort foods from his food truck, sent me into a keep-my-hands-busy spiral.

Maybe I'm a glutton for punishment.

All of the above, I decide, a few mouthfuls of Reisling in.

I investigate the fuzzy image of Seth. His legs are covered in dark denim, crossing at the ankles, his classic white tee with his business logo "By The Cook" printed in black and yellow lettering. The curve of his bicep peaks out from the sleeve, and I trail my gaze down his forearms to his hands casually resting in the front pockets.

My mind's responding like a teenager as I complete a full-body scan, pinpointing what exists beneath the blurry clothing. Thankfully, the forty-one-year-old in me slaps my palm over my mouth and tells me to get a grip. What do I think I'm going to find? Some clue to confirm he hasn't forgotten me after he explicitly told me to forget him.

Chels, stop torturing yourself.

He was heartbroken over his restaurant, and I was heartbroken for him. Seeing him back where he belongs in the community is all I could ask for. To see him happy again.

I suppose the past has been on my mind lately. Making plans and decisions have been on my mind, too.

The kids don't need me in the same way. My business runs itself. It's unfamiliar territory I'm in, with all this extra time. Running helps me work through it, but most nights, I'm right here, with a glass of white, wondering about the choices we make and don't make. Wondering *what if?*

"Mom." Paige interrupts my crushing on my forever crush. I scoot over on the lounge chair, making room. She puts her laundry basket down and parks next to me. "What's all this?" she asks, staring at the crime scene . . . papers, images, evidence from a lifetime ago. She picks up a photo of me in my old red cardigan with those barely attached pom-poms I loved so much, and that yellow messenger bag I used as a diaper bag with Paige until the strap broke. "How old are you here?"

My half-smile reflects off the photograph's film coating. "Twenty-one."

"Before I was born?"

"Yes."

"Did Dad take this picture of you?" She puts the photo down on top of the others.

"A friend."

"She take them all?" Paige picks up another—of me and Seth at the baseball game, making silly faces, my chin and the top of Seth's head cut off. She stares at the image and then back at me. "A boyfriend friend?"

"Seth."

"The chef?"

I switch subjects. "We're leaving to check out colleges this weekend whether you have a change of clothes or not."

"I'm almost done. Hey, wait," she notes, observing a different stack of photos, "these are of the city. Wow, I love them so much."

"They're my favorites, too," I share, my voice sticking. I hold one in my hand, tracing his face. The memory's soft, in a safe place. "I actually took these with the first nice camera I owned. Seth had given it to me as a loaner. He said until I upgraded, but I never did upgrade. I don't think he ever intended on me returning it anyhow."

Paige twirls Nan's heirloom chai pendant she's wearing between her fingers while I play with the ends of her curly hair. She reaches for the small pink music box, lifting open the lid. "Are these dried flowers?"

"Daisy chains." I tuck that photo under my thigh.

"Mom!" she exclaims. "There are two here."

"Hmm. Hmm," I mumble, finishing my glass of wine.

"Who knew you were such a hoarder?"

That draws a laugh from my chest. "I'm like Nan." I reminisce.

"This is all super sentimental and romantic."

"Okay, that's enough." I take the box from her hand and toss it on top of loose papers and notes. "You should finish packing."

"Mom." Paige chews on her lower lip. "How do you know if you're in love?" Her eyes unknowingly traipse over the proof of its existence.

I pull her in close, and she rests her head under my chin. "I think you know it's love when you can't describe it as anything else."

She looks confused.

"When your heart runs to that person faster than your legs can carry." It takes me another moment to formulate my thoughts, breathless at the realization. "You know it's love when you don't ever want to stop trying."

"You and Dad stopped trying."

"We did." I exhale.

"Did you ever love each other?"

"We loved each other so much we made you and Jonah. And then, loving you two was what held us together. It was better if we did that apart."

"Definitely better." Paige chuckles, peeking up at me. "Will you braid my hair before bed, please?"

"Always," I reply, kissing the top of her head. "Your dad's the best dad," I add. "In case I haven't said that enough lately."

"That's what he says about you. Except, as our mom." Paige's back rattles in my arms. "So, Seth. He was pretty cute."

"You know, he still is." I gather Paige's hair, smoothing her crown of curls with my palm. "He had this smile that bent a little. It was pretty adorable at eleven. Even as he aged, that smile stayed the same." I twist each row, crossing the strands until they're secure at the base. Seeing him online recently, I guess it got me thinking about life, and how quick it all goes.

"Were you really close?"

"We didn't spend a lot of time together." I consider that point.

"Does the amount of time matter? I only see Alex once a year at summer camp for two weeks, but she's still my bestie. You're always telling me quality over quantity, right?"

I drag an elastic from my wrist with my teeth and wrap it at the end of the braid. "I guess the little time we had over the course of a life added up."

Paige turns to face me. "I hope love finds you again, Mom. You know, the kind where you can't run fast enough into their arms—kissing love."

"Oh, kissing love—I see. Well, that comes with maturity, too," I whisper and rub the tip of my nose over hers. Paige's dimples grow more pronounced as she smiles.

"Jackson Whitlock kissed me in drama club once, and it was kinda chaotic and gross. Not how I imagined."

My kid has been kissed, and she's telling me about it. I'm relieved and honored she's telling me, and I'm painfully aware of those early years I was so lucky to have with them when all that mattered was playtime and cutting crusts off sandwiches. The days were sometimes long, but I wouldn't trade a second of it for anything. "Paigey, with the right person at the right time, it'll be better. I promise."

"I hope so. Otherwise, I'm not interested in kissing anyone ever again."

"I'm on board with that plan. But I'm also here if you ever want to talk about it."

"I know, Mom. Thanks for the braid."

Paige gives me a reassuring peck on the cheek. Her embrace envelops me. The future she has ahead of her is one for the books. I can't wait to sit in the audience and cheer for her onstage. My mom's ecstatic. Already planning her trips to visit Paige for every audition in New York.

As she gets up to leave, I decide to stop punishing myself with ghosts. "Paigey, can you put all this stuff by the trash before you go to bed?" I compile everything from the floor and hand her the pile.

"You sure?" she asks, stepping back.

I push in closer. "It's collecting dust. Sweet dreams."

Paige takes it, and I return to my empty room and my rabbit hole.

She pauses in the hallway that leads to her room. "There's a shirt in here, and you want me to throw away this tape?"

"Who is it?"

"The Police," she says. "Are they old?"

Seth would have a field day with this conversation. "As old as me."

She holds up the case, facing the album title at me. "What does Synchronicity mean?"

I raise my eyebrows and shrug my shoulders, reveling in the bright eyes of my curious and confident child, knowing that we all deserve a life with adventure and love and someone worth sharing it with.

"It means something a little different for everyone."

"What does it mean to you?"

My voice hums in my throat. "It's kind of like magic. It's believing in something, even if you are the only one who sees it."

40

SETH

"Hey, buddy, thanks," I say, locking up the truck for the day. David hooked me up with a lot a few blocks from my place, and the rent is only minimally outrageous.

"You always kiss your truck goodbye?" David asks, shoving a handful of potato chips into the compost pile that's his mouth, chomping in my ear.

"You always eat garbage?"

"Anyone ever tell you not to bite the hand that feeds you?"

We walk toward my building. "Thanks for the offer, but I'm not in front of the camera anymore. I like my quiet."

"You're killing me," he says, sulking. "You ever change your mind, make me your first call. I can see it now—the rebound story, how Chef Seth got back in the game. We could make a series of videos for TikTok and—"

"David."

"All right, all right. At least consider getting on TikTok for all this. We could make merch. Sell your logo on hats and shirts, bumper stickers, water canteens. You want more people to find you?"

"We thrive off of word-of-mouth—people showing up because their friends love it or they've heard about Free Meals Friday. It's better this way. Trust me. *I'm* better this way."

He crumples up his wrapper, the flimsy foil crunching louder than our conversation. "That face, though." He smiles at me. I stare over his shoulder at the late afternoon sun bouncing off cement and the pair of cyclists passing by.

"Don't you have other clients who need attention," I add, nodding at Freddy as we open the main door simultaneously.

"Not any who are also my friend."

"Mr. Hansen, you have a package," Freddy says, holding the door open for me.

"David, I'm good. I'm more than good."

He throws up his hands and steps back on the sidewalk. "I'll see you for dinner next week."

"Go to the market before then and buy yourself some actual food. Stick to the perimeter." I walk through the door. "Thanks," I say to Freddy, eyeing the medium-sized navy-blue package in his hands.

"This showed up today."

I inspect the surface. It's a dated Major League Baseball box with a decent amount of weight to it. "No return address?"

"Sorry, sir. I didn't get a name. Or a look. It was here on the desk when I arrived."

"Did you inspect it?"

"Aside from a light shake, no. We used to get so much fan mail for you, I assumed it was that."

"Yeah. Used to." I remind us both.

"You worried there's a head in that box?" Freddy jokes, referring to a nineties thriller with a twist no one saw coming.

"Thank you for that visual."

He laughs, pushing the elevator call button for me.

I carry the box under my arm to the apartment, propping the door open with my elbow and tossing my keys and knives onto the hall table. Once inside, Koufax cackles to be fed. It's been our nightly routine to cuddle up and watch Sportscenter after she's eaten. I pick up her thirteen-year-old frame, reminding her how much I missed her today. "Mangiamo," I say.

She meows back.

———

"Hey," I answer the call, shutting off the game.

"You see that last play?" My dad's voice stretches thick through the airwaves.

I drop both feet to the floor and pick up my empty glass off the table. "Terrible call. Kimbrel made it less painful to watch at the end."

"Sure glad I'm not stuck in the post-game traffic," he adds.

"A silver living to taking in games locally. No traffic with the bike." I toss the phone on the counter, put the call on speaker, and flip on the faucet.

"You try out that sandwich combo I suggested?"

"I ran it as a special. Sold out, actually. Thanks for the pickle tip."

"Oh, yeah? Well, how do ya like that?" he replies. "What ya got going on over there?"

"Washing a glass," I tell him, finishing rinsing it out.

"No, fool, I mean, how's your week been?" He alternates between low laughter and consistent shallow coughs, clearing his throat while I talk.

Lately, we've been doing more of this—talking. He'll check in, and I'll run through my day at the truck or the center. Sometimes I tell him about the pick-up basketball game I play on Wednesdays and the guys I meet up with. Since I've stopped catering and working nights, I'm free when he calls and grateful.

We stay in safe territory, building our relationship, avoiding tearing down bricks that are cemented in place. It took me some time to get used to answering. First, my forearms had to loosen enough to pick up. Then, my shoulders needed to roll back from their locked position. Eventually, the rest of my limbs and organs followed suit, relaxing enough to explore this new dynamic while accepting a past that can't be changed.

A shrill distress meow from Koufax in the front hall has me wrapping up the call quicker than planned. "Dad, the cat's got into something."

"Sure thing, Seth. Hope it's nothing serious."

"Nothing serious."

"Nice talking with ya," he adds, something he always says before we disconnect.

"Yeah, you too."

We hang up as I make it to the crime scene. The package I received earlier has fallen upside down on the floor. Koufax conveniently didn't stick around. My knees protest a little as I squat to grab it.

"You can come out now," I say aloud, bringing the box back over to the couch. The pocket-size Leatherman is sharp enough to break the seal, which, at closer glance, is definitely painter's tape. Not shipping tape. It's odd, but now I'm curious. I shake Freddy's joke from my thoughts. It's not heavy enough to be a—

The second my fingers graze a piece of paper, my stomach tumbles like a trust fall. I'd pick that scratchy handwriting out of a line-up any day.

I dump the contents of the box onto the coffee table. Our photos, daisy chains, the mix CDs, the Police cassette, my Dodgers shirt. What the fuck?

The envelope rattles in my grasp, edges curling against their will. Koufax hops up onto the couch cushion and nestles in beside me.

"Thank you for joining the party. Ready to get our hearts

stomped on one more time?" Pessimism, my choice of comfort when it comes to this subject.

I've tried to accept that whatever we had was over. Thought I'd done a solid job convincing myself of it, too. My life was rock bottom. She was thriving. I refused to disturb her peace.

Her persistent stare at Nan's funeral never escapes my memory. It bladed through me as if there were no such thing as space or time or laws of nature—we were the only two people in that cemetery.

Being with Chelsea, challenges were opportunities, mornings were brighter, and everything made sense. That kind of person's hard to let go of. And though I've been able to slowly move forward with my father, moving on from Chelsea . . . I don't know. There's only so much I can accomplish in one lifetime.

I wipe my eyes and pull out a lined piece of paper. My eyes instantly flood again when I see how much she's written, how hard I know that once was for her. And pride takes over, squashing my pessimism, stifling it enough that I read Chelsea's words with an open heart.

Dear friend,

I like to think of you that way. Someone who's a part of my life, and we're picking up where we left off over a cup of coffee. Someone with whom I could share anything and go anywhere with—in life and in our imaginations.

It's been many years.

At first it was impossible to not think of you and our memories. Rollerblading in the sunset on the wet streets of Los Angeles. My music and your awful taste in music—I'm partially kidding. Our first kiss, each time we had one. Sharing pizza. Swapping stories. Baseball games. Classic movie marathons.

The way you always had my back, especially when I didn't.

The moment you knew it was all worth it.

It's easier now. I think of our time together with fondness. My kids are older, too, and in many ways, I grew up with them.

I understand my place in the world a bit better.

Seth, you were my first friend, and I wanted to say thank you, and I miss you.

I miss you in the quiet moments, under a sky full of ominous clouds, desperate to release the rain. I miss you breathing in my first sip of coffee in the morning, and when I let my hair dry naturally. I miss you in the spring and on opening day, when wine lingers like tart cherries, and at night—always in the dark. I think of you, a light in my life, and carry you with me.

I've wanted to reach out so many times, but I never could manage to choose courage over fear when it came to you. I made so many excuses. Since the day I met you, you shined like a star I wasn't meant to keep, only to be admired from afar.

I know what we had wasn't some fleeting thing. I understand the gravity of that now more than ever. Where distance and time snap and sever for some, with us, they stretch.

I didn't know if I'd ever be able to give you what you gave me for all those years. The way you encouraged me in the loudest and most gentle ways. I've never forgotten.

When it came time that I could finally do something, I knew you'd never accept it, so I made a choice, the right choice, without telling you. I contacted David and had him sign an NDA. It's what Nan would've wanted. It's what I wanted. And I'm so happy for you. Seeing you back at it, doing what you love, what you're meant to do. Making your corner of the world so much brighter. Giving people a home with each meal you provide.

I know, what's the point of an NDA if I'm breaking my own contract by writing you this letter, but this letter is just for me. It's been hard to live in the present when I'm holding onto the past. I need to forgive myself for the way I handled things with us over the years. And my therapist encourages me to write down my feelings, practicing how to be in my own discomfort. I'm definitely getting better at it.

Writing this letter is self-acceptance. Knowing you'll never read it makes it easier for me to put it all down.

I hope somehow, someway, you know how cherished and loved you are.

You changed my life, and I'll never not smile when I think of you.

It finally makes sense to me, that everything we went through happened exactly as it needed to, so we could recognize each other and be there in life when it mattered most.

Always,

Chels Bells

The Pacific's breathtaking from this vantage point. The late afternoon sun glistens off the rolling waves as they crash into the coastline below. We're forty-five minutes out of the city, and it's a completely different world, untouched by modern technology or tragedy. The appeal of living out here settles in my lungs as my motorcycle tires grind against the gravel drive. I slow my speed, driving through a tunnel of pines until the house comes into view, glass windows that wrap around the front of the property.

I kill the engine, remove my helmet, and stretch the open road off my shoulders. My boots crunch on the dirt path that leads to the front door. I comb my fingers—stiff from the ride— through my hair, when two people exit, carrying small duffel bags and engaged in their own conversation.

These are her kids. It's been years since I've seen them, but the resemblance is unmistakable. Chelsea's daughter looks just like her around the eyes, same unruly hair, and when she smiles as she notices me, it rubs a sore spot in the center of my chest.

"Hey," she says, nodding.

Her brother waves and forces a polite smile. His face, full of braces and glasses, the way he walks slightly uneven, reminds me of his mom, too.

"Hello," I reply, pausing in my tracks, making way for them to pass.

Her daughter looks back from where they came from. "I left it open."

As I continue to the front door, their conversation carries within earshot. "Who's that dude?"

"Nevermind, Jonah. It's a friend of Mom's."

"Mom has friends?" he replies sarcastically.

"You only need one when it's the right one."

She has her mom's spirit, too.

The car rumbles as I reach the welcome mat. I peek over my shoulder at the drive and catch tail lights and a layer of dust sticking midair. When the dust dissipates, I take a deep inhale and a cautious glance into the house, bracing my palm over the pineapple handle. The door pushes open with minimal effort.

Barefoot in a white cotton dress, her hair brushing the middle of her back in long untamed ropes, she's humming a tune, something I recognize, and it tugs the sore spot harder.

I can't do this, I tell myself while knocking on the open door, once, twice, her movement matches the rhythm of the song, the beat, arms swaying in the air. She's cleaning and dancing. And she has no idea I'm standing here taking in the show. Suddenly, my presence feels invasive and premature.

I pull out my phone and dial her number. If she doesn't answer, I'll leave, and she'll never know I was here. If she answers . . . as it rings, she taps the Bluetooth in her ear.

"Chelsea, here," she recovers her breath.

"Chels."

Her back stiffens, body stills. "Seth?"

"Turn around." I count, *one, two, three, four*, exhaling as her feet rotate over the tile floor.

Chelsea's chest rises and falls like she's just run a marathon or seen a ghost or both.

Holding up my cell, I power it off and slide it into my front pocket. "What are you listening to?"

She tucks her hair behind her right ear, then removes an earbud, holding it out for me. Her parted lips suggest she's in shock.

I step out of my boots when I notice the mop, polished floors, and sheen on Chelsea's cheek. "Your place is beautiful." I'm enveloped by the warmth of her space. Bright and natural and colorful like her. I lay the bouquet I'm unintentionally squeezing the life out of onto the counter, next to a potted plant in a blue mason jar.

"It's home." That word grips the center of my chest. *Tug. Tug.*

For Chelsea, home is here. And for me, home has always been wherever she is.

I take the earbud, holding it up to listen.

"Daisies?" she asks, eyes on the counter.

The music barrels through me. I nod my head along to the lyrics that always take my breath away. "Didn't want to show up empty-handed." I return the earbud to Chelsea, dropping it into her waiting palm

"Thank you—they're lovely. Can I get you a drink or anything? White wine, beer, water."

I step in closer.

"There's fresh lemonade—it's homemade from our tree—or some random flavored energy drink Paige likes." She lays a hand over her chest, switching her weight from one hip to the next, her cheeks blushing like a blooming pink rose.

One more step.

"There's banana bread I baked earlier," she gasps.

And another.

"Seth." Her gaze clouds over.

One final stride, and her cheek brushes my chin.

"I'm here for answers." I hoist her up by her thighs, sliding her gently on top of the counter.

She leans back. "I don't understand." Her wet, gray eyes land eagerly on mine.

"I think you do."

She looks from me to the flowers, back to my hands beneath her, squeezing her thighs. "Why did you do that for me?" I demand to know.

It takes her a moment. "How did you find out?"

"Does that matter?" I steal her cool hand from the counter and hold it between mine. "Chels, that money. Nan's money was yours."

"Yes. To choose what to do with. And now it's yours," she replies, resolute and unyielding. "You can't fight me on this, Seth Hansen." She tries to make light out of changing my life.

"This isn't funny. It's too much. I'll repay it all, I promise."

"Seth, my whole life I've seen that money either does things *for* people or does things *to* people. Please don't make this the latter. I've always believed in you, and it's that simple."

"It's the most giving, generous," I graze my thumb against her jaw, "thing anyone has ever done for me."

The intensity of my stare has a throbbing pulse. All it will take is one whisper of affirmation. One smile in my direction, one hitch of breath, and nothing will stop me from consuming her right here on this countertop, her bare feet in the air.

Her mouth remains undetectable, a contemplative line. She's rolling her thoughts around on her tongue.

"Seth, you put a camera in my hands. Without you, I'd still be jumping around puddles, afraid to make a splash. You bought out my entire first show. I can stay here all day—I've got nowhere to be, if you want to play this game. Lov—"

Her final word hitches as her breath skims through her teeth. I run my fingers up her tanned arms. She trembles beneath my touch.

Her skin pebbles. A single tear of pride rolls over her cheek. "Loving you has always been an act in loving myself, too. It isn't complicated anymore, not for me."

"Chelsea, all the reasons I've always wanted to be near you, they've never changed. Not as a kid or at twenty-one or thirty-one or now. My love for you is endless. An hourglass that will never see its final drop of—"

She captures my lower lip, and I tighten my grip on her hips.

"Fuck," I swear against her open mouth, swallowing hard, breathing her in. My shoulders sink, dragging with them the burden I've been carrying for most of my life. I refuse to waste a single second past this one.

The pressure of our kiss matches the force of my fingers. I'm wasted in a haze of all the time we've missed, all the pain we've put ourselves through. She tastes like sweet caramel and crisp green apples, like a smooth bourbon lingering on my tongue.

Her body slacks into the caress of my hands slipping beneath her dress, my fingerprints melting into her thighs. Our embrace grows powerful and hungry. I'm devoured, and once again, alive.

I take her hand and lead Chelsea through the maze of her own house. Her bed's covered in pristine sheets, perfectly made, perfectly Chelsea. A deep satisfaction takes hold, knowing we're about to destroy it.

"You and me," I growl into her neck. "We're not leaving this room for the entire weekend."

"Promise," she teases.

"We're taking our time."

41

CHELSEA

I stroke Seth until he's ready to feel me again. His voice is deep, low and scratchy, whispering desires into my neck, and I accept them all—straddling his waist and lowering myself slowly down the length of him.

Seth stalks my every rock and roll as I build against his upright posture, cradling my back, his fingertips play with the ends of my hair. He brushes his lips over my shoulders.

This isn't chasing a high or escaping an expiration date. We're savoring and sweating, pausing to kiss, stalling to suspend our climax.

We spend the weekend swept away in soft touches, swapping stories, laughing and crying in each other's arms, in our insulated world fueled by joy and playfulness and multiple orgasms.

A guitar strums through the speakers. Seth holds my hands in his. A montage of all the years we were desperate to catch up on swirl in the air, soothing scars—a gentle thumb over the stitches until the sun begins to rise. The shore laps against the rocks loud enough to drown out our words of forgiveness.

When I think I know how Seth kisses me, he switches it up, keeping me on the edge, and I like it here.

Sunday morning smiles through the window over the gathered sheets around my waist. Seth steps out of the shower, the steam evaporating off his slick skin and broad shoulders. I trail the length of his arm, tearing up my lower lip. His full biceps and corded forearms are covered in freckles and faded oil burns.

I cover the receiver of my phone as the ringing stops. "You're using my hair towel, Chef Handsome," I point out, the terrycloth barely covering one thigh.

"This look not doing it for you?" His smirk and the spark in his eyes are enough to break me into a million pieces. He's threatening to drop the towel, having no idea who's on the line.

"Mom."

"Hey, sweets. How are the kids?"

"They're good, Mom, they're good." I try to conceal the taunting view of this dripping-wet man in my room, not a shy bone in his body.

"Are you crying, Chelsea? Is everything okay? Tell me this minute."

I press my fingers to my cheek. I *am* crying. Seth's smile disappears as he crawls under the duvet, gripping my ankles, trailing his lips up my legs. I gasp, biting my fist. I whisper the word to her.

"What? Speak louder, Chels. I can't hear you."

"The word, Mom. Remember?"

"The word." It takes a moment as my words surely were muffled. "Oh." It clicks. Her hands make a clapping sound in my ear. "Come talk to your daughter," Mom summons Dad, volleying between two conversations. "Hold on, Chels, we're putting you on speakerphone. Why can't I find the button? Where's the button?"

"It's right here, dear," my father chimes in. "Chelsea, Dad here, what's up?"

"She said the word," Mom whisper-screams.

"What's the word? ... Ah, yes. *The word.*"

I'm certain Mom has written out the word on a piece of paper and is holding it up for him as we speak, frantically pointing at it and mouthing it for him.

I swallow my ragged breaths as Seth inches closer.

"We couldn't be happier for you," Mom cheers.

My dad, a man of few words, adds, "Mazel Tov."

Seth drags me under into a sea of sheets. Probably not the ideal moment to squeal, but his hands are a force of nature, and Dad's hearing isn't at its prime.

"I'll call you later," I manage to get out as the phone drops to the floor.

Seth slides his strong body over mine, pushing up on his arms, a lazy smile on his lips.

"That smile. It does things to my heart, Seth Hansen."

He angles his head slightly, his chin tipping down and his brows lifting in amusement, like he already knows the answer but asks the question anyway. "What's this word business?" His breath tickles my nose.

"Top secret stuff."

"Chels?" Seth's magic touch aims to persuade me to spill.

"We made a deal."

"And?"

My breathing speeds up. "When I found the one, I'd say the word."

His register drops. "What's the word?"

"I chose a word," I gasp as his hands explore. "And she's been waiting," I inhale sharply, "a very long time to hear me say it." My back arches.

His fingers work with urgency. "What's the word, my love?"

I wrap my arms around Seth's neck, pressing in close, my

teeth grazing the sensitive spot behind his ear as I whisper it to him.

Dear Mr. Hansen,

Do you prefer Chef Seth? Whatever it is, hi, I'm Paige. You know my mom, Chelsea Bell. Do you remember me? We met once at your restaurant. You gave me and my brother a hat and a tour.

Mom had this box of stuff she asked me to recycle. I don't think she could bring herself to do it. I'm also pretty sure she'll be mad at first when she finds out I sent it to you, but I know Mom, and she'll eventually understand why I couldn't throw it all away, either.

See, the thing is, I held onto it because I hadn't seen her smile that way before, the way she was smiling in these photos with you. Truthfully, I had shoved it under my bed and kinda forgot about it until I was searching for my stuff for college. And I thought you'd know what to do with it.

My mom has always been the best mom ever. She makes pancakes, she sews costumes, she's never missed a single one of my plays or dentist appointments. She brushes out my tangles, and she tells me she loves me every day.

She always makes sure me and my brother believe in ourselves. And I know Mom doesn't regret a thing about her life, but sometimes I catch moments where she's far away. Maybe she's lonely for that place.

I wonder now if that place is somewhere in time with you.

She's never made herself a priority. I didn't even know she had a friend aside from Aunt Steph and our Corgi, Pebbles. So that day, when she showed me these photos and told me who you were to her, it made me want to know you better.

She's spent her entire life doing everything for everyone. And I have a feeling in this letter addressed to you—which, as you can see, is sealed, I swear I didn't read it—she might have been trying to do something for herself, and I couldn't let her back down.

She deserves to be happy. The kind of happiness that looks forward together, not backward apart.

So, if doing something for herself happens to include you somehow, then please, Mr. Hansen, come to our house on Friday afternoon at 3:30 p.m. We'll be heading to our dad's for the weekend. She'll be home.

Oh, and in case you don't know, her favorite flowers are daisies.

If by chance, you aren't the same Seth we met at that restaurant when I was twelve, and you aren't the same Seth who owns a food truck, or the one I looked up on Instagram, and if this letter isn't meant for you, and you have no idea who my mom is or what I'm talking about, please don't tell her I'm sending strangers mail. I'd be mortified and also grounded for life.

One last thing. I can't explain why I feel this way, but she always says to trust our gut and so, I wanted to say . . . I hope it's you.

Sincerely,
Paige Jacobs

42

CHELSEA

The playground swings sat happily atop deserted asphalt. Chelsea couldn't take her eyes off them. Smiling at the scene, she saw two eleven-year-olds sharing a song.

Seth firmly grasped Chelsea's hand in his left, hanging onto a large reusable sack in his right. He squeezed once, his gaze fixed on the same miraged memory.

"It's smaller." Her eyes roamed the open space, noting the field, which now resembled a backyard more than the vast expanse she used to escape to. The cracks in the cement she once was able to jump over gathered like tiny hair fractures. And that chain link fence they passed on the way in, she could skim the rough top with her fingers. She sighed at the reliable sky, overcast and threatening. "You plan the weather too?" She nudged Seth in his side with her elbow.

"Nah, that was pure luck."

Chelsea caught Seth's lips in a gentle tug. Unmistakable confidence feathered on both sides of her eyes as she smiled at him. "First kiss on a playground," she said, satisfied.

Seth smiled, stealing one more. "Second kiss." He pulled

back slightly, then dove back in, peppering her face with as many as he could, "Third, fourth, fifth, sixth, infinity," he spoke between kisses, a little winded from the rush of contact.

"Always competing with me."

"You're my fiercest competitor. My favorite playdate. My favorite everything."

Chelsea's toes tingled. She shifted the subject, eager to learn what Seth had planned. He'd been talking about it for a month leading up to their birthdays. Though it was still a day away, he had surprised Chelsea with this trip, bringing her and Jonah to visit her parents, even flying out Paige for the special occasion, but she didn't know that part yet.

"So, what's in your bag of tricks?"

"Nope, you're not rushing this, Chels."

Chelsea wrestled with insatiable impatience when it came to surprises. It used to be that she hated them or the lack of control she felt not being able to forecast what came next, but with Seth, she was safe to let that go. This impatience was the unbridled enthusiasm variety. She stuck her tongue out at Seth, taking off toward the swing, snagging the one closest to the field. Chelsea's fingers gripped the chains. They groaned as her hips settled unevenly, shifting until her adult frame fit as best it could into a child's seat.

"You ready?" she asked Seth.

"I was born ready," he replied, dropping the bag and his gaze to Chelsea's mouth. Before Chelsea finished laughing, Seth was settled in the seat next to her, closing the space between them with one more kiss.

"Focus, Hansen."

"Yes, ma'am." He smirked, winking to make his point.

In her eyes, she let Seth know it was time. They alternated counting down, "Three, two, one." Both pulling hard on the chains, sending their legs soaring in front of them.

Higher, faster, legs stretched out, knees bent in . . . they were flying.

Chelsea's hair swam freestyle behind her, lashing in the wind. Seth's smile beamed under a royal blue Dodgers cap. Together they climbed higher, and Chelsea could see it all so clear—the years together, their lives apart . . . it all surfaced with each blink, a flash of recognition in the darkening clouds, like specks of sunlight being swallowed whole.

As their legs tired, slacking into pendulums, Seth reached a hand into the air, and Chelsea's cramped fingers released her grip from the warmed metal, seeking relief in his hold.

It was going to be fine, more than fine, she thought. She recited the words in her mind. *It was going to be what it was always meant to be—theirs.*

They hopped off the swings, and Seth led Chelsea to the field.

He handed her a corner of a plaid blanket, and they smoothed it into a square over a patch of overgrown grass.

Seth plopped down, pulling out the contents. Chelsea took inventory. Two bottles of grape soda, a package of iced lemon cupcakes, two pairs of neon green and yellow roller blades, and a wrapped box with a red ribbon.

"What's all this?"

Seth stuck a candle in each handheld frosted cake, passing one to Chelsea.

"My birthday isn't until tomorrow."

"I won't tell if you don't." He smiled. "Figured we could, if you want to . . . rewrite the end of our beginning."

Chelsea's shoulders trembled like a good hard laugh, but she wasn't laughing. The seriousness in Seth's tone demanded to be taken seriously. Seth never regretted anything. He always moved forward, clearing obstacles to pursue what he wanted, and now he was asking her to go back in time with him, to the birthday he didn't get to finish, and indulge in a little make-believe.

It's one thing to devote yourself to a person. To fight with a person. To stand by a person—for love—motherhood had taught her that. Above all, in those early years of late nights and bruised feelings, uncertainty and brutal self-doubt, her children had also taught Chelsea what it meant when a person you love asked you to play with them.

"Hi." She stretched out her arm, offering her open hand. "I'm Chelsea Bell. I like swings and storms and taking photos and kissing men named Seth Hansen."

"Men?" He froze, wetting his lower lip.

"Okay, okay," she backtracked, smiling. "Only one man named Seth Hansen. It's nice to meet you."

"Well, hello. This is going to work out well for us because my name happens to be Seth Hansen, and the woman who holds my heart also happens to love swings and rain. She's an incredible visual artist, my best friend, and her name is Chelsea Bell."

"You don't say?" Chelsea deadpanned. "So, you wanna make a wish, Seth?"

"I want you to open that box."

Chelsea's spine straightened, and she inched closer.

"But first, you're gonna have to earn it." Seth laughed from the gut, pulling off his hat, securing a black helmet over his head.

"Seth."

"Coincidence or fate?" He dropped the question like they were picking up a puzzle they hadn't completed.

"I don't believe in coincidences anymore."

"Oh no. What do you believe in?"

"You. Me. Us," she stated, resolute.

He tucked a flyaway curl behind her ear, guiding her chin in his hand. "You take my fucking breath away, Chels. Always have." Seth dropped a kiss on the tip of Chelsea's nose before handing over the box.

Chelsea's fingers couldn't move fast enough to untie the ribbons. She tore apart the packaging, breaking for the occasional glance at Seth. She knew he wouldn't disappear, but habits have a way of holding strong.

The lid landed on the pilled surface of the blanket beside her dessert. Chelsea's eyes flooded upon seeing what was inside. Yellow, pink, and aqua letters floating on a white helmet, with zig-zag confetti, the band's grayed-out faces shining like newspaper sealed beneath varnish. The details of the helmet faded behind her tears. "Where did you find this?" she whispered, swiping the back of her palm at her cheeks, bringing her childhood dream helmet close enough to kiss.

"You want to wear it?"

"Yes! Yes!" she shouted. "I'll never want to take it off. Seriously, how, why, where . . ." It didn't even matter. He had done it, and that's all she needed to know. It took a moment to sink in— Seth didn't just want to change the end of his chapter, he went back for her too.

Seth's hands shook as he secured the clasp beneath Chelsea's chin. He leaned in for a kiss and was blocked by their helmets bumping.

"This tracks," Seth commented, and they both laughed in agreement.

He took Chelsea's face in his hands, positioning her head to the side. The sky filled with thick clouds overhead as he strategically maneuvered his own neck, meeting her lips in the middle, as Chelsea's tears of joy stuck to their cheeks.

"I love you," Seth said. As simple and true as any words could ever be.

"You loved me even when I didn't know how to love myself. Thank you for finding me all those years ago on this playground, and every time after that."

"You found me, too."

"I thought I dreamed you up and at the same time, I knew. I think I always knew."

"Oh, I'm pretty sure the evidence would suggest that I knew first." Seth traced an hourglass shape on her knee. "I knew we'd always find each other. And when I dared to forget, the universe liked to remind me."

Seth picked up their cakes, giving Chelsea hers, lighting both candles with one match. Chelsea's heart tumbled, staring at Seth's glowing face, set back from the orange light, flames dancing in his copper eyes.

His steady voice joined in with hers, counting down a final time, "Five, four, three, two . . ." each blowing out the flames. Chelsea took a bite, exposing the marshmallowy center. She moaned at the nostalgic burst of processed vanilla.

"You want to spend your pretend birthday behind bars, moan like that again."

"Public indecency not high on your bucket list?" Chelsea teased.

Seth had always cooked everything from scratch, except when it came to marathon movie nights and, apparently, reliving your eleventh birthday. She loved his stoic expression, as he swallowed enough to maintain tradition and quickly shoved the remaining cake into its plastic wrap.

"Now that we've settled I was always right about us," he wiped the corner of his mouth with his thumb, "I've got one question left for you."

"Bring it on," she dared, licking the lemony vanilla frosting off her pointer.

"Come here." He pulled Chelsea into his lap, removing their helmets and dropping them on blades of bright green grass. Seth polished off the remaining icing from Chelsea's finger, dragging the artificial confection onto his tongue.

He pried open her palm, gently placing one dried daisy

strand, followed by another, into her hand. She wrapped her fingers around the old vines, finally reunited, two parts of a whole, kids making good on their promises.

Seth motioned to the far end of the field, where the green folded into distinct aisles of yellow buds and white wings.

"Wanna make daisy rings?" he asked.

Chelsea's lashes lifted from the center of their joined hands to Seth's freckles over the bridge of his nose. She rubbed them with her thumb. "Not dirt." She smiled.

Seth raised his brow. "You're an odd duck, Chels."

"So I've been told."

"The sexiest odd duck and, to be clear, mine."

She balanced her hands against his knees, squeezing those old daisy chains to dust, bracing herself for the sprint of her life. "Race you there!" She kissed his cheek. "Ready, set," and Chelsea took off, trailing "go" into the wind.

Seth gave her a solid start, then picked up speed.

Chelsea knew he was gaining on her as his laughter grew louder, and her heart responded as it always had with Seth.

"I win. I win. I win," she playfully gloated, crossing an invisible finish line.

He looped his arms around Chelsea's waist, sweeping her off her feet. She buried her flushed face into his chest, closing her eyes, waving her bare fingers through the warm air.

The faint sound of street traffic mixed in with Seth's raspy laugh as he triumphantly sang in Chelsea's ears. "My master plan all along."

Chelsea let the earth brace her fall, her chest rising and falling, as she recovered from the impromptu sprint. It was the best birthday she ever had with the best person now lying beside her. Chelsea turned on her side, facing Seth. She propped her head on her hand, her elbow pressing into wildflowers. She watched as Seth released his bottom lip from his teeth, holding his breath.

He handed her a single daisy. She twisted the stem between her thumb and pointer, the petals twirling like a pinwheel.

She positioned her free hand on his chest, and Seth covered hers with his own. In her haste to race, Seth's question had absorbed in her head out of order. She was missing something. In the time it took for Chelsea's pulse to return to normal, she pieced together his question.

Seth hadn't asked Chelsea to make daisy chains at all.

Removing her hand from his hold, she flipped it over to reveal his palm. Her fingers pressed into Seth's skin, a bit sticky from frosting, using the daisy to trace three letters, over and over and over, until his exhale revealed an arching smile—soft at the corners—his happy smile.

Opening his eyes, Seth squinted from the light. "Yes?"

Chelsea nodded. What else could she say? She didn't know the exact words to express herself, not when there were so many combinations to choose from. So she kept it simple. Simple was best. She learned that from her fiancé.

And like any great recipe, if it didn't work out on the first try, she'd happily try again.

Chelsea released the daisy. She had exhausted all of her wishes—couldn't think of a single one. The most valuable wishes, she learned, were the ones she didn't know to ask for anyway—the answers showing up in life when she needed them the most. Like Seth had a lifetime ago.

They had found each other, again and again.

They had love.

They had their family, blended and colorful.

Side by side, they tackled their fears, repairing Seth's relationship with his parents, sending Paige off to college, supporting Jonah in his growth.

They were making it work between Seth's schedule and Chelsea's projects. It wasn't black and white. It wasn't perfect, but it never needed to be. It was something infinitely more beautiful than extremes and expectations.

It was loving each other in the gray.

The voices hung around, but they had lost their power the more time she spent doing the things that excited her heart, turning monsters into muses. Chelsea fell asleep and woke up next to Seth every day. She lived in a place that inspired her. She knew herself and liked what she saw. That was a gift Seth gave in his steadfast loyalty and heart. He stood her in front of the mirror and made Chelsea face the truth. And that's something she never took for granted.

DEAR READER

After college, I took a road trip with friends from the east to west coast—mapquest directions and Trader Joe's snacks included—stopping in some of my favorite cities, and a couple weeks later, landing in San Francisco. We spent our time there walking the windy streets, tasting the incredible cuisine, and getting lost in its cultural and artistic landscape. You can say I fell in love with the city much like Seth does.

A lot of this story is about timing. Right and wrong places. Right and wrong people. And within this idea of timing, our connection to home. What home looks like in a place, a person, and how we find ourselves through home. Before I took my trip at twenty-two, I'd been searching for those answers in myself and collecting the details that would eventually become Synchronicity.

When something greatly influences a creative, they'll often work that inspiration into their creation. Sometimes it's fun to be very obvious about those details. Like in Synchronicity, I chose to pay homage to two films I grew up with, for the impact they made on me as a young person. Maybe you noticed those scenes and lines in the story, maybe they blended in. I highly encourage you to watch them.

First, Dream for An Insomniac, directed by Tiffanie DeBartolo, who was so gracious when I asked her if I could use Café Blue Eyes in the fictional world I built. I felt so connected to Tiffanie's film back in 1999, the characters, and the café family she built. I was ready to pack my bags and move out west with my poetry and dreams. I did eventually move out west, and imagine my surprise two decades later, I'm following this incredible novelist who wrote books like Sorrow and God-Shaped Hole, and one night, in the midst of folding laundry, I see DFAI on a streaming device, and there in bold letters under the director's name is Tiffanie. I freaked out! As in I immediately abandoned the piles of clothes and got on social media to share my story. And she responded! I can't even begin to tell you how that eighteen year-old Sam felt. What are the chances?

If you're reading this, you've probably just finished Synchronicity, so you know, maybe it wasn't a coincidence. Maybe the universe is smiling on us.

The other moment is during Part II, in 2001, before Seth leaves to return to school. They're taking a final walk around the city, and Chelsea says, "You, me, and two cups of coffee." That line is inspired by Reality Bites, where Ethan Hawke and Winona Ryder's characters, Troy and Lelaina, are doing what young people in love do: talk about the stuff that matters to them while skirting around their vulnerability when it comes to each other.

Both films planted seeds of ideas years ago, the way great stories do, and it was such a treat as a creative to go back in time and get to play make-believe in those worlds through Chelsea and Seth.

There are multiple relationship dynamics and personal triumphs in this story that I explored and tried to shed light on. I hope you, the reader, felt seen in some way.

Early motherhood years are a scramble of joy and exhaustion. They say the days are long, and the years are short. And it's absolutely true. It was important for me to write a story about a woman who embodied all the roles so many of us hold. And to write a man who is strong and empathetic enough to support her and love her through it all.

I also aimed to hold space for neurodiverse minds in this

story. I chose to focus on sensory processing, and within that spectrum, no two cases are the same. It was my intention to highlight the experience of individuals living and navigating with sensory challenges and strengths. My heart recognizes what it takes for these children and adults to simply exist in a loud world.

Writing about mental health is important to me, and I hope I was able to do that in a sensitive, thoughtful, and inclusive manner. Through storytelling and transparency, we're all invited to venture outside our regularly scheduled programming through a lens different from our own. This is the magic and power words have. To expose. To foster empathy. To unite.

For those who've read The Hope of You, did you find all the easter eggs "Rory" left for you? They're there! For any reader who hasn't read my debut yet, Synchronicity is the book that the main character, Rory, writes in the story. You don't need to read both, but if you have, there are little nods to Reed and Rory throughout.

Thank you for journeying with Chelsea and Seth through the decades. These two have hearts of gold. They're helpers in the world, and like Fred Rogers tells us to do: "Look for the helpers." I imagine these two are cuddled up on the couch on a cool fall night after enjoying a home-cooked meal, watching a classic movie, holding hands, and sneaking in kisses. They are living life on their own terms, absolutely in love.

And I'm so happy for them. Xo Sam

ACKNOWLEDGMENTS

This year has been a happily-ever-after kind of blur, with sprinting sessions, writing retreats, book events, and life at home. One thing I know for sure, this story was no solo adventure.

To my Critique Partners, Krysann & Sarah, you both gave me the 'engine that could' energy I desperately needed to keep chugging along. Your notes, conversation, and cheerleading were an essential piece of the experience and end result. Thank you for being my first readers, but mostly, thank you for being my friends.

Kim. You changed my life a year ago. I know it seems like a bold statement, but that's what one act of kindness does for a person. There will never be an adequate amount of words to thank you for the generosity and guidance you have given to me. You are a special person in this world, and how lucky I am to call you a friend. You're stuck with me now.

Beta readers are the bread and butter queens of any book. Ashley, Ashley W., Kelsey, and Kim, you were able to see through the clutter to the heart of this story, helping me to shape it into the best version of itself. Having each of your insights and unique perspectives, at different stages, equally challenged and encouraged me so much. Thank you for loving Seth and Chelsea with me and answering all of my follow-up questions. Talking through the story with you all made this process possible, and fun.

Thank you so much to all of the ARC readers who took the

time to read and review. There's no S.L. Astor books without you.

To my editor, Sarah Peachey, your attention to detail is unmatched, and your eye for story is something you don't find every day. You made Synchronicity shine. Thank you for the gift of your time and expertise.

Tracey Barski, thank you for your proofreading talent, combing through the story in fine detail, and helping me to tie a bow around this book and get it out into the world.

Thank you, Ashley, for taking SY into your magical Vellum hands, and making this story look so beautiful. You added years onto my life.

Dominique, Korrie, and Michelle. Having your feedback on sensitive scenes helped me to understand the characters as their most authentic selves. Thank you so much.

Once again, Murphy Rae, you made the cover of my dreams for this story. Thank you for being so flexible when I have ideas I want to experiment with. I hope everyone judges my book by its cover, because it's absolutely stunning.

Alyse, thank you for the beautiful cover reveal video. I've watched it no less than a million times. And it was such an honor to share your creativity with everyone.

Sometimes the writing process is isolating and bumpy, but not once have I ever felt alone in this. Amanda, Ashley, Ashley W., Eve, Jen, Laurie, Melissa, MK, Sunny, and Tracey, thank you for always being up to talking shop with me, writing sessions, brainstorming, replying to all my messages and DMs when I have a last minute idea or thought (or meme) I have to share. And for picking up the phone when I call, that's true friendship! Thank you for just getting it.

To my dear Coho Support group, Amber, April, and Kelsey, you never let me forget I have a seat at the table and you never let anyone else forget it either. Thank you for cheering so loud for me and my books. All the virtual hugs for now.

Erin, you gave me Dermot, and it was only then I truly heard Seth.

Gabby, Elaine, S.J., Zooms, and Denver made this book happen. Period. The cheesecake, jeweled crowns, and duck sweater helped, too. Looks like my one sentence acknowledgment will have to wait for the next one.

To the readers and bookstagram accounts in the past year that helped The Hope of You soar and spread its wings, there will never be enough thank yous in the world to express my gratitude. You shared my book, made content, left beautiful reviews (Yes, I know I shouldn't, but I read them all). You took care of her so I could write Synchronicity. Thank you.

Megan, thank you for everything you've done for our family. Thank you for helping me to synthesize SPD for this story, so I could talk about it from a distance.

To my husband, thank you for sharing me with my make-believe worlds and Turkish dramas, and making this all possible for me. You spin me right round. And to G & A, one day you may read this story, and when you do, I hope you find places that feel familiar, and know how proud I am of you both, and how much you are loved. You make the world a better place.

There was quite a bit of research that went into this story, and it was important to me that I honored the heart of San Francisco as best as I could. That's easier to do when you've spent a lot of time in a place, but I don't have a time machine (sadly) to transport myself back to 2001 and 2011. Big thanks, Chloe Benjamin, for being my virtual tour guide, for meeting with me and answering my questions about the city, its climate and culture, during those years. I hope to one day enjoy a cup of coffee at your favorite coffee shop and chat some more.

We all need breathers when we're immersed in writing our stories. I definitely did with this one, and I have to thank two

Turkish series, Erkenci Kuş and Sen Çal Kapımı, for reminding me that love takes time and slow burns are where it's at.

Finally, Rory Wells. If it weren't for her story, Synchronicity wouldn't exist. It was a fun creative exercise to write this book from "her eyes."

BOOK CLUB QUESTIONS

1) Is it possible to fall in love with your first crush? What is it about young love that holds so strong for these characters?

2) Do you think Summer could've done anything different when Chelsea was younger to make her daughter feel seen? Are parents responsible for their children's self-confidence?

3) What coping mechanisms did Chelsea develop to navigate life without a diagnosis? How did her experience prepare or hinder her for parenting a neurodiverse child?

4) What would you name the shade of Chelsea's red lipstick? If you had a signature shade of lipstick, what would its name be?

5) If you found hundreds of thousands of dollars stashed away in a house, what would you do with it?

6) What was your favorite line of Nan's? Is there anyone in your life that reminds you of Nan, someone who fiercely loves without a filter?

7) How did Steph and Chelsea find common ground being from such different backgrounds? Do you think our commonalities or our differences make for great friendships?

8) The contents of Paige's letter was written to resemble the healing relationship of parents and children. What did Chelsea do differently in her parenting that both her parents and Seth's parents didn't do? How did it make a difference?

9) Chelsea and Seth are playful, and Chelsea says, "... her children had also taught Chelsea what it meant when a person you love asked you to play with them." How do the ways we love others also inform us on how to love ourselves?

10) One of the themes in this book is timing—how the past steers the future. Are there any moments in your life you would go back and relive? What role has synchronicity played in your life?

11) Chelsea tells Seth, "... we forgive people for ourselves, not for them." How did both Seth and Chelsea ultimately learn to forgive themselves?

12) One of the epigraphs in the book reads, "What we have once enjoyed we can never lose. All that we love deeply becomes a part of us," by Helen Keller. Do you believe this to be true? How has love shaped you?

13) Do you have any special mementos (daisy chains, mix cds, notes) that you have saved?

14) Chelsea whispers a word in Seth's ear, meant to be a word she chose when she found the one? What do you think the word is?

THE HOPE OF YOU

CHAPTER ONE

Rory

Second chances don't show up every day. And they definitely don't show up in mailboxes on Saturday morning with my name attached to them.

The envelope rattles in my grasp, edges curling against their will. I triple-check the label from Eden Publishing, then hold it up to the sun in hopes of discovering a hint of its contents, a single clue, but the brutal rays force my eyes to the ground, where flecks of silver and opal embedded in the pavement dance around in my vision.

There were hundreds of applicants. I'm sure it's a standard courtesy letter, rejecting my submission and encouraging me to try again next year. But for me, there is no next year. There is only this one.

I force a diaphragm breath to settle the shaking, half-expecting to exhale myself from one of my lucid dreams. Typical brunch traffic in Boston competes with a pounding pulse in my chest, alerting my system that this might not be a drill. On the off chance this is actually happening, there is no way I'll look back at this moment, where my life changes forever, and replay some sad story about how the sole witness was a weathered mailbox in front of my apartment with its mouth hanging wide open.

Sorry, mailbox, it's not you, it's me.

I sprint across the street to Memory Lane, the café my best friend Kat owns. The racket of welcome bells and steel crashes in my wake. It takes all of two seconds to spot Kat behind the counter. Her platinum wavy hair with lavender ends piled on top of her head bounces as she bops along to classic rock music playing throughout the café.

Waving the envelope in the air like a white flag, I rush the counter, practically knocking a latte from her hand.

"Goooooood morn—" Kat says, leaning over the counter. She takes in my state from head to toe—last night's leggings and messy bun, her eyes saucers of concern. "Are you," Kat lowers her voice, "having an anxiety attack? The kitchen's clear if you need a quiet place. It's all yours."

Kat's lips keep moving, but whatever she's saying isn't computing. I woke up this morning as ad sales Rory. Rory with a journalism degree collecting dust. The same Rory with the same coffee order, who spends her days in the same four-block radius.

I didn't let myself believe I could be chosen. Not for something this competitive or prestigious. I'm potentially a signature line away from being a full-time writer.

My hands shake as I slam the envelope down on the counter in front of a bewildered Kat.

"I can't open it."

"Can't open what?" Kat shoots me a quizzical glance. "I've never seen you this way, before coffee, ever."

I'm waiting for Kat to tap into her BFF radar and read my mind, because all I'm coming up with are jumbled consonants and vowels flashing in neon. I wipe the stray hair away from my face while spilling the unfiltered contents of my head.

My tongue scrapes like sandpaper, from the sprint and apprehension.

"The answer to whether I've been selected as Eden's debut writer is in this envelope. Whether I'm going to finally finish my book, and query agents, and commit to my dream." I'm nearly shouting now, riding an escalator of elation, making pit stops for shock and relief along the way. "And I'm too scared to open it and find out."

Kat's eyes pop open like cash registers. "I sure as shit am not!" She swipes the envelope from the counter, loosens a pencil from her hair, and rips right through the seal.

My stomach plummets. I steady my other hand on the counter.

At first, she stares intensely. Her brows pull in and her lips hold a straight line. After counting five Mississippis in my head, convinced I can't wait another second, as if on cue, Kat's lashes lift and her expression slowly reveals a smile. She's smiling. Kat is smiling. At me.

"Congrats, Rory, you're officially—wait, let me read it—here we go, Eden Publishing's Annual Aspiring Author Mentee! Well, that's a mouthful."

"I got in," I choke out. "I got in," I repeat in disbelief. "Wait, but I wasn't supposed to."

"Ha. That's what she said."

"C'mon, I'm serious."

"I am too. Dead serious," she points out, laughing while flipping the letter to face me, pushing the hard evidence into my trembling hands.

"Dear Ms. Rory Wells. Welcome to Eden. Accepted. Writing Mentorship. Reed Ashton."

The words I'm reading escape in whispers as I race through the details.

Kat's voice grabs my attention. She's raising a brow at the paper to-go cup in her hand, giving it a hard stare. "Alta . . . lune, your mocha is all set." She leaves the cup on the pick-up bar and comes over from behind the counter. "These double names kill me," she sighs, shaking her head. "I swear, at this rate, I'm gonna need to order thirty-two-ounce cups to fit them."

She yanks me into her cinnamon-infused embrace, giving me her signature squeeze, genuine and strong. Waiting for this decision has been eating at me for months. I've made wishes on every star in the sky.

When we stop hugging, Kat catches me off guard in a rare moment of seriousness, saying, "Don't look so shocked. I knew you'd get it."

I wipe my hoodie sleeve gently across my eyes. Kat's confidence in me is something I've never gotten used to. I swear she laces her lattes with loyalty and support, maybe a splash of courage too.

It was terrifying to subject my work to be judged, and I told myself that if this didn't work out, I'd take it as the final sign it was time to put the pen down, let go, and accept reality. I'm thirty, which isn't a death sentence for dreams, but I also know that when something isn't working, you don't hold on tighter.

"Thank you for pushing me to apply and for being my friend."

She waves my affection off with a brush of her hand, like her steadfast friendship is no big deal and thanking her for it is almost an insult.

"You know what this means? I'm going to march into Doris's office on Monday with a fuck-you-very-much resignation letter."

"You're absolutely recording that." She scans the café tables. The place is half-full, mostly regulars. "Seriously, this is the best news for my best non-paying customer."

I deadpan, both of us familiar with our established friendship charades. She's been my best friend, and also my barista, for close to a decade.

Kat strides over to the shelf of vinyl records in the corner, lifting the needle off the run-down record player. She's been talking about getting a replacement for forever.

The music stops. The music never stops at Memory Lane.

"Hey, listen up, everyone," she commands. The handful of patrons scattered around the café stop their conversations and look up. "This ridiculously talented romance writer is gonna be a bestseller-list-making household name."

The silence is deafening, followed by a few halfhearted claps. I feel thirteen again, eating in the bathroom, avoiding the riotous lunchroom at all costs.

Kat drops the needle back down. The music kicks on. The regulars, and my heart rate, return to business as usual.

"Hot pink's a good color on you," Kat says, with a winged-tipped wink.

I touch my cheeks. They're on fire.

"C'mon, we're celebrating." She raises her voice again. "Lattes on the house."

The room erupts in applause. Sharp whistles startle me. I turn to see Kevin Donnelly, a retiree with a head of silver hair that sticks out from his navy and red ball cap. He peeks up from his paper with a pleased grin that is his full smile.

"Hey, hey. That's what I'm talkin' about."

"Dad, you don't even drink lattes," Kat remarks.

"How about ah dahk roast then? One sugah."

She sends a smile over her shoulder. His grin slips behind the crisp shuffling of paper.

"Grab your spot" Kat directs and passes me a bottle of water.

When she returns behind the counter, Mr. Donnelly starts chatting.

"Rawry, how's yah faucet workin' these days?"

"Haven't had a leak since you fixed it," I reply. "Thanks again."

"Don't mention it."

"Fitz is still terrified. I had to move his litter box away from the bathroom."

Mr. Donnelly chuckles. "Bet he is. That cat of yahs was soppin' wet."

Poor Fitz caught the brunt of a pipe burst. Luckily, Kat's dad was on the scene to help, like he does with all the neighborhood residents.

"Congrats, kid. When will I get to read yah book?"

"You read romance, Mr. Donnelly?" I ask, concealing my shock.

"Yahs will be my first."

"Thank you. Well, you'll be the first person on my advanced copy list." I knock on the wood table in front of him, not wanting to get too ahead of ourselves here.

Kat returns, dropping off her dad's coffee and linking her arm through mine. "I want all the details."

We make our way to the best view in the house. I sink into the ruffles of a matted-down velour armchair. It's positioned behind a large storefront window. "Memory Lane" is painted in swooping powder blue letters that mirror the sky's soft edges when they blend into low-hanging clouds. The street is lined with triple-deckers, foot traffic, and at a distance, the lights at Fenway Park are visible at night.

"Hello, neighborhood," I whisper.

It's quintessential fall in New England. The postcard kind, with hints of burnt orange and apple yellow foliage. A nipping invitation in the air to step outside and be a part of it all.

This is my favorite season in Boston—distinct flavors, hometown pride, traditions and trophies—a potion crafted of nostalgia and that intoxicating feeling of connection I've got to every sight, smell, and sound. And it's not solely about its incredible, rich history etched in every brick, on every building, on every street. It's a city I can get lost in and still call home.

"I'm gonna grab our coffees and scones." Kat hops up and heads back to the counter. It doesn't take long to hear the frother sputter and hiss.

When Kat bought this place, she turned the key to a dump. Wall-to-wall red shag carpeting stained from winter street slush. Where I would've lit a match and never looked back, Kat saw potential. She gutted the space and restored its original flooring. She added mismatched chairs, tea tables, and a collection of vintage cups and plates. The walls are decorated with postcards, concert stubs, and photos. A low bookshelf with the sign "bring and borrow" rests against the right side of the wall. It operates on the honor system. Kat says, "Books are meant to be shared." I think her memories are too.

Shortly after I settled into my place on Chelsea Street, I'd walk by construction on my way to work, inhaling the fumes of paint sticking to summer air. Until one day, the magical scent of dark espresso roasting wafted all the way up into the tiny kitchen window of my third-floor apartment.

I ran into Memory Lane much like I did today, ordered a cinnamon latte, and fell in love with a bulletin board with a few scraps of paper tacked on. These days, those scraps overlap in a mosaic of pastels and permanent ink, displaying a collection of lyrics, one-liners, and words to live by.

Sometimes, I reach to reorder them, like a curator, so that they can be fully appreciated. Yet, I know there's something in Kat's cluttered chaos that makes this wall of quotes a piece of art, and altering it would be like removing a wild animal from its natural habitat, a travesty.

The iron table base wobbles as Kat places our scones and lattes down.

"Hey, when you get all fancy and famous, we'll take a trip to

Ireland. We can check out the scone scene and pub hop our way across the island. Kiss the Blarney Stone."

"You had me at scone," I say.

Kat laughs. "Yeah, maybe even find ourselves lucky."

"Can you imagine meeting *the one* in such a romantic country? One decision away from a happily ever after." My lashes bat over my latte.

"I think the lack of caffeine has caught up to you."

"Perhaps," I confess, in a daydream of hand scenes and meet-cutes.

"I'm talking about a guy to grab a Guinness with, maybe shoot some darts. Definitely not ride off into the sunset material."

"Hazard of the job," I rationalize, defending the fairy tale fantasy tendencies I often find myself in.

"I'm so excited for you, Ror. Let me check out this letter again."

I pass it to her, wondering if living in my head for most of my life has skewed my view of romantic relationships. Ideas start off in your subconscious and become aspirations over time. I'm not naive, but I also believe in something I can't define, so writing is how I work through it. And I'm not the only one. There's a billion-dollar industry looking for answers.

"We've talked about this so many times. Love in real life," Kat grabs her latte off the table and leans back, "is like baking. You can't throw random ingredients together. It has to be the right mix of timing and chemistry and compatibility. And the kiss. The first kiss has to be hot. None of this pecking nonsense like my parents do." Kat nods over at her dad drinking his coffee and finishing his paper.

"You can't break it down like that. Love isn't fixed. Love is the variable." I cut my scone into quadrants, picking up a quarter, and add, "*The one* describes a feeling. Like slipping into the most comfortable sweater, it simply fits better than the rest."

Kat's blank stare says what she's thinking. I almost reach over and roll her eyes for her.

She places her cup on the table and leans in closer into me. "Tillie let you watch too many princess movies growing up. Love is not always romance. Relationships are work." She pauses for a bite of her scone. "You better be taking notes, so you can use all this in your book."

"Well, if your theory is true, I don't have to write any of your realist relationship tips, because I'm writing fiction." I shove a piece of scone into my mouth and chew in pride, while my foot rattles under the table.

The mid-morning sun is warm on my legs, and my cinnamon latte is perfection. The steam coaxes a genuine smile from my lips, and for the first time since I held the letter myself, my shoulders relax too.

I've read about the places I want to travel to. As a kid, during recess, I'd make wishes on weeds, plucking petals. *If only I could be invisible, left to my imaginary worlds and words.* That's all I wanted then. To escape into stories.

I do think perhaps I made that wish one too many times. And I can't help but wonder if maybe we spend our entire lives on the receiving end of all that we ask for.

"Hey, so have you told your mom yet?" Kat asks.

"I will," hesitating, "tomorrow night at dinner."

"Can I tag along?" She's salivating for the free entertainment. "I'd never say no to her cooking and a Rory-Tillie showdown."

Because she knows—my mom will have a reaction.

"She's going to flip out. Maybe I shouldn't tell her."

"Maybe she'll be supportive."

"Maybe the sky is orange."

"Maybe she'll surprise you."

"Who's spinning fairy tales now?" I tease, shaking my head.

"By the way, this sounds pretty amazing. You're going to be

working with a mentor who also writes romance. I didn't realize that was part of the program, but it definitely makes sense now why that would be so appealing. So, are we excited about your match?" She peeks under the table at my feet rattling the base. "Nervous?"

I press my shoes firmly into the floor.

"He's a really big deal," I reply, chewing on my lip.

"And that's bad?" she questions. "And we don't like this because?"

"I wasn't expecting my mentor to be that guy. One whose books I've read too many times. I mean, they're all bent spines in my bedroom, Kat."

"And?"

"Stories I know by heart."

My thoughts sound irrational. My eyes dart around the room.

"And?"

"It's just, I guess, I wasn't prepared to be matched with an author of his caliber . . . you know, with so much," I stumble over my uncertainty, "experience."

"Isn't that a good thing?" she presses, as I continue to dance around denial. "So what if you fangirl a little? I'm sure all authors are used to that. You could totally get him to autograph those books by your bed."

I want to come up with an equally sarcastic retort, but I'm running on post-adrenaline empty.

The bell on the front door chimes. Kat checks and waves goodbye to the people leaving. There's only a few of us left in the café.

"I'd be more comfortable talking to a woman. You know, about certain scenes."

"You mean sex scenes, Rory?"

I roll my eyes.

"Well, my guess is you gotta get real comfortable, real quick.

And so what? He's a professional. I'm sure he's done this a million times."

Kat starts vigorously typing into her phone.

"What are you doing?" I ask, shifting in the chair.

"While you're busy taking all your nerves out on the base of my table, I'm taking action."

I pry over her shoulder and see she's pulling up a browser with Reed's name in the search engine. "You're cyber-stalking him?" I spit out.

"It's the age of digital research. It's not like I'm driving by his house."

As Kat scrolls, my insides twist. I turn back to the window. Vetting someone online before meeting them has never settled with me. It feels invasive and meeting someone naturally and discovering who they are, layer by layer, is where the magic exists. There's not much in this world that we get to be surprised by anymore, but slowly learning about someone as they choose to expose themselves to you feels like one of the last sacred rituals on earth.

But she's right. It's the twenty-first century and people do their research. Anyway, it's harmless and probably smart to know a little bit about the person I'll be working with, aside from his jacket bio.

"I see what's really going on here," Kat says, and I scooch closer to get a better look. It's a photo of Reed Ashton by a lake, crouched down next to a golden retriever. He's wearing a navy blue and gray plaid shirt. The sleeves are rolled up to his elbows. His eyes are covered under a faded Red Sox hat. A warm smile nestled in the middle of shadowy stubble.

Kat side-eyes me and returns her attention back to the screen. "This guy could grace the covers of his books. You're not worried about his bestseller status. You're freaking out that Reed Ashton has Rory Wells written all over him."

"You're so off the mark." I see her radar has finally switched on. I chug my coffee.

She raises her eyebrows at me, not buying a word of it.

"Obviously I see what he looks like. But I only care about how he can help my book."

"Maybe he'll come and rescue you from the depths of the writing trenches."

"You need to stop right now," I beg, swallowing amusement I shouldn't be entertaining.

"I've never seen you at such a loss for words. I bet that he's—"

"I'm not into him." My voice cracks and is unconvincing at best.

"With a face like that, he could sell me thin air."

I throw my head back in defeat. "It's fine. It'll be fine. I'm fine."

She puts her hand on mine.

"Listen, you've wanted this for so long. You're not going to let a hot guy or me giving you grief get in the way. Anyway, it's all online, right?"

"Good point." I stretch my legs. "I bet that's why their previous mentees land agents so quickly too, because of how awesome their mentors are."

"His last post is dated two years ago. That's odd," Kat points out.

"He hasn't published a book since then either. It's like he fell off the map."

Kat hops up and takes our empty cups to the counter. She returns with a paper sack and places my half-eaten scone inside it. She rolls the top down and hands it to me.

"You may have hit the mentor jackpot. Think about Stevie," she adds, gesturing to her concert tee. "Her mentor was Tom Petty."

"A true collab made in the music heavens."

The bells chime again. Two men in charcoal suits head to the counter.

"I'll talk to ya later," Kat says.

I get up and give her a hug.

"I don't know if I'm prepared enough."

"This is your moment, and sometimes it's good to go off-script. Hey, especially with a costar that looks like that."

"You're never going to stop, are you?"

"Probably not. Love ya."

She might not extract the admission she's looking for from me, but she definitely earns a smile.

I wished for this opportunity and everything it comes with. I'll write until my fingers fall off. I'll eat, sleep, breathe this story. Nothing else matters but finishing, and nothing will get in my way this time.

I wave, then step outside. Traffic has picked up. My eyes close. I tilt my face toward the sun, soaking in what's left of morning. I count on an inhale, *one, two, three, four*. Kat always finds a way to remind me that I won't lose my balance if I look up every once in a while. I release the breath, *five, six, seven, eight*, and check both ways before crossing.

ABOUT THE AUTHOR

S.L. ASTOR writes emotionally driven stories with characters who love big and don't always play by the rules. She lives (and bakes) in NorCal with her husband and their cookie enthusiast children. When she's not in meetings with her chatty imaginary heroines and heroes, you'll find Sam on the beach, reading and dreaming, with an iced latte in hand. She mostly hangs out on Instagram.

s.l. astor
author

Stay Connected
for updates and bonus content.

www.authorslastor.com
Instagram @sl.astor.writes
TikTok @slawrites

Printed in Great Britain
by Amazon

49650575R00229